A TASTE OF PASSION

Isabel crossed the room, found the brandy, and poured a quarter inch into a snifter. More soft laughter came from behind her. "Nervous already?" Mr. Julian asked. "You haven't come near me yet."

She recapped the decanter, straightened her shoulders, and turned. In the dim light he cast quite a spell. Untamed hair, open collar, and lips parted in a wicked smile. She walked to him and held out the glass.

"Oh, no," he said. "My hands are soapy. Bring the drink to my mouth."

Isabel hesitated. He asked no more than she had done dozens of times before. To lift a cup to someone's lips. Yet he made the act seem intimate somehow, indecent. She took a small step toward him and raised the snifter. He stared at her, singeing her with the fire of his gaze. And he stood absolutely still, not bending an inch to help.

Slowly she approached until she stood nearly on top of him, surrounded by steam from the water and his own scent of musk and spice. She lifted the glass higher, her hand trembling. His smile broadened, and then, without warning, he dipped his head and took the glass between his lips. He tipped it up, sending the amber liquid to his mouth. "You surprise me, Miss Gannon," he murmured. "Now let's see just how much backbone you have."

His eyes closed, dark lashes brushing his cheeks. He lowered his head again, this time toward hers.

ALICE GAINES

Waitangi Nights

LOVE SPELL ◆ NEW YORK CITY

For Hal, *mein guter Geist, mein besseres Ich.*

LOVE SPELL®

December 1996

Published by

Dorchester Publishing Co., Inc.
276 Fifth Avenue
New York, NY 10001

If you purchased this book without a cover you should be aware that this book is stolen property. It was reported as "unsold and destroyed" to the publisher and neither the author nor the publisher has received any payment for this "stripped book."

Copyright © 1996 by Alice Brilmayer

All rights reserved. No part of this book may be reproduced or transmitted in any form or by any electronic or mechanical means, including photocopying, recording or by any information storage and retrieval system, without the written permission of the Publisher, except where permitted by law.

The name "Love Spell" and its logo are trademarks of Dorchester Publishing Co., Inc.

Printed in the United States of America.

Chapter One

Bay of Islands, New Zealand, 1888

Isabel Gannon straightened her skirts, which needed no straightening, and settled her reticule on top. Trust her to end up halfway around the world from home—penniless, alone, and at the mercy of a man she'd never met. And to make matters every bit as bad as they could be, fate had decreed that she sit here, in this terribly proper, terribly stuffy drawing room, waiting to learn what would happen to her.

Isabel took a deep breath and tried to concentrate on the serenity of the landscape she'd seen on her way from the ship. Waitangi seemed welcoming enough, despite its exotic name. Not English, certainly. Not even Spanish, like the names of so many towns in Central and South America she and her father had visited. And yet the place itself appeared British enough, almost.

Unable to sit a moment longer, Isabel rose from her chair, her reticule dangling from clenched fingers by

Alice Gaines

her side, and crossed the parlor to the open window. The scent of newly mown grass floated to her on a warm breeze. She gazed out across a flagstone terrace to a formal garden, a semicircle of topiary chessmen, and then to a long expanse of lawn. The scene resembled a stately British home except for the palms swaying in the breeze from the bay, the huge ferns with ten-foot and taller trunks, and the trees beyond, trees with names like *ngaio, rimu, kauri*.

Yes, Harrowgate Manor was a lovely place, quite agreeable in fact. But what of the man, her new employer? Would Vernon Julian send her packing when he discovered that his new nurseryman was a woman? And what in heaven's name would she do if he did? After all, she'd spent the last of her modest inheritance getting this far. She couldn't go back to England unless she swam there.

From out in the hall came the sound of footsteps and Isabel couldn't help but jump. She turned to find Samuel, Mr. Julian's valet, emerging from the next room. He walked across the corridor and entered the drawing room where she stood.

He closed the door softly behind him, pulling it shut by crooking a finger into the hole where the knob should be. Strange, but all the interior doors she had seen so far in the manor were like that, latchless and incomplete. They lent the house a discordant note, as though something weren't quite right behind the proper British appearance of things.

Before she had a chance to ask Samuel about the lack of knobs, he smiled at her—almost reassuring her, but not quite.

"Few more minutes, miss," he said.

She did her best to smile back. "Thank you."

The man was clearly Maori, with his dark skin and Polynesian features. And yet here he stood in full English dress. Isabel had met the indigenous peoples of many different lands, and she found them at least the equal of Europeans for intelligence and kindness. Nevertheless, she wasn't used to them looking as though she had interrupted them on their way to high tea.

But then, everything about Harrowgate Manor seemed just slightly off—a disconcerting combination of familiarity and differentness. Like tree ferns and warm, impossibly long days in January.

Samuel looked at her for a moment, his eyes full of an uncertain warmth that might have been meant to comfort or to warn. Finally, he cleared his throat. "Mind a bit of advice, miss?"

"Of course not."

"He can seem a mite fierce at times," Samuel said. "But if you stand up to him, you'll have his respect."

Just as one didn't show fear to a snarling dog? Dear heaven. She gripped her beaded bag in her hand, focussing all her tension in her fingers where, please Lord, it shouldn't show. She didn't dare reveal how badly she needed this position. Far better to let them all think they'd scored a triumph in getting Arthur Gannon's daughter to care for their orchids. And as soon as she'd convinced them of that, she'd retreat to the nurseryman's cottage and keep to what she knew, horticulture.

"Samuel," came a muffled bellow from the other side of the door. Samuel opened it, stepped across the corridor, and peeked into the next room.

"Send him in," the same dark voice ordered.

"Yes, sir," Samuel answered. He pushed the door to the other room fully open and gestured for Isabel to go inside. She crossed the hall, stepped over the threshold, and looked around.

The room might have been the study of an English mansion, the sort of place the aristocracy referred to as a "country house" but that could have entertained half of Parliament. It exuded luxury, with its oriental carpets, intricately inlaid grandfather clock in the corner, and floor-to-ceiling windows looking out over the sumptuous gardens. And there, in the center of it all, behind a huge mahogany desk, sat a lone figure hunched over some papers.

Without looking up, he waved a hand toward her. "Sit," he grumbled. "Sit, sit, sit."

Isabel found a straight-backed chair against the wall. She took a seat and crossed her ankles under her skirts. The clock ticked on, counting out a brittle monotone as she studied the man behind the desk.

Despite Samuel's little bit of advice on how to handle her interview, he hadn't actually told her with whom she would be speaking. This man didn't fit what she knew about Vernon Julian, the master. So, who could he be? A majordomo perhaps? But no. He didn't resemble a servant of any sort.

In fact, he presented a most singular picture, with his broad shoulders barely contained by a finely tailored, velvet frock coat and his hair curling wildly around his face. The afternoon sun danced in his curls, producing fiery, even golden highlights—as though the very color of his hair would defy description. And yet underneath all that wildness sat a starched collar, almost severe in its propriety.

Still intent on his work, the man scratched a few more figures onto the paper in front of him. Then he stopped abruptly and sniffed the air, like a jaguar detecting the scent of nearby prey. "What the hell?" he mumbled. "Rose water?"

He looked up then, and an ice blue glare met Isabel's gaze. "Who the devil are you?" he demanded.

Isabel gripped her reticule until her fingers curled it so tightly she might just break a few beads. But she raised her chin and returned his stare. "I'm the new nurseryman," she answered evenly.

"No, you're not," he replied. He studied her a moment longer, his stare as unblinking as an eagle's. "Gannon?"

Isabel straightened her skirt and adjusted her reticule

Waitangi Nights

on top of it—anything to avoid his eyes and still not give her nervousness away.

"Yes," she answered, evenly she hoped.

He harumphed loudly and shuffled through the papers in front of him. He lifted one sheet and looked at it. "Arthur Gannon?"

"Isabel Gannon," she corrected. "Arthur Gannon was my father. He died shortly after receiving Mr. Julian's letter, so I came in his stead." She cleared her throat. "I'm sure the master will find me an able substitute."

"I doubt that very much," he replied. "I'm the master of Harrowgate Manor."

"No, you're not." Isabel bit her lip. She hadn't meant to blurt that out, but she had understood Mr. Julian to be well into his seventies. She had so hoped that he would be a kindly gentleman, like her father. That he would take her on and perhaps even shelter her. A foolish hope. But still, this man couldn't be Vernon Julian. He couldn't.

Whoever he was, he dropped his pen on the desk and leaned back in his chair, interweaving his fingers over his waistcoat. He gave her a rather mirthless smile, flashing perfect teeth and creating a dimple in his cheek. The expression might have been pleasant if it hadn't made him look so like a pirate.

"I'm Richard Julian," he said finally.

"But I was expecting—"

"Vernon Julian," he finished for her. His gaze roamed over her in an appraising manner that caused her heart to beat the tiniest bit more quickly. "My father has also recently passed on," he continued. "It appears that you and I have both been saddled with the wrong generation."

Dear heaven, the man who had engaged her, engaged her father, in fact, was dead himself. And she had spent her last penny travelling halfway around the world and had braved a treacherous passage around the horn, only to find that her fate lay in the hands of a man who

Alice Gaines

looked like a pirate and stared at her as if she were something to eat.

But there had to be some way to salvage the situation. He must still have the orchids, the famed Harrowgate collection. They would still need to be cared for.

She looked him in the eye. "I'm sorry for your loss."

"And I for yours." He heaved a sigh. "I suppose we'll find something for you to do here. I can't very well pack you up and send you back to England, can I?"

Merciful heaven, something for her to do? There was only one something here for her, the orchids.

He gave her that look of his again, the one that glowed with a hint of indiscretion. The one that made her breath catch. "Can you cook?" he asked.

"No," she answered. *Honestly, the very idea*.

His eyes widened until he stared at her openly. "Can't cook?" he said.

"I won't cook."

He smiled at that, now clearly amused. "Why the devil not?"

"I'm not a domestic. I'm a nurseryman . . . er . . . woman." She took a breath and tried again. "I'm a botanist."

"University degrees and all that?"

And there lay the difficulty that would follow her no matter where she looked for employment. It was hard enough to convince the world that a woman should be taken seriously in the male realm of orchid horticulture—but a woman with no formal education? At least she had foreseen this problem, and perhaps Samuel's advice might help her with it. If only she could manage to "stand up to" the intense gaze now focused almost mercilessly on her.

She straightened her back and looked Mr. Julian square in the face. "I have something better than a university education," she declared. "Practical knowledge. I've grown orchids since I was barely tall enough to see over the glasshouse bench."

Waitangi Nights

He rested his elbow against the arm of his chair and placed his chin in his hand. Long fingers splayed over his cheek. Odd that she hadn't realized before how large his hands were. He watched her for a moment, letting the seconds stretch out in silence. Her stomach fluttered, but there was nothing to do but continue.

"I've collected orchids in the jungles of Yucatán," she went on, "and in the mountains of Peru. I know how they grow in the wild, which is more than most men in my profession can say."

"The position has never been filled by a woman."

She gathered a little more inner strength and gave him what she hoped was a confident smile. "Perhaps it's time it was," she answered softly.

"The job requires strength, Miss Gannon," he replied, leaning forward and studying her again, this time as if she were a prize mare he was considering buying. "You're small, even for a woman."

"I'm strong," she answered. "I've had to be."

"How do I know you won't be pulling my gardening staff away from their own work, getting them to lift this for you, tote that for you? I daresay those dark eyes of yours could convince most men to do all sorts of things."

"I can do the work, sir," she snapped. "Your prejudices against women are outmoded. And you must not have much command over your staff if they spend their days flirting with each other."

He sat back in his chair, a faint glimmer of triumph filling his eyes, as though by making her angry he'd won some victory over her. "Impertinent bit of work, aren't you?"

"I mean no disrespect, sir," she said. She paused, searching his face for some token of understanding, some sign that he might thaw. "A gentleman would give me a chance, Mr. Julian."

He laughed then, a short, unpleasant bark. "You may well know plants," he said. "But you don't know much

Alice Gaines

about men if you think me a gentleman."

"I beg your pardon?"

"Never mind," he said. "You probably haven't heard any of the stories about me yet."

She stared at him openly, at his eyes, the color of dazzling sapphires, and at the unruly hair that haloed his face. What in heaven's name had she gotten herself into? "If there's something I should know about employment here—"

"There's nothing you need to know, Miss Gannon," he said curtly. "And I've yet to decide that you're employed at Harrowgate."

Her back stiffened, her teeth clenched shut. If only she weren't so far away from England. If only she didn't need the position so desperately. If only her father or his father were still alive.

"In any case, I've brought along the plants your father requested in his letter," she said.

"So Samuel tells me. Are they in good condition?"

"Excellent," she answered. "I cared for them myself aboard ship. I may not know you or your reputation, but I know orchids, better than you do, I expect."

"You may be right there," he said. "Especially the *masdevallias*. No matter what we try, the bloody things wither after a few months."

"Then perhaps I shouldn't leave the ones I've brought," she said. "My father and I collected these plants ourselves. I won't have them killed by slipshod culture."

He sat straight up in his chair and gaped at her in amazement. "You won't what?"

"I won't sacrifice my orchids to someone who'll destroy them out of carelessness."

"My orchids," he corrected. "My father paid for those plants."

"And my father collected them," she replied. She paused, letting her determination penetrate behind his crystal blue eyes. "But if you like, I'll take a look at your

Waitangi Nights

glasshouse and see if I can identify what's killing your *masdevallias* . . . while you're deciding what to do with me, of course."

He stared at her, wide-eyed, for a moment longer. "It can wait until tomorrow," he said finally. "It's late, and you've only just arrived."

She sat and stared right back at him. "If I'm not to be employed at Harrowgate, I'll need to find someplace to spend the night. I can't stay here."

"For the love of God, woman," he grumbled. "You will stay here, and you'll like it."

"But—"

"I'm hiring you," he said. "Provisionally, of course. If you work out, you can have the job permanently."

"Thank you."

"I'm not quite as mired in outmoded prejudices as you may believe," he added. He rose and walked around the desk toward the door. "Now, I'll show you to your room."

Her room? Here in the house? "But your father mentioned in his letter . . . the nurseryman's cottage."

"It's in terrible disrepair." He smiled again, his eyes gleaming wickedly. "I couldn't let a lady stay there."

"I've slept in tents and leaky huts," she said. "I'm sure the cottage will be fine."

"Don't worry," he said, one eyebrow rising. "I'll put you in a guest room, not in the servant's wing."

She stood and gazed up into his face. Perhaps she'd be better off with the staff than anywhere near those blue eyes and that pirate smile. She gave herself a mental shake. What nonsense. "Very well, then."

He reached the door, and as Samuel had done before, he slipped a finger into the hole where a knob would usually be.

"Mr. Julian," Isabel said. "None of the doors I've seen here have locks, or even latches."

"Correct," he replied. "There are no locks anywhere in the interior of Harrowgate Manor."

Alice Gaines

"Why?"

"That doesn't concern you," he answered.

"But—"

He opened the door, ignoring her objection, or so it seemed. "You'll join me for dinner, won't you?" he asked. "I'd very much like to hear about your adventures in the Americas."

"Very well," she muttered. She glanced back at the emptiness where the door latch ought to be. What if her own bedroom door were the same? How would she ever get to sleep?

The doors to the elegant suite of rooms Mr. Julian expected her to occupy did all have the same gaping holes in them. And they all swung silently open under the lightest pressure. Isabel pushed the door that separated her sitting room from the main hall closed and noted that it stayed in that position without a latch, thank heaven. Still, would it stay that way?

Bookshelves stood nearby, and Isabel selected three large volumes. She set them in a pile on the floor and with her foot nudged them solidly into place against the door. Irrationally feeling more secure, she walked through the sitting room toward the bedroom.

Deep carpets swallowed up the sound of her footfalls as she crossed the threshold. Seldom had she seen such luxury, even in the great houses where her father had worked when she was small. Against the far wall stood an enormous canopied four poster, draped all around with velvet the color of champagne. The bed curtains flowed like fabric waterfalls to the powder blue of the carpet, filling the room with a soft brightness that would lift the spirits on even the dreariest day. Today, bathed in the slanted sunlight pouring in through towering windows, the room looked like something from a book of fairy tales—the enchanted princess's bedchamber, lovely.

And perfectly preposterous. Isabel Gannon was no

Waitangi Nights

princess, not even a proper lady by society's estimation. She belonged in a cottage, near the glasshouse where she could keep watch over the orchids. She should have a cozy hearth and furniture with enough nicks and scratches to testify to years of use. She didn't need the enormous hardwood wardrobe that stood in one corner, a piece designed to hold dozens of gowns. And she certainly had no use for the dressing table, its top littered with crystal atomizers and bottles for perfumed lotions, its banks of mirrors positioned to reflect the image of a lady at her toilette.

Arthur Gannon's daughter was a professional, a nurseryman, and she deserved respect and independence. The boudoir and its furnishings might prove that the master didn't plan to treat her like a domestic. But neither should he consider her a guest, or, heaven forbid, a dalliance. She would have to convince him that she needed her privacy. The nurseryman's cottage would have to be repaired, and soon.

That settled, she crossed to the bed and dropped her reticule onto it. She ran her hand over the silk comforter, outlining the richly embroidered images of fantastical flowers and birds with her fingertips. She turned and sat, testing the mattress.

From the sitting room came a soft thud, followed by muffled footsteps. Isabel jumped from the bed and folded her hands together in front of her skirt. A young woman appeared at the doorway, dressed in the sober clothing of a servant. She smiled warmly. "Hello, miss," she said. "The master had your trunk sent up."

"Oh, yes, my trunk."

"May we bring it in?"

"Of course."

The girl turned back toward the sitting room. "Come on, then," she called, "and mind you don't scratch the furniture."

Two laborers entered, each holding one end of Isabel's trunk and struggling with its weight. They huffed

Alice Gaines

and puffed their way to the center of the room and set the trunk on the floor. Their burden laid to rest, they straightened. One of them ran his arm over his forehead.

"I'm so sorry," Isabel said. "That's a quarter full of books. It must be dreadfully heavy."

"Not to worry, miss," the girl answered. "The lads aren't afraid of a bit of work." She glanced toward the workmen. "Are you?"

The man who'd mopped his brow looked at the girl with more than a hint of irritation. "No'm," he mumbled. He turned to Isabel. "Welcome to Harrowgate."

"Thank you," Isabel replied.

He nodded and then tapped his companion on the arm. The two of them turned and left the room.

The girl smiled at Isabel and dropped a little curtsy. "I'm Clarice," she said.

"How do you do?" Isabel answered. "I'm Isabel Gannon."

Clarice stood her ground, the smile never wavering on her face. "Well," she said after a moment.

"Well?"

"Shall I unpack your things?"

Oh, dear heaven. The child had been sent to act as her personal maid. Jungles held few secrets from Isabel. Mountains, bogs, even caves didn't mystify her. But boudoirs? Servants? Lady's maids? She had dropped down onto a foreign continent, indeed, and her only hope of regaining her equilibrium lay in spending some quiet time with her thoughts, soon. And alone.

"Thank you very much, Clarice," she said. "But I can manage on my own."

The sparkle in Clarice's brown eyes dimmed, and her smile faltered. "Mr. Julian would be quite displeased if you weren't given every consideration, and we don't have a lady's maid."

"Not even for the mistress of the house?"

Waitangi Nights

Her expression darkened even more. "We don't have a mistress, either."

No mistress of the house, and therefore no lady's maid. Clarice's predicament suddenly became clear. Isabel's appearance must have been the poor child's first chance to advance among the staff.

"What's your current position in the household?" Isabel asked.

"Second housemaid, miss," Clarice answered. She gazed up at Isabel, entreating with her eyes. "But I'll do a good job for you. I don't plan on staying a second housemaid forever."

Isabel didn't have to know much about wealthy households to know that second housemaid to lady's maid was quite a promotion. Clarice stood before her, pleading her case much as Isabel had done a few moments earlier with Mr. Julian. She could hardly deny Clarice as much opportunity as she had received, or thought she had received, at least.

"I'm sure you'll do wonderfully well," she said.

Clarice dropped another curtsy. "Thank you, miss."

"But I'll confess, I know even less about being a lady than you do about being a lady's maid. I'm afraid we'll have to help each other muddle through."

The girl's sunny smile reappeared, followed by a little laugh, clear as a bell and thoroughly pleasing.

"Now, then," Isabel continued. "What do we do first?"

"I'll unpack your trunk and hang up your clothes." Clarice extended her hand. "If I may have the key."

"No need. The lock broke years ago."

"You sit and rest, miss. You've had such a long journey." She clucked her tongue in sympathy—the perfect combination of admiration and solicitousness. Isabel took a seat at the dressing table and watched as Clarice opened the lid of the trunk, the ancient hinges groaning in protest. The girl lifted out the tray from the top, walked across the room, and set it on the bed. She returned, carrying Isabel's comb and brush, and laid

Alice Gaines

them on the table in front of Isabel.

Isabel pulled the pins from her dark hair and shook it free. Then she picked up the brush and dragged it through the tangles.

Clarice straightened from her work, one of Isabel's dresses draped over her arm. "I'll do that for you," she said.

"Let me," Isabel said. "You've enough to do with my trunk."

"Very well, miss. But later I'll do up your hair all pretty-like. I've a curling iron in my room."

Oh, dear. "All pretty-like" was *not* what Isabel had had in mind. She had planned to braid her hair and pin it back up, splash some water on her face, and then get through dinner as best she could. Would her newly acquired lady's maid let her get away with such a simple plan?

Clarice picked up another dress and raised a critical brow. "Which gown will you want to wear to dinner?"

"I thought I'd wear what I have on now," Isabel said. "I don't own any gowns."

"Oooh, this is pretty." Clarice draped the clothing in her arms over the top of the trunk and pulled out Isabel's only good dress. She held the blue silk in front of her and inspected it. "You should wear this tonight. Tomorrow I can take down the neckline a bit."

"I don't think—"

"You have such lovely skin. You should show it off."

"But—"

"And here's a tournure and underskirt," Clarice declared, peering into the trunk. "I'll have you looking pretty enough to turn the master's head, that I will."

"Clarice . . ."

Clarice didn't respond but proceeded to the bed, where she lay the blue dress out over the comforter. She hummed a little tune the whole time, in a high, reedy voice full of youthful enthusiasm, and Isabel smiled in spite of herself. Let the girl do her best. She'd find out

Waitangi Nights

soon enough that her mistress didn't have it in her to turn heads, not with her unremarkable figure and features.

To Isabel's dismay, at age sixteen she'd stopped growing entirely, never topping five feet two. Her hair and eyes had outstripped her stature, however—her hair trailing down her back in thick, unruly waves and her eyes half-filling her face. Cute was the only charitable way to describe the way she looked, along with nicknames like "pixie" and "crumpet."

But she had one great asset, her mind. And that didn't depend on pretty gowns or curling irons or any other sort of fluffery.

She'd long ago reconciled herself to her own appearance. But now she was rather curious about the master, and perhaps a little feminine gossip might tell her how best to deal with him. "What's Mr. Julian like?" she asked.

"He's a gentleman right enough, miss. Despite his roughness."

"And where does that roughness come from, I wonder?"

Clarice shrugged. "Some from what he's been through, I suppose. Some's just his nature. He's always had a sort of wildness abut him, or so the older servants say."

Isabel remembered how he had appeared in his study, the fire in his eyes, the sunlight shimmering in his hair. Most especially she recalled the economy of movement, the coiled strength underneath a gentleman's dress. *Dear heaven, such fancies.*

"What's he been through, Clarice?"

The girl hesitated, dropping the hem of Isabel's dress and straightening. "I have run on, haven't I?" she said quietly.

"Does it have anything to do with the doors not having locks?"

"I don't like to gossip, miss."

Alice Gaines

"But surely if something is wrong here, I need to know about it."

"There's nothing wrong. Truly." Clarice glanced about, avoiding Isabel's gaze. "There was an accident in the house some years ago. I don't know much about it."

Isabel studied her for another moment. Her expression had clouded, quite in contrast to her earlier delight. She was sincerely upset about something. "I'm sorry," Isabel muttered. "I didn't mean to pry."

"No matter." Clarice bustled back to the trunk, dispatching the gloom with a wave of her hand. "As stern as he is, Mr. Julian's an honest man and very fair with his staff," she said. "He doesn't toy with the females among us, either, even though there are some who wouldn't put up a fuss if he did."

"Are you one of those?" Isabel asked.

Clarice's brown eyes twinkled. "Not me, miss. Although I will admit I let my eye linger on him now and then. He's mighty fine to look at."

Isabel thought back to broad shoulders and long, graceful fingers. "Yes, I suppose he is."

"Hoping to rise above one's station can only bring a lass to grief, haven't I seen that often enough?" She gave Isabel a conspiratorial wink. "My ambitions lie elsewhere."

"I'm sure you'll fulfill them."

"Thank you, miss. Now let me help you out of that dress, and I'll draw you a nice, hot bath."

Isabel rose and turned so that Clarice could unhook her clothes. "You're sweet, but that's so much trouble," she said over her shoulder.

"No trouble at all," Clarice answered, her fingers loosening Isabel's dress until if fell into a heap at her feet. Then she started in on the stays of Isabel's corset. "I just turn on the spouts."

"Spouts?"

"In the tub."

Waitangi Nights

Clarice finished with the corset, and Isabel stepped out of the pile of clothing, unbuttoned her shoes, and kicked out of them.

Clarice led the way to a door on the far wall and opened it to reveal a smaller room. Sunlight from a tiny window danced off the white walls and the fixtures: a water closet, basin, and claw-footed tub. Clarice bent over the tub, dropped a stopper into the drain, and turned the spouts. After a moment, steam curled out of the water that ran from the faucet.

"Mr. Julian makes sure we have all the latest," she said. "None of us will ever have to haul water for baths again."

The room began to heat from the water filling the tub. Clarice reached to a large crystal bowl and poured some bath salts into the steaming liquid. Then she swished it around with her hand and turned off the taps. "Now, you climb in and have a good soak. I'll have your dress pressed and be back with a curling iron. We'll turn you into a real beauty, enough to catch the master's eye."

Humming again, Clarice left the room. Isabel slipped out of her chemise, stockings, and drawers. Fully naked, she lifted one foot over and into the tub. The water was hot and fragrant with rose petals. Heaven. She climbed the rest of the way in and lowered herself into the water. She scooped some up and over her shoulders and felt her muscles relax. Testing the miracle she had just witnessed, she reached out and turned the spout. More hot water splashed into the tub, setting up delicious currents between her legs. She leaned back against the porcelain of the tub and closed her eyes.

After a moment, the heat and scent eased her, preparing her for dinner and whatever lay ahead, whatever fate Harrowgate Manor and its master had in mind for her.

Chapter Two

Richard watched Sammy pour a generous shot of whiskey into a crystal tumbler. Then his longtime gentleman's gentleman and partner in crime placed the drink on a silver salver and turned toward him. He held out the glass to Richard, as properly as any English butler. But the same glint of mischief played in his eyes that had been there all afternoon.

Richard took the glass and did his best to glare at Sammy. "You knew, didn't you?"

"Knew, sir?"

"Don't use that 'sir' nonsense on me," Richard growled. "You knew about Miss Gannon and didn't tell me."

"Not me. The note said 'Gannon.' I thought her father had come."

"But you rode all the way back from the docks with her," Richard insisted. "You might have warned me."

"I saved her for a surprise. I thought you would like it."

Waitangi Nights

"Rubbish." Richard took a sip of whiskey, then paced across the balcony and sat on the stone balustrade. The last rays of the sun warmed him through the shoulders of his tailcoat.

Surprise indeed. The whole afternoon had provided one surprise after another, mostly of his own making. Very well, he had taken on a woman as nurseryman. But she very likely did know more about orchids than anyone else he would find, especially so far from England. And very well, he'd given her a room in the house. The roof of the glasshouse cottage really did leak, even in the most meager rainstorm.

He studied his whiskey. "What do you think of our Miss Gannon?" he asked.

Sammy put his hands behind his back and shrugged.

"She's rather an odd bird, wouldn't you say?" Richard continued. "With eyes a bit too large for her face."

"Whatever you say, sir."

"Dammit, man. You know I hate it when you do your servant's imitation. I'm asking your opinion."

Sammy smiled, sincerely this time. "I think she's a courageous young woman to travel alone all the way from England. She didn't know if you'd turn her around and send her right back."

Richard snorted. "I hate it even more when you're right."

Sammy laughed outright at that. In the six months since his father had died, Richard had assumed the position of master with the rest of the staff, but Sammy resisted intimidation. Oh well, one couldn't spend months in the goldfields with one's manservant—sleeping in the same hut, eating out of the same pot—without inviting at least some intimacy. And, truth be told, Sammy made a much better friend than valet.

Richard took another sip of his drink and studied Sammy's earnest, open face. "And you are right about Miss Gannon, of course."

Sammy grinned. "Yes, sir."

Alice Gaines

Oh, hell. What was giving him such gooseflesh, anyway? Just because there hadn't been a female in residence at Harrowgate since Louisa. Miss Gannon wouldn't have to deal with his father. She'd only have to deal with him. And only until the cottage could be repaired.

"Hello," came a tentative call from inside the house. The same soft voice that had echoed around his brain since the afternoon. Isabel Gannon. He rose quickly from his seat.

She appeared at the French doors that separated the library from the balcony and glanced around. There were those eyes again. He'd been right telling Sammy that they dominated her face, but whether her eyes were really so large or the rest of her features were really so petite, he couldn't tell. Whatever the cause, the overall effect was to force him to stare into the ebony depths of her gaze and lose himself. And damn him if he hadn't done it again.

He pulled himself back to the present. "So, you've found us, Miss Gannon."

"Clarice directed me to the library," she answered.

"Clarice is a very good girl," he said. "I hope you find her adequate."

"More than adequate," she said. "I appreciate your kindness, but you mustn't treat me like a guest. I'm your employee."

He let his gaze roam from her hair—which was now attractively arranged in a cascade of sable curls—along the length of her throat to soft, pale skin that stretched over a delicate collarbone. He lingered on the deep blue silk of her dress, her narrow waist, and the flare of her hips. Finally, he looked down at the toes of the slippers that peeked demurely out from beneath her hem. When he glanced back at her face, he noticed that her cheeks had turned a very appealing pink.

"I'm afraid Clarice got rather carried away with dressing me," she said.

Waitangi Nights

"Much to my delight, I assure you."

She took a breath. "But you will simply have to remember that I'm a professional woman."

"No doubt you'll remind me frequently."

She stared at him, her expression a mixture of apprehension and defiance. A gracious host would say or do something to put her at ease. Richard opted to stare right back at her instead.

"Sherry, Miss Gannon?" Sammy asked.

"Thank you."

Sammy filled a tiny, stemmed glass with Amontillado, set it on the salver, and presented it to Miss Gannon. She took it and brought it to her lips, tasted the liquid, and smiled. All very aristocratic and quite insincere. She was working hard to cover her uneasiness, but in fact, Richard had seldom seen anyone so tense. The way her eyes darted from place to place gave her away, as did the slight tremble of her fingers.

What the devil could be making her so nervous? Himself, no doubt. And why the hell not? Women with any sense at all kept well away from the men in his family. He took another sip of his whiskey and studied her over the rim of his glass.

"You have an impressive collection of books, Mr. Julian," she said. "Have you read any of them?"

Richard laughed aloud. An impertinent question, if ever he'd heard one. Impertinence would hold her in good stead at Harrowgate. "I try to read a little every day," he replied. "At least until my poor brain overheats."

Sammy snickered quietly.

The corners of the prim Miss Gannon's mouth quirked upward in a smile. Her lips curled into a tempting little morsel, as they had earlier in his study, reminding him of fruit just ripe enough to be sweet. But the same fierce pride he'd seen that afternoon still shone in her eyes.

"That was ungenerous of me," she said. "You must

understand—I've spent a great deal of time in wealthy households, where the people are surrounded with treasures they almost always fail to value, or even to see."

"I appreciate what I have."

"I'm glad to hear it." She took another sip of sherry. "You have several of Mr. Darwin's books," she commented after a moment.

"Do you approve?" he asked.

"Approve?" she repeated, raising one eyebrow. "That's an odd way to put it. One doesn't approve or disapprove of scientific theory. It simply is."

"You've been persuaded by Darwin's arguments?"

"They're very convincing," she answered. "The man himself was even more so."

"You knew him?"

"My father supplied several of his specimens."

So, here was the meat of her little presentation. She had met Darwin, and she supposed that would impress him. And he wasn't impressed, not by her name-dropping, but by the cheeky way she stood there, sipping his expensive sherry and looking about her as though evaluating everything: Sammy, Harrowgate, himself.

"Then you believe we're all animals?" he goaded. "Apes?"

"I believe humans and apes have a common ancestor," she corrected. "Please don't misstate the theory."

"Sir?" Sammy said softly, pointing to the pocket watch in his hand. "It's time."

"Ah, yes." Richard set his drink on the balustrade and extended his arm toward Miss Gannon. "We'd best go in to dinner, or Mrs. Willis will have my head."

"Mrs. Willis?"

"My cook. She demands punctuality."

A tiny gleam of amusement entered her eye. "Aren't you the master of Harrowgate?"

"Except for Mrs. Willis," Richard answered. "She's

Waitangi Nights

been here longer than I have. Now, will you take my arm?"

She handed her glass to Sammy and then turned back to Richard. She looked at his sleeve for a moment, suspiciously, as though expecting him to pull back at any moment, leaving her to look foolish. Finally, she placed her hand on his arm, but so lightly he could hardly feel the pressure of her fingers. Small they were, delicate and pale, like fragile china.

He covered them with his own and led her through the library and into the hall. "Did you like your rooms, Miss Gannon?"

"You have an odd way with words, Mr. Julian," she said, matching her stride to his. "Liking is hardly the way I feel about living in such splendor."

"I'm glad you approve."

They reached the dining room. He paused, and she dropped her hand from his arm. "But I don't approve," she said. "I'm afraid the rooms are quite unsuitable."

"The devil you say."

She didn't answer but simply stood, looking up at him as though he were some kind of oaf who had to have the simplest matters explained to him. Well, in this case, he did want an explanation, and he would have it, before they'd finished their soup. He gestured toward the dining table. "Please, have a seat."

She obliged, allowing Ned, the footman, to pull out her chair. Richard took his place at the head of the table, shook out his napkin, and put it into his lap. "Perhaps you'll tell me what in damnation is unsuitable about those rooms."

"I've lived a good part of my life among men," she said, "I'm used to profane language, and I won't be intimidated by it."

Curse the woman if she hadn't done it again. Just as she had in the study earlier—she'd caught him unawares with some bit of impudent nonsense. Unsuitable. What the devil did that mean? "Then I'll repeat," he snapped. "What in damnation is unsuitable about those rooms?"

"First, I shouldn't stay alone with you in this house."

He had to laugh at that. "Alone? I have a full staff of servants."

"Who are completely loyal to you and would say nothing against you, no matter what you decided to do. They can hardly be considered proper supervision."

"Supervision?" he repeated, his voice rising unpleasantly, even to his own ears. "You think I need to be supervised?"

"What do *you* think?" she asked quietly.

"Well, I'll be damned."

She stared at him in silence. Gone was the timid little creature who had barely found enough courage to touch his sleeve. The mouse had turned to face down the cat, confound her. "I'll be damned," he repeated.

She placed her own napkin in her lap. "What's more important, I should stay in the nurseryman's cottage so that I can be near the orchids."

"I've told you, the cottage is in no state for anyone to live in."

Ned set a bowl of soup before her, and she lifted her spoon, curling her little finger into a delicate arch. "I'm sure you have the wherewithal to have it fixed."

"Of course I do."

"Well, then?"

Ned served Richard and then retreated quietly. Richard stared at Miss Isabel Gannon over his own soup. "My carpenter is occupied with something else just now."

She took a taste of her soup and then set her spoon down, lifted her chin, and stared back at him. "What?"

"What do you mean 'what'?" he snapped.

"With what is your carpenter occupied?"

Of all the audacity. "That's none of your business, Miss Gannon."

She lifted a very disapproving brow.

Waitangi Nights

"You're my employee," he added, leaning toward her for emphasis, "and you will stay where I say you will stay. Is that understood?"

She looked down into her bowl and lifted her spoon again. "Yes, sir."

"Until I change my mind, you'll stay here in the house." He lifted his own spoon in triumph—perhaps. "With me."

Moonlight so intense as to be preternatural poured through the open window of Isabel's sitting room and bathed her in magic as she sat, composing her thoughts and breathing in the night smells. The air had taken on a chill, but rather than close the window, she had put on a shawl. She didn't want to miss the perfume of grass and flowers—or the light, the miraculous moonlight. The house had quieted and she had time to think in peace. The cool breeze felt like a balm against her skin.

What to make of it all? First, the house and her place in it. She'd been ordered to remain in these rooms, fitted out as elegantly as the Queen of Sheba. And yet her lack of choice in the matter made the suite into a sort of prison, an opulent, gilded prison, a prison with no lock on the door.

She'd been right, of course. Under no stretch of the imagination could the world consider it proper for her to stay under the same roof with Mr. Julian. His own servants could not make adequate chaperons, no matter how many of them he had. But then, she'd never let propriety rule her behavior in the past. If she had, she'd never have traveled down the Amazon with her father or lived among the half-naked Indians there. She wouldn't have altered a pair of boy's trousers for herself so that she could scramble into trees after orchids when her father had grown too old to do it.

In any case, the master of Harrowgate wasn't likely to trouble her, not in the way men usually trouble women prettier than her.

Alice Gaines

Isabel put her chin in her palm, rested her elbow on the sill, and gazed out over the formal gardens. Richard Julian might be the very devil himself, but he had a fortune and looked like a dashing pirate. Men like that seldom even noticed women like her—untitled, unmoneyed, and unimposing.

A man like that donned his charm for any woman, even a bookish spinster of twenty-five. He put it on as easily as he dressed himself in that impeccable tailcoat and blindingly white shirt. And he took it off again at the first challenge to his authority, as she had learned firsthand over the soup course.

Well, so much the better for her. With no indecent proposals from him, she'd have an easier time attaining her status as nurseryman. As soon as she made him see the reason of giving her the cottage, she could go about her business undisturbed. Isabel straightened and pulled her shawl tighter around her. Yes, things would settle right into place as soon as she got out of the main house and into her own little cottage.

A board creaked out in the hallway. Isabel turned and glanced in that direction. A circle of light spilled through the hole in the door into the sitting room. Someone was out there, with an oil lamp, if she could judge from the flickering. She gathered her shawl around her tightly and sat as silently as she could, not moving, hardly breathing.

The door moved, opening a foot or so, until the top book fell off the pile onto the carpet. Isabel took a deep breath and held it. But the door stayed where it was, light now shining along its entire length. Then came a sigh, deep and soft, and the light moved away. More boards creaked as footsteps resounded down the hall.

Isabel waited a moment to let the intruder put some distance between them. Then she padded barefoot to the door, inched it open a bit farther, and stuck her head into the hall. She only saw the man's back, but she

Waitangi Nights

couldn't mistake the broad shoulders or the wild curls. Richard Julian.

He wore an ankle-length nightgown as shockingly white as his dress shirt. Lace at the cuffs made the garment appear feminine, in marked contrast to his height and the strength of his hands, one of which held a lamp high. He reached the end of the corridor and descended the stairs to the floor below, taking the light with him.

Warm sunlight teased Isabel's eyes open on her first morning at Harrowgate and revealed yet another surprise: a little girl of five or six sitting cross-legged at the end of her bed.

Dear heaven, another interloper. Isabel sat up, pulling the covers over her night dress. "Who are you?"

"Beatrice," she answered. "But everyone calls me Bunny. Isn't that silly?"

"Well, I don't know." Isabel didn't normally think about names being silly. But then she wasn't accustomed to being quizzed by children before her breakfast. And she didn't plan to get accustomed to it.

The child leaned toward her and scrutinized her face, giving Isabel a close-up view of blue eyes set off by dark, glowing skin. "Cousin Richard was right," Bunny said solemnly.

"Right?" Isabel asked. "About what?"

"He said there was a pretty lady sleeping in this room and I wasn't to disturb her."

Isabel's cheeks warmed with pleasure, thoroughly unwarranted, of course. "Did he now?"

Bunny backed away again, and her eyes grew wide. "I didn't disturb you, did I? I was very quiet."

"A well-behaved little girl doesn't go into people's bedrooms uninvited."

"But I couldn't wait," Bunny protested. "It's very late in the morning, you know."

"You're up, miss," came a voice from the sitting room doorway—Clarice. Perhaps the footman would come next and then the gardener's staff. Perhaps the master of the house himself might follow. They could all have a cup of tea and discuss plans for the day.

"I could hear you talking from the hall," Clarice said, apparently unconcerned with what must have been some exasperation in Isabel's expression. "And here you are, too, little Miss Bunny," she added. "Nanny wants to start your lessons."

Bunny drew herself up to her full height, which wasn't much, and pointed toward Isabel. "But this lady is going to take me to play with the orchids."

Clarice walked to the dressing table and set her burden, a small tray with tea cup and pot, onto it. "Did Mr. Julian tell you that?"

"No." Bunny worried her lower lip for a moment and then turned back to Isabel. "But I may play with the orchids, mayn't I?"

Isabel looked into those blue eyes, filled with the urgency of a little girl's request, and felt herself begin to thaw.

"Orchids are living things, and we don't play with them," she said. Bunny's brows knitted together. "But I'll be happy to take you to the orchids," Isabel added quickly, "and show you how they grow."

A dazzling smile spread over the girl's little face, a smile that went straight into Isabel and warmed her heart.

"Thank you, Miss . . ." Bunny said.

"I tell you what. I'll let you call me Isabel if I may call you Bunny."

The smile grew even wider. "All right."

"Now, you get yourself to the schoolroom, Miss Bunny," Clarice said. "I'll send Miss Gannon along when she's dressed and has had her tea."

Bunny climbed from the bed and scampered out of the room. Clarice followed her with her eyes, smiling indulgently. Then she turned to the dressing table and poured a cup of tea. That, at least, was entirely appropriate, even welcome.

Isabel threw back the covers and got up. She took the cup Clarice offered and sat at the dressing table. "Does everyone come and go as they please in this house?"

"Bunny does, I'm afraid," Clarice answered. "Mr. Julian's her guardian, and he spoils her something awful."

"She seems polite enough otherwise."

Clarice dug her fingers into Isabel's braid, unplaiting it. "Her own sweet disposition, miss. The way the master dotes on her, she could be a little harridan if she wanted, and he'd never say a word."

"Besotted, eh?"

"Don't you know it?" Clarice clucked her tongue. "One tear out of her and he'll come quite undone, turn the house inside out to find some way to get her smile back. Happily for us all, she doesn't cry often."

Isabel took a sip of her tea and watched in the mirror as Clarice pulled her brush through her hair. "And what of Mr. Julian himself?"

"Hmm?"

"Does he come and go as he pleases?"

The brush paused mid-stroke. "I suppose so." Clarice shrugged, an unconvincing attempt at nonchalance. "Why do you ask?"

"He nearly let himself into my sitting room last night."

"Are you sure?"

Isabel turned and looked up at Clarice directly. "I saw him with my own eyes. And I'd like to know what he thought he was doing."

Clarice avoided her gaze, instead concentrating on Isabel's hair and renewing her brushing with some vigor. "He likes to look in on us from time to time. He doesn't mean anything by it."

"It isn't proper."

Clarice laughed. "Mr. Julian doesn't concern himself with proper, miss."

"So I gather. But why does he feel it necessary to check on everyone?"

Clarice hesitated for just a moment. "Samuel says he gets restless at night. It eases him to know all's well in the house. Helps him to sleep."

Helps him to sleep, does it? His prowling didn't help *her* to sleep. Especially if he did it at will and with the tacit permission of the household staff. And especially if she couldn't lock her door, couldn't even close it properly. "I'll have to speak to him."

"Please don't do that, miss."

"But the situation is untenable," Isabel said. "People slipping into and out of my rooms while I'm asleep, or ought to be asleep. Prudery is one thing, but this just isn't done."

"There's no harm in it. Truly there isn't," Clarice implored. "And questioning Mr. Julian's actions would only upset him."

Isabel turned back again and studied Clarice. Her mouth had narrowed into a nervous line, and she held onto the brush tightly with both hands. What could be worrying the girl so badly?

Isabel put a hand on Clarice's intertwined fingers and gave them a gentle squeeze. "I'll be tactful, but the man simply must learn that there are boundaries even he dares not cross."

"If you say so," Clarice answered. But she didn't sound convinced, not one bit.

Chapter Three

"The devil you say." Richard stormed across the terrace and descended to the garden, Quinn and Mrs. Willis right behind him. "She opened the glasshouse doors?"

"And all the vents," Quinn, his gardener, answered. "The wind's whipping through there, sir. You should only see the poor plants swaying in it."

Of all the idiotic, reckless, purely stupid things to do. He'd hired Isabel Gannon to care for his orchids, not to murder them. He proceeded through the roses and onto the lawn. "What could be wrong with the blasted woman?" he growled.

"That's not all she's done, sir," Mrs. Willis said. Despite her sixty or so years, the cook kept pace with him, the ribbons on her cap bobbing furiously. "Tell the master the rest, Mr. Quinn."

The gardener's legs were considerably shorter than Richard's, and he had to trot to keep up. He bounded alongside Richard's elbow, gasping for air. "She's had my whole staff working to . . ." Quinn's face grew quite red. "To . . ."

Alice Gaines

Richard stopped in the middle of the croquet court and glared down at him. Mrs. Willis had to step aside smartly not to crash into his back. "Out with it, man," Richard demanded. "To do what?"

Quinn took another breath. "To move the orchids out of doors, sir."

"Out of doors?" Was the woman insane? "My orchids? Out of doors?"

Mrs. Willis nodded in righteous indignation, giving the ribbons on her cap more nervous fits. "I could scarce credit it when Mr. Quinn told me," she said. "I brought him straight to you to repeat the tale."

"Damnation." Richard marched to the edge of the yard, through the topiary chessmen, to the path that led to the glasshouse. He continued between the hedgerows, his footsteps crunching angrily in the gravel.

"I've cared for those plants myself, Mr. Julian, ever since Mr. Turner died," Quinn panted. "And now a female, a female, comes in and undoes all my hard work."

"This is what comes of elevating a domestic above her station," Mrs. Willis added, now rather short of breath herself. "I might have told you something like this would happen."

Quinn grunted in agreement.

"An employee acting like a guest upsets the balance of things, sir," she continued.

Damn it all, Mrs. Willis was right. He had given the impudent Miss Gannon too much freedom. But that could be corrected. "We'll have the balance of things restored soon enough, Mrs. Willis," he growled. "Soon enough."

They rounded a corner in the hedge and came within view of the glasshouse. Richard stopped dead and took in the scene in front of him. The doors had indeed been thrown open, and the better part of Mr. Quinn's staff bustled in and out carrying plants and benches. Several score of plants had already been removed from inside and sat in rows along the gravel path—exposed to the elements. The woman must have lost her mind. "Miss Gannon," Richard called.

All activity ceased, the gardeners stopping in their tracks, some holding his plants, his precious orchids, like so many petunias in their hands. "Miss Gannon," he roared.

A small figure appeared at the door, not his upstart nurseryman, but Bunny. Her face broke into a grin, and she ran to him. He lifted her onto his hip, where she settled, slipping her arms around his neck. "You've been a very bad boy, Cousin Richard. Isabel says you've been boiling 'sparagus in the glasshouse."

"Isabel is it? We'll just see if she responds to her given name." He took a few steps toward the glasshouse. "Isabel," he shouted, even more loudly than before.

She finally deigned to show herself, and quite a sight she made. Sweat had soaked through her bodice and ran in rivulets down the side of her head, caking wisps of hair to her temples. She had rolled up her sleeves, exposing her forearms and very dirty hands. When she spotted him, she straightened, pushed her hair from her face, and walked toward him stiff-backed, as though she were royalty, damn her.

"There you are," she declared. "I don't know how you can show your face after what I've found here."

"I?" Richard sputtered. "Show *my* face? What in hell do you mean by that?"

Bunny giggled.

He took a breath and tried to compose himself. "What do you mean, show *my* face?"

"This glasshouse is a disgrace, sir. When I opened the door I thought I'd crossed the portal to Hades, the heat was so fierce."

"Damn."

Bunny wiggled in his arms.

"For heaven's sake, woman. Of course the house is hot, there are orchids growing inside."

Alice Gaines

"Dying inside," she corrected. "Because of your ignorance."

He looked down into her face and found it full of haughtiness and nerve. Bloody hell. In another minute he'd bust a gusset if he couldn't swear out loud. He set Bunny onto the ground. "Mrs. Willis, would you please take Bunny into the house?"

"But Cousin Richard," the girl protested.

"Run along now," he said. "Back to your lessons."

Mrs. Willis took Bunny's hand and led her along the path toward the house. Richard watched them until they were out of earshot. Then he turned back to Isabel Gannon. "Damn it all to hell, woman. Explain yourself."

She bristled, straightening her back and planting her hands on her hips. "You've been suffocating your orchids in this heat, steaming them like vegetables for your dinner."

"That's what Bunny meant about asparagus?"

"Don't have none of it, sir," Quinn burst in. "Everyone knows orchids grow in jungles. Hot jungles."

Isabel Gannon turned on him. "Everyone is wrong, Mr. Quinn."

"Ezekiel Turner, God rest his soul, a man who worked for your father for years, told me so, Mr. Julian." Quinn's voice caught with emotion. "Told me on his death bed, 'Quinn, keep the orchids warm.' And that I done, sir."

Richard put his hand on the man's shoulder. "Of course, you have."

"It's a common misconception, Mr. Quinn," Isabel Gannon said more quietly. Apparently the display of emotion had taken a bit of the fire out of her. "Some orchids do grow in very hot climates, but not most. The *masdevallias* especially wilt in that sort of heat."

"You can believe her if you want, Mr. Julian," Quinn said. "But to my way of seeing things, it's a sad day when a slip of a girl can come in here and contradict Mr. Ezekiel Turner."

Waitangi Nights

Miss Gannon bristled again and opened her mouth. Before she could say anything, Richard raised his hand, commanding silence. "No one's contradicting Mr. Turner."

"But he's wrong," she said.

Richard fixed her with a look that ought to be good enough to melt tallow. She shut her mouth and crossed her arms over her chest.

"Now, perhaps you'll explain all this to us poor males, Miss Gannon," he said. "Calmly."

"*Masdevallias* are cool growers, Mr. Julian. They don't even like a warm day, and they can't tolerate heat at all."

"How can that be?" he asked. "Even I know they grow at the equator."

"At very high altitudes." She gestured with her dirty hands. "Bathed in clouds—cool, moist air. Cool, sir."

Richard studied her. She had that same look of determination in her eyes that he had seen the day before: fierce, proud, admirable even. And after all, she had no reason to harm the orchids. She'd only hurt her own reputation.

Richard glowered at her a bit more, just to make sure she knew who owned the orchids, who was really in charge. "All right, Miss Gannon. We'll grow them your way, but if any of these plants die you'll find yourself out of a job."

"They won't die," she said.

He turned back to Quinn. "Perhaps we should give Miss Gannon's methods a try," he said. "We *have* lost quite a few of the *masdevallias* by following Mr. Turner's instructions."

Quinn looked from Richard to the still fuming Isabel Gannon.

"If you say so, sir," he grumbled finally, "but I wash my hands of it."

"Of course," Richard answered. "My responsibility entirely."

Alice Gaines

"Then I'll just be back about my own work, sir." Quinn walked away, shaking his head at the insanity of it all.

One of Quinn's assistants cleared his throat. "What do you want us to do, Mr. Julian?"

Richard looked around at the rest of Quinn's staff. Some were staring at plants in their hands, others at their feet.

"I'll need help with this," Isabel Gannon said softly, "or it will take me all day."

"Finish this work and then report to Mr. Quinn," he said. The men went about their chores, and Richard turned back to the cause of the disturbance. "Well, Miss Gannon," he said. "You've upset my cook and my gardener, taken my ward away from her studies, and spread my orchids all over the place. None of the men in this position ever did that."

"None of them ever showed you something like this, either, I'll wager," she said. She turned and led him to a large barrel. She bent over it, her torso disappearing inside, and her rump sticking most indecorously into the air. Damned if she couldn't act like a perfect prude at one moment; then behave in a deliciously indelicate manner at the next. Oblivious to the view of her nether regions she had just given him, she reemerged from the barrel, holding a small plant that was covered with pristine, white flowers. "*Tovarensis*," she declared, handing it to him.

"*Tov—*"

"One of the plants I brought. With love and a little luck I'll have all your *masdevallias* covered with blooms like these, in every color of the rainbow."

Richard took a closer look. The orchid was truly a remarkable specimen. Less than six inches tall, it held twenty or thirty blossoms—each a perfect white triangle with starched tips standing at attention at the corners. If she had cared for it on a long ocean voyage and could still coax results like this from it, if she had hundreds more plants, his plants, at her disposal, if she really could manage all that, she might turn out to be worth much more than her salary. Maybe even more than a few ruffled feathers among the older staff. "Do you truly think you can grow my plants to do this well?" he asked.

"Of course. That's what I was trying to tell Mr. Quinn." She pushed a wisp of hair away from her face, leaving a smudge of dirt on her cheek. "You have the perfect climate here, out of doors, in the breezes from the bay. Perfect."

"Hmm."

She walked, almost waltzed, to where Quinn's workers had set a few benches along the gravel walk. "For now, we'll set up here and cover the plants with some shade cloth. But we'll need lathing as soon as it can be constructed."

"Lathing?"

She looked up at him, pure excitement in her eyes. "Slats set up above the plants to filter the sunlight." She walked the length of the benches, holding out her arms as though to measure them. "All along here. Then we'll redo the inside of the glasshouse."

"Now, see here."

She grabbed his hand and pulled him toward the glasshouse. Despite their delicacy, her fingers were very strong, and she gripped him with none of the shyness she had shown the night before. She walked along with him, hand in hand, as if they were dear friends. And curse him if he didn't like the feeling.

She had to step aside to let one of the gardeners out of the glasshouse, and she dropped his hand. After letting the man by, she stepped across the threshold without even looking back at Richard. He followed her inside, keeping himself close enough to her side that she could take his hand again if she wanted. He was acting like a blasted schoolboy and enjoying himself thoroughly.

She didn't touch him again but instead walked to the far end of the house. A large space was now empty because of all the plants and benches outside. But the area where she stood, near the heater, still held rows of orchids.

"You have several nice specimens that like the heat," she said. "I propose to erect some sort of moveable barrier, curtains perhaps." She spread her arms, demonstrating where the barrier would go. "This part of the house can be kept warmer than that part."

"And the *masdevallias* can be moved in here during colder weather," he said.

She smiled at him, her dark eyes sparkling. "Exactly. So of course, we'll need more benches built."

"Of course." He turned and stepped outdoors again. He glanced at the length of benches outside and the empty space inside. Quite a lot of work fulfilling her demands. "I want to be sure I understand everything you need," he said. "Everything."

She joined him and gestured toward the benches. "Lathing, that whole length."

"Solidly built."

"Certainly."

"And more benches for inside," he added, "like these?"

"If a second shelf could be built underneath for shade plants, it would give us more room."

"And you'll need all this soon?"

She took his hand again and squeezed it. "Oh, yes. As soon as possible."

"Then I'm afraid your cottage will have to wait."

She dropped his hand. "The cottage?"

"My carpenter will be busy with all this," he answered, making a sweeping gesture with his arm. "Lathing and benches."

"But—"

"Busy for quite some time I imagine." He put the orchid he still held into her hand, turned, and strode off down the walk toward the house. "I'll see you at luncheon, Miss Gannon."

"Mr. Julian," she called after him. He didn't stop but went on, smiling to himself.

Hours later, after a solitary, unsatisfying luncheon, Richard went looking for Miss Isabel Gannon. Perhaps she thought he'd merely invited her to take the midday meal with him. Perhaps she thought her attendance at table—punctual attendance, mind you—was optional. But Mrs. Willis didn't fancy spending all morning making splendid dishes only to have them fed to the dogs, and Richard had to agree. From now on, when he told Miss Gannon he'd see her at luncheon, he'd damned well better see her at luncheon.

He rounded the bend in the gravel path and caught sight of the glasshouse. Where all had been madness earlier, now method reigned. His plants sat in orderly rows on benches, covered by some gauzy fabric. The glasshouse door stood open, and he approached, glancing at the orchids inside. Leaves waved in the gentle breeze, seemingly quite content in the currents of air. A fresh, green scent wafted to him, settling sweetly in his nostrils and making him smile.

Maybe she did know what she was doing with the orchids. God knew he'd never wanted to set foot in the glasshouse when Turner had had the air shimmering with heat. Maybe the plants felt the same way.

He stepped inside and looked down the rows of benches. No sign of the woman. Very well, she'd worked her little miracle. Now, where in hell was she?

He walked back outside and looked first toward the house and then down the path into the wooded part of the estate. Soft laughter—lovely, warm, and feminine—sounded from the direction of the little clearing where his mother used to spend long afternoons. He headed toward it.

Miss Gannon was there, all right, sitting on the marble bench, facing away from him and looking downward. She laughed again and bent toward the ground. "What a silly little thing you are," she said. "Have you found your way into the master's whiskey?"

A flutter of feathers answered, as a tiny bird danced around her feet. "Drunk at this hour of the day?" she continued. "What sort of bird would behave so disgracefully?"

"A fantail," Richard answered.

She turned abruptly, straightening and placing her hand over her breast. "Mr. Julian. How long have you been there?"

"Only a moment."

"You shouldn't come up on people unannounced."

"And you shouldn't ignore invitations to luncheon."

"I'm sorry," she answered. "I was busy."

She turned and looked back at the fantail, which still danced crazily at her feet.

Dammit, he'd scold later. Right now he wanted to hear more of her laughter. He walked to the bench and sat down beside her. "Your little friend here's a fantail."

As though to illustrate Richard's point, the bird hopped about a bit more, spreading its tail feathers, and flashing its white ear patch at her. She smiled at it, an expression of uncomplicated delight. "An enchanting creature, and so tame."

"They live all over New Zealand—both islands. The Maoris call them *piwakawaka*."

A low, clear note, like the sound of a flute came from among the trees, only a few yards distant. Miss Gannon tipped her head, listening. "And that call?" she said. "I've been hearing it all afternoon."

"A *tui*, no doubt."

"What does it look like?"

"I'll call it to us, and you can see for yourself."

Her eyes widened in surprise, as though he'd said something very clever. "You can do that?"

"Sammy taught me." And indeed, Sammy had, over

Waitangi Nights

twenty years before when they'd both been boys. Richard hadn't tried the trick for almost that long. But with any luck this particular *tui* would turn out to be a gullible bird that could be lured by even a poor imitation of its call.

Richard cupped his hands around his mouth and pursed his lips. He whistled for a moment, the noise coming out rather rusty in contrast to the purity of the *tui's* tone. He waited for a moment, watching the woman beside him. She had twisted her fingers together in her lap and sat completely still, perhaps even holding her breath.

Together they waited another few seconds. And then the answer came. Another sweet note, closer to them this time. Miss Gannon gave Richard a smile like liquid sunshine. "He's coming nearer."

Richard called again and then rested his hands on his thighs and sat back, inordinately pleased with himself. He'd never imagined that women might be charmed by bird calls, but this woman clearly was. If she showed much more delight in his performance, he'd end up puffing out his chest and strutting for her as the little fantail had.

Wings fluttered overhead, and the *tui* appeared, perching on a small branch and settling its feathers into place. Richard called to it again, and it cocked its head. Then it opened its beak and answered. This time the fluid single note ended in a croak and a gurgle.

Isabel Gannon brought her hands together and giggled into them. "Oh, he's lovely," she declared. "The ruff at his throat makes him look quite the gentleman."

"Ah, but appearances often deceive."

"He's such a dignified bird," she objected.

"Watch for a moment."

Catching its cue with the precision of a paid actor, the bird dipped its head and swung around, hanging from its perch almost upside down. Miss Gannon giggled again. "I see. Do all the birds of New Zealand act as though they've been tippling?"

"Not all. The *kiwi*, for example, is a very dull brown and walks about at night as carefully and soberly as a barrister."

"Can you lure *kiwis* by aping their calls, too, Mr. Julian?"

"I'm afraid not," he answered. "Only *tuis*."

The *tui* lifted itself from its branch with a loud whirring of its wings and flew off. "Perhaps not even *tuis*," Richard added. "That one seems to have tired of my conversation."

"Silly bird."

Richard studied her. Was it possible that Miss Isabel Gannon enjoyed his company? She took a deep breath, and her mouth curled into a gentle smile. A perfect expression of peaceful contemplation, her head cocked to one side as though listening to something. How could she look like that? She'd been here less than a day, had already weathered a storm of criticism from the senior members of his staff, and then had worked for hours without even stopping to eat. No one could have settled into a strange situation so quickly.

"You appear quite content, Miss Gannon."

"Hmm?" She shook herself out of her reverie. "I'm sorry?"

"What were you listening to?"

"I don't know. All afternoon, I've been hearing something like music. Very faint and far away. Do you hear it?"

Richard sat in silence, watching her. Other women on his staff had occasionally mentioned hearing music, or thinking they heard it. But he could never make the sound out. Even now he heard nothing except for the murmuring of the breeze and calls of birds.

"No, I don't," he answered finally.

She smiled. "Probably only my mind playing tricks on me. You were saying?"

He studied her another moment, watching as an easy

Waitangi Nights

smile replaced her pensive expression. "I had just remarked that you appear content here."

"Why shouldn't I be?" she asked. "Harrowgate is a lovely estate."

"But still, your life has been rather uncertain of late."

"Life is always uncertain," she answered. She looked at him, perfect assurance in her eyes. "We all must make our own contentment."

"That's easily said but more difficult to put into practice."

"Difficult or not, we have no choice."

As simple as that. She truly believed that one decided to be happy and then just did it. But how could she? She was without family, without funds. If he turned her out tomorrow, she'd most likely have nowhere to go, no one to go to. And yet here she sat, on his property, dependent on his whim, insisting that she was master of her own happiness. If she really could make her own place in the world, find her own peace, that would be a trick he'd pay dearly to learn.

"I'm afraid I don't see how that's possible," he said.

"You'd need to see a bit of the world, the non-European world, to understand. The Indians of the Amazon, for instance."

"You have been there?"

"Oh, yes." She paused for a moment. "The people of the Amazon live in conditions no proper Englishman could tolerate. Insubstantial shelter, no plumbing at all, very little privacy. Their clothing, if you can call it that, barely covers their most intimate parts, and the children go completely naked most of the time."

"And these people taught you about contentment?"

"For the most part, they're very happy and healthy, at least where the white man hasn't introduced his weapons and diseases."

"The noble savage?" he said.

"Nonsense," she answered. "They're no more noble than you or I."

"And not savages?"

"Certainly not."

Richard sighed. "Then I'm afraid your lesson still isn't clear."

"There's no mystery, Mr. Julian. One learns to be happy with what one has."

"Even if one has nothing, or next to it?"

"You have missed my point." She turned to him and looked into his eyes. "The Indians have a great deal—the beauty of their jungle, the love of their families."

"And what do you have, Miss Gannon?"

He shouldn't have asked that, had no right to ask. But dammit, he needed answers. She gazed at him evenly, seemingly unperturbed. "I have my memories," she answered after a moment. "I have myself."

And an easy conscience, no doubt. One that let her sleep at night, with no horrors to haunt her dreams and no fears for the future to set her to wandering the halls, listening and waiting for the old madness to return. "What if you've done things of which you're not proud?" he asked, still staring at her. "What if you've hurt people?"

She looked right back at him, not the slightest hesitation in her gaze. "Then you make things right."

Bloody hell. How was he supposed to do that? He needed forgiveness, and she offered simplicity. He needed assurances, and she offered rectitude. He couldn't ask her for more, at least not yet, maybe later when he understood the fierce independence in her eyes and how she'd arrived at it.

He sat, just looking at her, until she began to fidget.

She folded her hands in her lap and studied them. "You were in my rooms last night," she said quietly.

"No, I wasn't."

She lifted her chin and stared straight ahead of her to the trees beyond. "I saw you."

She had been awake. He'd felt her, even though he

Waitangi Nights

had no idea how that could be possible. "I stayed in the hall."

"Very well," she answered. "You opened the door to my boudoir. Why?"

"I needed to know you were safe."

"Safe from what?"

What could he tell her? He hardly knew the answer himself. Safe from demons—his demons? He sat in silence, his brain refusing to form coherent thoughts, his tongue refusing to form words.

"You mustn't do that again," she went on. "It isn't proper."

"Damn it all, woman. You just told me you've lived among half-naked Indians, and now you'll lecture me on propriety?"

"We're in New Zealand, not the Amazon."

"I don't give a damn where we are," Richard snapped. "And I care even less about what proper people think."

"You've made that quite clear," she answered, her voice still quiet, but now with a cold edge to it.

"Then why can't you accept my hospitality and the devil take the outside world!"

"I don't want your hospitality." She glared at him, her eyes flashing anger. "I want your respect."

"Bloody hell," he growled. He rose from the bench and paced a few feet to where a sapling *kauri* struggled upward toward the sunlight. After a moment, he turned back to face her. "You have my respect."

"Do I?"

"Yes, damn it." He ran his hand through his hair, a stupid nervous gesture, and he hated himself for doing it. "Of course you have my respect."

"Thank you," she said quietly. She set her jaw into a rigid line and looked away, her shoulders tensing as she gazed into the distance. She'd shut him out with that simple movement, closed an invisible door and left him on the other side. He wanted to say something but couldn't, for the life of him, figure out what. So, instead

Alice Gaines

he turned and headed back up the path toward the house.

The study wasn't empty when Richard got there. Sammy stood by the window, looking out. At the sound of Richard's footsteps, he turned. He studied Richard, and his welcoming smile faded, his eyes widening in concern. "Richard, man, you look like hell."

Richard walked to the desk and dropped into his chair. "I must. You never call me by my given name anymore unless I'm in deep trouble."

"What trouble?" Sammy asked.

Richard sighed, suddenly exhausted. "I was up most of the night."

"No, not that." Sammy approached the desk gazing keenly into Richard's face. "I've seen you sleepless before, mornings after we took a few taverns apart, you and me."

Richard raised his hands to his face and rubbed his eyes. "I'll be fine."

"Something's shaken you, bad. What?"

Richard dropped his hands and studied the ledger before him. He'd been working on the figures only that morning, but now they appeared to be in some stranger's hand, not his own work at all. He felt rather than saw Sammy walk to the chair on the other side of the desk and sit down.

"I know," Sammy said quietly. "Miss Gannon."

Richard looked back at him. "I'm that transparent?"

"I watched you with her last night."

"And what did you see?" Richard asked.

"I saw the Richard I used to know, a little bit maybe."

"I didn't mean me," Richard snapped. "What did you see in her?"

Sammy hesitated, as if measuring his response. "Nervous at first. Then quiet, in command, like."

"Exactly." Richard pounded his fist softly onto the papers in front of him. "You feel you understand her, hold

Waitangi Nights

the upper hand, then she turns to you, all surety and composure, and says something so outrageous you really ought to laugh. But she somehow manages to make it sound like the most reasonable statement in the world."

A slow, knowing smile crossed Sammy's face. "And what did she say to you?"

"That I must make my own contentment."

Sammy laughed softly, and Richard glared at him. "Damn it, not you, too. You and the Gannon woman could make a bloody pair of Buddhas with your smiles and riddles. What's so blasted funny, anyway?"

"Nothing, old friend," Sammy answered. "I'm just surprised she could see into you so quick."

"There's nothing inside me to see."

"You think?" Sammy rested back in his chair and studied Richard, like a schoolmaster who knows the truth but wants to watch his student squirm anyway. "I think she looks into you and sees a man who won't let himself be happy," he said finally.

"Rubbish."

"That's what I see."

"You know me." Richard rested his elbows on the desk and leaned toward Sammy. "You know what I've done."

"What have you done?"

"Louisa—"

"Richard, Richard." Sammy bent forward, placing a palm on the edge of the desk. "When will you let that go?"

Richard rose from his seat and paced to the window. "She's dead, Sammy."

"She killed herself."

"Because of what I did to her."

"You loved her."

"No." Richard turned and faced Sammy, his old friend. "I thought I loved her, but I only lusted after her. I used her until I had a child with her, and then I aban-

53

doned her to my father and his abuse."

"Mr. Vernon was one powerful man, but even he couldn't talk a person to death."

"He picked at my mother, criticized, harped, and badgered until she doubted her own sanity. Until she slipped away even from me."

"Richard—"

"I watched him do it. I watched him until I couldn't stand anymore, and one day I raised my hand to strike him, just to shut him up." Richard clenched his hands into fists by his side. "He looked at me, and—I'll never forget that moment—I realized he was afraid of me. I'd grown big enough and strong enough to murder him if I wanted. And I wanted to. God, how I wanted to. So, the next day I left for Otago."

Sammy's dark eyes widened. "That's why we went looking for gold, you and me?"

"It wasn't because the family needed money."

"Good thing, too," Sammy said. "Because we didn't find gold, just trouble. Fun trouble for two man-boys growing up."

"We cut a rather wide swath through the south, didn't we?"

"We?" Sammy repeated. "You more than me. Some lady's man you were. I almost killed myself keeping up."

"You did well with the ladies, as I recall."

Sammy shook his head. "Not like you. You were one hot-blooded fellow."

"That was a long time ago."

"Not so long." Sammy reclined in his chair, smiling at him, Buddha-like again. "And now there's a woman in the house, and your blood's running hot again, I think."

"What if it is?" Richard replied. "I'm older now. I can control myself."

"But why?"

"I won't use anyone for my own pleasure ever again. I won't hurt another woman."

Waitangi Nights

"Miss Gannon's not Louisa TeKea. You could be good for each other."

Richard walked back to the desk, sat down, and picked up some papers. "The discussion's academic, anyway. The cottage will be repaired soon, and then I'll seldom see her."

"So, keep her."

Richard glanced at Sammy and found the old devilment in his friend's eyes. "Keep her?"

"Think of some reason to keep the cottage roof leaky. Keep her here in the house."

Richard sat back and gazed toward the window, glancing out to the gardens in the direction of the glasshouse. Only hours before he'd told Miss Gannon that she shouldn't expect repairs on the cottage soon. He'd been joking then, teasing her. Or had he?

Maybe he could delay her departure from under his roof. Not so that he could have an affair with her, not to satisfy some lusty urge. He'd control that on his own. No, he'd learn from her, take lessons in making his own contentment, as she had put it.

Sammy rose, walked to Richard's side, and placed his hand on Richard's shoulder. "Keep her with you," he said. "It's not good for a man to be alone so long. You'll end up a sour old fellow like your father."

"Maybe you're right," Richard said. "I'll think about it."

Chapter Four

A week, an entire week, and the lathing had scarcely been started. Isabel stood at the glasshouse door and glared at the carpenter's back, willing him to get on with the work. But the stooped old man moved so sluggishly that if he got any slower, someone might just toss dirt over him and erect a stone monument at his head.

The delay was Richard Julian's fault; she could feel it in her bones. During the past two weeks, she'd asked four times when the work on the glasshouse might be done so that the carpenter could repair her cottage. All four times, the master had glared at her, that piercing blue gaze seeing right inside her, beneath her clothing to where her heart beat as rapidly as a rabbit's.

Then, each time, he'd demanded to know in that charming way of his what the devil was so blasted bad about staying in the house with him. And she'd repeated each time: she wasn't his guest, wasn't his guest, wasn't his guest, wasn't his guest.

"I'm not your plaything."

Waitangi Nights

"Excuse me, miss?"

The carpenter was staring at her, his hammer dangling from gnarled fingers. "You're not my what, Miss Gannon?"

Oh, dear heaven. Mr. Julian had her talking to herself now. "Nothing, Mr. Davis," she answered.

He scratched his head for a moment, still looking as though he expected more erratic behavior, and he didn't want to miss the show.

"Hadn't you better get back to your work?" she said.

He grumbled something and bent to lift another board. Curse the male breed, anyway. Isabel turned and went back inside the glasshouse.

And curse Mr. Ezekiel Turner, wherever he was. If orchids ran the afterlife, he'd be roasting in hell right now for the atrocities he'd committed against this particular group of plants. He'd kept the glasshouse tightly closed, preventing any hint of air movement inside and encouraging every kind of rot imaginable. Then he'd overpotted nearly all the plants. Naturally, the medium had broken down, turning into a mush that no orchid root could live in. Only the innate toughness of the plants had saved them. She'd found over a dozen that had managed to survive by growing on top of their sour compost, their roots hanging free to the air, as they did in nature.

She had months of work ahead of her, and the gardener, Quinn, wouldn't be any help. She'd found that out soon enough. Sighing, she moved back to the bench, picked up the *cattleya* she'd been working on, and tried one more time to pry it loose from its pot.

"Hello," came a tiny voice from the doorway. Isabel glanced over and found Bunny on the threshold, paint brushes and watercolors in one hand and a sketch pad in the other. "Nanny brought me down to visit you."

Not again. Isabel set the plant down. "How nice," she said. "Is Nanny still outside?"

Bunny stepped inside and headed for the workbench.

Alice Gaines

"I think she's going into town."

Of course she was, leaving Isabel to watch her charge. But this time she wouldn't get away with it. Isabel wiped her hands on her apron. "I'm going to talk to Nanny for a moment," she said, reaching out and ruffling Bunny's hair. "You stay here. And don't touch anything."

"I won't," Bunny answered, childish indignation in her tone.

Silly of her to worry. Bunny always behaved herself, which was more than Isabel could say for her nanny. She walked to the door and looked outside, down the path toward the house.

Miss Partridge was just disappearing around a curve in the gravel walkway.

Isabel called out to her, "One moment, please."

Miss Partridge stopped and her back stiffened. She turned slowly. "Yes, Miss Gannon?"

The woman obviously was going to town, but probably not to visit the butcher or the bookseller. She had dressed up in a walking costume trimmed with ribbons and lace. Fashionably bustled and corseted and smelling faintly of lavender, Miss Partridge appeared readier for a tryst than a shopping trip.

"Is this your afternoon free, Miss Partridge?" Isabel asked.

The nanny at least had the decency to blush. But she raised her chin, golden curls bobbing around her heart-shaped face. "I have business in Paihia," she answered.

"No doubt," Isabel said. "But I have work of my own to do, and I don't need a child underfoot."

"I sent Bunny's paints with her. She'll occupy herself."

"Bunny is a dear child. I have no problem with her." Isabel straightened to her full height. "But I resent your treating me as your substitute. Bunny is not my responsibility."

"Surely you wouldn't mind—"

Waitangi Nights

"But I do mind. Very much. Did you send Bunny to sit with Mr. Turner when you went to town?"

"Of course not."

"Then don't do it with me."

"Very well." Miss Partridge fidgeted for a moment. "But I really must leave now. You'll watch her for me today?"

"Today," Isabel answered. "For the last time."

Miss Partridge breathed a sigh of relief. "Thank you. She can have her luncheon with you and Mr. Julian. I'll be back in a few hours."

The nanny walked off down the path, leaving Isabel with a snail-slow carpenter to supervise, a child to watch, and a glasshouse full of orchids to repot. Only a miracle would allow her to get the Harrowgate collection into order before next Christmas. She turned and went back inside.

Bunny had pulled a high stool up next to the work bench and had installed herself with her brushes and paints there. She looked up at Isabel and held out a chipped tea cup. "May I have some water for my paints, please?"

Isabel took it, filled it from a nearby bucket, and set it in front of Bunny. "What are you going to paint for your Cousin Richard today?"

"He says he has a whole houseful of my art." Bunny looked up at Isabel with her sparkling blue eyes, so like her guardian's, and yet so full of innocence and joy. "Would you like me to make you a picture?"

"I'd like that very much."

"An orchid plant?"

Isabel didn't quite manage to stifle a groan. "Not when I'm up to my elbows in them," she said. "Paint something else."

Bunny shrugged. "What?"

"I don't know. Use your imagination."

Bunny's face broke into a grin, her plump little cheeks dimpling. "Really?"

Alice Gaines

"Really," Isabel repeated. "Don't tell me what it is until you're finished."

Bunny dampened the bristles of her brush and ran them over a pot of brilliant blue tint. She bent over her pad and applied herself to her painting with gusto. Isabel went back to the recalcitrant *cattleya*. She grabbed the two largest pseudobulbs firmly in one hand and the lip of the clay pot in the other. She pulled as hard as she could, but the plant still wouldn't budge. "Bunny, would you pass me that hammer, please?"

Bunny set her brush into the cup of water and looked across the bench. She found the hammer, grasped it in her small fingers, and handed it to Isabel.

"Now, cover your face," Isabel said. "I'm going to smash this thing, and I don't want a piece flying into your eye."

Bunny giggled and did as she was told, firmly pressing her hands over her eyes. Isabel lifted the hammer and brought it down on the pot—once, twice, three times. Finally, it broke into segments that could be pulled away from the orchid's roots.

Bunny lowered her hands and gazed wide-eyed at Isabel's handiwork. "You broke it to bits, Isabel. Won't Cousin Richard be angry?"

"Not if he values the plant more than the pot."

Bunny looked at the destruction, and a gleam of mischief very much like her guardian's flashed in her eyes. "May I smash the next one?"

Isabel laughed. In Bunny's gaze the devilment played out as pure delight. On Richard Julian that delight hinted at danger of the type that many women found alluring, the type that Miss Partridge might be enjoying any moment now. Thank heaven she herself was too levelheaded for such trifling.

"I think I'm through breaking things for now, Bunny," she said. "Why don't you go back to your painting?"

"All right."

Waitangi Nights

Isabel put down the hammer and began to pry pieces of clay away from the *cattleya's* roots. This plant had somehow escaped Mr. Turner's tender ministrations, and even though she had had to take drastic measures to get it out of its pot, the root system seemed quite healthy. Maybe she could coax it into blooming on the new growth. Mr. Julian would love this species, with its wild purple spots. Maybe he'd give her one of his piratical smiles, complete with dimple. Oh, dear heaven.

"Isabel?"

She glanced down at Bunny. The little girl stared back, her eyes filled with curiosity.

"I'm sorry," Isabel said. "What did you say?"

"Do you like it here?"

"Of course I do."

"Good." Bunny dipped her brush into another pot of paint, bright green this time. "Do you like Cousin Richard?"

Isabel picked up the orchid again and resumed separating the roots from pieces of pot. "What a question."

"Do you?"

"I suppose so."

"He likes you," Bunny said.

Isabel's cheeks grew warm. "Why do you say that?"

"When you're around, he swears."

She had to laugh at that. "He swears all the time."

"Not with Mrs. Willis or Nanny," Bunny answered. "Or with Mr. and Mrs. Farnsworth."

"Who are they?"

"The people who live at Willowbrook." Bunny pointed with her brush. "Down the road that way. Cousin Richard's very polite with them."

"And you think that means he doesn't like them?"

Bunny shrugged. "He swears when he's with Sammy, and I know he likes Sammy."

"But he doesn't swear when he's around you."

Bunny looked up at Isabel as though she'd said something very stupid. "I'm not supposed to know those words."

Isabel studied the determination in her little face. "Did Cousin Richard tell you all this?"

"I figured it out myself."

Ah, yes, childish logic, Isabel thought, airtight, immutable, and utterly off the mark. Isabel dusted her hands together. "Now, let's see your painting."

Bunny turned the sketch pad, revealing a picture of something that looked for all the world like a very colorful lizard. "It only needs a bit of red here," the child said, pointing to where the eye would go. "And black claws for feet."

"What is it?"

Bunny glanced over her shoulder, as though to check that they wouldn't be overheard. "A *taniwha*," she whispered.

"And what's that?"

"A Maori dragon. Sammy told me about this one. It lives in the mountains near Rotorua."

"Have you ever seen it?" Isabel asked.

"No." Bunny crooked her finger, and Isabel bent her face toward her. "But I've seen a *turehu*," Bunny confided. "The spirit of a Maori lady."

"Where?" Isabel whispered.

"In my room at night. She dances at the foot of my bed."

Isabel straightened. That music sounded at the back of her mind again. Not real, imagined more likely. The insubstantial suggestion of a flute that had accompanied her off and on since her first afternoon at Harrowgate. Nothing, an extra whisper in the breeze. Nothing at all.

"Good day, Miss Gannon," came a voice from the doorway. Mrs. Willis stood there, as much starch in her backbone as in her spotless apron. "Luncheon is ready. You'll dine with the adults today, Miss Bunny."

"Oh, good." Bunny squirmed down off her stool.

Waitangi Nights

"I'll just wash my hands and be right there," Isabel said.

Bunny scampered out of the glasshouse and down the path toward the house. But Mrs. Willis stood her ground, staring at Isabel. Isabel turned, feeling the other woman's gaze on her back, walked to the washstand, and turned on the tap.

"Bunny should be at her schoolwork," Mrs. Willis said, "not out here with you."

Isabel lathered her hands and scrubbed them thoroughly. "You can be sure it wasn't my idea."

"You needn't encourage her."

Isabel turned off the water and glared back at Mrs. Willis. "You don't care for me, and I'd like to know why," she said.

Mrs. Willis arched an eyebrow. "I don't even know you."

"You don't approve of me, then."

"I don't."

Isabel crossed her arms over her chest. "Why?" she asked.

"I don't approve of a servant trying to rise above her station."

Isabel's jaw tightened. In another moment she'd be swearing like the master. "I'm not a servant."

Mrs. Willis raised her hand dismissively. "I know. You're a professional woman, whatever that means."

"It means that I'm here to do a job, not to wait on anyone's pleasure."

"I see."

Something besides disapproval lay behind the cook's eyes, something like skepticism, disbelief, perhaps suspicion.

"And just what is it you think you see?" Isabel demanded.

Mrs. Willis straightened her shoulders. "I've worked for the Julians since before the master was born. I won't allow anyone to take advantage of the family, especially Mr. Richard."

"I? Take advantage of him? That really is too laughable, Mrs. Willis."

"It's been done to wealthy men before," Mrs. Willis replied. "And Mr. Richard has never acted wisely where women are concerned."

"Well, I intend to act wisely where he's concerned," Isabel said. "You may depend on that."

"Then why are you staying in the house with him, two doors from his own bedroom?"

"I'm staying in the house with him because he refuses to have the cottage fixed for me." She stared at Mrs. Willis for a moment. "As you damned well know."

Dear heaven, that felt good, she thought.

Mrs. Willis bristled. "If this is how you plan to carry on the conversation, I'm afraid it's at an end."

"It certainly is." Isabel brushed past Mrs. Willis and out the door. "And I don't intend to have another one like it."

Some little girls charmed the ear with the sound of their laughter. Others caught the eye with their beauty, the way a deeply faceted gem traps the sunlight and pulls it inside. But Bunny, Richard's own little girl, could enslave a heart with a single one of her smiles.

His Bunny, his daughter. Every time Richard looked at her, a lump formed in his throat. To think that he had had a part in making her, that such a treasure could come from his affair with Louisa. A miracle of Bunny's magnitude really ought to turn him to religion. It really ought.

Right now his little miracle sat at the table with him, her chin held high, her napkin covering her lap and draping over her knees like a skirt. Her pinafore hid the two fat books that raised her so she could lean her elbows on the linen tablecloth. But she'd never do that, of course. Ladies didn't rest their elbows on the table,

Waitangi Nights

and his Bunny was every inch a lady in spite of her parentage. He, himself, was no more than the son of a social climbing merchant, and Louisa had been a half-Maori tavern girl with a spotty reputation. Bunny wouldn't find much to brag about in her father and mother, but that wouldn't interfere with his plans for her.

Only, please God, don't let her share her mother's weakness. Please. He had to keep her safe from her mother's fate, from the madness. He couldn't bear to watch her slip away from him as Louisa had.

No, she'd be fine. He had to believe that or lose his own sanity. And he'd overcome the problem of her breeding, or lack thereof, with the one thing the upper classes respected about people in "trades," money. He'd send her to school in England with a fortune so immense it would guarantee her gentility. The swells would find her dark complexion exotic, and they'd drown in her blue eyes, his eyes. She'd win herself a titled husband, some impoverished earl or other. And she'd come back to him Lady Somebody, trailing a blueblood behind her.

Ned set her luncheon in front of her, a meat pie in the shape of a half-moon. Nicely browned and with its flaky crust almost crumbling before her eyes, the dish was Bunny's favorite, as Richard had well known when he had asked Mrs. Willis to make it. Bunny looked at it, and her eyes widened with delight. "Thank you, Cousin Richard."

"You should go to the kitchen and thank Mrs. Willis, too, when we're through. She says she hardly sees you now that you're quite grown-up."

"I will." She looked up at him, the very picture of poise and gentility.

Richard beamed back at her. Bunny's grandfather would spin in his grave if he knew of Richard's plan for his carefully hoarded money. After the years Vernon Julian had spent trying to buy and then bully his way into the nobility, first in England and then in New Zealand, his bastard granddaughter would use his fortune to simply marry into it. The justice of it all was too rich.

Ned served Richard's meal next, local mussels in cream sauce inside a pastry *vol au vent*. Richard shook out his napkin and picked up his fork.

"Shouldn't we wait for Isabel?" Bunny asked.

"She's late," he answered. "Again."

"Are you going to scold her?"

"Of course not. She's an adult. When she's eaten enough cold food she'll learn to be on time for meals."

Bunny stared at him for a moment. "You look as if you're going to scold her."

As much as Richard adored his little girl, he sometimes wished she were a little less perceptive. But then he probably did look as if he was about to scold someone. After another restless night prowling the halls checking on everyone, even Sammy, he must look bloody awful.

He'd stopped by Miss Gannon's suite, too, for all the good it had done him. The woman slept only two doors down from him and yet remained so distant, self-contained, detached in a way he could never be.

He never set foot inside her rooms when he checked on her. He only stood at the doorway listening, straining his ears until he could convince himself he heard the sound of her breathing. Maybe one night he'd find her awake. They could sit up in her boudoir, and she could explain to him how she had acquired all that self-reliance.

As if summoned by his thoughts, his stubborn nurseryman appeared in the doorway. "Here you are finally, Miss Gannon," he said.

She didn't excuse her lateness but simply walked to the table and took her seat, placing her napkin in her lap as Ned pushed in her chair. "It isn't easy to drop whatever I'm doing to join you, Mr. Julian. I should think you'd want the orchids to take precedence over luncheon."

"You have to eat."

"Not necessarily," she answered. "Or if I get hungry, some bread and cheese would suffice until dinner."

Ned set her plate in front of her, and she looked down at it the way she always did. As though she wasn't quite sure whether she approved or not. "I'm not accustomed to such rich food," she said. "My tastes are really rather simple."

"Then I'll have Ned take your luncheon back to the kitchen," Richard snapped. "Perhaps Mrs. Willis could find some gruel for you."

Ned approached her, ready to take her plate, but she raised a hand to stop him. "It looks delicious," she said. "I didn't mean to offend you. Dear heaven, what a to-do over a meal."

"Damn it—"

Bunny giggled and gave Miss Gannon a knowing grin. Miss Gannon's cheeks turned that delightful pink he'd seen before, and she lowered her eyes, trying to stifle a smile of her own. The two "ladies" were obviously engaged in some female conspiracy. No man stood much of a chance in the face of all that deviousness.

He stared at Miss Gannon for a moment, and her skin reddened even more. Then she giggled, and Bunny joined her.

Damn her. She did upset the balance of things. That's what Mrs. Willis had said about her the first day she spent at Harrowgate, she upset the balance of things. Mrs. Willis had no idea how right she was.

"I'm glad the two of you find me so amusing," Richard huffed, sounding more like his father than he'd ever thought possible. "Now perhaps you'll eat your food before it turns cold."

"I'm sorry," Miss Gannon said, picking up her fork. She took a taste of her mussels and smiled. "Delicious."

Alice Gaines

Richard glanced at Bunny, who had dug into her meat pie and was now happily devouring it. "What did you learn this morning?" he asked.

She thought for a moment, and snuck a peek at Miss Gannon. "I watched Isabel smash a pot."

"Oh really?" he turned to his nurseryman. "Is pot smashing one of your specialties, Miss Gannon?"

"The plant was root bound. Taking the pot off in pieces was the only way to save it."

"And what else did I miss by sitting at my boring desk going over the boring books?"

Miss Gannon smiled. "Bunny made me a painting, very colorful and creative."

Bunny's eyes grew wide, and she set her fork in front of her, suddenly subdued, as though she'd done something wrong and knew it.

Miss Gannon seemed oblivious, though. "It was some sort of lizard or dragon." She looked at Bunny. "What did you call it?"

A dragon? Not that nonsense that Sammy had filled her head with. Dammit, the man knew how Richard felt about fantasy and legend, Maori or European. "What was it Bunny?" he asked quietly.

Bunny just stared in her lap, and Miss Gannon smiled at her. "The dragon had a lovely Maori name," she went on. "A *tan* . . . ?"

Richard rested his arm on the table and studied his daughter. "What was it Bunny?" he repeated.

"A *taniwha*," she mumbled.

"Yes, that was it," Miss Gannon declared. She looked back and forth between them for a moment. "Have I said something wrong?"

Richard turned to her. "Did Bunny mention anything else, a spirit perhaps, a *turehu*?"

"Perhaps." She straightened and dropped her hands into her lap. "I really don't remember."

Dammit all. The one thing that could ruin all his plans for his daughter. The one thing he couldn't fight.

Waitangi Nights

But he didn't dare frighten her. That might only make matters worse. "We've discussed this, Bunny," he said softly. "Haven't we?"

"Yes, sir," she muttered.

"What on earth—?" Miss Gannon started to say, but Richard glared at her so fiercely that she let it go. Richard looked back at Bunny. "And what did we decide?"

She stared down into her lap. "There are no spirits," she recited. "There are no dragons."

"That's right." He picked up his fork again. "And we won't have any more of this nonsense. Now, finish your meal."

"Yes, sir." Bunny gulped down the last few bites of her meat pie. "May I be excused?"

"Go to the kitchen and thank Mrs. Willis for making your favorite dish."

Bunny nodded and climbed down from her chair. She silently crossed the room and disappeared into the hall.

"That was quite a display."

Richard glanced at Miss Gannon and found that expression of disapproval again, pursed lips and fire in her dark eyes. "What on earth did Bunny do to deserve that?" she continued.

"I didn't raise my voice," he answered.

"So much the worse," she replied. "Everyone's used to your cursing and blustering. But this—"

"This is none of your concern."

"I'm sorry, but if you're going to persist in involving me in your household affairs—"

"I've done no such thing," Richard said. He stood, nearly knocking over his chair, and paced to the window. "I've only tried to make you comfortable."

That was a lie, a transparent lie. But what could he tell her, the truth? That the longer she stayed under his roof the more he depended on her solidity, her quiet confidence that everything could be made to be the way it ought to be? It was idiocy to need her that way, but he did, and he couldn't get away from the need.

As if sensing his weakness, she rose from her seat and quietly approached him. She touched him, her fingers just grazing the back of his shoulder. "What on earth are you afraid of?" she whispered. "All little girls dream of dragons and knights to slay them, of pixies and spirits. We all grow out of it."

"You don't know what you're talking about." He had meant the words to come out like an accusation, but instead they sounded like a plea.

"But I do. I grew up as Bunny is growing up, surrounded by adults, with no playmates my own age."

"You didn't escape into fantasy."

"Of course I did."

"Not like this, not like..." Not like Louisa. Isabel Gannon could never be like Louisa. He turned to stare at her. "No. You don't understand."

"Very well, then. I don't understand." She threw her hands into the air. "I don't understand you or your household. I don't even understand why I'm here."

"You're here because the cottage roof—"

"Leaks. Oh, yes, I've heard that one often enough." She put her hands on her hips and lifted her chin in the defiant manner he was getting to know so well. "And it's a lot of hogwash. I don't know what your real reasons for keeping me in the house are, but I find the situation impossible."

"What the devil do you mean by that?"

"I have no status in this household. I'm not a servant. I'm not a guest. I'm not a family member. I don't belong anywhere."

"You belong where I say you belong."

"The noises of a petty tyrant. How easily you make them," she said, her eyes flashing fire. "Shall I tell you what Mrs. Willis thinks of me? She thinks I'm hoping to trap you into marriage."

"Bloody hell," he answered. "I'll straighten her out on that score."

Waitangi Nights

"By all means, curse at her. That'll do wonderfully well. Even you can't order people what to think."

"Then what do you want of me, woman?"

"The cottage," she said, as she had said at least half a dozen times since she'd arrived. The one thing he couldn't give her. Not yet. Not until he understood her.

"Soon," he said.

"When?"

"Soon." He glared back at her. He was still the master, and she the employee. "And that's all I have to say in the matter."

"All right." She straightened her shoulders. "Soon."

He turned back to the window. Behind him her quiet footsteps moved to the door and out into the hall.

He slapped a fist against his palm. Dammit all to hell. One way or another every female he'd brought to Harrowgate managed to twist him into knots. First Louisa, then Bunny, and now Isabel Gannon.

Louisa had marched over him like a conquering army. One look into those sultry eyes, one glance at those generous lips, and his blood had gone directly to the simmer. He should have known trouble would come of their coupling. He'd already made enough mischief for two lifetimes, and he understood the consequences of blindly satisfying the fire in his loins. But he'd felt so alone after his mother died. And Louisa had been there, and he'd lost himself in her for a little while.

If only he'd loved her, maybe he could forgive himself for what happened afterward. She'd loved him. At least, she'd always insisted she did. Lord knew he'd never meant that love to cost her so dearly.

"Shall I clear these dishes, sir?" Ned asked quietly.

Richard shook himself and stepped away from the window, turning back to the table, to the ruins of what should have been a pleasant luncheon. "Yes, thank you."

Ned left his corner, where he'd stood, forgotten, through the whole painful scene. He gathered up the china and silver, turned, and disappeared through the swinging door that led to the kitchen. The man was a gem. His whole staff was top drawer—Sammy, Quinn, Mrs. Willis—the lot of them. He didn't deserve them, didn't deserve the house, the orchids, the wealth. He didn't deserve Bunny.

Before Louisa died, she'd given him Bunny, Bunny, who looked at him with his own eyes and gave him her mother's pout. Bunny, who dazzled him with her wit and common sense and generosity of spirit. She wouldn't share her mother's fate. Somehow he'd protect her if he had to exorcise every spirit from the whole of New Zealand. If he had to find every *taniwha* and personally kill it, he'd keep his daughter safe.

No, Isabel Gannon didn't understand. How could she? She hadn't seen the savagery in Louisa's eyes at the end, hadn't heard her screams, her laughter. She might have explored the jungle, but she hadn't seen true wildness.

He walked to his chair and gripped the back in his fists. He couldn't do anything for Louisa, to his everlasting misery and regret. But he could save his daughter and he would.

Chapter Five

Isabel chewed the last of the bread that had been sent to her in the glasshouse. Then she poured herself a cup of tea from the pot that had accompanied her modest meal. After Mr. Julian's odd performance over luncheon the day before, she had begged out of the midday meal altogether. And, surprise of surprises, the master hadn't argued but had sent Clarice to her with a tray of bread, cheese, and sausage. She had stood at her workbench eating but hardly tasting her food. Instead she'd been imagining Mr. Julian at his own luncheon, hearing his rich baritone in her mind and picturing how his long fingers would curl around his water goblet when he took a drink.

In the normal course of things, Isabel could always lose herself in her work. Each orchid had its own personality, its own rhythms of growth, flowering, and then rest. The secret to caring for them lay in understanding those tempos, in allowing the plants' cycles to rule the grower rather than the other way around. And

Alice Gaines

Isabel had a natural ear for the orchids' music—how the *cattleyas* could blare a *fortissimo* of purples in one part of the glasshouse while the *aerides* set a quieter undertone of continuous blossom. And the *masdevallias*, her little treasures, smoothed out the rough edges of the other flowers, piping an *obligato* over, under, and around the bigger plants surrounding them.

Oh, dear heaven. She straightened and glanced around almost guiltily, as though someone might have entered and caught her engaged in pure fantasy. As though an intruder might have heard her thoughts. The plants sat and stared back at her.

Plants, you silly woman. Vegetable matter, no more. She lifted her cup to her mouth and took a sip. The liquid had already cooled; she'd stood that long, lost in foolish notions.

What on earth had come over her? Harrowgate had worked some magic on her, had sent her mind off in flights of fancy like those of her childhood, when she really had believed in dragons and rescuing knights on white chargers, When she really had believed that, through the goodness of her heart, a little girl might grow up to become a beautiful princess and enchant the heir to the kingdom.

Richard Julian lay at the bottom of her confusion, of course, just as he disrupted a room simply by entering it. The wildness of the man, from his impossible, shining curls, to the crystal blue ice of his eyes, to the heat of his smile, made her yearn to believe the fairy tales that men really could talk to birds and slay dragons.

And how was she to understand his behavior? His prowling in the night, stopping outside her door in silence, and then moving on. And the locks he wouldn't allow inside the manor house. And his alarm at Bunny's innocent imaginings. He'd gone deathly pale and ominously quiet at the mere mention of the word *taniwha*. He'd been truly frightened.

She'd had to comfort him, of course, even though

Waitangi Nights

every ounce of her common sense knew that was a mistake. She'd had to ease the tension in his broad shoulders, even though the contact was forbidden. And for good reason. By touching him she'd broken through a barrier. By allowing her fingers to brush the wool of his coat, she'd given herself a feel of his strength, his power, his wildness.

Merciful heaven, more fancies. She set her cup down, the tea nearly untouched, and picked up the pots she'd been working on. She walked to the sink, turned on the tap, and grabbed the stiff brush she used for scraping old bits of compost from the clay. After a moment, she found herself staring at her hands, as though she had to remind herself of how to perform the simplest tasks. And the water ran on, unused and unimpeded, down the drain. She set her work aside, turned off the faucet, and sighed.

It seemed the more she tried to stay within reality, the more she slipped into impossible images, the music that waited just outside consciousness and the extra light in the garden at night, moon or no moon. Perhaps they were just perceptual tricks of the atmosphere at these latitudes. After all, she'd never lived this far from the equator. That wouldn't explain the innate wrongness she felt in those perceptions, although how a sound or light could be wrong escaped her.

Whatever was happening in Harrowgate manor frightened the master, that was sure. Memories from the day before still pulled at her: Richard Julian standing at the dining room window staring out, hands clenched behind his back. Needing something. Needing her.

"Hallooo inside," his dark voice called from outside the glasshouse, reality this time. "Is anyone at home in there?"

Bunny's giggle followed. A horse nickered, and leather tacking creaked. All happy sounds, as though the day before had never happened.

Alice Gaines

"Come out, come out," Mr. Julian continued, accompanied by more childish laughter. "All work and no play, etcetera."

"Come out and play," Bunny called.

Isabel laughed to herself. What a silly goose she'd become, standing there imagining wildness and power when he was no more than a man who worried about the little girl in his charge.

"I don't think Miss Gannon's in there," he declared with exaggerated solemnity. "I think we'll have to leave without her."

"Oh, no," Bunny cried. "Please come out, Isabel."

"Very well, I'm coming," Isabel answered. She headed for the door. "Honestly . . ."

She stepped outside, and the rest of her sentence flew straight out of her head. Richard Julian in riding clothes, seated atop a sleek, coal-black stallion made a picture that would disrupt any woman's thoughts.

His costume was perfection, from the snowy neckcloth at his throat to the high polish of his boots. Precise tailoring allowed his jacket to spread over his broad shoulders and then taper down to his waist. Snug breeches clung to his muscular thighs, giving her a view of him that his more modest everyday trousers didn't afford. And, try as she might to avert her gaze, the vision held her riveted.

His eyes widened as he smiled at her. He'd caught her staring, and he was sure to enjoy the embarrassment the knowledge would bring her. Sure enough, her cheeks warmed, but what was she to do when the reality of the man made even her fantasies pale in comparison?

"We're going riding," Bunny said, breaking the lengthening silence. "You will come, won't you?"

Isabel glanced at her. She was dressed in a riding habit that was a perfect miniature of an adult's costume and sat her pony with the dignity of a princess.

A third horse trailed behind the stallion, saddled but

riderless, a small chestnut mare. Meant for Isabel, no doubt. "I have work to do," she answered.

"Rubbish," Mr. Julian declared. "I let you toil through luncheon. Now it's time you had a ride."

"You pay me to care for the orchids, Mr. Julian, not take rides."

"Lord spare us," he grumbled. He swung his leg over his mount and dropped to the ground. "I'll put you bodily on your horse before I listen to that tired old song again."

"But—"

In three strides he covered the ground between them and took her elbow in his hand. "No buts, Miss Gannon. This is for your own good."

Bunny giggled. "For your own good," she repeated.

Mr. Julian grasped Isabel's arm firmly and led her to the mare. The pressure of his fingers lay well within the realm of courtesy but still conveyed a determination that would tolerate no opposition. What choice did she have? She went with him.

He paused beside the horse, bent, and wove his fingers into a step. Isabel stared down at him. "What on earth do you think you're doing?"

"Offering you a leg up."

"I can mount on my own, thank you."

"Don't be silly," he said. He glanced up at her, evil mischief in his eyes. "I promise not to peek at your ankle."

"Honestly—"

"Dammit, woman," he snapped. "Put your precious little foot in my hands and get on your horse."

Bunny giggled again and Isabel surrendered. If she didn't do as he said, they'd be here all afternoon, battling about ankles and mounts, much to Bunny's amusement.

She put her foot on his fingers and took a step to raise herself up. He lifted her almost without effort, settling her into the saddle before she could even get her balance. Then he picked up the reins in one hand, grabbed her own hand with his other, and shoved the reins into her palm. "Enough foolishness," he said. "Let's ride."

"Very well," Isabel responded, mustering as much dignity as she could after being tossed about as though she weighed no more than a feather. She crooked her leg over the horn and slipped her foot into the stirrup. "I'm ready."

"Good." He walked back to his stallion and remounted, swinging his leg over the beast's broad back in one fluid movement. He picked up the lead to Bunny's pony and clucked to his own horse. The two of them set off down the trail. Isabel nudged her own mount's ribs and trotted until she caught up with them.

Mr. Julian studied her out of the corner of his eye, and she would have sworn she caught a hint of admiration in his smile. "I like the way you sit a horse, Miss Gannon," he said after a moment. "Not like a prissy woman at all."

She raised her chin and stared resolutely down the path ahead of them, determined to hide her pleasure at his compliment. "I rode horseback through large parts of South America," she said. "Although I'll admit I'm not well accustomed to sidesaddle."

His eyebrow rose. "You rode astride?"

"It seemed the practical thing to do."

"But your skirts—what did you do with them?"

"I wore trousers."

"Really." His grin grew positively evil. "Whose trousers?"

Oh, for heaven's sake. When would she remember not to get into a war of words with this man? "You can take that smirk off your face, Mr. Julian. They were boy's trousers that I bought for myself."

"Still . . ." His gaze roamed over her and settled where her bottom rested against her saddle. "I don't imagine a boy's pants would fit your build."

"I took in the waist."

Waitangi Nights

"And let the seat out a bit, I imagine."

"Mr. Julian," she sputtered. "How can you?"

He settled his face into an expression of pure, wide-eyed innocence and glanced pointedly toward Bunny. For her part, the little girl peered around her guardian, staring first at him and then at Isabel with unmasked curiosity.

Isabel gritted her teeth and set her shoulders. "We'll discuss this later, sir," she whispered.

"I'm sure we will."

He laughed and nudged his horse into a faster trot. Bunny followed suit, her pony working hard to keep up with the stallion. For a child, Bunny rode like an accomplished equestrienne, and the two Julians soon left Isabel behind.

"Oh, no you don't," she muttered. She tapped her heel against her mare's ribs a few times. The animal accommodated willingly, breaking into a spirited canter that covered the distance to the other horses easily. Isabel matched her breathing to the rhythm of the horse's gait and relaxed into her ride.

She pulled abreast of Mr. Julian and Bunny and then left them behind, passing beneath stately trees, darting from their shade into sunlight and back again. Finally, she broke into a clearing and pulled up. The mare danced beneath her, impatient for more freedom, but Isabel held the reins tight and looked out over a small meadow.

Incredible that the world could hold so many hues of green: emerald for the hedge that stood around the pasture, jade for the grass, deep kelly-green for the pines in the distance. And the sun kissed it all, deepening the colors and setting them apart from the red of a flowering shrub across the valley and the sapphire of the stream that meandered through it. Isabel took a deep breath, filling her senses with the perfume of the warm pasture and the calls of birds. As she watched, a small flock of sheep appeared from over a rise and headed in the direction of the clearing where she sat.

"Here they are," Bunny called from behind Isabel. "The lambs."

Mr. Julian and Bunny came up beside her. Bunny squirmed in her seat, all childish enthusiasm and impatience. "May I go see the lambs, Cousin Richard?"

"I'm afraid they aren't lambs anymore, precious," he answered. "You won't be able to tell them from the others."

"I'll remember the little black-faced one."

"Very well." He dismounted and walked to the pony. He lifted Bunny out of the saddle and bent to set her on the ground. "Don't go far. Miss Gannon and I will wait for you here."

Bunny threw her arms around Mr. Julian's neck and kissed his cheek. He held her for a moment, rocking her back and forth. Then he stood, letting her slip away from him and trot off toward the sheep. He turned to Isabel, an embarrassed smile on his face, as though she'd caught him at something. He walked to her and held up his hands to help her down.

She took one look into his blue eyes, and a chill ran down her spine. "I can manage, thank you."

"Will you please stop acting like a silly female, Miss Gannon?" he replied, still holding out his arms to her. "I won't bite."

Did she dare slip into his grasp? After all, men helped women down from horses all the time. She unhooked her foot from the stirrup and placed her palms on his shoulders. His hands came up, his fingers splaying over her ribs. His touch was firm but not coercive, warm but not overwhelming. It was pleasant, seductive, tempting.

He lowered her to the ground and removed his hands immediately. "There. That wasn't so bad, was it?"

"Not at all," she mumbled. In truth it hadn't been bad, quite the opposite, in fact. Exactly the sort of contact she would have to avoid in the future if she was to remain independent of the man and his charm.

"Help me tether the horses," he said, grasping the pony's bridle and then walking to his own stallion. "Sit with me for a while."

"Of course."

She picked up the mare's reins and followed him to a nearby tree, where they fastened the horses' leads to a low branch. Mr. Julian removed a rolled-up blanket from behind his saddle, tucked it under his arm, and extended his other arm to her. She took it, curling her fingers around his sleeve, and let him escort her to a grassy knoll.

In the shade of a small tree, he shook out the blanket and spread it over the ground. Isabel sat, crossing her legs in front of her and gathering her skirts over her ankles. Mr. Julian dropped to the blanket and stretched out on his side, casually propping himself up on one elbow only inches from her lap. He crossed one booted foot over the other, extending his legs for what seemed like yards, his snug riding breeches outlining every muscle of his thighs.

Isabel shaded her eyes and searched the pasture for Bunny. She finally found the little girl, running between the sheep and laughing.

"Is this your entire flock, Mr. Julian?"

"Only a small part," he answered. "Still, we'll need many more hundreds of animals to put my plan for Harrowgate into action."

"And what is that?"

He shifted slightly, gazing out over the meadow, and an almost boyish eagerness filled his eyes. "New Zealand has always raised sheep for wool, but the new methods of refrigeration offer many more opportunities for selling lamb as meat."

"To England?" Isabel asked.

"England, the United States, anywhere," he answered. "The possibilities are limitless."

"That's quite an undertaking."

He smiled. "I plan to organize a cooperative of my

Alice Gaines

father's tenant farmers. At first the capital will come from me and a few other investors, but in the end we'll all be filthy rich, if I can get my father's people to trust me."

"Why shouldn't they?"

"Because my father was a perfect bastard to them," he answered. He rolled onto his back, tucking his hands behind his head and stretching his legs out even farther. "He set up a personal fiefdom here, treating his tenants like serfs."

"But, why would he behave that way if he wanted their cooperation?"

"Logic had nothing to do with it," he replied. "My father always pictured himself a feudal lord, never mind the fact that he was only the bastard son of a petty aristocrat."

"That's a terrible way to talk about your parent."

"It's true," he said. "Vernon Julian bought people with the money he managed to wring out of a small counting house, and then he ruled their lives."

"Dominating them?" she said softly. "Ordering them about?"

His head snapped up, and he glared at her. "Like me, you mean?"

She shrugged. "I'd never say you were cruel."

"But I *am* domineering."

"You can be rather overwhelming."

"Oh, hell." He rested his head back against his hands and sighed. "Now and again I worry that I'll end up to be just like him. The thought sometimes frightens me right out of a sound sleep."

"Is that when you go prowling?"

He didn't answer but instead closed his eyes, retreating inside himself, or so it appeared. Perhaps she shouldn't have pried, but time had come for some explanations, and he really had appeared ready to confide in her.

Isabel looked up and scanned the meadow again.

Waitangi Nights

Bunny had broken away from the flock and was headed in their direction at a full run. "Cousin Richard," she called.

Mr. Julian sat up, immediately on the alert, as though sensing something was wrong. "What is it, Bunny?"

She trotted up in front of him, clear distress in her expression and a threat of tears behind her eyes. "I can't find the little black-faced lamb," she said. "Did something happen to him?"

"I'm sure he's here, pumpkin," he answered. "He was in fine health the last time we visited."

"But where is he?" she cried.

Isabel studied the sheep, trying to pick out each individual face. Finally, she spotted the lamb. "There, Bunny," she said, pointing to a cluster of large ewes. A smaller animal, with a black face hid among them. "Over there."

Bunny's gaze followed the direction of her hand. "Where?"

"Miss Gannon's right, Bunny," Mr. Julian added. "See?"

"Yes," Bunny exclaimed. The clouds lifted from her face, leaving a bright-as-sunshine smile. "Thank you, Isabel."

Bunny threw her arms around Isabel's neck and pressed her moist little mouth to Isabel's cheek. On instinct, Isabel drew her closer for a moment. Just a moment. Then Bunny pulled away, turned, and ran, laughing, back toward the herd.

"Blue eyes must run in your family, Mr. Julian," Isabel said.

"I beg your pardon?"

"Bunny is related to you, isn't she?"

"Well, I'll be damned," he said, then chuckled for a moment. "You've bought all that cousin rubbish. How delightfully naive of you."

Isabel looked at him, and he stared back at her, his

Alice Gaines

eyes dancing with amusement. "I don't understand," she said.

"Bunny's my daughter. I assumed you'd reasoned that out."

Of course, why hadn't she seen it? He'd called her naive—a monumental understatement. A blush warmed her cheeks, as it always did when she'd said something stupid. Curse her fair skin.

"Wrong side of the blanket, I'm afraid," Mr. Julian continued. "But then, what else would you expect from a scoundrel like me?"

Her blush grew even hotter, and she looked down at the plain wool of her skirt, averting her face from his gaze.

"There now, I've gone and shocked you," he said. "Goodness, what you must think of me."

"No need for sarcasm, Mr. Julian. I sometimes forget that the upper classes have their own moral code."

"Upper classes?" He threw back his head and laughed. "Good God, woman. I'm a mutton merchant."

"A very wealthy one."

"And an absolute villain who takes advantage of innocent young girls at every opportunity."

"You're raising Bunny," Isabel replied. "That speaks well for you."

"Pure selfishness," he said. "I love her too much to be parted from her."

Isabel stared at him. "How will you keep her parentage a secret?"

"No chance of that." He plucked a blade of grass from beside the blanket and twirled it between his thumb and forefinger. "Everyone in these parts is aware of whose child she is. They all knew her mother."

"But then—"

"I don't give a damn what they think, as long as they keep their mouths shut around Bunny."

"That can't work forever," Isabel said. "She's bound to find out."

Waitangi Nights

"Oh, hell, I know that." He tossed the twisted blade of grass from his hand. "I plan to send her to England to school as soon as she's old enough. It'll kill me, but I'll do it."

"Won't you ever tell her that she's your daughter?"

"Maybe someday. I don't know." He took a breath and let it out on a sigh. "What the devil would she gain from knowing?"

"Her father," she said softly.

He snorted, a dismissive, unpleasant sound. Then he lounged back against the blanket and propped himself on his elbow again, looking up at her out of fathomless blue eyes.

"So," he said slowly, drawing the syllable out into a lazy question. "Now that you know about my sins, do you suppose we could be friends?"

She gazed down at him, at the shine of his hair, the heat of his eyes. "I don't think that would be appropriate," she said.

"No, I suppose not." His lips curled into a smile, full of challenge and temptation. "Companions, then?"

He was teasing now. Isabel smiled back. "That sounds like two elderly ladies," she answered.

"I have it," he declared. "Dinner partners."

"Very well," she replied. "But I make no promises about luncheon."

"Agreed," he said, holding out his hand. "Give me your hand on it."

She slipped her fingers into his, and he grasped them firmly. He turned her hand over and stared at it. Then his thumb began to move, tracing a path over her knuckles, generating warmth. Back and forth, back and forth.

The sunlight slanted into late afternoon when they reached the stables. On her mare, Isabel followed Mr. Julian's stallion into the courtyard. In the hand she didn't need to hold her own reins, she gripped the lead

Alice Gaines

to Bunny's pony. The little girl herself rested in Mr. Julian's lap, fast asleep, her face nestled against his chest. The two of them made a picture of such tenderness and beauty, Isabel's throat constricted every time she looked at them.

A young groom Isabel hadn't met before stood at the stable door. When they approached, the lad ran to her and took the pony's lead. Isabel slipped her foot from the stirrup of the sidesaddle and dropped to the ground. She handed her own reins to the groom, and he disappeared into the stable, the mare and the pony trailing behind him.

"Miss Gannon," Mr. Julian called. "May I have your help here?"

"Certainly." She walked to the stallion and glanced up. Mr. Julian gathered Bunny into his arms and then bent in the saddle, lowering the little girl toward Isabel. She took Bunny and held her against her breast. Bunny squirmed and mumbled something, but she didn't wake. Isabel held her breath and stood perfectly still, afraid to move, as though Bunny were made of fragile china and might break.

Mr. Julian dismounted and reached for his daughter. Isabel relinquished her burden and then extended her hand toward Bunny's face and brushed a few baby-soft, dark hairs away from her eyes.

When Isabel looked up again, Mr. Julian was smiling at her. "Thank you," he whispered.

Isabel nodded.

"I'll see you at dinner?"

"Of course."

"Wear the blue silk gown," he said. "The one you wore on your first night here."

"But . . ." Oh, dear heaven—the dress Clarice had altered to lower the neckline. Isabel had tried it on only once since then. She had taken one look in the mirror and had buried the dress in the bottom of her trunk. She couldn't wear that, especially not for Mr. Julian.

Waitangi Nights

But how could she explain her reluctance?

He studied her face, and his eyebrow rose. In curiosity? Amusement? "Please," he said.

She looked at him, standing there with his daughter in his arms and an innocent smile on his face. As innocent as *his* devil eyes could manage, anyway. How could anyone deny this man anything?

"Very well," she answered. "The blue silk."

Chapter Six

Shadows hung like spiderwebs from the corners of Harrowgate Manor as Isabel, candle in hand, found her way to the dining room. Not a lamp had been lit, though the sun had set over an hour before, and not a soul remained to light them now, no one Isabel could find, in any case. Even Clarice had disappeared, leaving the blue silk dress neatly pressed and lying over the bed.

Isabel walked the length of the first floor corridor, listening to her steps echo from walls almost totally hidden in blackness and feeling for all the world as though she were creeping along a hidden passageway in a penny dreadful novel. It didn't help that the same odd, discordant melody had haunted the back of her mind ever since the sun had set. Flutelike, it seemed to linger in corners, teasing her with its ghostly presence.

A floorboard creaked under her foot and she jumped, nearly extinguishing her candle.

Honestly, what would make her start like that? she thought. A little darkness? Not likely after the places

Waitangi Nights

she'd lived. She'd simply have to get her mind back to reality if she hoped to navigate the dark hallway.

"Miss Gannon?" Mr. Julian called from the direction of the dining room, "Is that you?"

"Where is everyone?" she answered,

"Don't be afraid. Just follow my voice."

"Afraid?" she grumbled. "The very idea."

"I beg your pardon?"

"Never mind," she called. "I'm coming."

"This way, Miss Gannon," Mr. Julian said. "Take the next turn to your left."

Didn't the man think she knew that? Hadn't she spent every dinnertime with him for the past week? And curse him for keeping her here, anyway. It hadn't been her idea to stay in this enormous house where one could rattle around the rooms and lose oneself in the hallways. If she had her cottage she'd find her way about it easily enough.

She rounded the corner and found firelight spilling from the dining room into the hall. At least that offered comfort. She lowered her candle and made for the doorway. Once there, she paused and peeked inside.

Not only had a fire been lit, but so had several large candelabras, their tapers adding a warm glow and turning the room into a very cozy haven, indeed. Mr. Julian stood at the hearth, gazing into the flames. When Isabel crossed the threshold, he turned and straightened in one motion. He looked at her, and his eyes widened. "Your hair," he said. "What have you done with your hair?"

She reached a hand to her head and smoothed her fingers over her braids. "I'm sorry. I don't know anything about curling irons. Without Clarice, this was the best I could do."

"Don't apologize," he answered quickly. "It's just that with all your hair on top of your head like that, your neck looks . . . oh, hell."

Suddenly her fingers got a nervous flutter to them

and slipped away from her braids, over her temple, to her throat. Mr. Julian's gaze followed their progress, finally resting on her bodice—or what Clarice had left of it after the alterations. Her heart fluttered in her chest, and what breath she could manage came only erratically, making her breasts rise and fall under her palm.

Mr. Julian's lips parted, and he stared at her until heat flared in her cheeks and along her neck. Until all the air seemed to empty out of the room.

"And your dress," he said roughly. "I don't remember it being so . . . that is, showing so . . ." He raised his arm in her direction and made futile little circles with his hand.

Isabel clutched her candle and stood there, unable to speak, unable to move. Mr. Julian didn't move, either, but continued to stare, a decidedly hungry gleam in his eye.

After a moment he cleared his throat and smiled. He assumed that easy composure he seemed able to summon at will. "Forgive me for staring, won't you?"

"Of course," she answered. But in truth, she had no idea really what she was forgiving. She had no idea what had just happened between them. Something had gotten loose inside him, and her first image of the man suddenly came back to her, that of a jaguar, tensed and ready to spring.

Nonsense, pure and simple. She walked to the table and set her candlestick down next to a breadbasket and a huge china tureen. She looked up at Mr. Julian again, half expecting to find the predator gazing back. But the jungle cat had disappeared, to be replaced by a normal human male. He was a stunning example of the species with his broad shoulders, shining hair, and long eyelashes that in the fire's glow cast shadows at the corners of his eyes. But he was normal nevertheless, from his very civilized collar and cravat, to his burgundy satin waistcoat, to his cutaway jacket and tapering trousers.

Waitangi Nights

He smiled and gave her a little bow. "What a miserable host I've become all of a sudden," he said, walking toward the sideboard. "Allow me to pour you a glass of wine."

"Wine?" she asked. "Not whiskey or sherry?"

He lifted a bottle in one hand and a stemmed goblet in the other. "Claret tonight," he answered, pouring a ruby liquid into the glass. "The best accompaniment to my dinner."

"Your dinner?"

"In the sense that I cooked it," he answered. "It's ours to eat, of course."

"You cooked it?"

He lifted an eyebrow and gave her his full pirate smile. "Do you always speak in questions, Miss Gannon? I thought you had a wider repertoire."

"I never expected you to cook dinner," she said.

He poured a second glass of wine and approached, holding one goblet out to her. "I gave the staff the evening off. The Ngapuhi tribe invited them to a feast at their *marae*, the meeting ground."

"They're all gone?"

"Except for Nanny, who's upstairs watching Bunny."

"And me."

"And you." He lifted the wine glass to her, prompting her to take it. She did, carefully keeping her fingers away from his. "The Ngapuhis specifically asked for the household staff," he went on, "and since you aren't a domestic . . ."

She raised her chin and glared at him.

He shrugged, all innocence. "I didn't want to offend you by including you with mere servants."

"I've never referred to servants or anyone else as 'mere,' " she countered.

"Still, I didn't want to take a chance with that temper of yours."

"Of mine?" Isabel sputtered. "I do not have a temper."

Chuckling softly, he set his glass on the table. Then

he pulled out her chair. She sat, put down her own glass, and shook out her napkin. "Really," she muttered. "Of all people to complain about someone else's temper."

He laughed outright at that, still holding the back of her chair, his fingers grazing her nearly naked shoulders. "Calm yourself, milady. I meant no offense."

She huffed for a moment and then picked up her glass. "So, that's why the house is dark."

He took his seat. "I forgot to ask Ned to light the lamps before he left, and afterward I was far too busy preparing dinner. I settled on candlelight instead."

"And a roaring fire," she added. "A lovely idea."

"I knew I couldn't ask you to make dinner."

"I should hope not. I'm not a cook, I'm a—"

"Professional woman," he finished.

"Professional woman," she said in unison.

He lifted his glass, and his gaze rested on her face, penetrating and oddly intent. "Here's to your profession," he said quietly.

An innocent enough toast, why did it seem to carry a hidden meaning? Perhaps the answer lay not in his words but in the way his eyes appeared to take on a wicked gleam as he looked at her. But surely she must be mistaken. That was just a trick of the light from the flickering candles, from the warmth of the fire. She stared right back at him, raised her own goblet to his, and clinked the lip against his glass. "To the orchids of Harrowgate," she said.

"The orchids," he repeated. Then he put his glass to his mouth and took a sip.

Isabel tasted her wine, too, and a chorus of flavors exploded on her tongue. Herbs and fruit, honey and wood smoke. She swallowed, and the memory of flowers lingered in her mouth. "Delicious," she said.

"Now, let's taste my dinner." He lifted the lid from the tureen, allowing steam to escape, along with a tempting aroma of vegetables and spiced meat.

Waitangi Nights

"My, that smells good," Isabel said. "What is it?"

Mr. Julian smiled and extended his hand to her. She gave him her dish, and he ladled a concoction from the tureen onto it. "A simple mutton stew," he answered, putting her plate in front of her.

Isabel looked down at a mixture of chunks of meat and tiny potatoes and yellow onions, all glazed with a rich gravy that actually gleamed in the firelight. "This may be mutton stew," Isabel said, "but it hardly looks simple. You made this?"

His grin widened, nothing complicated about the expression now. He felt only pleasure at her approval, as ridiculous as that seemed. "Taste it," he urged.

Isabel lifted her fork and helped herself to a morsel of meat. It presented only the most tentative resistance to her teeth before melting into perfect tenderness and releasing the slightly gamy flavor of mutton. That gone, she speared an onion and ate it greedily. "Oh, my," she mumbled, barely having cleared her mouth. "Oh, my, yes."

"Wonderful," he declared. "Now, try the claret with it."

Isabel raised her goblet and took a mouthful of ruby liquid, slurping slightly and not caring a whit that he might find the sound unladylike. The nuances of the wine made a perfect contrast to the earthy flavors of the stew. She took another drink and looked at her glass. Empty.

Mr. Julian took it from her hand, rose from his seat, and walked to the sideboard. She watched him go, watched the power and economy of his movement. He returned with the wine bottle in hand and sat down again.

Isabel took another bite of her stew, let it linger on her tongue for a moment, then swallowed. "Where on earth did you learn to cook like this?"

"In Otago, South Island," he answered, lifting her glass and refilling it with claret.

She waved a hand toward him. "You mustn't," she said, "that is, I mustn't."

"A little wine won't hurt," he said. "We're having our own feast tonight."

He pressed the glass into her hand, and she brought it to her lips and took another taste of ambrosia. "I suppose just a bit more."

"That's my girl."

"Tell me, is Otago where rich young men from Waitangi go to learn to cook?" she asked.

"Otago is, or was, where restless young men went looking for gold and adventure," he answered, filling his own plate with food. "Sammy and I wandered most of the province together, sleeping in tiny huts and doing our own housekeeping."

"Did you find gold?" she asked.

"No. We were too late for the good strikes."

"Adventure?"

"Some." He lifted his glass and took a drink. "The less said about that, the better."

Isabel ate some more stew and washed it down with wine. Mr. Julian did the same, spearing meat and vegetables and chewing them slowly. Then he dabbed at his mouth with the snowy linen of his napkin. Finally, he brought his goblet to his generous lips, almost caressing the glass as he did. Isabel stared at him, intent on watching him eat, of all things. How could he make such simple, everyday actions so compelling? So dangerous?

He glanced up, and the crystal fire flared briefly in his eyes again. "There are rolls," he said.

Isabel jerked back to reality. "Excuse me?"

He nodded toward the breadbasket. "Rolls," he repeated softly.

"Of course." She reached for the basket, lifted the napkin that covered it, and peeked inside. Half a dozen or so perfectly browned rolls stared back at her. She took one and handed the basket to him. "Did you make these, too?"

"Good God, no," he answered, helping himself. "After many attempts, Sammy managed to produce some little flour stones that we called biscuits. But I never tried baking."

Isabel broke her roll and dipped a scrap in her gravy. She brought the dripping chunk to her mouth and chewed slowly, enjoying the buttery flavor of the stew as it coated the substantial crust of the bread. "So, did you conjure the rolls out of thin air?" she asked.

He swallowed another forkful of stew. "Mrs. Willis made them before she left."

"Mrs. Willis might have made a stew, too, and set it aside for us," Isabel challenged. "She might have made any number of dishes that could have waited for our dinner."

"I suppose she might have done, at that." He took another sip of his wine and appeared to consider the question. "But I wanted to cook for you."

"Why?"

He grasped the wine bottle and refilled both their glasses. How had hers gotten empty again?

"I wanted to," he repeated, as though the flat assertion explained everything. An intriguing question lay under his actions, one that she really should probe. But the warmth from the fire was so soothing, and the food so delicious. And the wine made everything perfect. She brought her glass to her lips and sipped it. Was this her third glass or her second? It was her third, his second.

"It took some doing getting Mrs. Willis to agree to let me into her kitchen at all," he went on. "She fluttered all around me, laying out every possible argument for why I shouldn't trouble myself. She was worried about her territory, she's seen the results of my cooking before."

"Messy?"

"Disastrous," he answered. "I had to promise to clean

up after myself so that everything would be spotless by the time she got home. Otherwise I doubt she would have budged from the kitchen all night."

"You? Cleaning up after a meal?" The very idea—Mr. Richard Julian, ruler of the very splendid Harrowgate Manor, owner of everything within sight, lordly master of profanity—washing dishes? She brought her fingers to her mouth and covered a laugh.

"I've done it before. Sammy and I often woke up in the morning to find the remains of dinner dried into the pot. You can't imagine the mess."

"No, that I can imagine." She laughed again. "I just can't believe that you're going to wash dishes here in your own empire, with a whole staff of people to do your bidding."

He bristled, positively bristled. "Finish your dinner and see if I don't."

"I won't help, you know."

"Of course not," he replied. "Your sensibilities are far too delicate for that."

"They are not."

"Oh, yes they are."

"A woman in my position can't afford sensibilities, Mr. Julian," she said, sitting up as tall as she could in her chair. She took another drink of wine, to fortify her for the lecture she'd obviously have to deliver. "I've slept in tinier huts than you, cooked coarser meals, and scrubbed out dirtier pots."

"Rubbish."

"I've scared snakes out of my tent and shaken scorpions out of my boot. I've bathed in rivers where I had to look over my shoulder for alligators."

"Nasty beasts, alligators," he said.

For heaven's sake, the man hadn't the faintest idea what he was talking about, she thought. "I've seen a good deal more of life than you, with your manor house and your domestic staff," she continued. "All sides of life."

Waitangi Nights

"So you say."

Isabel glared at him in answer. They'd see who knew more about living and cleaning up messes. They'd just see. As soon as she finished her dinner. She dipped her roll back into the stew and swirled it around. She ate it happily, at the same time scooping up more meat and vegetables, with her soup spoon this time. They followed her roll into her mouth.

He watched her for a moment, a smug grin on his face. Then he set to with his own meal. After a moment, he poured a bit more claret into her glass. How had it emptied again?

This time the bottle came up empty, too, and probably just as well. She certainly didn't need any more. In fact, a pleasant tingle had already spread from her spine out to her limbs, as though the fire's warmth had reached into her to loosen muscles and nerves. But instead of limp, she felt alive. Her senses were keenly aware of the beauty around her, from the aroma of the stew, to the crackle of burning wood in the grate, to the indecently good looks of the man sitting next to her.

Dear heaven, a nurseryman didn't think of her employer in that manner. But on a night like this who cared?

Mr. Julian finished the last of his stew and ran his napkin over his lips slowly, as if to tempt her, to lead her mind off in directions where it didn't belong. He caught her watching him and smiled. "Are you ready?"

"Ready?" she echoed. "For what?"

"To witness me washing the dishes."

"I'm looking forward to it."

"Then finish your wine."

Isabel lifted her glass and took the last swallow. There wasn't much left, thank goodness. "Ready," she declared.

He pushed back his chair, rose, and picked up the tureen. "Bring the wine glasses," he said. Then he walked to the swinging door and nudged it open with his shoulder. Isabel picked up the goblets and followed.

He led her down a dark corridor to another room lit by candles—the kitchen—and what a dreadful mess it was. Vegetable parings lay in piles on top of the main work table. Pots of every kind and description sat in drunken disarray in the scullery corner. And flour was scattered almost everywhere, coating half the room's work surfaces with a fine, white layer of dust.

"Oh, dear heaven," Isabel gasped.

Mr. Julian looked around, and his grin faltered. "I suppose I outdid myself with the mess this time."

"I should say so."

He set the tureen onto the work table and headed back toward the dining room. "I'll get the plates."

Isabel walked to the sink, put down the wine glasses, and looked around. So, the great Richard Julian was going to clean this up, was he? She lifted the lid of a pot that lay nearby and peeked inside. She found scalded-on food, their stew most likely, several layers thick. The lord of the manor would be scrubbing until morning before he got that off. Well, she didn't have all night to watch him, but she'd certainly enjoy his first few attempts. Imagine the profanity.

She gazed at it all, the entire disaster of a kitchen, and giggled. Mr. Julian reentered, carrying their dishes. He glowered at her for a moment and then joined her at the scullery. His broad shoulders filled the corner, and she stepped back to give him room, or perhaps to give herself room to breathe with him so near.

After setting the plates down next to the wine glasses, he slipped out of his jacket, turned, and made as if to toss the splendid garment onto the work table on top of potato peelings and a layer of flour.

"Stop," she cried. She held out her hand. "Give me that."

"This?" he asked, glancing first at the jacket and then at her. "Do you think it proper for you to handle my clothes?"

Waitangi Nights

"Better I handle it now than Samuel spend hours tomorrow picking vegetable matter out of it."

He lifted an eyebrow. "Still."

"Oh, for heaven's sake." She took the jacket from him, turned on her heel and went in search of a clean surface. She found one finally, clear across the room, on an out-of-the-way corner of a sideboard. She folded the wool fabric carefully and put it down. That done, she looked back across the room.

The enormous stove poured soothing heat into the kitchen, and candlelight glowed all around. It danced over the master's features and into his unruly mop of hair, painting a most appealing picture, that of a wild male beast who had at last succumbed to domestication.

Mr. Julian turned on the taps, running water into a basin until it steamed up around him. He added soap and swished it around with his hand. Then he loosened his tie and rolled up his sleeves, exposing muscular forearms covered with dark, curling hairs. A beast, indeed. And yet one, Isabel fancied, that might be kept for a lady's amusement, if the lady were very, very careful. A beguiling thought and a wicked one. She covered her lips with her hand, but laughter escaped, anyway.

"What do you find so funny?" he said.

"I was only thinking what a homey portrait you make, readying yourself for soapy water."

"You really won't help me?"

"Certainly not," she answered. "As I told you before, I'm your nurseryman, not your scullery maid."

"Only a heartless woman would make me wash and dry all these by myself," he said, gesturing to the array of pots at his elbow.

"If you hadn't given the entire staff the evening free, you'd have plenty of help."

"Now she'll punish me for my generosity," he grumbled.

Such a pained expression he presented, the very image of a poor fellow who has done his best and has received nothing but criticism in return.

"Very well," Isabel conceded. She crossed to the sink and picked up a towel. "I'll dry."

"Thank you." He grabbed a handful of cutlery, dropped it into the basin, and plunged his hands in after. "Damn," he cursed. "This water is hot."

"The better to get things clean," she answered. She picked up a wine goblet and held it out toward him. "You'd best start with these."

He took the glass and put it into the basin. Then he lifted a cloth from the drain board and began to wash. "Did you enjoy my dinner?"

"Very much."

"Mutton stew isn't normal fare for a lady."

"I found it delicious."

He smiled that devil grin that she was coming to enjoy much more than was good for her. "You do have appetites, don't you, Miss Gannon?" he said. "I'm never quite sure."

She averted her gaze, found the other goblet, and picked it up. He reached for it, too, and his fingers brushed hers. She jerked her hand back, almost dropping the glass.

He grasped the goblet and slid it into the water, laughing softly all the while. "Yes, I think you're every bit as human as the rest of us."

"I've never denied that," she answered. "I've lived under primitive conditions and seen things that would shock even you."

"Of course. The naked savages."

"I never called them savages," she replied. "I've generally found that, when it comes to savagery, no one equals the European male."

His eyes flashed delight again. "But they were naked."

"Nearly so."

"Even the men?"

"I've told you that before."

Waitangi Nights

He chuckled. "So you have. I simply find it hard to credit the story."

"I'm not a liar, Mr. Julian."

"But you are the most disgraceful charlatan, Miss Gannon."

She placed the towel on the drain board. "I won't stand here and be insulted."

"Don't get your feathers all aflutter. I didn't mean that as an insult."

"I fail to see how it could be taken any other way," she replied.

"I should have said 'delightful charlatan.'" He quirked a brow in that evil manner of his. "Your fake sophistication amuses me more than I can tell you."

She put her hands on her hips. "Well, I really—"

"You know nothing about men and how they respond to women," he said. "For example, I doubt you could do something as simple as giving me a drink of brandy without your innocence betraying you somehow."

"What a ridiculous thing to say."

"As a matter of fact, I'll wager that if you got any closer to me than you are right now, a cautious arm's length, you'd turn bright red and dart away like a scared deer."

Isabel glared at him. Men in general didn't frighten her. She had seen the South American natives as God had made them, whether this particular man cared to believe her or not. She found him rather different, however. But he needn't know that.

"Where is the brandy?" she asked.

"On the sideboard. There are glasses, too."

She crossed the room, found the brandy, and poured a quarter inch into a snifter, the lip of the decanter tapping audibly against the glass as she did. More soft laughter came from behind her. "Nervous already?" he asked. "You haven't come near me yet."

She recapped the decanter, straightened her shoulders, and turned. In the dim light Mr. Julian cast quite a spell around him. Untamed hair, open collar, and lips parted in a wicked smile. She walked to him and held out the glass.

"Oh, no," he said. "My hands are soapy, bring the drink to my mouth."

Isabel hesitated. He asked no more than she had done dozens of times before. To lift a cup to someone's lips. Yet, he made the act seem indecent. She took a small step toward him and raised the snifter. He stared at her, singeing her with the fire of his gaze. And he stood absolutely still, not bending an inch to help.

Slowly she approached until she stood nearly on top of him, surrounded by steam from the dishwater and his own scent of musk and spice. She lifted the glass higher, her hand trembling. His smile broadened, and then, without warning, he dipped his head and took the glass between his lips. He tipped it up, sending the amber liquid to his mouth, and letting a bit escape from the side.

She lowered the snifter and watched in fascination as a golden drop formed at the corner of his mouth and nestled between his lips. Slowly, slowly the tip of his tongue emerged, ran along the length of his mouth and retrieved the errant brandy. He swallowed and smiled again. "You surprise me, Miss Gannon," he murmured. "Now let's see just how much backbone you have."

His eyes closed, dark lashes brushing his cheeks. He lowered his head again, this time toward hers.

Dear heaven. The man planned to kiss her, and she wanted him to. How she hungered to take the taste of that brandy from his lips to hers. With her free hand she reached for him, her fingers touching the satin of his waistcoat. Her own eyes fluttered closed, and she tipped her face up to his. If this was sin, then let her be a sinner. But she would know the feel of his mouth on hers.

"*Mr.* Julian," came a voice from the hallway. "What have you done to my kitchen?"

Waitangi Nights

Isabel rocked back on her heels, catching the drain board behind her for balance. She looked toward the sound of the voice and found Mrs. Willis, absolutely the most logical person to show up in the kitchen and positively the last person in the world Isabel wanted to face.

Mrs. Willis's gaze made one full circuit of the room and then settled on Isabel. "This is a disgrace," she said quietly.

"There you are, Mrs. Willis," Mr. Julian replied cheerfully. "I'm afraid I haven't had a chance to clean up yet."

"What are you doing in my kitchen, sir?" Mrs. Willis demanded.

The woman might claim later that she was referring to the mess. But Isabel knew very well what she really meant, she thought the upstart domestic had intentionally trapped the master in a compromising situation.

"I hope you had a pleasant evening," Mr. Julian went on, making things even worse. "But aren't you home rather early?"

Isabel set the brandy snifter down and gaped at him. Curse the man. What on earth had possessed him to say the single most incriminating thing possible? She could happily kick him in the shin. And then if she could only manage to dissolve and reappear somewhere on the opposite side of the planet, she might salvage the evening, after all.

Mr. Julian rested a moist hand on her shoulder. "Why don't you go up to bed, Miss Gannon? Mrs. Willis and I will take care of things here."

Isabel continued staring at him until he removed his fingers. Then she glanced at Mrs. Willis. The cook glared at the exact spot on Isabel's skin that Mr. Julian had just touched, and the disapproval in her expression could sear flesh.

"Yes, I think I'll do that," Isabel said. "I'm rather tired."

Mrs. Willis made a little huffing sound. Isabel lifted her chin and headed across the room, making her steps slower than the run that she would have preferred. The sooner she got out of the room, the better. And never, no matter what, would she allow herself to be caught in a predicament like this again. Never.

Chapter Seven

Bloody fool, bloody empty-headed fool. Richard climbed the last two stairs and started another circuit of the second floor, lamp held high. He'd been awake all night, playing the evening over and over in his head. Now his heart raced, his blood pounded in his ears, and something gnawed at his gut.

Something? Fine joke, that. He knew damned well what was eating at him.

He'd acted like a lout, of course. First he'd given the staff the evening off so he could be alone with Miss Gannon. Then he'd isolated her in a huge, dark house and tried to take advantage of her. What a fine chap he'd been, a perfect prince of a fellow.

What in hell had made him taunt her, anyway? They'd reached a sort of understanding that afternoon. She had allowed him to take her hand, had let him circle her waist with his fingers, however briefly. She'd shown him some kindness, and instead of returning kindness, he'd gone and lost his head. He'd let lust cloud his reason, and now he was paying the price.

He walked a bit farther and found himself at the door to her boudoir again. This time something froze him to the spot, absolutely not allowing his feet to take another step, and he stood and looked down at the latchless brass plate where a knob had once been.

Why not go in if he wanted? Why not wake her quietly and apologize? For the most part she seemed a sensible enough woman, not the type to suffer the vapors because a man in his nightshirt showed up in her sitting room to beg forgiveness for behaving like an ass.

But what the devil would he say? *I'm sorry I teased you. I'm sorry I tried to kiss you. If only you hadn't gazed up at me with those eyes. If only you hadn't looked so vulnerable, so hungry, so impossibly delicious.*

She'd made him hard then, and now she had again, just by haunting his mind. After only a moment of standing outside her door remembering how her fingers had clutched at the fabric of his waistcoat, how her breath had fanned his cheek, and how she had closed her eyes and tipped her face to his, here he stood, swollen and ready for her, like a green schoolboy getting his first taste of female passion.

There was only one thing to do about that schoolboy with his overactive imagination, get the hell out of here, go to bed, and make his mind and body behave themselves. He turned and headed back to his own room.

Before he had gone more than a few feet, a door opened behind him, her door, of course. Then a few quiet steps followed, her steps. She stood right behind him. He knew that in his bones, could feel the heat of her body in his blood. If he turned now and looked at her . . . Oh God, if he looked at her . . .

"Will you never settle down and let me get some rest?" she demanded in a whisper.

He gripped the lamp until his arm shook. "I'm sorry."

"What on earth is the matter with you?"

"Nothing," he snapped. "Go back to bed."

Waitangi Nights

"You must stop doing this, Mr. Julian," she said, her voice rising into a tiny plea. "You must."

That plea undid him. It was so full of her own uncertainty, her own need for comfort and safety. He had to convince her he wouldn't hurt her, wouldn't let anything hurt her. He wouldn't let anyone come to harm at Harrowgate, ever again. She had to be made to believe that.

He lowered the lamp and turned.

One glance at her and every rational thought flew right out of his head. She looked so small, standing in their private circle of light, yards of white nightgown draping from her shoulders, over soft curves, to the floor. Her hair fell in a tangled mass of sable down her back, begging his fingers to bury themselves in its silk.

What had happened to the braids that had sat so severely on the top of her head, emphasizing the length of her throat? What of the fierce light in her expression when she had pretended to sophistication? Gone, both of them, leaving behind only a delicate woman, unclothed and unprotected.

And if she kept staring up at him out of her fathomless dark eyes, how would he keep himself from pulling her into his arms and taking the kiss he had almost stolen in the kitchen, that kiss and quite a few more? Instead he took a deep breath. "Go back to bed," he said.

She crossed her arms over her chest, the action lifting the hem of her gown just high enough to allow bare toes to peek out from underneath. From there Richard could imagine tiny feet, delicate ankles, slender legs, and then . . .

"Go back to bed," he repeated, his voice coming out in a croak this time.

"Not until you either explain your behavior or promise to leave me in peace in the future."

He ran his free hand through his hair, anything to keep himself from reaching out for her. "You've every

Alice Gaines

right to be angry," he mumbled. "I've been a perfect bastard."

"Oh, for heaven's sake." She dropped her arms to her side. "I'm not angry with you. I just don't understand you."

"There's nothing about me worth understanding, Miss Gannon." He tried to laugh, but his voice cracked. "I'm only a boor, I'm afraid, a cad who takes advantage of his female dinner guests."

"No," she answered softly. "You're a great deal more than that."

"Don't read too much into me." He turned away from her. "Now, go back to bed."

Her hand caught his arm, her fingers gentle but persuasive. She pulled him back to face her. "Tell me what's wrong here," she said quietly. "Maybe I can help."

He gazed again into her face and once more lost himself in her eyes. How easily he could forget all of himself in her woman's warmth. How easily he could find comfort in her embrace, if only for a moment.

But no. He could pleasure her, but he could destroy her, too. "You don't know what you're asking," he whispered.

"There's something terribly awry in this house," she went on. "And it's time you told me what."

"It's none of your business."

"You're afraid of something, and Bunny's afraid of you for some reason."

"My daughter is not afraid of me," he answered.

"Perhaps not of you."

"I'm not like my father, dammit," he grumbled. "Bunny is *not* afraid of me."

"Very well," she replied. "But Bunny greatly fears upsetting you. Why?"

"Leave it alone, Miss Gannon."

"Why are there no locks on the doors? Why do you prowl the house at night?"

Waitangi Nights

Damn, but she was persistent. She stood there, barefoot, in the middle of the night, absolute determination in her expression. And all he wanted to do was crush her against his chest, take her lips, and devour her one little piece at a time.

A soft cry whispered down the corridor, insinuating itself around corners and reverberating through the darkness. Richard held his breath, listening. It came again, the sound he dreaded: a high pitched crooning and then laughter. Little girlish and yet not quite right. Not quite innocent. It came from Bunny's room, of course.

Miss Gannon's eyes widened. "What is that?"

"Go back to bed," he ordered. "If you value your position here, do as I say. Now."

The laughter sounded again, louder this time and even more discordant.

"Dear heaven," Miss Gannon gasped.

The laughter continued, now soft and seductive, but still somehow wrong, unhealthy. Richard turned on his heel and headed to Bunny's room. Isabel Gannon trailed right behind him, but he didn't have time for her now. Tomorrow he'd deal with her. He'd fix the blasted cottage, or he'd give her the sack altogether. Tomorrow. Right now he had to get to his little girl.

He covered the distance as quickly as he could, Miss Gannon trotting to keep up. At the nursery door he hesitated, holding the lamp high and listening. Soft humming continued inside, now clearly Bunny's normal voice, off-key, reedy, and infinitely precious. Richard pushed the door open and thrust the light over the threshold.

Bunny sat in her little bed. At the intrusion of the lamp, she let out a cry and retreated, pressing her back against the paintings of lambs on the headboard and gathering her covers under her chin. "Cousin Richard," she gasped.

"What's happening here?" Miss Gannon demanded.

Alice Gaines

"Who made the noise we heard before?"

Idiotic question. There wasn't anyone in the room but Bunny. Just as there had never been anyone else in sight when the demons had visited Louisa. Like mother, like daughter. But oh God, why?

"You can't think Bunny made those sounds," Miss Gannon insisted, as though reading his thoughts. "She couldn't have."

"Damn you, woman. Leave us alone."

Bunny looked from him to Miss Gannon and back. He took a step toward her, but Miss Gannon grasped his arm again. She pulled him back into the hall, her grip no longer soft.

"What are you going to do?" she demanded.

"I'm going to see to my child," he whispered back, dropping his voice on the last word so Bunny wouldn't hear. "Then I'm going to find out why Nanny isn't here, and may heaven help her if she doesn't have an acceptable explanation."

"Never mind Nanny. What are you going to do to Bunny?"

"Whatever I have to."

"You must be gentle with her," she went on. "She doesn't mean any harm."

"How do you know what she means?"

"She's just a child." She gripped him with both hands now, gazing up into his face, entreating. "Don't frighten her."

"I'll handle this."

"Please, Mr. Julian," she said.

He pulled free of her grip, turned, and went into the nursery.

"Richard," she called after him.

He kicked the door shut behind him and walked toward his daughter.

Isabel lifted the silver lid of a chafing dish and glanced inside. Sauteed kidneys stared back at her, making her own innards do a little cartwheel. She carefully replaced the top and took a breath. The next dish revealed scrambled eggs. A third held fried tomatoes—somewhat more appealing, but still not enough to tempt her. Not after the night she'd just spent. Instead she picked up a teacup and filled it from the nearby pot. Finally, she took a dry piece of toast, carried her simple breakfast to the dining-room table, and sat down.

Long rays of sunlight flooded in through the windows, trapping dust motes in a frenzied dance. It all looked so cheery: the lace draperies, the tiled terrace on the other side, and the gardens beyond. Harrowgate had assumed its serene mantle of normality, hiding the darkness of the night before, just as its master donned and doffed his effortless charm, his easy command of everything around him. By the bright light of day all seemed in order with the man and with his household. But at night, at the least provocation, the tables turned. Shadows took control, their power only held at bay by the glow of an oil lamp. And little girls made noises like . . .

No. Bunny had not made those sounds, no matter that the nursery had stood empty except for her small form huddled in her bed. Mr. Julian had gone deathly pale at the sight of his daughter, as though he believed her capable of demented laughter and disembodied song. But Isabel wouldn't believe it.

She took a bite of her toast, but her mouth had gone dry. She took a sip of tea and swallowed with some difficulty. Her mind raced with possibilities, none of them pleasant.

If Bunny hadn't made those sounds, then someone else had. But who? Could one of the servants have crept into her room and hidden behind a curtain or under the bed? The staff members Isabel had met seemed normal enough, but perhaps she hadn't met them all. Perhaps one of the employees wasn't quite right mentally. If so, that person could be a danger.

Alice Gaines

And if the intruder came from outside the household, so much the worse. No one from the outside had any business in Harrowgate after bedtime, no legitimate business in any case. How could they get in and out? What did they want? What might they do, especially to a defenseless child?

Hot liquid spattered over her fingers, and Isabel glanced down to find that her hands were trembling. She set her cup onto its saucer carefully and clenched her fingers together in her lap.

For his part, Mr. Julian appeared unable to realize the true danger here. He seemed to think that something was wrong with Bunny herself, perhaps something related to the Maori folklore that had frightened him so badly over lunch that day. Could he really be so gullible, so superstitious as to believe that supernatural forces were at work in his own terribly correct British country house?

If he did, Isabel would have to convince him of his mistake. Otherwise he could spend precious time searching for hobgoblins and dragons when the real danger came from a human adversary, a flesh and blood person, perhaps unbalanced, who planned to scare the Julians—or worse. She'd have to make him see that.

But how? He might not take advice well from a member of his staff. He might even think that she offered her opinion in order to get closer to him and his daughter. For heaven's sake, he needed only to remember her overly familiar behavior at dinner to become convinced that she hoped to insinuate herself where she didn't belong.

Mrs. Willis hadn't been entirely wrong when she pointed out that female employees sometimes ended up embroiled in intimate relations with their masters. Sometimes such liaisons ended in matrimony, but usually they led to disgrace, especially for the hapless girl. And even if a wedding did result, such marriages had more than a hint of impropriety to them. They often

Waitangi Nights

involved suspiciously premature babies and ugly whispers among the family and the neighbors.

Isabel could hardly consider herself innocent in the events of the previous night. She hadn't discouraged his advances, far from it. She'd had too much wine, but that was no excuse. The man hadn't poured the stuff down her throat.

She'd giggled shamefully, too, like a love-struck girl. Never in her life had she giggled like that before, even when—very briefly—she had been a love-struck girl. Worse, she'd put her face up to him to be kissed. He hadn't touched her, hadn't even removed his hands from the dishwater, and she'd given in to him completely. How laughable she must have looked standing there, waiting, no, begging, for an illicit caress.

Given her disgraceful behavior, he'd be entirely justified in believing she had improper designs on him and his estate. Under the circumstances, how on earth would she convince him that he needed to question his staff, search the grounds, search the neighbor's grounds if need be? How could she even face him, when she'd barely managed to look at her own reflection in the mirror this morning?

Isabel put her face in her hands and rubbed her eyes. She'd have to try, somehow, just try.

"Not feeling well, Miss Gannon?"

She turned in her seat and glanced toward the hallway. Mr. Julian stood on the threshold dressed in a cashmere cutaway frock coat and trousers, impeccable as always. He rested a shoulder against the door molding and studied her, the light of his blue eyes cold and distant—unreadable.

Isabel sat and gaped at him and her heart nearly stopped. What had he done after he kicked the nursery door closed in her face? And what would he do this morning to the employee who had behaved so intemperately?

"I see you're not," he said quietly.

"I beg your pardon?"

"Not well," he answered. "In fact, your complexion's taken on a rather green tinge."

She turned back in her seat at stared into her teacup. "I'm fine."

"Didn't you sleep soundly?"

Sleep soundly? How on earth could she have slept at all, given everything she had seen and heard? Everything she herself had done?

Behind her Mr. Julian picked up a plate from the pile on the sideboard and began to make very ordinary breakfast noises. Lids to chafing dishes lifted and closed. Spoons scraped inside them and then tapped their contents onto his dish. The aromas of rich food wafted to her nostrils, making her stomach turn. She picked up her cup and took a sip of tea.

Mr. Julian set his plate on the table and sat down at his regular place at the head, and yet too close. Much too close. He shook out his napkin and lifted his fork.

He had filled the dish with everything on the sideboard: kidneys, eggs, ham, toast, and tomatoes. He couldn't possibly mean to eat it all. Even on the best of mornings no one human being could consume so much breakfast.

He speared a kidney, studied it briefly, and set it down again. Instead of eating anything, he raised his coffee to his mouth and took a loud sip. "Very well, then," he snapped after a moment. "What's wrong with you this morning?"

"Nothing's wrong with me," she mumbled.

He set his cup down and glared at her. "Dammit, woman. Don't give me that puny lie again."

She took a deep breath. "Last night—"

"What is it you'd like to discuss about last night?" he demanded.

"What happened?" she whispered.

His eyebrow rose. "Do you mean in the kitchen?"

"No." Dear heaven, no. She didn't want to even think

about that, let alone discuss it. "I mean later, upstairs."

"I couldn't sleep, so I took a little stroll around the house."

"Little stroll?" she repeated, incredulous. "You made at least two full circuits of the hallway outside my bedroom."

"How like you to keep count."

"You knew what you were searching for, didn't you? What you were listening for?"

"Don't be absurd," he answered. He took another drink of his coffee, staring into his cup as though to shut her out of his thoughts.

"You looked distressed but not surprised," she went on. "You expected to hear something in Bunny's room."

He set his cup down, clattering it into the saucer. "She has bad dreams sometimes."

"What we heard was no dream," Isabel replied. "And where was Nanny? She couldn't have slept through all the noise we made, not if she was in her room off the nursery."

"Nanny was 'out,' as it turns out. Just 'out.' I sent her packing this morning."

"Do you think that wise, firing her before you can find a replacement? Who will watch Bunny, give her her lessons?"

"Her lessons can wait. I'll 'watch' her, and so will Sammy and Mrs. Willis. Mrs. Willis mothered me enough when I was Bunny's age. She's rather good at it."

"Someone will have to sleep near Bunny, to protect her from whoever got into her room last night."

Mr. Julian glanced at his plate for a moment and shoved it away from him. "You have no idea what you're talking about."

"Then why don't you tell me?"

"Because Bunny is not your concern."

He was right, of course. She had no business prying into his relationship with his daughter. Still, until she

Alice Gaines

could assure herself that he hadn't acted cruelly toward Bunny, she couldn't let the matter drop. She rested her hands on the table and looked into his face. "What did you do to her?" she asked quietly.

"Do to her?" he repeated.

"When you went into her room last night, what did you do?"

His eyes widened with disbelief and more than a hint of anger. "What the devil do you think I did?"

He could get as furious at her as he liked, but she wouldn't back down. "Some parents believe in corporal punishment," she said quietly. "Are you one?"

"You think I beat my daughter?"

"I didn't say beat."

He stared at her, his eyes now flashing like ice and fire. "You must have one hell of an opinion of me."

Isabel held his gaze, returning his fury with calm determination of her own. At least she hoped she looked calm, despite the pounding of her heart. "Then what did you do?"

"I reasoned with her, if it's any of your business."

"And what was her explanation for those noises?"

"Her explanation was nonsense," he grumbled. "As it usually is."

"What did she tell you?" Isabel persisted.

His fist came down on the table top, shaking the silver and rattling the cups. "Dammit, woman," he roared. "How many times do I have to tell you to mind your own affairs?"

Isabel jumped. Then she settled back into her seat, placing her hand on her breast. "I'm sorry, sir, but it isn't that easy. After what's happened here—"

"What exactly do you think that is, Miss Gannon?" he demanded.

She took a breath to steady herself. "Last night someone let himself—no, herself—into Bunny's room. That someone made the sounds we heard."

"Did you see that someone?"

Waitangi Nights

"No."

"Not even when I shone the lamp into the room? Not even when you leaned inside to pull me back into the hall?"

"No," she admitted.

"Then how can you be so bloody sure someone else was in there?"

"Because Bunny didn't make those noises," she answered. "That was not a little girl's voice."

He rested his elbow on the table and put his face into his hand. "Oh, Miss Gannon," he muttered into his palm. "You can be so relentlessly naive."

"Mr. Julian," she began. What could she say next? What would penetrate? "I'm afraid your judgment has been clouded, perhaps because Bunny is your daughter."

He made a sound that might have been swallowed laughter or a sob, but he didn't lift his head. Dear heaven, how could she reach him?

"Someone, either an employee or an intruder from outside, has gotten into Bunny's room at night," she continued. "You need to question the staff, take steps to secure the house."

"Don't tell me how to protect my own child."

Isabel reached out and touched his arm. He jumped as though she had burned him and glared at her. Then he rose and walked to the fireplace. After a moment, he turned back to her and settled his face into the charming mask she had seen so many times before. "Thank you for your concern, Miss Gannon," he said. "But when I want your opinions, I'll ask for them."

His control was firmly back in place, and all she'd get from him now would be superficial banter or even sarcasm. Still, she couldn't give up. He had to see the danger. "You must listen to me," she entreated. "Someone is trying to frighten your daughter."

"I said thank you," he answered icily. "Now, perhaps you should be about your work."

Alice Gaines

Curse him for being an arrogant, pig-headed male. She rose slowly, fixing him with her own frigid glare. "Very well, sir."

She turned and headed toward the door.

"Miss Gannon," he called from behind her. "I expect you to appear promptly for dinner."

Isabel stopped in her tracks and gritted her teeth. How could he ignore her warnings and then order her about like this? How could he? Because he was her employer, and she was there entirely at his whim. But he didn't own her, and he wouldn't have a civil response from her, not this time. She raised her chin and continued out into the hall.

Richard rested a forearm against the mantlepiece and sagged into it.

Damn the woman, he thought. Damn her for being awake last night and hearing the noises in Bunny's room. Damn her for trying to intrude between him and his little girl. And damn her for seeing his weakness this morning.

A few pleasant afternoons in her company, and he ended up daring to hope that life could be normal for himself and Bunny. Then, when the ugliness reared its head, Miss Gannon refused to see it. Intruder indeed.

Miss Gannon hadn't searched the nursery for the twentieth time, looking for someone who was never there. She hadn't sat with Bunny, trying to make sense of the fantasies. She hadn't tried to convince Bunny that there was no such thing as a *turehu*, or any other sort of spirit, only to have her look back out of innocent blue eyes that didn't believe a word of the explanation. Miss Gannon didn't have to worry about her daughter's sanity.

No, Isabel Gannon hadn't the first clue about what went on at Harrowgate Manor, nor did she need to. She made interesting conversation and was devilishly nice to look at. And from now on, Richard would talk to her and look at her, and that was all. And he'd do it when he damned well pleased.

Chapter Eight

Freedom to move—how Isabel had missed it. Finally, without the long skirts that soaked up water at the hem and knocked over small plants on the lower shelves, she could roam around the glasshouse easily. She glanced down at the men's trousers she had bought over a year ago through a mail-order catalog and then tailored to her woman's hips and thighs. Now, after many wearings and washings, the once-heavy twill molded itself perfectly to her body and felt like silk against her skin.

Isabel smiled to herself. What would the rest of the staff of stately Harrowgate Manor think if they saw her like this? Her hair had worked itself out of her braids and hung in wisps around her face, clinging to the perspiration at her temples. Mud and bits of orchid compost clung to her fingers. Her dishevelment, combined with her most decidedly, improperly, shockingly masculine dress would certainly raise eyebrows. How she'd love to stand in the middle of a circle of them and declare her independence loudly. *This ought to convince you all that I don't give a fig for your precious Richard Julian and all his blessed money*. And if it didn't convince them, the devil could take them.

"And the devil take him, too," she said aloud; Most especially the devil could have the master.

Isabel picked up a *cattleya intermedia* and carried it to the potting bench. The plant might well be the type discovered by Aquino, with the lovely splash of color on the petals. Mrs. Willis, the cook, wouldn't know about that. Mr. Quinn, the gardener, wouldn't either. Even Mr. Julian, with all his lordliness and fine clothes, wouldn't recognize a rare and beautiful orchid until it bloomed, if then.

Only Isabel knew the plants, and they, after all, were why she'd come to Harrowgate. Not to try to make sense of a wealthy autocrat with shining blue eyes and a foul temper. Not to ingratiate herself with a staff of disapproving snobs. She'd come to Harrowgate to care for the orchids, and care for them she would. The rest of the household could slide down the long, slippery slope to perdition, for all she cared. She'd spend every possible moment in the glasshouse and ignore the lot of them.

She peeled back an old, dried flower sheath from the center of a leaf and checked carefully for pests. No sign of insects, and the new growth seemed healthy enough, fat and succulent. After she'd repotted the orchid, it should do well in a spot with intermediate temperatures. Maybe in a few months it would bloom, and she'd discover whether it was the *aquinii* variety of the species or something more ordinary.

"Miss Gannon," said a female voice from the doorway, the same voice Isabel had heard in the kitchen the night before, and just as full of starchy disapproval.

She set the plant down and willed her shoulders to relax. "Mrs. Willis," she acknowledged, making her tone as light as she could.

"The master requires your presence."

Waitangi Nights

"Does he, now?" Isabel turned slowly, planting her hands on her hips as she did.

Mrs. Willis looked Isabel up and down, and her mouth dropped open. "What in heaven's name are you wearing?" she gasped.

"They're called trousers, Mrs. Willis. You must have seen trousers before."

"Never on a lady."

"But we both know I'm no lady," Isabel answered.

Mrs. Willis's face grew even more scornful, if that were possible. "And the rest of you is so, so . . ."

"Unkempt? Disorderly? Unladylike?"

"Dirty," Mrs. Willis finished.

"Horticulture is dirty work, but it's my job," Isabel replied. "Now, was there something you wanted? Or did you only come out here to check on my appearance?"

Mrs. Willis straightened. "Mr. Julian is waiting luncheon for you."

"Then he can wait until the sun comes down," Isabel said. "I agreed to attend dinner, not luncheon."

"He's your employer."

"Not my owner," Isabel replied. "I'll stay here and do my work, if it's all the same to you."

"What will I tell the master?" Mrs. Willis demanded.

"Tell him . . ." *to go to hell*. Isabel took a breath. "Tell him anything you want. He'll see me at dinner, not a moment before."

Mrs. Willis stared at Isabel for several seconds. "I'll tell him that you're not dressed for polite company," she said finally.

"Fine," Isabel answered. "That's certainly the truth."

Mrs. Willis huffed, spun on her heel, and left. Isabel turned back to the bench and smiled. Let the old biddy tell her master whatever she wanted, the more disgraceful the better. Let His Arrogance fuss and fume until nightfall. That would serve him right for his highhanded ways. He'd ordered her to mind her own business. Fine, she wouldn't bother him. He wouldn't even

121

Alice Gaines

see her except for the short time it took her to gulp down an evening meal.

She picked up the plant and tapped the pot against the bench, loosening the roots. But what about Bunny? Bunny hadn't done anything wrong, hadn't ordered Isabel this way and that. She hadn't teased, hadn't drawn Isabel in only to push her away. Bunny was innocent and possibly in peril. Isabel couldn't abandon her.

But what could she do? She really had no right to question Mr. Julian's relationship with his daughter. But what if he continued to misunderstand the danger Bunny might be in? Isabel would have to do her best to befriend the little girl, but discreetly, without arousing Mr. Julian's hostility. She understood how it felt to be a child all alone among adults, and she would do whatever she could to help Bunny. She only needed to reason out how.

"Miss?" Another female voice at the door, this one gentle.

Isabel looked over and found Clarice. The maid lifted her fingers to her mouth and giggled into them. "Oh, miss, you almost look like a boy, you do."

"I showed you these trousers," Isabel answered.

"That you did." Clarice laughed again. "But, oooh, I never thought you'd go and wear them. No wonder Mrs. Willis got all red like that."

"Angry?"

"As mad as a stewed witch."

Isabel laughed too. At least she'd accomplished something this morning. "Did she send you out here?"

"No, miss, the master did. He says you're to come in to luncheon."

Isabel set the *cattleya* back onto the bench and dusted her hands against each other. "Is he as mad as a stewed witch, too?"

"Nearly so," Clarice answered. "He's been into the kitchen several times looking for you. Mrs. Willis told

Waitangi Nights

him you refused his order. She called you an insubordinate snippet, she did."

"Insubordinate snippet, eh?" Isabel said. "The woman has her master's way with words."

"The two of them agree about you, right enough. When I left they were standing over the stove, waving their arms and shouting."

What a picture. It would almost be worth going inside to see. The lord of the manor and his stiff-backed cook debating what sort of oil to boil the uppity nurseryman in. "So they sent you out to get me?"

"Had to, miss. Everyone else slunk off."

"And no doubt you'll get into trouble if you don't produce me."

Clarice shrugged. "Not to worry. I'm your maid, not your mistress. If you don't want to come, I can't make you."

Isabel walked to the sink, turned on the tap, and ran her hands under the water, washing away the worst of the grime. "But I think I will go, after all."

Clarice's eyes widened. "Do you think that's wise, miss? The way you're dressed and all?"

"I'm sure Mr. Julian's seen a woman's limbs before, probably naked."

"Maybe he has, but should he see yours now?"

Isabel turned off the water, walked to the doorway, and crossed in front of Clarice to the gravel walkway outside. "It's time he realized that I have a real job to do here, that I don't sit about tatting doilies and waiting for his summons to meals."

Clarice darted a few steps ahead of Isabel and spread her arms, blocking the path. "Think about it, miss. You're not exactly clean. Why don't we go to your room and get you freshened up?"

"Nonsense," Isabel replied. "I've already made luncheon quite late. If Mr. Julian wants my presence, he'll have to take me as I am."

"But . . ."

Alice Gaines

Isabel brushed past her and charged up the path toward the house. Confronting the man in her present state might be fun. He could eat his midday meal sitting across the table from a woman with dirty clothes and hair hanging in her eyes. He probably hadn't worked a full day in his life and hadn't witnessed the mess that resulted from real labor. Even in the gold fields he'd most likely lounged around camp looking for pretty Maori girls to seduce. Let him see for once how the common people lived.

She reached the lawn and headed toward the topiary chessmen. Clarice did her best to trot alongside, but with her skirts tangling around her ankles, she had a harder time covering ground. Isabel smiled at her. "Perhaps you should try trousers yourself, Clarice."

"Not me, miss," Clarice gasped. She took another gulp of air. "Before you go into the house, there's something I should tell you."

"Something else I should learn about Mr. Lord-of-the-Manor Julian?" Isabel replied. "I know all I need to know about spoiled children."

"Not about him."

After the long expanse of lawn, passing among the rose bushes only took seconds. Then came the terrace, and Isabel took the steps two at a time, leaving Clarice to lift her skirts and follow at a run.

"Please, miss," Clarice panted. "Can't you wait a moment?"

Isabel crossed the flagstones and reached for the knob on the front door. Before she could get it, the door swung open on its own. Samuel stood on the threshold. His dark eyes took her in for one brief second, and his face broke into a grin. "There you are, Miss Gannon," he said.

"Good afternoon, Samuel," she responded, breezing past him into the hallway. "Where is luncheon being served?"

"The library terrace, other side of the house."

Waitangi Nights

"I remember where it is." Isabel continued down the corridor, now with an entourage of two. Samuel and Clarice mumbled to each other, something Isabel could barely make out. Something like "tried to tell her."

She'd find out later what they were talking about. Right now she was headed toward the library, and nothing would stop her. In fact, this storming about in a snit felt rather good. No wonder Mr. Julian did it so often. Maybe she'd take up the habit herself.

She reached the library and nudged the door open with her foot; it had no latch, after all. She proceeded across the deep carpet, leaving tracks of dirt behind most likely, heathen that she was. She had almost reached the French doors that led to the balcony, when a hand caught her arm. She turned and looked into Clarice's face, now quite red with exertion.

"Don't go out there, miss," Clarice begged. "Not like you are."

"Why on earth not?"

"Because the master . . ." Samuel began—

Isabel pushed open the closest French door and stepped onto the balcony.

". . . has company," Samuel finished behind her.

Three heads turned as Isabel crossed the threshold. There was Mr. Julian, of course, and a petite blond woman seated at a table that had been set for luncheon. By her side sat a mustachioed, balding man, his mouth hanging open as he studied Isabel. "I say, Richard, this is . . . ?"

"My nurseryman," Mr. Julian said. "Miss Isabel Gannon, finally."

Isabel looked at him. His own eyes had widened, and he stood there, staring at her. Oh, dear heaven, what must I look like? "If you'll excuse me, I think I'll go and tidy up," she mumbled.

"Oh, no," Mr. Julian said, skirting the table in two strides and catching her elbow in his hand. "Not after all the trouble it took me to get you here."

125

Alice Gaines

She scanned her clothes quickly, and her cheeks warmed. There was mud on her shoes, quite a bit of it. Somehow she had even managed to smear some on her pants, making them not only worn and faded but grimy as well. Disgraceful. Here she stood among strangers, looking like someone who slept in a ditch. "Please, Mr. Julian," she whispered. "I'll only be gone a minute."

"Too long," he answered. "The soup is getting cold, and I want you to meet our neighbors, Mr. and Mrs. Edward Farnsworth."

Reluctant to meet Mr. Farnsworth's frank amazement head on, Isabel nodded instead toward his wife. "I'm sure your guests don't want to dine with someone who hasn't cleaned up after her work."

Mrs. Farnsworth smiled without a hint of irony or sarcasm, just an honest, warm greeting. "There's no need to be ashamed of the sweat of your brow, Miss Gannon," she said.

"Still, I could find some clothes more in keeping with the occasion," Isabel offered.

"Certainly not on our account," Mrs. Farnsworth replied. "Isn't that right, Edward?"

Mr. Farnsworth blustered for a moment, small, disgruntled coughing sounds. "Certainly not, my dear. If you say so."

"There now," Mr. Julian announced. He guided Isabel by the arm, not very gently, to the table, pulled out the chair next to Mrs. Farnsworth's, and pushed her into it. "Sit, Miss Gannon."

"I asked Richard to invite you to join us," Mrs. Farnsworth said. She reached over and patted her husband's hand. "Edward and I are hoping to establish a collection of orchids, you see, and I'd like your advice as to how to go about it."

"Mr. Julian might have told me you were here," Isabel said. "I'd have come sooner."

"Not bloody likely," Mr. Julian grumbled. He sat down, glowering at Isabel.

Waitangi Nights

Isabel looked away from him and into Mrs. Farnsworth's soft brown eyes. The lady was a beauty, with her golden hair and delicate skin. But her loveliness comforted rather than dazzled, and her expression held the promise of intelligence, the most attractive attribute a woman could possess.

"You're interested in orchids?" Isabel asked.

"Oh, yes," Mrs. Farnsworth answered. "Such intriguing plants, such splendid flowers. I've always wanted to learn about them."

"I'm sure Miss Gannon will be happy to instruct you," Mr. Julian said. "She's quite free with her opinions on orchids and any other subject."

Isabel glared at him. Very well, she'd arrived late for luncheon and in unconventional dress, but he didn't really have to act like a petulant child, did he?

"My husband has decided to indulge me with a small glasshouse of my own," Mrs. Farnsworth said. "I'll need help with the design of the structure and with stocking it."

"I've been repotting many of Mr. Julian's plants," Isabel said, turning back to Mrs. Farnsworth. "I'm sure he'd be happy to give you some of the divisions."

"Honored," he said. "And of course, you'll borrow Miss Gannon for consultation. I can have her in the carriage and off to Willowbrook at a moment's notice." He glanced at Isabel, his eyes full of fire and wickedness. "If that's quite acceptable to you, of course."

"Of course it is," Isabel answered. "Why on earth shouldn't it be?"

"There, then, that's all settled," Mr. Farnsworth proclaimed. "Let's have our luncheon and discuss that other matter."

Mr. Julian signalled to Ned, who served steaming bowls of soup. It hadn't gotten cold, despite all of Mr. Julian's complaining. Isabel tasted hers and found it a delightful concoction of vegetables and cream.

Mr. Julian shook out his napkin and placed it in his

lap. "I hope 'that other matter' isn't the damned ball, Edward."

"What else would it be?" Mr. Farnsworth replied. "Waitangi Day is only a few weeks off."

"Waitangi Day?" Isabel said.

Mrs. Farnsworth turned toward her. "The holiday commemorates the signing of the treaty between Her Majesty and the Maoris."

"All of New Zealand's best assemble at the Treaty House to compare clothing and tell stories about each other," Mr. Julian added. "With yours truly supplying the best grist for the gossip mill."

"You're being over sensitive, dear boy," Mr. Farnsworth said.

"Not at all. I don't know what the idle tongues have done without me these last several years."

"Richard," Mrs. Farnsworth chided softly. "No one takes pleasure in your personal tragedy."

Personal tragedy? Isabel looked from Mrs. Farnsworth to Mr. Julian, and an awkward silence followed.

"I'm sorry," Mrs. Farnsworth said after a moment. "I've overstepped myself."

"No matter." Mr. Julian dropped his napkin onto the table, rose, and paced to the balustrade. He turned back toward them, lounging against the stone behind him. "Then there are the husband hunters. Odd how the combination of money and scandal can make a man so blasted attractive to empty-headed little females."

Mr. Farnsworth gazed at his wife, love written all over his face. "So, get married, man. That will put an end to that."

"What a cruel thing to do to some poor woman foolish enough to have me."

"Now you are being silly, Richard," Mrs. Farnsworth said. She turned to Isabel. "Prevail upon him to attend, Miss Gannon. He needs to get out and see people."

"I'm sure I have no influence over what Mr. Julian does," Isabel answered. And of course, she didn't. Be-

Waitangi Nights

sides, leaving Bunny alone to attend a fancy dress ball wasn't the wisest of plans. Not after hearing an intruder in the nursery. And Isabel could easily understand any reasonable person's dislike for formal affairs like a ball. She certainly would avoid it like the plague.

"Perhaps if you allowed Richard to escort you . . . ?" Mrs. Farnsworth said.

"Oh, no," Isabel said. "That's out of the question."

She looked over to where he stood, leaning against the balustrade, his lips curled into a devilish smile. Oh, no. Impossible.

Richard looked with more than a little amusement at Miss Isabel Gannon where she sat stiffly in the straight-backed chair across from his desk, her dark eyes full of demands. To be let out of attending the ball, no doubt. Too bad. If he had to attend, so did she. In any case, she owed him some consideration after showing up for luncheon covered with grime.

"Well, Miss Gannon," he began. "Perhaps you'd like to explain your behavior this afternoon."

Her chin came up in defiance. "I?"

If only she could see how preposterous the gesture made her look—like a dirty, naughty child defying her parent. One he'd dearly love to put across his knee and spank. "What in hell possessed you to come to table looking like that?" he demanded.

"I hadn't planned to come to table at all," she answered. "You ordered me."

"I'm your employer."

"Not my master," she snapped.

Bloody hell. They'd see about that. They'd just see. He leaned his elbows against the desk, steepled his fingers together, and glared at her over them. "Olivia asked specifically to speak with you."

"You might have told me you had company."

"And wait another half an hour for you to make yourself presentable? When I issue an order, I expect you to obey it. Is that clear?"

She crossed her arms over her chest and stared out the study window.

He pounded his fist on the desk. "Is that clear?"

"Yes, sir," she mumbled.

Calm. He had to be calm, even with this infuriating female. He rested back in his chair. "Am I such an ogre that you can't bring yourself to share meals with me?"

Her head snapped around, and her gaze met his. "No, of course not."

"Has it never occurred to you that I might have a reason for what I ask?"

She shifted a bit in her chair. "I'm sure you have your reasons."

"Then why must you defy me at every turn?"

She heaved a sigh. "It was the way Mrs. Willis commanded me, I suppose."

"Yes, Mrs. Willis," he said. "Why in God's name can't you two get along? You're splendid women, both of you."

Her eyes widened; this was quite a compliment.

"Most of the time," he grumbled.

"What has Mrs. Willis said about me?" Miss Gannon demanded.

Mrs. Willis had given him quite an earful the night before, as a matter of fact, about a certain insubordinate snippet who didn't know her place in a quality household. But Miss Gannon needn't know the details. If she found out, he'd have to keep the two of them separated permanently.

"I'd no sooner repeat what Mrs. Willis tells me in confidence than I'd do the same to you," he answered.

She huffed, but settled her shoulders nevertheless.

"Now then, the ball," he went on.

"You can't seriously expect me to attend," she said.

"I do, indeed."

"I don't even understand why you agreed to go. Not

with Bunny having her bad dreams."

"Bunny has had her dreams for over a year," he answered. "One night isn't likely to make much of a difference."

She opened her mouth as though to say something and then shut it again. "Yes, sir," she muttered finally.

Oh hell, the woman was right. A fancy ball? Ordinarily he'd have dismissed such a ridiculous idea out of hand. But Farnsworth had been so insistent, and the idea of dressing Isabel Gannon up in a decent gown and perhaps even coaxing her into his arms for a waltz held quite an appeal, an appeal he oughtn't give in to, of course, but when had he ever worried about "oughtn't"?

"I need Edward Farnsworth's cooperation to form my sheep ranching cooperative. I don't want to offend him," he said.

"I don't see why I have to be involved in not offending him," Isabel said.

"Furthermore, I expect you to behave yourself when you visit Willowbrook to consult on the glasshouse."

"Of course I will," she replied, her shoulders tensing for battle. "What makes you think I won't?"

"Because right now you look more like a street urchin than a professional woman," he answered.

She glanced down at herself. "Oh."

Delightful. She'd puffed herself up, and then lost all her steam. Richard could watch the spectacle half a dozen more times without getting tired of it. In fact, the day had worked out far better than he'd imagined.

"I also expect you to make yourself presentable for the ball," he added.

"Presentable?" she demanded. "What on earth does that mean?"

"It means that you'll dress for the occasion."

"I don't see how. I don't have a single thing that's suitable."

"Easily fixed," he answered. "Olivia Farnsworth's given me the name of her seamstress. I've sent for the woman to come to Harrowgate to take your measurements."

"I can't afford a ball gown."

"You won't have to pay for it," he said. "If I require you to attend parties, I can damned well buy your dresses for you."

"It isn't proper," she protested. "It just isn't done."

Richard didn't answer but only stared at her.

After a moment, her eyes narrowed and her jaw set as she studied him. "But you don't care about that, do you?"

"What do you think?"

"Of course you don't," she mumbled. "Why are you doing this?"

Why? Because he'd had a tempting glimpse of her alabaster skin the evening before, the swell of her breasts above the blue silk. He wanted more, much more. Her snug pants gave him a wonderful view of perfectly rounded buttocks, of course. But he wanted to see her dressed as the seductive woman she really was underneath all her propriety and protestations.

"I think I'll have the seamstress make you several gowns," he said. "You can dress a bit better for our dinners together."

Her jaw dropped, and she made some noises in the back of her throat. Not words, at least not of any language he knew.

He straightened and opened the ledger on top of the desk. "That will be all for now, Miss Gannon."

She shot out of her chair and glowered down at him. "Yes, sir," she hissed.

Richard stared at the page in front of him, doing his damnedest to stifle a grin. Miss Gannon turned on her heel and headed to the door. He stole a peek at her rear as she did. Oh, Lord, yes, perfectly rounded.

Chapter Nine

That night, only slightly more than twenty-four hours after the sounds had come out of Bunny's room, the little girl herself appeared by the side of Isabel's bed. Isabel had just opened her eyes from a dream and found her standing there as quiet as a ghost. Isabel sat straight up. "Is something wrong?"

Bunny stared back, her wide blue eyes considering the question with all seriousness. "No," she answered. "Is something wrong with you?"

"No. Why do you ask?"

Bunny shrugged. "You look sort of scared."

Isabel glanced down at her hands and found that they were clutching the covers over the bodice of her nightgown. She settled the blankets on her lap. "You startled me."

"I'm sorry," Bunny said. "I'll go back to bed."

"Don't go, dear. Did you want to tell me something?"

"Not exactly."

"Do you want to visit for a while?"

Alice Gaines

Bunny looked down at her feet and shrugged her shoulders again.

Isabel moved backward until she rested against the headboard. Then she patted the mattress next to her. "Why don't we sit and talk, like friends?"

Bunny gazed back up at Isabel. "I'd like that."

"Come on, then."

Bunny scrambled onto the bed beside Isabel. She slipped her legs between the sheets and leaned against the headboard, staring straight ahead into the dark bedroom.

"Well," Isabel said. "What shall we talk about?"

"I don't know."

"You must have had something in mind when you came in here."

"Well, yes."

She certainly must have, and Isabel planned to discover it. She slipped an arm around Bunny. "Why don't you tell me what it was?"

"You came to my room last night with Cousin Richard."

"Yes." Isabel hugged Bunny lightly, encouraging her to go on, but the little shoulders just tensed. "And?" Isabel prompted.

"Did you see her?" Bunny whispered. "The *turehu*?"

"I didn't see anyone but you, dear."

"Cousin Richard never sees her, either." Bunny looked up at Isabel. "But she's real, I promise."

"Does she frighten you?"

"She did at first, but she's very nice," Bunny answered. "We sing songs together."

"What kind of songs?"

"I don't understand the words. I think they're Maori," Bunny went on, warming to her subject. "Then after a while she goes away."

"She didn't leave by the door last night, or Cousin Richard and I would have seen her," Isabel said. "Does she go out the window?"

Waitangi Nights

"No. She just . . ." Bunny spread her arms. ". . . goes."

Oh, dear. No wonder Mr. Julian thought Bunny made her *turehu* up. Real people didn't "just go," and they weren't invisible to adults. Maybe it was all a childish fantasy. But then, where had those sounds come from?

"You don't believe me, either," Bunny said softly.

"But I do."

"Really?"

Isabel put her other arm around Bunny and pulled her closer. No matter whether the spirit did or did not exist, this little girl needed a friend. "Really."

"Good," Bunny whispered. "I like you, Isabel."

"And I like you, very much."

"May I ask you something?"

Isabel stroked Bunny's hair back from her face and draped it over her shoulder. "Certainly."

"Do you have a mother and father?"

"I did. They're both dead now."

"What's it like to have a mother?"

What a question. That had been so long ago, when Isabel had been small and she and her parents had lived in a cottage on the Yardley estate. Then the influenza had killed Mary Gannon, and Arthur had taken to exploration, leaving his only child behind with various relatives until she had grown enough to join him.

"Most of the time, it's very nice to have a mother," Isabel began. "She takes care of you when you're sick, but she also punishes you when you're bad."

"If I could have a mother, I'd be very good," Bunny said.

"You already are very good," Isabel replied.

Bunny wiggled a bit closer.

"Let's see, what else?" Isabel went on. An image came back to her, very old. Really just a collection of senses—sunlight streaming in a cottage window onto a faded blue tablecloth, soft humming, baking smells. "My mother used to have me do my lessons at the table while she cooked. She made me treats out of cinnamon sugar

Alice Gaines

and scraps of pie crust as a reward."

"Mrs. Willis does that," Bunny declared. "I visit her in the kitchen sometimes, and she makes those for me, all rolled up and baked in the oven."

"Well, you see," she said. "We have something in common."

"Tell me about fathers. What are they like?"

"Fathers are great, good fun. They take you on adventures and buy you pretty dresses. They make funny faces to cheer you up when you're unhappy, and they take you riding when your mother's angry."

A bright smile crossed Bunny's face. "Cousin Richard makes funny faces, and he takes me riding."

"He took us both riding."

"That's right, he did," Bunny exclaimed, delight in her eyes. "And you should see his funny faces. They make me laugh."

"I'd like to see them some time," Isabel answered. Indeed she would, what a sight that would be.

"Maybe Cousin Richard could be my father," Bunny said.

"He'd make a wonderful father."

"And you could be my mother."

Isabel hugged Bunny against her. "We've only just become friends, why don't we give that a try first?"

"All right." Bunny stretched and yawned elaborately. "I think I'll go to sleep now. May I stay here with you?"

"I don't know," Isabel said. "I'm not sure your Cousin Richard would approve."

Bunny slid down between the covers and gazed at Isabel. "Please."

Mr. Julian certainly wouldn't like that, not after ordering Isabel to mind her own business. As a matter of fact, he'd better not find out about this midnight meeting at all. But then, she could simply let Bunny fall asleep and carry her back to her own bed. What would be the harm?

"Very well," Isabel said.

Waitangi Nights

Bunny closed her eyes, and Isabel bent and kissed her forehead. Well, now she had a friend, six years old and lonely. Trusting and vulnerable and so beautiful she might have been made by angels. But she hadn't been. She'd been made by a mysterious woman who hadn't stayed around to know her daughter and a man who loved his child but wouldn't own her publicly.

Such a perfect child deserved better. She shouldn't have to invent parents for herself, asking a near stranger to play mother. At the very least, she should know the father she did have. She should know the depth of his love.

And she should be protected from whatever haunted her room, whether reality or fantasy. An employee who had no standing in the child's life and no power to act on her behalf shouldn't serve as protector. She hadn't the means, hadn't the right.

But who else was there? A father who grew so upset at Bunny's imaginings that he couldn't listen to reason? A valet and other servants substituting for a nanny? Mrs. Willis could be of help, but would she believe a word out of Isabel's mouth? No, Isabel didn't even want to explore that possibility. She'd have to do what she could for Bunny on her own.

Isabel glanced down at Bunny, who had fallen fast asleep. She could start by carrying her new friend back to her own room. She slipped out of bed, threw back the covers, and lifted Bunny into her arms.

Bunny didn't stir as Isabel crossed the bedroom and tiptoed into the sitting room. Such a tiny thing made a light burden, and within seconds Isabel was in the hallway headed toward the nursery. That same music floated through the edges of her consciousness, seeming to grow stronger, though still quite faint, as she approached Bunny's room, and now there appeared to be light with it.

Isabel stopped dead halfway to the nursery and turned her head, trying to catch sight of the faint illumination, but it eluded her. She had to be imagining it, but it never quite faded from her consciousness. Instead, it lingered, an impossible illusion. That and more. A new sound, still too distant to make out, but sounding for all the world like laughter.

Isabel shook herself, trying to free her mind of the images. She'd never given in to such nonsense in the past, and she wasn't about to now. Nothing unnatural was going on at Harrowgate Manor, but a human being somehow had gotten into Bunny's room the night before, and Isabel could take this opportunity to discover how.

She walked the last few footsteps to the nursery, nudged the door open with her foot, and went inside. A setting moon cast dim light through the window, revealing what one would expect of a wealthy little girl's room, undersized but ornate furniture, a glass case holding at least a dozen dolls, more dolls and a china tea service set up at a small, child's-height table.

Isabel crossed the room and settled Bunny into the bed, lifted the covers over her, and tucked them around her chin. She touched Bunny's cheek gently. It was so soft, so precious. Bunny shifted and rolled onto her side, burying her nose into her pillow.

Isabel straightened and looked around her. How might a person get into the nursery undetected during the night? He, no she, that had been a woman's voice, might simply sneak into the room during dinner and hide, waiting for the household to go to sleep. The wardrobe might provide a hiding place. Isabel crossed to it, opened the door, and peered inside. She found nothing more than a little girl's clothing, the frocks hanging neatly, shoes arranged in pairs on the floor and bonnets on a shelf at the top. A person would have to be very small in stature, indeed, to fit under that shelf, and she'd leave quite some evidence of her presence if she had to disappear suddenly. Even a servant as lax as

Waitangi Nights

the former nanny would notice it if someone had been in Bunny's wardrobe.

Isabel closed the door and glanced around again. Someone could hide behind the floor-to-ceiling drapes at the window, and they wouldn't leave any trace there unless they dropped something. She walked quietly toward them and pulled first one and then the other away from the wall. Nothing.

For once she could have wished the staff to be less efficient. Any speck of dust might have shown whether someone had recently disturbed it. But then, did she have any idea what to look for, really? She'd been trained to investigate nature, not human behavior.

She dropped the second drape and stood for a moment, worrying her lower lip. The ghostly music started up again, clearly flutish now, but still too distant to make out clearly. It might have been coming from outside, and Isabel turned toward the window.

If a trellis ran up the side of the house, the window would be the easiest way in undetected. She pulled up the sash and stuck her head outside, looking downward. She couldn't make out anything that someone could climb, but she'd better check again from outside in the daylight.

With the window open, the sound of flutes should have been louder if indeed it had been coming from a distance. But oddly enough it wasn't. It still appeared to originate inside the house, or inside her own head, although that made no sense at all.

The light did come from outside, though. Faint moonlight, as she had noted before, but more, too. Something else shimmered above the horizon. The *aurora australis*, most likely, the Southern Hemisphere version of the northern lights. Having spent most of her time in tropical latitudes, Isabel had had precious little experience with auroras. Didn't they resemble streamers or waves, and didn't they contain different colors? This was just a pale glow, more like a huge bonfire

Alice Gaines

when viewed from a distance. And yet, it hovered in the air, where no bonfire could possibly be.

Somehow the light went with the music—they both were so insubstantial. How could the light come from out there and the music come from inside here? None of it made any sense, and yet . . .

Isabel turned and gazed back at Bunny where she slept beneath the image of two little lambs. Something wasn't right here, and it involved this precious child. Something. Something.

Of all the pretentious, overblown, purely ridiculous . . . Isabel stretched to glance over Madame Arlee's shoulder into the mirror on her dressing table. No, it was just ridiculous.

"Are you sure this is the dress we discussed, madame?" Isabel asked.

"But certainly," the dressmaker answered in a thick French accent.

Clarice glanced up from where she knelt at the hem of Isabel's gown and removed the straight pins from her mouth. "You look just lovely, miss."

"But I don't remember all these flounces," Isabel protested. "All this lace."

Madame Arlee poufed out the sleeves of the dress and stepped back to inspect her handiwork. "We embellish a little, *non*?"

Isabel stared at her image in the glass, a tiny woman surrounded by yards and yards of robin's egg blue satin, matching velvet ribbons, and sinfully expensive lace. "You've embellished quite a bit, madame, none of which I agreed to."

Madame Arlee smoothed an errant gray hair into the bun at the back of her head. Odd how someone who created such ludicrous excess for other women could herself wear a simple black dress and pull her hair into a severe style that emphasized her high cheekbones and beaked nose. "As I told you, mademoiselle, at the first

Waitangi Nights

fitting we see only the bare essence of the dress, how it will hang. The *dénouement* comes later."

Isabel stared at her reflection, forcing her gaze to travel down over her chest to where the dress plunged to reveal the valley between her breasts. "But this doesn't suit me at all."

"Oh, miss," Clarice said. "You look like a fashion plate."

"I look like something on the top of a cake."

"A sweet confection, *oui*," Madame Arlee answered. "In this gown you will capture every eye, mademoiselle, I stake my reputation on it."

"But I don't want to capture any eyes," Isabel moaned. "I just want to be left alone."

Madame Arlee grunted in disapproval. "Show me the profile," she ordered.

Isabel stood exactly where she was. This had gone on long enough, and she didn't have to perform like a trained dog for a puffed-up seamstress who probably wasn't really French, in any case.

Madame Arlee crossed her arms over her chest and glared at Isabel above the lenses of her half-spectacles in the most Gallic manner imaginable. After a moment, Clarice rose from her knees and gently turned Isabel around for madame's inspection.

A new perspective greeted Isabel from the looking glass, no more reassuring than the first. Madame Arlee's flounces trailed out behind her, held up by a horsehair bustle so stiff that a tea tray might have rested securely on Isabel's backside. In front, she protruded from the bodice of the gown, giving her form a top heavy appearance, despite the substantial anchor at her back. Below her bosom, her tightly corsetted rib cage narrowed to a waspish waist, and her skirts fell over a flat belly to the floor, revealing only the tips of slippers covered in the same satin as the gown.

"Do you think she needs a dress form?" Clarice asked.

"Dear heaven, you can't mean a pair of those fake

things," Isabel gasped. "Those pads that push one's breasts up and in."

Madame pursed her lips and studied Isabel. "*Non*," she said. "The mademoiselle has very lovely bosoms, very full and round without help."

How perfectly mortifying. The two of them were discussing her chest as though it were some sort of commodity. Isabel's cheeks warmed, and she glanced down at the flesh in question only to find that it had turned a fiery pink. Dear Lord, what if she blushed the night of the ball? Would everyone stare at her 'very lovely bosoms' in their very reddened state?

"You're so right, madame," Clarice said.

Wonderful. Now her own lady's maid was talking as if she weren't in the room.

"But wouldn't a little more shoulder show them off better?" Clarice continued.

"You think?" the older woman replied.

Clarice circled Isabel and took a bit of satin sleeve between her thumb and forefinger, pulling it down over her upper arm. "Like this," she said as she slid a pin into the satin. "A little pinch here and a tuck below."

"Ah, *bien*," the seamstress declared. "You have a very good eye, *ma petite*."

"Just one moment," Isabel interrupted. "These are my bosoms you're discussing, and if you lower this bodice one more inch, they'll fall right out of it."

"Not to worry, miss," Clarice answered. "The madame and I know what we're doing."

"Just so," Madame Arlee announced. "A little pinch and a tuck, and the gown she is finished."

"Now, see here," Isabel protested.

"What will you do with the hair?" madame continued, not even addressing Isabel anymore, but dealing directly with Clarice.

"Easy," Clarice answered, gathering Isabel's mop of dark curls and holding them around her face. Clarice glanced over her shoulder at madame for approval. "Up

Waitangi Nights

simply, with one lock dangling down her neck to her shoulder."

Madame tapped a bony index finger against her lips. "Up and simple, *oui*," she said. "But all of it up and held with combs, carved tortoise shell, perhaps."

"Or mother of pearl," Clarice added. "To go with the color of the satin."

"*Parfait*," Madame Arlee declared. "Now, off with the dress," she ordered, "and I make the pinching and tucking."

Clarice dropped Isabel's hair, stepped around her, and swiftly undid the buttons. Then she bent and pulled the entire ornate creation over Isabel's shoulders, past the bustle, and to the floor. Isabel stepped out of the pool of fabric and tugged at the laces that held the horse hair contraption in place around her waist. As soon as it was free, she handed it to madame, who had bent to retrieve the gown.

Clarice approached with a wrapper, and Isabel shrugged gratefully into it. Thank heaven this ordeal was over. Now she only had to survive the ball itself.

"One week," Madame Arlee said to Clarice. "The gown will be back in one week for the ball. You will obtain the combs by then?"

"But I don't have mother of pearl combs," Isabel protested.

"I'll get them," Clarice said.

"You are very lucky in your girl here, mademoiselle," Madame Arlee said. "Perhaps someday I steal her from you."

Clarice smiled broadly and dropped a curtsy. "Thank you, madame."

"One week then," the seamstress declared and breezed out of the room, a pile of blue satin in her arms.

Isabel turned to Clarice and put her hands on her hips. "Did you have to encourage her?"

"Just look at you, miss," Clarice answered. "All upset over nothing. Madame and I will make you the most beautiful woman at the ball."

"Haven't you been listening to me?" Isabel demanded. "I don't want to be the most beautiful. I just want to get through the evening without looking like a fool."

Clarice clucked her tongue. "Why would you look like a fool?"

"The other women, they'll be richer, more poised." Isabel walked to the dressing table and sat down. She picked up her brush and stared at it. "They'll be taller."

Clarice reached over Isabel's shoulder and took the brush. Then she pulled it through Isabel's hair. "You needn't worry, miss. The master will see no one but you."

"I don't give a fig for the master's opinion of other women. I don't give a fig for his opinion of me, either. And I won't give him a clue that I care about fancy dresses or balls or anything else."

Clarice stopped brushing Isabel's hair mid-stroke. "Oh dear, that will make things difficult."

"How so?"

"The combs, miss. I planned to get them from Mr. Julian."

Isabel turned in her seat and stared up at Clarice. "From him?"

"Well, not from him directly," Clarice answered. "But I could put a word into Samuel's ear about them. He could make a subtle suggestion to the master."

"No," Isabel said. "Mr. Julian has spent far too much money on these gowns. I won't have him put out another penny on my behalf."

"He wouldn't have to buy them, miss. The ones I had in mind were his mother's. Very pretty things, too. She wore them all the time."

"You mustn't even mention the combs to him," Isabel said. "Promise me."

"But madame felt so sure they'd be perfect. She expects me to produce them."

Waitangi Nights

Isabel grasped Clarice's hand. "You must understand. I can't ask him for anything like that."

"But I'd ask Samuel to ask him. You wouldn't be involved at all."

"No, I forbid it."

Clarice's face fell. "If you say so, miss."

"I know you want to impress madame, but you mustn't say anything to Mr. Julian about my appearance, combs or gown or anything at all. I'll blend into the crowd at the ball as best as I can and wait for it to be over."

"But, miss—"

"And you'll help me do that," she said. "Agreed, Clarice?"

"Agreed," Clarice mumbled.

But did she mean it?

Chapter Ten

The combs appeared, anyway, in a highly polished case of *kauri* wood lined with crimson velvet. Isabel took the box from Clarice and sighed. "How could you do this?" she moaned. "You promised me."

"I didn't ask, miss. Honestly, I didn't, not even of Samuel."

Isabel stared at the combs, and they glistened back at her, opalescent colors playing over their surfaces. "But then how?" Isabel whispered.

"The master must have sent them on his own."

"Why would he do that?" Isabel said. "He doesn't even know the color of my dress." She glanced at Clarice's reflection in the mirror of her dressing table. "Does he?"

Clarice shrugged. "I didn't tell him."

Isabel lifted the combs out of their velvet cradle and studied them. Such priceless treasures, and on top of their monetary value, they had belonged to Mr. Julian's mother. What on earth could have moved him to loan them to an employee? And what must he have thought as he went through his own mother's things looking for them? She didn't dare ask, so she'd probably never find out.

She handed one over her shoulder to Clarice. Clarice, in turn, nudged it securely into a grand sweep of hair she had piled on the top of Isabel's head.

As much as Isabel would never have believed it possible, Madame Arlee and Clarice had turned her into rather a beauty. The dress carefully skirted the border between respectability and overexposure. Ball gowns, after all, were supposed to show some flesh. And this one managed to bare just the right amount while still hiding the most interesting curves beneath discreetly positioned bits of lace.

"The other?"

Isabel started and glanced over her shoulder at Clarice. "I beg your pardon?"

Clarice held out her hand. "The other comb?"

"Of course." She gave the second comb to Clarice. She set the box aside and watched as Clarice worked the mother-of-pearl teeth into the hair behind her ear.

"If you don't mind, miss, I'll crow just a bit," Clarice said. "Didn't I tell you you'd be a vision tonight?"

"You've worked miracles, I'll admit," Isabel replied. "But a vision?"

"A vision, yes. Nothing less," Clarice declared. "I only wish they all could see you with your skin still pink from your bath."

"Oh, my gracious," Isabel answered. "Let's not go to excess."

"Right you are. I'm just so proud of myself and Madame Arlee." Clarice gave a lilting laugh. "And you, too, of course."

A soft knock sounded at the boudoir door, the one to the main hallway. This was a reminder that an outside world waited for her, beyond Clarice's flattery and soothing ministrations. A world not nearly so safe as

Alice Gaines

the one within the champagne glow of her own bedroom.

Clarice shook Isabel's shoulders gently. "There now, miss. You've gone all tense on me again. Relax. I'll send whoever it is away."

Isabel patted Clarice's fingers. "Thank you."

Clarice disappeared into the sitting room, and Isabel turned back to the mirror. She did still glow from the hot water of her bath, and the floral scent of the bubbles clung to her skin. Just the right amount of perfume by Isabel's reckoning, enough to make her feel clean and feminine. But so subtle as to give someone else only a hint of flowers, if he noticed the fragrance at all.

Clarice reappeared at the entrance to the bedroom, a small satin-covered box in her hand. Isabel turned around to get a better view than the mirror allowed. "What's that?"

"I don't know," Clarice answered. "Ned said it was for you."

"Who could have sent it?"

Clarice smiled slyly and removed an envelope from the pocket of her apron. "There's a note."

Isabel held out her hand, and Clarice quickly crossed the room and placed the envelope into it.

The paper was ivory in color, heavy and opulent although unadorned. "Miss Gannon" had been written on it in a firm hand. Isabel slipped the note out and unfolded it.

The ball will be full of pompous asses tonight, it read. *Don't disgrace us by calling us fools to our faces, even if we deserve it. Let this little fellow do it for you instead— Fondly, R.*

Fondly, indeed. Isabel's cheeks warmed, and she quickly folded the paper back up.

"Did the package come from the master?"

Waitangi Nights

"Hm?" Isabel looked up at Clarice. "Oh, yes. Yes, it did."

Clarice held out the box to her. "Then open it, miss. Before I just die of curiosity."

Isabel took it from Clarice and pulled the lid open. Inside lay a piece of jade, almost emerald in color, carved in a curious, primitive shape. The form appeared to be of a little man, sitting cross legged with his head turned almost on its side. He had two enormous eyes made out of luminescent shell, and his mouth hung open, his tongue protruding.

"A *tiki*," Clarice exclaimed. "What an odd thing to send to a lady on the evening of a ball."

"A *tiki*?"

"It's a Maori good luck charm," Clarice said.

"Did this belong to Mrs. Julian, too?"

"I've never seen it before," Clarice answered. "A right beautiful piece of greenstone. But, still, he's rather ugly, don't you think?"

"No, I don't," Isabel exclaimed. "I think he's absolutely perfect."

"Perfect, miss?"

Isabel grasped Clarice's hand. "Don't you see? Diamonds and such are stunning but wholly conventional. This little creature has magic in him."

"I suppose so," Clarice replied. "Is there a chain, or is it supposed to hang around your neck by sorcery alone?"

Isabel lifted the figure out of the box, and a long strand of tiny gold links followed. She set the box aside and handed the necklace to Clarice. Clarice fumbled with the clasp for a moment before fastening it behind Isabel's neck.

Isabel stared at her reflection in the looking glass. The Maori figure nestled just above the rounding of her bosom, glaring at the world and sticking his tongue out defiantly so that Isabel wouldn't have to. How simply right. Now for the entire evening, when the magnificence of the ball became too overwhelming, the manners too oppressive, she'd just run her fingers over her good luck charm. He'd thumb his nose at them all for her.

"I'll say this for the greenstone," Clarice remarked. "It picks up the color of your dress."

"Yes," she said, thinking that only someone who knew her could have sent a work of native art to comfort her. Only someone who could see inside her could realize how she would value the gesture. *Fondly, R.* Fondly.

A throat cleared at the doorway. Isabel glanced over to find Samuel standing on the threshold. "Mr. Julian is asking for you downstairs."

"Already?" Isabel asked.

"Yes, miss," Samuel said, smiling.

Isabel raised a hand to her chest and stroked her good luck talisman. The smooth stone grew warm under her fingertips, whether with the heat of her body or its own alchemy, she couldn't tell. But the warmth reassured, promised even, that this night would be full of magic, magic of her own making.

Clarice leaned over Isabel's shoulders and gave them a little squeeze. "Go on down now, miss. And have a splendid time tonight."

Isabel hastily slipped Mr. Julian's note into a small drawer in the dressing table. Then she smiled at her reflection in the mirror and rose. "I'm ready."

Blast Sammy and his punctuality. The man always managed to get Richard dressed early for social engagements. And somehow the more odious the occasion, the more time he found on his hands before the bloody thing got started. He pulled his watch from his waistcoat pocket again and lifted the lid. They wouldn't have to leave for the Treaty House for another twenty minutes.

Richard put his watch back in his pocket and turned

Waitangi Nights

to the crystal decanters. He poured a generous shot of whiskey into a tumbler and took a comforting sip.

"Miss Gannon," Sammy announced from behind him.

Richard turned back to find his valet at the entrance to the parlor, a mischievous grin on his face. Sammy stepped back into the hall, motioning with his arm as he did. Miss Gannon crossed the threshold and stood there, motionless. For several heartbeats time froze into one crystalline moment as Richard studied her.

Damn, but she was beautiful. Despite her small stature, she dominated the room with her perfection. Silken, ebony hair; pale, shimmering skin; a square set to her naked shoulders that set off the softness of her breasts. And there, between them, hung the greenstone pendant. "You wore my *tiki*," he said.

"Certainly," she said. "Isn't that why you sent it?"

"For all I knew you'd send it back with a note explaining its unsuitability."

She smiled at him slowly, all sleekness and confidence. "Why would I do that?"

Why indeed? His prim nurseryman would have found some reason, but not this creature. This vision in satin and lace might do anything. He smiled back at her and took another sip of his whiskey. "I never know what to expect from you, Miss Gannon."

She raised her hand to her breast and ran her fingers over the *tiki*. "It's exquisite. Thank you."

"And the combs look wonderful in your hair."

"How kind of you to loan them to me. Clarice tells me they belonged to your mother."

"She would have been pleased to see them so gracefully worn."

A light blush of color climbed from her throat to her cheeks. "Thank you for them, too."

"There now," he said softly. "Was that so bloody hard?"

Alice Gaines

Her chin rose, and her smile broadened. "Was what so 'bloody hard'?"

"Thanking me," he answered. "Being pleasant."

She didn't answer, but merely lifted an eyebrow and huffed.

Bless her, she hadn't changed all that much. "Have a drink with me before the nonsense gets into full swing, won't you?"

She walked across the room to join him. "And thank you for that."

He picked up the glass that he had filled for her before she entered the room. She took it and sipped the liquid inside. "This isn't sherry."

"Whiskey," he replied. "We're both going to need it."

"Why, Mr. Julian, you sound as if you're dreading this more than I am."

He bent toward her. "I have a small favor to ask of you."

She pursed her lips into the most tempting curves imaginable. "Now, what on earth could a lowly employee do for the master of Harrowgate Manor?"

He leaned closer, until his nose brushed the hair at her temple. A fragrance of wild flowers filled his nostrils, light and pleasing. "Protect me," he whispered directly into her ear.

She shivered—just the slightest tremor and over so quickly someone else might have missed it. But not Richard. He'd been watching this woman for weeks.

She rested her free hand against his chest and rose on tiptoe, bringing her lips to his own ear. "Protect you from whom?"

Her breath pricked at something deep within him, racing down his spine to parts of him that had nothing to do with cutaway coats and ball gowns and polite conversation. And everything male inside him responded predictably. Good grief, what had he started?

She rested back on her heels and gazed up at him.

Waitangi Nights

Her hand rose to her throat and then came to rest over the *tiki*, her fingers fondling it in a way that both mesmerized and inflamed him. This wasn't the woman he'd hired to grow his orchids, the timid little creature who had sat in his study clutching a beaded bag in her hand as though to squeeze the life out of it. This wasn't the dirty-faced female in boy's clothes who had shown up for luncheon, sparks flying from her eyes. This wasn't even the woman who'd stood in the steam of the dishwater in the scullery and innocently turned her face up to his for a kiss. This woman held a power over him, and she knew it.

"You're not going to tell me?" she asked.

"I'm sorry," he answered. "Tell you what?"

"Who poses such a threat to you that you'd ask for my help."

He cleared his throat. "Some of the female guests tonight may have ideas," he began. "About me and my, shall I say, availability."

She arched a brow. "Designs on you?"

"Perhaps."

"And you want me to rescue you if any of them circle in too closely."

At the moment he couldn't think of anything more dangerous than her dark eyes, but he needn't tell her that. He took another sip of his whiskey. "If you would be so kind," he answered.

"What should I do?"

"Simply come to my side. Any other woman will slip away rather than bear comparison to you."

She tipped back her head and laughed. No, this wasn't his Miss Gannon. Had the *tiki* entranced her? Or was it working some black magic on him instead, reducing him to the helpless animal all men really were under the trappings of civilization? No matter the cause, he would enjoy the effect. Perhaps not right now, but later. Much later.

Alice Gaines

And yet . . .

Her lips parted ever so slightly, as though she were having trouble breathing, a feeling he quite understood, suddenly having to work for air himself in the closeness of the parlor. Yes, he might have a taste of her now, something to hold him until he could be rid of polite society and its nattering. He lowered his face toward hers, half afraid that she might pull back or simply evaporate like the apparition she surely must be.

Instead she leaned into him, and the gentle pressure of her palm rested against his chest. He breathed in the scent of her hair again. The perfume penetrated his brain, fogging what little reason he had left. Nearer and nearer she came, until his heart raced and he could taste desire on the inner sides of his lips.

A throat cleared—Sammy's. "Time to go, don't you think, sir?"

Richard straightened and caught a ragged breath. Bloody hell, why did he have to go to a ball tonight? Tonight, when he'd discovered this enchantress, when every ounce of his flesh ached to play satyr to her nymph.

Miss Gannon's chest rose and fell erratically, too, as she discreetly put some distance between the two of them. She lifted her glass to her lips and took a healthy swallow. Then she placed it on the tray next to the decanters and took Richard's arm. He set his own drink down and guided her toward the doorway.

After the majesty of Harrowgate Manor, the Waitangi Treaty House looked small, indeed. Isabel wasn't quite sure what she had expected, but this cozy, rather charming structure didn't seem the sort of place where an entire nation would be founded. In fact, the house and the *marae* nearby couldn't contain the scores of guests, let alone serve as a ballroom. So, with Kiwi ingenuity, local officials had set up a temporary dance

Waitangi Nights

floor on the lawn outside the Treaty House, festooned it with paper lanterns, and spread a banquet of local delicacies on tables nearby.

Isabel stood to one side of the dance floor, hiding out in shadows and enjoying the pleasantly cool evening breezes. If she'd allowed herself any more cowardice, she would have disappeared into the darkened gardens all together. But she'd promised Mr. Julian to "protect" him from eager young women, as preposterous as that sounded.

He'd coerced her, of course, plying her with whiskey and the seductive music of his voice whispering into her hair. Still, she had promised to help him extricate himself from feminine attentions, and she really didn't relish the idea of watching him act as recipient of some other woman's flirtation, as he surely would, for he was so handsome a figure in his formal dress, so wildly, excessively, maddeningly handsome.

Isabel took a slow breath. Why, oh why, did she have to have those thoughts? Why did she have to melt inside every time the man looked at her? Why did her breath have to quicken whenever he got near? Most of all why did her own lips have to part every time his did?

Enough. She would get her thoughts under control. She'd watch him discreetly from the shadows, and if he appeared to need her assistance, she'd "rescue" him somehow, even though she hadn't the faintest idea how. And she'd stay well away from the other men who'd asked her to dance. A few hours—she could manage that. Then the whole ridiculous affair would be over.

Just stay away from the other men. So many had asked her to dance, she'd lost count. And they gaped, too—down the front of her dress, until she reddened under their scrutiny. Then they really stared, not listening to her excuses at all but ogling her flesh as though they had some right to do so. She'd had to repeat herself at least a score of times. *I don't dance. No, thank you very much, but I don't dance. I don't dance, don't dance, don't dance.*

Oh no, another one. A tall blond man separated himself from the crowd around the buffet and headed toward her. His limbs dangled from his torso as he did, as though he hadn't been put together securely. But that didn't stop his progress, as his long strides quickly covered the distance between them.

Isabel turned, scanning the area for rescue. She didn't know a soul besides Mr. Julian, of course. And the Farnsworths, if you could call that knowing. The three of them stood together across the dance floor. Mr. Farnsworth and Mr. Julian were deep in conversation as Olivia looked on, worshiping her husband with her eyes. But she glanced briefly at Isabel and then at the tall blond approaching her and smiled.

Mr. Julian looked in her direction, too, and a frown creased his brow. His eyes sent off some message Isabel couldn't fathom—anger, perhaps, or some warning. Before she had a chance to puzzle his expression out, the other man neared her, blocking Mr. Julian and the Farnsworths from her view.

He grinned at her, revealing a gap between his front teeth. "I say, would you care to dance?"

"No, thank you very much," Isabel answered. "I don't dance."

"Well bless my soul, a kindred spirit," he declared. "I don't dance, either."

"Then why did you ask?"

"It's expected at these things, isn't it? Dancing, I mean."

"Yes, I suppose so." Isabel snuck a peek around his shoulder to Mr. Julian again. His expression had taken on a decidedly dangerous sparkle, his blue eyes flashing. For heaven's sake, what could be the matter with the man? Her attendance at the ball had been his idea, not hers. She raised her hand to her *tiki* for comfort and turned back to her companion.

Waitangi Nights

The man slid a finger inside his collar and tugged on it, jutting his chin out in a ostrich-like move. "Ripping party, this. Wouldn't you say?"

"Yes, I suppose so," she muttered, repeating herself.

"Have you seen the grounds?"

"No, I haven't."

He extended his arm. "Care to give them a stroll?"

A nighttime stroll with someone she'd just met? While her employer looked on, scowling at her? "It's rather dark."

"Of course. Quite. Silly of me not to think of that."

She stared up at the stranger. His smile beamed back down at her out of soft brown eyes, very much like Olivia Farnsworth's. In fact, he bore a striking resemblance to that kind lady with his pale skin and easy smile. His hair sat on top of his head like a haystack, in contrast to Olivia's neat coiffure, but otherwise they might have been brother and sister.

"Are you here with the Farnsworths?" Isabel asked.

"Oh, my yes. Didn't I introduce myself?"

Isabel shook her head.

"Dashed awkward of me, as usual," he replied, sticking out his hand. "Hugh Upton, your obedient servant. Olivia Farnsworth's impoverished cousin from London."

Isabel slipped her own fingers into his. No wonder she had thought him gangly; his wrist poked out of his sleeve by a few inches. But his grip was warm and pleasant, his smile reassuring, just like his cousin's.

"I'm Isabel Gannon," she said.

"Then you are the one," he announced, his grin growing even broader. "Livvie's told me all about you."

"Good evening, Upton," a male voice boomed.

Mr. Julian stood right behind Hugh Upton, topping that gentleman's considerable height. He wore his pirate's smile, the disquieting expression Isabel hadn't seen on his face for some time. It still gave her a chill.

Mr. Upton didn't seem to notice the darkness behind

Alice Gaines

Mr. Julian's eyes. He extended his hand with as much enthusiasm as he'd just shown Isabel. "There you are, Julian. Splendid evening, what say?"

"Glad you're enjoying yourself," Mr. Julian said.

"I've just met your Miss Gannon." Mr. Upton nudged Mr. Julian with his elbow. "Dashedly unsporting of you to keep such a lovely lady to yourself, old fellow."

Mr. Julian turned to Isabel, outright devilment now flaring from his eyes. "To the contrary, Upton. She's made herself more than a little public this evening."

Really. Isabel raised her chin and glared at him. He stared back, his gaze never wavering. Curse the man.

Hugh Upton looked from Mr. Julian to Isabel and back again. "I say, Julian, is that any way to speak of a lady?"

"Please leave us alone," Mr. Julian answered.

Mr. Upton cleared his throat. "Certainly." He turned toward Isabel and nodded politely. "I hope we can not-dance again later, Miss Gannon."

"Of course, Mr. Upton," she replied.

The man backed away, as awkwardly as he had approached. Isabel turned on Mr. Julian. "How could you?" she sputtered. " 'Made herself more than a little public,' indeed."

"You bloody well have," he snapped. "I thought I asked you to protect me from the female predators here."

"That was a ridiculous request, and you know it."

He leaned toward her, his eyes gleaming wickedly. "Was it, now?"

She tipped her head back, sticking her nose right up into his face. "Yes, it was."

"Damn," he grumbled. He caught her elbow roughly in one hand. "You'll dance with me. At least that will be one thing every other man in the room hasn't enjoyed yet."

"No."

His eyes widened, their color darkening to a truly

Waitangi Nights

threatening deep blue. "What in hell do you mean by no?"

"I don't dance," Isabel declared.

"All women dance," Mr. Julian grumbled. "It's the bane of man's existence."

"Then you'll be spared tonight, because you won't dance with me," she went on. "You've trussed me up and put me on display, but you can't force me to make a spectacle of myself on the dance floor."

"Why would you make a spectacle of yourself?"

"Because when it comes to dancing I have two left feet."

A smile played across his lips, not the dark, threatening sort this time, but an expression of pure amusement.

Surely he wouldn't drag her onto the dance floor and expose her clumsiness to the entire crowd. She reached up and clutched her *tiki*. "Please, Mr. Julian," she whispered.

The orchestra chose that exact moment to start up a new piece, and Mr. Julian tipped his head, listening. "A waltz," he said. "Anyone can waltz."

She tried to pull out of his grip, but his fingers tightened on her arm, telling her in no uncertain terms that she wasn't going anywhere. "*One*, two, three," he chanted in time to the music. "*One*, two, three. Simple, Miss Gannon."

"Please," she repeated. "I can't, really."

"Nonsense," he answered. "You simply haven't had the right partner. Tonight you will."

He started for the dance floor, pulling her along with him. They passed among gaily dressed ladies and their elegant partners, pushing aside bustled skirts of every possible hue until they reached the center of the whirling throng. Mr. Julian turned her around and placed his palm at the small of her back. He took her hand in his, holding it out to her side. Isabel hesitated and then reluctantly reached up to place her other hand on his shoulder. He began to move.

The music swelled, filling the night with its lilting beauty. It was a waltz, perhaps Viennese. Gowns swished by in a kaleidoscope of colors. The gentle pressure of Mr. Julian's fingers against her spine urged her to move to the rhythm, and she followed him for a few steps.

He smiled at her, reassuring this time. "There now, you see?"

She smiled back and promptly stumbled over his foot. "Oh, dear," she mumbled.

"We'll try again." He hesitated for a moment and then started with a new beat.

Isabel looked over his shoulder into the darkness and counted silently. One, two three. One, two three.

Mr. Julian bent his mouth to her ear. "You're fighting me, Miss Gannon. Relax."

Relax? He'd wasted his breath with that bit of advice. How on earth was she to relax with his hand at her waist and her own fingers on the smooth broadcloth of his tail coat? With the scent of his shaving soap in her nostrils? She tried, she really did. But she only succeeded in tripping over his toes for a second time.

She pulled away from him. "I told you this wouldn't work," she said. "Now, please let me go."

His eyes flashed fire again. "It would work if you'd give in and let me lead."

"I don't know how."

"Simple," he replied. "Do as Bunny does when we dance. Stand on my feet, and I'll waltz for both of us."

"I'll do no such thing," she gasped.

"Then you give me no choice." He grasped her chin between his thumb and forefinger and tipped it up to him. "You will look at me, not your feet or the shrubbery around us."

"Oh, dear heaven, Mr. Julian."

His arm slipped around her and pulled her hard

against his chest. His fingers splayed over her ribs, stealing her breath and crushing any resistance she might offer. She looked into his face and fell, helpless, into the blue light of his eyes.

Chapter Eleven

Heaven or hell, Isabel couldn't tell which, but one thing she knew, floating in Richard Julian's arms was an intoxicating experience. The scent of the man, his strength, the heat of his body—all of it was too much—and much too right, too perfect.

He twirled her once again, pulling her hard against him. She nearly lost her footing, he lifted her that high. But she didn't stumble, joined as she was to him and as one with the grace of his movements. The grace of the jungle cat, he had that certainly, and the strength and the predatory instincts. She'd seen that in the fire of his eyes. Cold blue and hot all at once. Dangerous.

His arm tightened around her waist, moving her even closer until her breasts pressed against him. And that felt right, too. As wrong as it was, she wanted it. She wanted the friction that set up a slow ache in her bosom. She wanted her flesh to come alive to his touch. Wanted that and more. But she couldn't. She didn't dare.

Waitangi Nights

"Mr. Julian," she whispered, his name coming out of her on a rush of breath.

He lowered his mouth to her ear. "You're doing splendidly, Miss Gannon. Stay with me."

"Please, sir." Oh dear, that was a plea. Weak, plaintive, female. "That is, I can't."

Laughter rumbled through his chest. She could feel it, for heaven's sake.

"Oh, but you can," he murmured into her ear, his own voice dark and laced with hints of the forbidden. "You most certainly can."

Please. Please, let me go. She didn't dare say it. That would betray too much. Begging him would give him even more power over her, and he already owned her breath, the beating of her heart.

Don't let me go. Not now. Not ever. Worse. Far worse.

He straightened and looked down into her face, the light in his eyes burning, feverish. His lips trembled, and she felt her own respond, parting to let at least some air into her lungs. His expression turned ravenous as he watched her. He wanted her. Dear heaven, he wanted her as much as she wanted him.

"I think we should sit down," she said.

"I disagree," he answered smoothly. "We've plenty of time for sitting later, and this is such a pleasant waltz, wouldn't you say?"

Pleasant? Hardly. "Some food, then. Something to eat."

"So, you're hungry." He laughed again, more softly this time, a sound meant only for the two of them. "I noticed some of the local oysters on the buffet. I'd be happy to feed them to you slowly and watch you eat them."

"That isn't what I meant." How could he? How could he even entertain ideas like that? "I only thought—"

"Don't think, Miss Gannon. Dance."

He twirled her again, and Isabel clutched at his shoulder. She needn't have, for he showed no willingness to release her. And in truth, everything was wonderful: the music, the way he guided her in the movements, the warmth of exertion, and the delicious closeness, the sense of knowing how he would move and how she would respond. Only, how could he make her feel this way? And could he make her want more and more?

"You can dance," he murmured. "In fact, you move quite well."

"I do wish you wouldn't say things like that."

"Why not? Afraid of your own nature?"

"My nature is most decidedly not your concern."

He smiled, and his gaze swept her face and lower, his lashes brushing his cheeks. "To the contrary, your nature does concern me. Very much, in fact."

"Mr. Julian—"

"Come now." He looked back into her eyes. "Where's my brave explorer who lived among the naked tribesmen of the Amazon?"

"I don't see what bravery has to do with this situation."

"You don't?"

"No."

"Then you obviously have no idea what effect your closeness is having on me."

She didn't answer that. She wouldn't answer that. Instead she stared at his shoulder and did her best to draw in a breath. She couldn't let him know that the mere idea that he might desire her set up a fluttering in her belly—and below.

"I could show you, I suppose," he said. "One move, a little extra pressure of your hip against me, and you'd be convinced well enough."

"That would be rather crude, don't you think?"

"Quite. Well then, I imagine I'll just have to tell you how alluring I find you."

Isabel concentrated on the music, the steps, the images of other dancers blurring past. Why on earth did

Waitangi Nights

this waltz have to last so long?

"You really are quite ravishing," Mr. Julian continued. "You looked delicious in my parlor with your hand pressed against my chest and your lips just begging to be kissed."

"They did not."

"They certainly did," he countered. "Dishonesty isn't like you."

She pressed her lips together. If she pressed hard enough, she might be able to erase the memory of that interrupted kiss.

"And now, so close to me." He increased the pressure at the small of her back, where his hand held her captive against him. "You tempt me sorely, Miss Gannon. Such an intoxicating form of torture. Surely you must feel the same way."

"No."

"Yes. I can see your excitement in the way you breathe, in the flush to your skin."

He couldn't, could he? Oh please, no.

"I know when a woman wants to be kissed," he went on, "and you're more than a little kissable right now."

"I'm not."

"Stop contradicting me."

The waltz ended, finally, with a little flourish of violins. Polite applause followed. It filtered to Isabel only vaguely where she stood, staring up at Richard Julian and the infuriating certainty in his eyes.

"Thank you for the waltz," she said. "It was most amusing."

"Good, then we'll dance another."

"No."

He caught her elbow in his hand. "Don't tell me 'no.'"

She eased out of his grip. "I'm tired. I think I'll go sit down."

"I'll escort you."

Alice Gaines

"I'd rather go alone," she said from between clenched teeth.

"Nonsense." He took her elbow again, not gently this time, and led her from the dance floor. "And sitting isn't what you have in mind. Not at all."

She had to sit, though, and breathe deeply a few times and try to concentrate on the party all around them. She had to get away from the man who held her elbow so close to his side, who held her fate in his hands.

He didn't head toward the chairs or the buffet or even the Treaty House. Instead he left the dance floor, stepping down onto the lawn and "helping" her to follow.

"We mustn't do this, Mr. Julian," she said.

"Do what?" he demanded.

"We can't leave the ball together, not to disappear into the darkness. What will people think?"

"They can bloody well think whatever they want to think. They always do."

"Everyone will see us leave," she said.

"Only if you set up a racket."

It was too late to worry about being seen, in any case. They'd left the party goers behind, and whoever had observed them leaving had observed them. She couldn't do anything about that. What she could do, what she had to do, was stop Mr. Julian somehow. But stop him from what? Where was he taking her? And what did he plan to do when they got there?

They continued across the grass, his long strides covering ground so quickly Isabel had to trot to keep up. The night air tickled at her skin, cooling and pricking where it penetrated the fog of heat his body had thrown up around her. They entered a grove of trees . . . Isabel couldn't tell what kind. Whatever he planned to do, the trees would provide cover. She had to stop him now or surrender, not only to him but to the fire in her own blood.

She dug in her heels and finally called a halt to their progress. He stared at her, his features caught in the

Waitangi Nights

last stray beam of light from the bank of lanterns. His eyes glowed, fierce, beautiful, wild.

"Mr. Julian, please," she cried. "Richard."

"Dear God," he whispered. He pulled her into the shade of a tree and pressed her against its trunk, the entire solid length of him pinning her there. Then his mouth came down on hers.

The world exploded around her into a thousand different sensations, all of them created by the movement of his lips as they danced over hers. Music and moonlight, the scent of flowers and the sweetness of their nectar, fire and fury and thunder. She slipped her arms around his neck and rose onto her toes to get even closer to him. Her mouth fit itself to his, moving in rhythm with his urgings, surrendering to the heat, the hunger.

This was what she'd needed when he'd taken her into his arms on the dance floor. This sharing of breath, this melting together until boundaries lost their meaning and dissolved. Her body had understood before she had, and now her body would be her teacher.

He pulled back then—too soon, much too soon. He took his lips from hers and buried his face into her neck, his harsh, uneven breaths heating her skin. "Isabel," he muttered. "Ah, Isabel."

She took his head in her hands and lifted it until she could look into his eyes. She found a world of feeling there—hunger and desire, but also a dark knowledge and something deeper. Something like pain.

She pushed his hair out of his face, the strands as hot as silken flame in her fingers.

"Richard," she whispered. She rose up on her toes again, bringing her face to his, offering herself as sacrifice to whatever burned inside him.

He groaned and took her mouth again. This time his touch held a universe of tenderness in it. Softly, smoothly, his lips moved over hers—coaxing, cajoling, drawing a sigh from deep inside her. His tongue probed her lips, parted them, and then slipped into her mouth, wreaking gentle havoc with the beating of her heart.

She answered with her own tongue, and all sanity fled. This gentleness was far more insidious than his earlier force. It could steal her soul along with her breath. And, heaven help her, she didn't care. She leaned into the kiss and took from him, and took and took and took.

He straightened, suddenly and awkwardly. His hands gripped her shoulders, holding her away from him, as he drew in a wrenching breath. "Damn, but I'm an ass," he cursed.

She placed a hand against his chest to steady herself. Her world had taken on a wicked tilt, and Richard Julian was the only solid figure in it.

He looked down into her eyes. "Are you all right?"

All right? The question made no sense in this new world of sensation. He might as well ask if she could taste colors, hear heat. She nodded.

"I'm so bloody sorry," he continued. "When you said my name, I suppose I went a bit wild."

Isabel stood, mute. Barely able to breathe, she gazed up into his face and watched the darkness return to his eyes. Helpless, she nodded again.

"I have no excuse, of course." He put a hand to her cheek and stroked it. "Nothing like this will ever happen again. You have my word."

Never again.

He lifted her chin. "Please say something. Say you'll forgive me."

"Yes." She managed the word somehow through a throat that felt rusty, as though she hadn't used it for weeks.

He heaved a sigh. "Shall I take you back?"

She shook her head. "I think I'd like to stay out here a while and clear my head." *Clear my heart.*

"Of course. I'll have the carriage brought around. We'll go home."

Waitangi Nights

"Thank you. I'd like that. In a moment."

He nodded. "In a moment then."

He turned and stepped around the tree, heading back toward the Treaty House and the ball. Isabel rested against the trunk and closed her eyes, waiting for her heartbeat to return to a normal rhythm.

How did the man do this to her? How did he make her act in direct opposition to every demand of professionalism and propriety? To dance with him like that, to kiss him like that, such monumental folly. Inviting disaster over and over again. And she hadn't even stopped herself. He'd separated them. Lord knew how far she would have gone if he hadn't.

What would happen now? He had all the options, and she had none. He could fire her outright if he wanted, just as he'd fired the nanny, and she'd have no recourse. She certainly couldn't tell anyone about what had happened between them. That wouldn't do her any good, and it would be too humiliating to bear.

He might try to seduce her. And after the way she'd behaved in his arms, so shamefully eager for his touch, he had to feel sure that she'd accept his lovemaking. Then, when he tired of her he might sack her anyway. He could take her innocence and turn her out. She'd be ruined, in every sense of the word, if he did that. And again, she'd have no recourse.

Or maybe, if she were very lucky, he'd ignore the whole incident. He'd apologized, after all, and that said he accepted responsibility for what had happened. As wild as he could be at times, as unreadable, he acted like a decent enough man. He didn't seem the type to punish her for his own sins.

Yes, maybe he'd let the whole embarrassing thing go. Put it down to the madness of an ill-conceived evening. It was a party that neither of them had wanted to attend. He might forget the incident entirely. If he did, she'd have a second chance at keeping her job, and

Alice Gaines

she'd take it. No more ball gowns and kisses—no matter how pretty the gowns, no matter how sweet the kisses.

"There you are, Miss Gannon," Richard said, enjoying the mere sight of her, damn the woman. "You have a visitor."

She stood on the threshold to the parlor and glanced around, cautiously. Only one day after the ball, and she had already reverted to her usual manner of dressing. He really ought to be grateful for the plain cotton of her dress, the bodice that buttoned up to her neck with the collar of lace at her throat. But he couldn't help longing for the feminine creature who had caught fire in his arms the night before. The woman who had . . . oh hell, best to forget about all that.

The visitor, that bothersome cousin of Olivia Farnsworth's, bolted out of his chair and covered the distance to Miss Gannon . . . Isabel. After the ball she would always be Isabel.

"Decent of you to have me, Julian," Upton declared, extending his hand toward Isabel. He gazed at her, pure adoration in his eyes. "I did want another chance to visit with Miss Gannon."

She took his offered hand and shook it, lowering her eyes demurely, the very image of feminine modesty. "You're too kind, Mr. Upton."

"I say, won't you call me Hugh? I'd be most honored."

"Very well," she replied softly. She peeked at Richard out of the corner of her eye, as though asking for his permission. "Hugh."

Damn. Richard had only heard his own name from her lips on two occasions. And he'd acted like a perfect bastard both times. Once he'd kicked Bunny's bedroom door closed in her face. The second time he'd tried to ravish her. She deserved better, much better, and Hugh Upton was exactly what she needed, as much as Richard hated to admit it. "Have a seat, both of you. I'm sure Miss Gannon is delighted to see you again, Upton."

Waitangi Nights

She glanced toward Richard and raised a questioning brow. "Of course."

Upton escorted her to the loveseat and joined her there. Richard resumed his own seat in a wing-backed chair and did his best not to notice how close Upton was to her. The man was practically breathing on her.

"Livvie's told me so much about you," Upton said, gazing into her eyes. "I was hoping to hear about your travels. And then perhaps to ask a favor."

"What would you like to know?"

"Everything," Upton declared. "Julian says you've been to the American West."

"Yes."

"My dear lady," Upton said. "Isn't it full of wild Indians? Weren't you afraid of being scalped?"

"The North American natives aren't wild. They've been suppressed, very viciously and effectively. And they learned scalping from the white man."

"Do tell," Upton said.

"Real native customs are disappearing. Entire languages may be lost. The Indians in the Central and South American jungles have fared somewhat better because of their isolation. But that will not last forever."

"Fascinating," Upton declared, still staring at her, rapt. "You've heard all this before, Julian, I'm sure."

"No, actually I haven't," Richard answered. In fact, he'd learned little about her past. He'd been too preoccupied with her present, with her eyes and skin, the sweetness of her breath. But all that had to end. And it would, soon. "Miss Gannon and I haven't discussed her voyages."

Upton's eyebrows shot up. "Really? Well, I intend to learn as much as she is willing to teach me." He turned back to Isabel. "In fact, I'd like you to address my students. That's the favor I mentioned."

"I didn't know you had students, Upton," Richard said.

"I don't, yet," the man answered. "I've come to Wai-

Alice Gaines

tangi to establish a boy's academy. Along the lines of an English public school."

"A noble undertaking, I'm sure," Richard said.

Upton studied him, uncertainty in his eyes, as though he suspected that he'd been insulted. *He could take the remark any way he wanted. As long as he stopped staring into Isabel's dark eyes.*

The ploy didn't work for long. Upton turned back to her, and an idea struck. Richard could read it plainly on his face.

"I say, you'd make quite an addition to my faculty, Miss Gannon."

"Is it customary now for women to teach at English public schools?" she asked. "It never was when I lived in England."

"Well, no," Upton answered. "But this will be a New Zealand school. We can start our own customs."

"I don't hold any university degrees."

"But as headmaster, I can hire whomever I wish."

"Miss Gannon already has employment," Richard said.

"I'm speaking of the future." Upton took her hand in both of his, all exuberance and innocence. "Do tell me you'll consider the proposition. I won't release your hand until you do."

She glanced at Richard. He did his damnedest to meet her gaze evenly. He'd die before he'd let her see what another man touching her did to him. She looked back at Upton and blushed. "Very well, Mr. Upton—Hugh—I'll consider it."

"Splendid," he crowed. "Splendid. Quite a find for my academy, wouldn't you say, Julian?"

"Absolutely. Miss Gannon knew Darwin. Did she tell you that?"

"No." Upton's eyes grew round with astonishment, and he gripped her fingers even more tightly. "My dear Miss Gannon, you knew that great gentleman?"

"I met him a few times. When I was very small."

Waitangi Nights

"I say, how absolutely marvelous. You must tell me all you remember about him. What he looked like, every word he said."

"I'm afraid I don't remember much."

"I want to hear whatever you do remember." Upton's gaze hadn't moved from Isabel's face. Nor had he released her hand. "But what say we have our talk in the garden? I'm sure your employer wouldn't mind. Would you, Julian?"

"Not at all," Richard answered. "The gardens are at their best now. I'm sure Miss Gannon would enjoy showing them to you."

Isabel's chin came up, and she stared at Richard, no doubt surprised at how easily he handed her over to Upton. Could he blame her? Only last night he'd held her against his chest and devoured her lips with his own. He'd cried her name into the pulse at the base of her throat. Now here he was, pushing her at another man.

She couldn't know how he ached to show Upton the door. To have that walk in the garden with her for himself, to take her into his arms among the roses and rekindle the passion they'd shared. She couldn't know, and she wouldn't know.

He looked back at her and smiled, pleasantly he hoped. "Go along now, Miss Gannon," he said. "It's a lovely afternoon."

"Yes," she said. She rose a little too quickly, almost losing her balance. Upton shot out of his seat, caught her, and steadied her.

"Thank you, Mr. . . . Hugh," she said.

"My pleasure." Upton held out his arm to her, and she rested her hand against it. She didn't hesitate as she had the first time she'd taken Richard's arm. But then, Upton didn't pose any threat to her. Upton was a gentleman, through and through. Upton would behave himself, or Richard would murder him.

They left him. They walked, arm in arm, into the hall

and toward the front of the manor house, Upton's voice growing more distant. Finally, as the heavy door closed behind them, the man's nattering ceased entirely.

Richard's stomach clenched, again. His insides had been churning ever since the night before, when he'd managed to pull himself back out of Isabel's embrace.

How that had hurt. Turning down passion like that, denying himself the sweet release she had offered. He'd wanted her so much the frustration had been a physical pain. He still wanted her, and he still couldn't have her.

But soon at least he'd remove her from the house. He'd made that decision near dawn. He wouldn't have to spend many more nights like the last one, lying wide awake in his bed, aching for her, knowing she was only a few doors away. Doors with no latches. Doors that couldn't be closed against him.

Isabel rested her hands on the balustrade and leaned against it, gazing out over the garden. Fingers brushed her shoulders, and she glanced back. She expected Richard, of course, the man whose kiss had stolen her breath the night before. The man who could never be Mr. Julian to her again, not after that embrace. But instead she found Hugh. He dropped her shawl over her and then stepped back, shyly, as though he'd done something wrong.

"Thank you," she said. "The breeze is rather cool. Did Clarice have any trouble finding my wrap?"

Hugh skirted her and took a seat on the balustrade. "None at all. The girl's a gem."

Isabel studied him as she had several times that afternoon. How could she have helped it? He'd been at her elbow the entire time. He gazed back at her now, apparently satisfied just to sit and look at her.

So, here was Richard's way of dealing with what had happened between them the night before, making a match for her with Hugh Upton. Why not? She and Hugh occupied more or less the same station in society

Waitangi Nights

and shared the same interests. Certainly, she could do worse than this kind, attentive gentleman with the gap-toothed grin and soft brown eyes. And his company would help her to maintain a discreet distance from the man she really wanted, her employer.

Well, no use dwelling on the impossible. She smiled at Hugh. "Now, shall we have that walk?"

"I say." He slipped a finger under his collar and tugged on it, loosening it a fraction of an inch. "I don't really care about the garden. I saw enough gardens in England to last a lifetime."

"Then why did you ask for a guided tour?"

He leaned toward her, an impish grin on his face. "To spend some time alone with the guide. Dashed clever of me, eh?"

"I suppose so," she answered. "I really wouldn't know." And, heaven help her, that was the truth. Ever since she'd arrived at Harrowgate she'd come to realize that, despite what her travels had taught her about people as people, she knew very little of men as men. The evening before she'd thought Richard Julian wanted her, desired her. Now . . .

"I hope I haven't overstepped my bounds," Hugh said.

Isabel snapped back to the present. "I'm sorry."

"I don't do this very often." Hugh peered at her with a gentle expression that would amuse even the most fainthearted spinster. "Ask ladies for a tryst in the garden, that is. We can go back inside if you like."

She reached out, touching her hand to his. "No, no. Please excuse me. My mind was wandering."

He squeezed her fingers in reply, a warm, comforting touch. "To pleasant places, I hope."

She smiled again. Hugh made smiling easy, it seemed. "So, now that you've lured me out here, what are your intentions?" she asked.

He leaned even closer to her, still holding her hand. "To ask you to a picnic."

"A large affair?"

"Just the two of us," he answered.

"When?" she asked.

"Any Sunday afternoon of your choosing." His smile faltered, and his fair cheeks turned pink. "If you would do me the honor."

A picnic for just the two of them. Very formally and properly proposed—the way a gentleman courted a lady. "I'd be honored to accept."

He breathed a huge sigh of relief and delight. "Well, yes. I say. Splendid."

"Shall we make it this Sunday afternoon?"

"Splendid," he repeated. "I have so much I want to ask you."

"About Darwin?"

"And other things. I was serious about asking you to consider serving on my faculty, you know." He looked down at their intertwined fingers. "And I may have other favors to beg in future."

How absolutely perfect he ought to be. He offered her the hope of future employment—perhaps a great deal more, if she read him correctly. Why didn't that please her? Why did Hugh Upton fall so short of what she really wanted?

He cleared his throat. "And now that you've agreed to call me Hugh, might I address you by your Christian name as well?"

"Yes, I think that would be appropriate."

He took her hand in both of his then, giving her a smile that would melt the hardest of hearts. "Isabel," he said softly. "Belle. No, I don't like that—it sounds rather like a music hall girl."

"Really, I—"

"Bella—that's it," he declared. "Bellissima, most beautiful."

Honestly, an Italian endearment. Whoever would have thought that Arthur Gannon's tree-climbing pixie of a daughter was romantic enough to warrant a pet name in that passionate language? Dear man. What did he see when he looked at her? Obviously not what she saw when she looked in a mirror.

"Bella," he repeated, playing with her fingers in his exuberance. "My own Bella."

Isabel gently removed her hand. As sweet as he was, she had no wish to encourage him. They'd only just met, and she knew very little about him. But then, she knew nothing about men at all, as was fast becoming clearer and clearer.

"Until Sunday, then," she said.

He rose from the balustrade, suddenly all elbows and wrists. He took her hand again, this time for a very professional, very proper handshake. "Until Sunday. I'll bring everything, just be waiting for me."

"Of course."

He released her hand and started across the terrace toward the house with a sideways gait, leaving and yet still staring at her. At the doorway, he nearly tripped over the threshold. But he caught himself, smiled at her, and nodded. "Until Sunday."

Then he turned, finally watching where he was going, and went into the house. Isabel pulled her shawl around her shoulders and looked back out over the garden.

Everything would work out for the best. Richard . . . Mr. Julian . . . no, Richard showed every sign of wanting to ignore their encounter of the night before. She still had her job, and now she even had the possibility of a teaching position for the future, an opportunity that would have been unheard of in England. So, why didn't the rescue make her happy?

Because she'd been given a taste of heaven in the impossible, wild sweetness of Richard's kiss. And from now on, she would compare any man, any caress, with that forbidden delight. How could she not? Even today she could still taste him on her lips, still breathe in his scent. Preposterous but undeniable, the essence of him clung to her after all these hours. Would she ever be rid of it?

Isabel straightened and turned toward the house. She would have to be rid of him, or else she'd have to learn to live with the memory of his touch and get on with her life. He might always be with her, hiding in the back of her consciousness, clinging to the edges of her vision. But she would learn to adjust to the ache of not having him. Maybe in time the image of him standing in the soft glow of the lantern would fade into a pleasant recollection, a hazy reminder that for one brief encounter on a warm evening she had felt her heart beating in her chest, ready to burst with passion.

Yes, in time she'd be glad for having known his touch. For now she'd just have to endure watching him and wanting him and not having him.

Chapter Twelve

Dinner alone with Richard Julian had done nothing to make the man any less of a mystery. Would Isabel ever understand him? He'd been pleasant through the entire meal. Distant but pleasant. She'd told him of her planned outing with Hugh, and he'd encouraged her to go. Less than twenty-four hours since he'd kissed her with such abandon, and here he was giving her his blessing to keep company with another man. Oh well, she'd wanted another chance to maintain a professional relationship with her employer, and now she had it. She ought to be happy.

Isabel stood among the roses and gazed off into the distance. The light seemed closer tonight. Could it be a bonfire? Could the local Maoris be sitting around it, playing their flutes? Odd how no one on Harrowgate's staff mentioned the light or its ethereal music. After all, they had been invited to the Ngapuhis' *marae* before. Why remain silent now?

Isabel drew her shawl closer around her, cocked her

Alice Gaines

head, and listened. Another sound joined the music of the flutes. A human voice, chanting, and not far away. She headed toward it.

Halfway across the lawn, the chanting grew clearer. The bonfire or whatever it was might lie at some distance, but the chanting was nearby. She passed the topiary chessmen and found the source.

Holding a lantern, Samuel stood with a singular-appearing man. He was quite stocky of build and dark skinned. Despite the evening's chill, he wore no more than a Polynesian style skirt of grass. He carried a beautiful but lethal-looking jade warclub, and he was speaking in a singsong monotone.

He turned as Isabel approached, and the view of his face made her gasp. It was covered with tattoos—geometrical whorls and angles—all around his eyes and over his forehead and cheeks. As lovely as the patterns were, they gave him a fierce aspect. As she watched, he scowled at her, sticking out his tongue in a manner very similar to that of the *tiki* she'd worn the night before.

"Miss Gannon," Samuel said, turning toward her and raising his lantern. He had a decidedly sheepish expression on his face, as though he'd been caught at something. "Chilly out here. You should be inside."

The other man approached Isabel. He actually wasn't much taller than she, and he bent slightly to stare into her face. From this close, his tattooing really was remarkable, extending from his hair line to his chin, from one temple to the other. She held her ground and looked back into his unblinking stare. "Samuel, who is this man?" she asked quietly.

"Henga," Samuel answered. "The local *tohunga*."

"*Tohunga?*"

"Magician," Samuel replied. "Shaman."

Isabel raised herself as tall as she could manage and extended her hand toward Henga. He didn't take it, but straightened, removing his face from hers. He spoke a

Waitangi Nights

few words in a language she didn't understand—Maori, undoubtedly.

"What's he saying?" she asked.

"He says you must be the *hine*, the woman."

"What does that mean?"

"I wouldn't worry, miss," Samuel said. "It's superstition, no more."

"Still, I'd like to understand."

Henga began to talk again, pointing toward the light. This time Isabel made out the word *hine*. The man clearly meant to refer to her, while also indicating the light in the distance. "Do both of you see that shining?" she asked.

Samuel nodded.

"What is it?"

Samuel shrugged. "Who knows?"

"What does Henga think it is?"

"Don't concern yourself," Samuel answered quickly. "These things are best left alone."

"Do you hear the music, too?" she said. "Like flutes."

Samuel listened for a moment. "No music. I hear nothing but us."

Isabel stood in silence. The flutes were there, still faint, but definitely discernible. She looked at Henga. He might have been a statue. No way to tell if he heard anything without asking Samuel to translate, which he seemed most unwilling to do.

"Don't worry about that light, miss," Samuel said. "Someone built himself a big fire, that's all. The rest is imagination, yours and Henga's."

"I suppose you're right."

Henga looked into the distance and then back at Isabel. He finally said a few words to Samuel, turned, and strode off. Samuel laughed.

"What did he say?"

"The first thing sensible. He said the night was too cool to be standing here. We should be in our *whares*."

Isabel just looked at him.

Alice Gaines

"Our houses, miss. Let me take you back inside."

"Very well."

Isabel turned and headed back toward the house, Samuel at her side. He cleared his throat. "No use telling the master about Henga being here," he said. "It would only upset him."

"I can't lie to my employer."

"But you don't have to tell if he doesn't ask, no?"

"I don't know, Samuel. That seems dishonest."

"You don't understand all." Samuel stared resolutely ahead of him. "Richard, he lost someone, someone he loved."

Richard. Samuel had called Mr. Julian by his Christian name. None of the other staff had done that, at least not in Isabel's hearing. And he'd mentioned a loss. Could that be the "personal tragedy" Olivia Farnsworth had mentioned that day at lunch? But what could that have to do with Henga and his pronouncements? And of course, the most important question . . . "Samuel, is any of this related to Bunny and her dreams?"

Samuel stopped, and his eyes grew wide. "You know about that?"

"Not really," she answered. "I heard something coming from her room the night before Nanny left."

"What did Richard tell you about that?"

"Not much more than to mind my own business."

"Do what he says, miss. Please."

"But perhaps I can be of some help."

Samuel stared into her face. "You can help. Just be with him. Don't question. And don't mention Henga was here. Please."

What on earth? Why shouldn't Richard know about the shaman's visit? Samuel seemed so certain, so concerned. She touched his arm. "Very well, Samuel. I won't volunteer any information."

He let out a breath. "Thank you."

"I only wish I understood the man."

Waitangi Nights

"You will someday, and the understanding will give you joy."

And what in heaven's name could that mean? So many questions, but the answers would have to wait for another day. Her head was still spinning from the night before. She squeezed Samuel's arm and resumed walking toward the house. When they reached the terrace, Samuel accompanied her up the stairs and across to the door. He pulled it open for her. "Good night, miss."

"Aren't you coming in?"

"I'll check out front first."

"Good night, then."

She went inside and let the door close behind her. The house had darkened to nearly black. And the light of only one lamp shown into the hallway from a doorway, the doorway to Richard's study. He often worked there after dinner. Would he be there now?

Did she want to see him now? She'd just agreed to keep something from him, and she'd never been good at keeping secrets. They always showed on her face. Then too, being alone with him in near-darkness would be too much like the night before to be comfortable. But the only way to the staircase that led to her bedroom was right by the study door. If he were inside, he'd see her go.

Such nonsense. Of course, he would see her. He was going to see her around the manor house constantly and every night at dinner. And she would encounter him, too—to expect anything else would be ridiculous. She would simply have to get used to it.

She headed down the hallway, keeping her eyes straight ahead of her. She wouldn't glance into the study, wouldn't act as though she even cared where he was. She'd go up to her room and get to bed.

A few feet from the door, her step faltered for a second. But she continued, head held high. She crossed the pool of light and emerged on the other side. Success. She'd be spared speaking to him, for tonight at least.

"Isabel," his voice called softly from the study.

She stopped dead in her tracks and squeezed her eyes shut. Not tonight, please. Not while the feeling of his lips on hers still burned so brightly in her mind. Please.

"Isabel," he repeated. "I'd like to speak with you for a moment."

She opened her eyes, turned, and stepped into the study.

The light from his desk lamp barely touched the corners of the room, leaving all in shadow except for the papers in front of him and the orchid at the corner of the blotter. She'd brought the plant in from the glasshouse a few days before as a surprise for him. But he'd never mentioned it or its flowers with their vibrant purple spots. What a fool she'd been to think she could please him. The orchids were merely possessions, and she was merely an employee.

"There you are," he said quietly. He gestured for her to come farther inside. "Don't stand there in the dark where I can't see you."

She stepped forward, just until the lamp light fell onto her skirts. Better if he didn't see her face. "I was on my way to bed."

"I won't keep you," he answered. He opened a drawer and pulled something out. He set the object onto the desk, and the light revealed it, the satin box with the *tiki* inside. "I expected you to return my mother's combs, but I meant for you to keep this."

He pushed the box across the blotter toward her. She stared at it, half wanting to take it and half wanting to run away. "I couldn't," she whispered.

"Why the devil not?"

Because I can't withstand its magic. Because it makes me want what I can't have. Because it makes me want you. "It isn't right."

He rested his elbows on the desk top and leaned forward. The light from the lamp danced in his hair and caressed the planes of his face, emphasizing the perfect geometry of his features. His eyes glowed with a deep blue weariness, a sadness that tore into her and made her fingers itch to stroke his brow.

He took a deep breath. "I've behaved miserably toward you."

"No, you haven't."

"Don't say that," he answered. "Your generosity only makes me feel more like an ass."

She looked down to her hands where they were clenched in front of her skirt. He had devilled her, challenged her, tempted her ever since she had set foot in his house. But how could she call that miserable behavior when all she wanted was more of the same?

He opened the satin box and turned it toward her. The *tiki's* iridescent eyes shone up at her, and its tongue stuck out, as Henga's had a few moments earlier. Just last night she had considered the little figure a protective talisman. Now it mocked her.

"Please," he said softly. "It's a good piece of greenstone, traditional handwork. I'd like for you to have it."

She held her fingers tightly together. One moment of weakness and she might give in, take the *tiki* from him, take his hand in hers. She stared at the box, willing it closed, begging for freedom from its temptation. From the temptation that was Richard Julian. She shook her head. "I . . . can't."

He sighed and closed the box. "Perhaps later, after you've been here for some time—a gift to a valued employee."

"Perhaps."

He placed the box back into the drawer and pushed it shut. The sound had a final ring to it, like a door closing on a part of her life.

A valued employee. The night before he had signed a note "fondly." Where had that fondness gone? Had it evaporated in the heat of his kiss? Maybe it had never existed at all.

"And I do value your work," he said. He lifted his hand to the orchid and stroked a petal with long, graceful fingers. "The orchids are in splendid condition. I'd hate to lose you because of an indiscretion."

Indiscretion? So, that was all their intimacy had meant to him. She should have known. She had known, but had wanted to pretend that he wanted her as she did him. Somehow the pain of denial would have been easier to bear if she could only know he shared it.

"I won't lose you, will I?" he asked.

Her gaze travelled from his hand where it rested against the orchid flower to his face. But he had leaned back in his chair, hiding himself from her in the shadows. Did she read the plaintive tone in his voice correctly? Or was she only hearing what she wanted to hear? "No, you won't lose me," she answered.

"When Upton opens his academy you'll take him up on his offer, of course. It'll be a great opportunity for you."

"Yes, then, of course."

"I'll let you go with all best wishes, references, anything you need."

"Thank you."

"In the meantime, I think we've reached an understanding."

And indeed, they had. She'd keep her job, her status as a valued employee, and that was all. She'd care for the orchids, and she'd want their owner. At least until Hugh took her away, and then she wouldn't see Richard Julian again at all.

He shifted in his seat, a restless move, as though he suffered the same discomfort she did. "I've spoken to Davis," he said.

"Davis?"

"My carpenter. He's finished his other work and had a chance to look at the nurseryman's cottage."

Waitangi Nights

"Oh yes, Mr. Davis," she mumbled. "The cottage."

"The roof isn't as bad as I thought. You should be able to move in by the end of the week."

Thank heaven for that at least, a clean break, not having to be so near him.

"Clarice will want to continue as your lady's maid," he continued. "She's grown very attached to you."

"And I to her."

He shifted again, moving from one side of his chair to the other. Then he cleared his throat. "You'll dine with me as usual."

"Why?"

"Because I want you to."

What in heaven's name was wrong with the man? Why couldn't he just let her go? Isabel stared into the shadows but still couldn't make out his face. "I'd rather not," she said.

"I didn't ask your preference," he snapped. "I won't have my staff carrying your dinner out to the cottage."

"I can cook for myself."

"You'll dine with me," he said.

"Please, Mr. Julian," she said.

"I haven't heard about any of your travels yet," he replied. "If Upton is to know all there is to know about you, then so will I."

"But—"

"I sounded like a bloody fool this afternoon. I hadn't even heard that you'd met the red Indians."

"I haven't, not really."

He leaned forward again, finally revealing his face, his eyes. The old fire blazed in them, the heat that stole her breath, her logic, her heart. It wasn't gone, after all.

He rested a fist against the desk top and stared up at her. "You'll dine with me," he said for a third time. "I'll hear all your stories, every last incident."

"Very well," she mumbled.

He stared at her a moment more, as though he wanted to burn his image into her brain. As though he hadn't already done exactly that, dozens of times. Then he sighed and sat back again. "That's all for now."

She turned and headed toward the hall. What on earth was she to do with the man? He pushed her away and then ordered her to attend him, to entertain him with her life. He sent her gifts and then called her an employee. He granted her independence and then took it away. Maybe tomorrow she'd make sense of him. Right now her head was beginning to ache.

Just as she reached the doorway, he cleared his throat again. "Isabel?"

She stopped but didn't turn. "Yes, sir."

"I'd very much appreciate it, when we're alone..." He hesitated. "If you'd call me Richard."

"Richard," she whispered.

Without waiting for an answer, she stepped into the hallway and headed toward the stairs and the quiet of her bedroom.

Isabel dropped a filth-encrusted dish back into the sink and gazed through the dusty windowpane to the cottage garden. Overgrown. Apparently her predecessor, Mr. Ezekiel Turner, had made a mess of everything he touched.

"Lord, miss," Clarice declared from behind her, "are you sure you want to live out here?"

"It's where I belong."

"So far from the main house? With the rats and all?"

Isabel spun and scanned the floorboards. "Rats?"

Clarice lifted an end of the moth-eaten braided rug in front of the fireplace and peeked under it. "Bound to be something living in here—something that scurries about at night."

Isabel glanced quickly into all the corners of the room. "But surely not rats. Field mice maybe."

Clarice shuddered. "Rats, mice—they're all the same to me."

"Not to me."

Waitangi Nights

Clarice dropped the rug back into place, setting up a cloud of dust. She wrinkled her nose and sneezed loudly. "Oh miss, come back to the house. Please."

"I can't. Mr. Julian has had this cottage fixed for me, and I'm moving in."

"As you say," Clarice grumbled.

Isabel glanced around the one room that would serve her as sitting room, bedroom, and kitchen, and she tried to imagine how it would look after some cleaning. The fireplace was perhaps the best feature of the cottage, made of large fieldstones and almost big enough to walk into. Inside hung several hooks and swinging arms that would allow her to do rudimentary cooking, making tea for herself and even a nice stew or soup. The heat and the odors of simple homemade fare would provide comfort on cold, rainy nights. All she would need would be a rocking chair and a cat curled up, purring, in front of the flames, or maybe in her lap while she read a book. Harrowgate had extensive stables and must have a mouser somewhere. Where there were cats, there would be kittens. She would select one for a pet—a calico, preferably.

Clarice walked to the bed and dropped onto it. The springs creaked loudly under her weight. "I don't know how you'll ever sleep with all this noise," she said.

"I'm sure I won't even hear it after a while."

"Humph." Clarice lifted a corner of the bedspread, glanced at the mattress underneath, and made a face. "Ugly, lumpy old thing. We'll get you a new one from the house."

"The bed itself looks adequate," Isabel said.

It was large with a lovely hardwood headboard. It was no doubt a castaway from the manor house that after a few years of service had been deemed not suitably elegant and had been given to the staff. Nestled into a corner across from the fireplace, it would make a soft and warm haven.

Yes, this cottage would make her a cozy home, exactly what she had been wanting since she arrived in Waitangi. She'd merely become distracted by the elegance of Harrowgate Manor and by a certain pair of fiery blue eyes. Now that she would have more privacy, she could get on with her work in peace. Maybe even dinner could become a pleasant affair—interesting company and lively conversation between two individuals who treated each other with respect.

Richard had been nothing if not respectful for the last few days. Respectful, courteous, boring even. He had ensconced himself in his study and appeared to have little time left for fits of temper with her.

Clarice heaved a sigh. "I'll go back to the house and get some cleaning things. If you insist on staying here, we've our work cut out for us."

"Oh, no," Isabel protested. "A lady's maid doesn't make beds and clean floors. I'll do it myself."

Clarice laughed with her usual pleasant lilt. "Saints, miss, listen to yourself. You're the lady here, if you don't mind my pointing it out."

"That's right," Isabel answered. "I keep forgetting."

Clarice put her hands on her hips and looked around. "I doubt the rest of the staff will lift a finger. None of them ever came out here when Mr. Turner was alive. Rumor was the man didn't even bathe much."

"I certainly appreciate your help."

"Just you and me, then." Clarice dusted her hands together. "I'll hunt up a new mattress, brooms, mops, and such and be right back."

"And I'll look around for mouse holes."

"I only hope you won't find any," Clarice said and shuddered. "Nor any rats." She walked toward the doorway and went outside.

Could there really be rats in the walls? Isabel looked around. Oh well, what choice did she have? This was her home now, and if it had vermin, that only made another good reason to have a cat.

She crossed to the fireplace, picked up the poker, and

Waitangi Nights

headed to the far corner where some old journals and newspapers stood in a top-heavy pile. If she were a mouse, she'd hide her entrance behind them where no human with any sense would intrude. She'd get spiders to stand guard over it. But please, not rats—anything but rats.

She gingerly poked at the papers. Several inches of faded newsprint slid off the top, sending up dust from the floor where it landed. Isabel stood, absolutely silent, listening for the scuttle of little rodent feet. Nothing. Maybe the creak of a floorboard. Or could that be a mouse's squeak?

She took the poker in both hands and pushed harder against the base of the pile. It all moved in an avalanche of yellowed paper, dust, and cobwebs. There, something moved, or maybe not. Some creature might have darted out from under the newspapers and then hidden again. Or maybe not. She brought the poker down on the spot where she had last seen movement. Nothing responded, no animal cry, no darting and hiding.

She inched closer and tapped the wall behind the papers. No response. She knocked again, harder, first at the dingy corner and then along the baseboard toward the fireplace. There might be something living in the hollow behind the wall for now, but it had better learn that a human was moving in. A human who was soon to be joined by a cat.

"Isabel?"

Oh, dear heaven. Isabel stood bolt upright and placed her hand over her breast. She took a breath and turned.

Bunny stood in the doorway dressed in her riding costume. She looked at Isabel with wide, blue eyes. "Did something bite you?" she whispered.

"No, thank goodness."

"Then why are you standing there with the poker?"

"Just foolishness." She leaned the poker against the fireplace. "Why don't you come in?"

Bunny took two small steps inside and glanced

Alice Gaines

around. "Are you really going to live here?"

"Don't you like my cottage?"

Bunny shrugged.

"It doesn't look like much now, but when it's cleaned up it'll be very nice, don't you think?"

"I guess so." Bunny shifted nervously and looked down at her feet. "Are you angry with me?"

"No, dear," Isabel answered. "Why on earth would you think that?"

"You moved out of your room," Bunny said, nudging the edge of the battered rug with her toe. "Maybe I made too much noise or I was naughty or something."

Isabel walked to Bunny and crouched down, lifted the little girl's chin, and stared into the clear blue of her eyes. "You're never naughty."

"But you left," Bunny said. "We were going to be friends. If I couldn't have a mother and father, at least I could have a friend."

"We are friends." Isabel hugged Bunny to her chest. "You can come out here and visit me whenever you like."

"Whenever I like?"

"Of course." Isabel closed her eyes and drank in Bunny's little girl scent—soap and wildflowers, innocence.

A throat cleared. Isabel glanced up to find Richard on the threshold. He wore his riding outfit, including the tawny breeches that showed off the definition of every muscle in his thighs. Such clothes ought to be outlawed, tempting as they were to any poor female's imagination. What rugged beauty would lie just under the camel's hair? What sleek strength would reward the exploration of curious fingertips?

He smiled down at her where she crouched, still hugging his daughter. His gaze held an intimate knowing in it, as though he could read her thoughts and would answer them with similar notions of his own. And yet the light of his eyes offered a welcome, too, an invitation to closeness with his flesh and blood. Through his

Waitangi Nights

daughter, through his own person.

It was an invitation Isabel didn't dare accept, a temptation she would have to learn to resist. She rose slowly. "Mr. Julian."

He nodded toward her, politely, oh so politely. "Miss Gannon."

They stood in silence, looking at each other for a long, awkward moment. Finally Bunny fidgeted by Isabel's side, her shoe scuffing against the rough planking of the floor.

"There you are, precious," Richard said, although he surely must have noticed her before. "Are you ready for our ride?"

"Is Isabel riding with us today?" Bunny asked.

"Would you like her to?" Richard replied.

"Oh, yes," Bunny said.

Richard smiled tentatively, with no hint of his usual mischief. "Well, Miss Gannon, would you like to ride with us?"

Of course, she would. She'd like to canter off through the woods with them, laughing and then bristling at Richard's improper remarks. She'd like to lounge in the shade of a tree with him, watching Bunny at a distance. She'd like to hear his imitation of a *tui* and then rest back against a picnic blanket, reaching up to invite him to kiss her. She'd like to lie there, smelling the grass, feeling the sun in her hair, and taking the nectar of his lips. But she wouldn't.

"I have too much to do with the cottage right now," she said. "Maybe some other time."

Bunny looked up at her, hurt clearly written in her face. "Please."

How awful it was to disappoint her. Bunny couldn't possibly understand that it was Richard Isabel had to pull away from. There was simply no way of explaining the agony of being close to the two of them and yet not close enough. She needed some time, some distance, some objectivity.

Alice Gaines

"I'm sorry," Isabel stammered. "Not today... I can't."

"See all the work Miss Gannon has to do on the cottage before she can live here?" Richard said. "We wouldn't want her living in a dirty house, would we?"

Bunny shook her head.

"We want her to be happy in her new home, don't we, precious?"

Bunny worried her lower lip for a moment. "Yes."

"Miss Gannon will come with us another day," Richard said, holding out his hand. "Now, let's have our ride."

"All right," Bunny muttered. She walked to her father and slipped her fingers into his. "I hope you're happy here, Isabel."

"We both do," Richard added. They left, Bunny lagging behind him a half-step and looking over her shoulder in a wordless accusation.

Isabel watched them go and then walked to the table, pulled out a chair, and dropped onto it. Happy. They wanted her to be happy. She rested her elbows against the tabletop and put her face into her hands, determined to stop the tears before they started.

Chapter Thirteen

The very next Sunday afternoon, Hugh Upton appeared at Isabel's door in a one-horse shay that was upholstered in Cordovan leather. Behind the seat he had stowed a blanket, cushions, parasols, and an enormous picnic hamper. They rode to a sunny meadow on the Willowbrook estate, and he spread everything out in the shade of a majestic *kauri*. He installed her on a pile of cushions, surrounding her in luxury until she felt like Cleopatra cruising the Nile on her barge. She should have loved the setting with all its elegance and attention. But in fact, it made their afternoon into a good deal more than she had bargained for, a lovers' rendezvous rather than an outing in the country for friends.

"Now, let's see," Hugh said, opening the wicker basket. He lifted out bone china plates, two crystal goblets, and finally some linen napkins. "Livvie's cook isn't as good as your Mrs. Willis, but we won't starve."

"I'm sure we won't."

He pulled out a parcel and tugged at the string that

held it together. The brown paper fell open, revealing two tiny, perfectly roasted birds. He placed one on a dish and handed it to Isabel. He served himself the second. After dropping the paper back into the basket, he rummaged around inside.

"Drat," he mumbled. "Cook seems to have forgotten the silver."

"No matter," she answered, taking one napkin for herself and handing another to Hugh. "We'll use our fingers."

He looked at her and smiled. "The lady's resourceful," he declared. "What else would I expect of an intrepid explorer?"

"You really must stop flattering me," she said. *And stop gazing at me like love-sick puppy.*

"Not at all," he answered.

"Really you must." She took her bird's drumstick between her thumb and forefinger and pulled. The entire leg came away easily, and she lifted it to her mouth and took a bite.

She glanced up to find Hugh staring at her as though she'd done something terribly clever. No, more as though she'd done something exotic, something slightly naughty and rather tempting. He blushed lightly and turned back to the picnic hamper. "I say, if I can find that loaf of bread, we can tear it apart with our hands, too."

"Yes, let's."

"The cheese may offer a bit of a puzzle, though, what say?"

"I'm sure between the two of us we'll muddle through somehow."

"That's the spirit." He pulled out a long French bread and set it onto a plate with the ends sticking out several inches on each side. From the basket he produced another parcel and unwrapped the paper, revealing a large chunk of cheddar. He put the cheese next to the bread, which promptly fell off the plate and onto the

Waitangi Nights

blanket. Poor man. If he had anything else to retrieve from the basket, who knew where it might end up?

"There I go," he said. "Fumble fingers as usual."

"No matter." She grabbed the end of the loaf and pulled off a bit of bread.

Hugh laughed and did the same, helping himself to quite a hunk. He brought it to his mouth and tore into it with his teeth. "Splendid," he mumbled around the bread. "Just splendid."

Isabel resumed her meal. Hugh grasped his own hen, the little bird almost disappearing in his large hands. He split it clean in two and bit off some white meat, wolfing it down, and grinned at Isabel. "I say, let's leave the cutlery behind every time we go on a picnic."

She set down her food and wiped her fingers on her napkin. "All right."

"Then you'll come out with me again?"

"Shouldn't I?" she replied. "Do you plan to disgrace yourself later this afternoon?"

"Not at all, my dear Bella." He put down his food and took her hand in his. "Although a man could go quite off his head for you, you know."

A trace of grease from the bird clung to his fingers, but then hers probably weren't entirely clean, either. She pulled her hand out of his grip and picked up her napkin again.

"You see?" he said, reaching for his own napkin. "I've already forgotten myself."

She wiped her fingers. "You're forgiven."

"Dashed decent of you," he said. "Now, let's see if I can find us something liquid."

He peered into the basket again and produced a wine bottle wrapped in a linen napkin that was soaked through with condensation. After a bit more searching he pulled out a corkscrew.

"I'm afraid I don't drink much wine," she said. "Especially during the day."

"Oh, but you must have some today," he objected.

197

Alice Gaines

" 'Tain't a proper decadent picnic without the gift of the grape."

"I don't suppose you have some tea in there."

He turned the corkscrew down into the neck of the bottle. "Not a drop—not continental enough for my first afternoon with a world traveller."

"You've travelled around the world, too," she answered. "To get here from England."

"Right you are," he proclaimed. "Now, let me pour you a glass. Bacchus must be served."

"Very well."

The neck of the bottle tapped against the glass as Hugh poured. After a moment, he pressed a cold goblet into her hand, and she raised the rim to her nose to sample the wine's bouquet: berries, honey, and oak. She took a sip and leaned back against the cushions, letting her gaze wander over the sun-drenched landscape of the meadow.

Here she was on a delightful picnic in a perfectly lovely setting. Every comfort imaginable. Good food. Pleasant company. She ought to be happy. Why couldn't she be satisfied?

Why couldn't she find Hugh Upton more than just agreeable? What perversity made her insist on pining after her employer, a man who wasn't the least bit appropriate for her? Who didn't even want her?

Hugh poured himself a glass and sat in silence, staring into the distance. Overhead a bell-like call rang out—one sweet note. A whirring of feathers followed, and a white-ruffed bird came into view, settling on a branch of the *kauri* nearly twenty feet up.

"A *tui*," Isabel exclaimed.

The bird tipped his head and studied her out of one eye. Then he opened his throat and called again.

"Oh, listen," she said. "Isn't he beautiful?"

Hugh glanced upward and scrutinized their visitor. "Member of the *meliphagidae* group by the looks of it."

"He's a *tui*," she said, correcting his Latin with Maori.

Waitangi Nights

After all, this was a New Zealand bird, not a Roman one.

"Probably a fruit eater," Hugh added. "Maybe nectar, too, by the shape of the bill."

"The Maoris can talk to them."

"Do tell." He smiled at her. "Charming myth."

"But they can," she protested. "I've seen it done."

"Really? By a Maori medicine man?"

No, by Richard Julian. On an afternoon much like this one, her second day in Waitangi. Back then he'd been a mystery to her, a difficult master to be satisfied, an enigma who roamed the halls at night. Now? Now, he was a positive danger, a threat to her equilibrium and a great deal more.

"Bella?"

"I'm sorry," Isabel answered. "Did you say something?"

"Nothing important." He raised his glass. "Have a bit more to eat and drink."

"Oh yes, of course."

Hugh ate more bread and then some game hen. He chewed slowly and finally washed it all down with a gulp of wine. "I was talking to an old Maori the other day," he said, "a retainer at Willowbrook. He told me that all this land used to be covered with *kauris*. Most of them even bigger than this one."

Isabel looked up into the giant tree, so straight and tall. Imagine, an entire forest of them, pointing right to heaven.

"Told me a man could swing from one to the other across the entire width of the island," Hugh went on, "never even touching ground."

"What happened?"

"All harvested," he answered. "They made wonderful masts for Her Majesty's ships. Also they had to be taken out for agriculture and sheep grazing."

"All of them?"

"Well, not all, but most of them."

Alice Gaines

"It seems a shame, a terrible waste."

He gazed into her face, the warmth of his brown eyes registering concern. "Bless you. You would see it that way, being a woman and all."

"I don't see what my gender has to do with cutting down such magnificent trees."

"Tender-heartedness, don't you see," he answered. "Wonderful trait in women, but it makes it hard for you to face the demands of progress."

"Progress?"

"Oh my, yes. Ask Richard Julian. Sheep ranching will bring prosperity to all, Englishmen and Maori."

"I suppose so," she answered. But she didn't really suppose so, not at all. The loss of the trees was a terrible waste. And certainly white New Zealanders must think of themselves as New Zealanders, not Englishmen.

Hugh stretched out, leaning an elbow against a cushion, and propped his wine glass on his hip. "That prosperity is what I'm counting on," he said. "When people have the wherewithal, they'll want a good, classical education for their sons. We who live in genteel poverty have that to offer, if nothing else."

"What about their daughters?" Isabel asked. "Don't they deserve a good, classical education?"

"Well, yes. Them, too. As much as they really need."

"Knowledge isn't squandered on girls, Hugh."

He blushed and smiled shyly. "But women have so many more delightful things to do with their lives than the humdrum business of men."

"And for that they're to be denied the joy that comes with learning about the world? Learning about themselves?"

He sat straight up. "There, I've gone and offended you. Put my foot right into my mouth."

"It's a myth that women require less schooling than men."

"I have upset you," he said. "I could cut my tongue out."

"If only I could tell you how much I would love to have a university education, some formal recognition."

"And you should have had it, with your intelligence and wit," he said, taking her hand. "But you must realize that most women forget all about book learning when they become wives and mothers—as well they should."

"But some of us never have husbands and children. What are we left if we don't have an education, either?"

He set his wine glass onto the blanket and rubbed her fingers between both his hands. "That could never happen to you, Bella, not as lovely as you are."

"It shouldn't happen to anyone."

"And we won't let it," he declared. "If you want, we'll have a girls' school, too. You can be headmistress if you like. Anything."

Dear Hugh. He didn't really understand. She'd become upset, and he would offer her the moon if it would make her feel better. Still, no matter what his reasons, if he did open his school to the girls of New Zealand, they'd have a better chance at an education than she herself had had.

"And that other bit, about not having a husband and children." He paused for a moment, staring down at their intertwined hands. "It won't happen to you. You have the promise of Hugh Bridgewater Upton on that."

"Hanging on trees? Roots free to the air?" Richard Julian demanded. He pushed away his dessert plate and tipped back in his chair. "How in hell could a plant grow like that? Especially something as substantial as an orchid."

Isabel studied his expression. She saw skepticism, warring with curiosity, warring with outright disbelief. He glared back, his blue eyes narrowing, his brows furrowing together in frustration. For the last half hour she'd been telling him the absolute truth but couching it in the most sensational terms she could think of.

She'd watched him as he found himself torn between his usually reliable nurseryman and his own, very fallible common sense. And she'd delighted in every moment of his discomfort.

"The roots not only hang in the air, but they trap things," she said, keeping her face as impassive as she could.

"Trapper orchids?"

"Some species."

"Now, how could plants do that?" he said. "Do they use miniature saw-toothed snares? Tiny bows and arrows?"

"I didn't say they hunted," she answered, letting a note of exasperation enter her voice, as though she were speaking to a difficult child. "Their roots grow into a tangle, like the mesh of a wire wastebasket, and they trap forest detritus—falling leaves and such. That rots, making food for the orchid."

"Humph." He picked up his coffee cup and took a swallow, scowling at her over the rim.

"Why is it men have to believe that every other creature on earth does things exactly the way they do? If I say an orchid traps things, a man immediately thinks of human weapons."

His eyebrow shot up, and he abruptly set his cup into its saucer, making a distinct clatter. "Men do that, do they?"

She shrugged, feigning nonchalance. "This particular short-sightedness does appear to be a failing of the male constitution, like color blindness and a marked tendency toward self-aggrandizement."

"Bloody hell," he muttered.

Isabel bit the inside of her lip, stifling a grin. In her lifetime she'd sat through countless lectures from her father's pompous colleagues—the same type of flowery nonsense, but about the frailties of womankind. As the very pinnacle of human perfection—the rich, white male of British extraction—Richard had never had his

Waitangi Nights

inborn flaws shoved into his face before. Tonight he would. Perhaps she could think up some more before they finished their coffee and it was time for bed.

"Self-aggrandizing, am I?" he snapped.

"I didn't say you were. I said that men often were. You aren't color blind, are you?"

"No."

"There, then," she replied. "I say something about men in general, and you assume I must be talking about you."

"Rubbish."

"You ask me to tell you about my travels, and then you refuse to believe what I relate."

He leaned toward her, resting his elbow on the table and bringing his face close to hers. "Let's see. You've told me about singing frogs that live in the tops of trees and never touch the ground."

"Yes."

"And monkeys that howl so loudly they can be heard for miles. And flowers with petals half the length of a fully grown man, dangling to earth so that ants can climb them."

"And snakes thirty feet long and as big around as a woman's waist," she added.

"So, my dear little yarn spinner, is it any surprise that I doubt you?"

She lifted her coffee cup in a toast. "Doubt whatever you want. I'm telling the truth."

He harumphed again, but he smiled at her this time, flashing a hint of the pirate in the shining perfection of his eyes.

These dinners with him, lately stretching out to entire evenings of shared stories, would lead her to misery eventually. Hugh would build his school, and she'd take the position of headmistress. The job would be the opportunity of a lifetime, a gift she would never have dreamed possible. But she'd miss the master of Harrowgate and his daughter. How she'd miss them.

Or Richard would marry some proper lady, who would never tolerate discussions of frogs and snakes at her table. Isabel might still dine with them, but the conversation would turn polite, stifling. She might sit right across the table from Richard, but she'd still miss him. Paradoxically, he might seem even more distant in that close proximity than if she left Harrowgate altogether and only saw him occasionally in town.

In either case, misery. But what choice did she have? She'd have to fight a battle with him to be excused from his company in the evening. And she'd already become so attached to the man, so caught up in the magic of his eyes, so bewitched by his sounds and scents, all she'd gain by refusing to dine with him would be to bring on the misery now and get it over with that much earlier. That hardly seemed worth sacrificing the laughter and companionship, the memories of him she would take away with her. If only she could keep her head and not fall too completely under his spell.

She gazed at him where he sat, still smiling at her, his curls a halo in the lamplight, his lips set in devilishly tempting curves. He ran his forefinger around the rim of his cup, toying with the delicate china in a frankly suggestive manner. She only had to follow the sinuous movements with her imagination to dream of the heat of his hands on her skin, playing over her softly until she went up in flame.

"Miss?"

Richard started, taking the subtlest of jumps in his chair, and turned toward the doorway. Isabel looked in that direction, too.

Clarice stood on the threshold, a lantern in her hand. Her eyes were drooped half shut, and she brought her hand to her mouth to stifle a yawn. "Will you be retiring soon, miss?" she asked. "I've brought a light to take you to the cottage."

"Thank you, Clarice," Richard answered. "We didn't

realize it had gotten so late. Why don't you go on to bed?"

Clarice looked at the lantern in her hand. "But . . ."

"I'll find my own way," Isabel reassured her.

"Nonsense," Richard said. "I'll escort Miss Gannon. Just leave the light."

"Yes, sir." Clarice set the lantern on the sideboard, turned, and smiled at Isabel. "I'll see you in the morning as usual."

"Good night, Clarice," he added.

"Good night." Clarice disappeared into the hall.

"I can get to the cottage on my own," Isabel insisted.

"I didn't say you couldn't." Richard rose and went behind her to pull out her chair. "But we can continue our discussion on the way there. I'm not through with you for tonight, not yet."

"Ghosts," Isabel said as Richard walked her home.

Richard looked down at Isabel, a diminutive figure who nevertheless matched his stride perfectly, who felt so absolutely right on his arm. "Impossible," he said.

"You asked what the most remarkable thing I saw in the jungle was," she said. "Well, I saw ghosts in the jungle."

"Now you are telling stories, Isabel."

In the moonlight, he had no trouble making out her smile. She looked resolutely ahead of them down the path, but the corners of her mouth turned up, in pleasure it appeared. Perhaps at hearing her name from his lips. But then, that might only be a reflection of his own fancy. After all, his heart still skittered a bit when she called him Richard.

"Isabel?" he prompted. There, he'd said it again.

Her gaze was still fixed far ahead of them, but her smile widened. She'd been having great fun with him all evening—the little tease—telling him impossible tales about her travels. At first her behavior had incensed him, as had all her insubordination ever since she set foot under his roof. But after a while he had recognized the sport and even enjoyed it. In fact, he'd never seen her more animated, more lovely, more tempting.

He stopped, pulling her to a halt, and turned her to him. "Ghosts," he said softly. "I don't believe they exist in Central America any more than they do in New Zealand."

"No, of course not. But, if you'd only seen—"

"Seen what?"

"It was the moonlight, I suppose." She looked up at him, and her dark eyes shone with their own glow. "Very much like tonight."

"You're speaking in riddles."

She took a breath and stood in silence for a moment. He waited with her. Patience had never been one of his great virtues. But over the past several evenings he'd discovered that if he waited for Isabel to gather her thoughts, she often repaid him with revelations about herself, rare and sparkling, like jewels.

"There's a place on the Yucatán peninsula, called *ooszh-máhl*," she said finally, or at least that was what it sounded like.

"*Ooszh . . . ?*"

"U-X-M-A-L," she spelled. "Pronounced *ooszh-mahl*."

"The place is haunted?"

"It's a ruin of an ancient civilization," she answered. "I stood in the middle of the city on a night when the moon was full, and I swore I could see the people who built it."

"A very romantic notion. Rather unlike you."

She placed her hand on his sleeve, her fingers gripping his arm with gentle urgency. "No mere human could resist the magic of Uxmál. At its center stands the most magnificent palace you could imagine."

"An ancient palace in Central America?"

"A building that would dwarf your manor house if they stood side by side," she answered, her face radiating the moon's light back to him. "Indeed, Harrowgate would look like a pitiful little thing in contrast to the Palace of the Governors."

He'd heard something about lost civilizations in Mexico, but nothing that ought to make someone as sensible as Isabel take leave of her senses. And yet, here she stood, clinging to him as though she could transport him to the Yucatán through the force of her will. "Who built this enchanted city?" he asked. "Some race of super-humans?"

"The Maya built it, of course. Kings who portrayed themselves with the images of jaguars and smoke."

"And you saw them that night."

She tugged at his arm. "You must understand. When you first come upon the palace by day, it takes your breath away. It sits on top of a grand stairway and extends three times the length of Harrowgate. Massive stones covered with sculpture, fantastical birds, entrances to the underworld."

He set the lantern on the ground carefully, bending only the slightest bit necessary to do so. He'd never seen Isabel quite like this before, and he had no intention of breaking the mood. He rose again, covered her hand with his own, and squeezed her fingers.

She rewarded him with a smile, with the heavenly light of her eyes. "At night, with moonbeams playing over it, the palace comes alive. If only I could show it to you."

"I'd like that," he said quietly. "Very much."

"I could see the kings on the staircase that night, dressed in their loincloths, draped with jaguar skins and feathers. Obsidian amulets and jade." Her eyes widened. "Like the *tiki*, Richard. Beautiful and powerful."

He lifted a hand to her face and stroked her cheek. God help him, he had no choice. He wasn't a dead king but a living man, a man who needed this woman so desperately he might just die if he didn't have her. And soon. "Beautiful," he murmured.

She gazed up at him for a moment. Then recognition

entered her eyes as his meaning registered. She bit her lip and looked downward. "I must sound rather silly talking about ghosts."

"Not at all."

He slipped his fingers under her chin and lifted her face to his. He was going to kiss her, bloody fool that he was. And she was going to let him. And after the kisses, after the sighs, with his body burning for her, what then? How would he pull himself away then, as badly as he already wanted her? Oh, hell. Some questions didn't have answers. But he was going to kiss her, that much he knew in his bones.

She held herself perfectly still, except for the slightest parting of her lips, a woman's invitation. He bent toward her slowly, his fingers barely grazing the soft angles of her jaw.

Her head turned abruptly, and her eyes widened. "What's that light?"

"The moon," he whispered, still lowering his mouth to hers.

"No, Richard, look."

He did look then and discovered alarm in her eyes. He turned toward the house following her gaze with his own, searching.

"There it is again," she exclaimed. "I've seen that light before, but now it's in the house. Dear heaven, it's in the house."

He finally saw it, a ghostly beam from one of the second story windows. Not lamplight, somehow it was colder than that, unnatural. But there shouldn't be any light in there at all. There hadn't been a moment ago. No one should even be awake on that side of the house. The servants all lived in their own wing. That only left Isabel's old suite, his own rooms, and . . .

He counted windows, frantically searching the floor plan in his memory. "Good Lord," he muttered. "The nursery."

He took off toward the house.

Waitangi Nights

Isabel followed right behind him, at a dead run. "Richard," she gasped, "what room is that?"

"Bunny's room."

"Are you sure?"

"I ought to know where my own daughter sleeps."

He increased his pace, now running at full speed. That light might mean nothing. Ella, who now slept in the next room from Bunny, might simply have gone in by candlelight to check on her charge. But what if she hadn't? What if Bunny were alone, singing her unnatural songs? Might she have set fire to the room somehow? Her insane mother had never done that. But if the madness started in childhood, who knew?

He reached the terrace, covered it in three strides, threw open the door, and entered the house. He had to get to Bunny, had to get to his little girl. Being too late again would kill him. Doors wouldn't stand in the way this time—he'd made damn sure of that on the fateful afternoon when death had beaten him to Louisa. But he could still arrive too late. Tonight's moon could mock him the same way the warm sun had mocked him on the day his lover killed herself.

He reached the back staircase and paused just long enough for a deep breath. His heart pounded in his ears, and his lungs burned. He gasped again and then headed up the stairs, taking them two at a time. Finally, he reached the corridor that ran by the main bedrooms, and he could see Bunny's door. He stopped in his tracks.

A flickering of light reached out from under the door, like tentacles uncoiling, now here, now there. Insubstantial but real, fingers of ice. And the singing, odd and off-key as usual, otherworldly. Oh God, his child, his beautiful little baby. What was she doing in there?

He ran to the door and flung it open. The sight that greeted him chilled him to the marrow of his bones.

Chapter Fourteen

Three heads turned as Richard entered the room. Three pairs of eyes, three separate greetings. Bunny, of course, gave him her familiar smile. Ella was a different matter all together. She cowered in a corner, her eyes wide with fright. But the other . . . the other.

It was female, human-like and yet not human, apparently naked, except for a waistmat of dried vegetation. Flaming red hair, white skin, colorless eyes. He couldn't make out her features plainly—all of her shimmered in the ghostly light. She was the light somehow. It came right out of her.

A childhood memory of Maori folklore came back to him in a rush. A *turehu*, a creature from the underworld. "Who are you?" he demanded. "What are you doing here?"

It . . . she . . . didn't answer but only fixed him with the cold light of her eyes. Evil shone from them, blind, unblinking hatred. He had to get between her and Bunny. He couldn't let that foulness touch his daughter.

Waitangi Nights

He took a step toward the creature, backing her away from the bed. She eyed him warily, not in fear exactly, more like caution, but it was enough to get her away from Bunny.

"Ella," he shouted. "Get Bunny out of here."

Ella didn't move from where she was huddled. She only whimpered.

"Damn it, Ella. Now."

"I have her, Richard," Isabel called. "Keep that . . . thing occupied. I'll get Bunny out."

He kept approaching the *turehu*, one slow step at a time, and she kept retreating. He'd have her backed against the wall soon, and then he could grab her. He didn't want to touch her. His flesh crawled at the mere idea. But he'd have to catch her if that would keep Bunny safe. He'd have to destroy this creature somehow.

One more step, and he would have her trapped. But she only smiled. Smiled, damn her, and opened her mouth to laugh. Instead of laughter, music came out of her mouth. Flutes: unholy, eerie. Now. He had to grab her, now.

He lunged for her, but she disappeared, evaporated in his grasp, disintegrating into a mist, the light from her body falling in on itself until nothing was left. Nothing but a memory of flutes.

Richard looked around frantically, unwilling to believe even his own senses. Had he just seen, heard what he thought he had? Or had it all been a nightmare?

The room still held a glow. But now the light was outside. Richard went to the window and lifted the sash. The light came from some distance, and it held that same music in it. The flutes he'd just heard. Whatever had just stood in his daughter's room hadn't vanished but only retreated.

A whimper from the corner brought him back to reality. Ella clutched her ribs, shivering. She stared into space, her expression blank, as though she were in

Alice Gaines

some sort of trance. He crossed to her and dropped to his knees, grabbed her shoulders, and shook her. Hard.

"How did that thing get in here?" he demanded.

"Saints alive," she mumbled, "I never seen nothing like that."

"How did it get in here?" he repeated.

Her eyes focused on him finally. "I don't know, Mr. Julian. I swear I don't. 'Twere just here when I come in."

"Bloody hell."

He rose and crossed the room. Isabel stood in the corridor, holding Bunny in her arms.

"Sammy," Richard bellowed. "Mrs. Willis."

"Shouldn't you keep your voice down?" Isabel whispered. "Bunny's been frightened enough."

"Not as badly as I've been frightened all this time," he replied. "But now I have a real enemy to fight, and by God, I'll win."

Isabel tucked Bunny's head under her chin and made shushing, reassuring sounds. Let her calm his daughter if she wanted. Bunny had listened to his hollering her entire life, and she wasn't afraid of his raised voice.

And tonight he felt like climbing to the top of Harrowgate Manor and shouting his throat hoarse. His little girl wasn't like her mother, after all. She wasn't mad. She'd been telling the truth from the beginning, but he'd feared madness so much he hadn't believed her. Now he'd find that whatever it was that had intruded into their home, and he'd take it apart, limb from limb. Then the whole bloody nightmare would be over.

Only, where in hell was everybody? "Sammy," he roared again. "Dammit, get up here!"

Footsteps sounded on the staircase behind them. He turned to find Sammy charging down the hallway. Mrs. Willis came right behind, pulling on her robe.

"Richard," Sammy said. "Man, what's the noise?"

"Get the staff together," Richard ordered. "Something's been in Bunny's room."

Waitangi Nights

Mrs. Willis's hand flew to her mouth. "Saints preserve us," she gasped between her fingers.

"Something?" Sammy repeated.

"I'll explain later, but gather up the men. Have them grab anything that can be used as a weapon. Then report back to me."

Sammy ran the length of the corridor and headed down the stairs.

"What are you going to do to the *turehu*?" Bunny asked.

He stroked her hair. "Never mind, precious."

"But she's very nice."

"Mrs. Willis, take Bunny and keep her with you tonight," Richard ordered.

"Yes, sir," Mrs. Willis answered. She took Bunny from Isabel and bustled off toward the servants' wing.

"Good night, cousin Richard," Bunny called to him over Mrs. Willis's shoulder. By all appearances she was taking the night's events with perfect equanimity.

"Good night, precious," he called back.

Richard glanced back toward Isabel. She crossed her arms over her chest and stared at him. "I think it's time for an explanation," she said.

"Yes, and a bit of a celebration, too."

Richard glanced at the decanters on the sideboard. As much as he'd like a drink, he had to keep a clear head. But Isabel would have some whiskey. She'd need it after she'd heard his tale. He hefted a tumbler and poured her a stiff one, finally shoving it into her hand.

"I don't want this," she said, setting the glass on the sideboard. "I want to know what's going on in this house."

"And that you shall," he answered. "Just as soon as I find out myself."

"Don't be coy with me, Richard," she said. "I want you to tell me, now, what you think is going on here."

"Ah, but what matters most is what's not happening

here. What's not happening to my daughter."

"Dammit," she said, "I'll have the straight story from you."

Oh, hell. He picked up her glass and drained it, tipping his head back to allow the burning liquor to slide down his throat. His Bunny, his daughter was *not* like her mother. She wouldn't leave him, as her mother had.

Isabel put her hands on her hips and stared at him. "Now," she repeated.

"My daughter is not going mad," he said.

"Well, of course she's not."

He stared at her a moment longer and then set the glass back down carefully. "You wouldn't be so sure of Bunny's sanity if you'd seen her mother."

"Her mother was mentally disturbed?"

He lifted his head, searching the ceiling for patience. "Disturbed?" he said. "She was a stark, raving lunatic. And until tonight I thought Bunny would end up the same."

"How could you?" she gasped. "Bunny's so dear."

"So was Louisa when I met her." He looked back at Isabel. How could he expect her to know about his family? It wasn't as if he'd told her anything about them. "She was gentle, loving, attentive. How can I tell you how I felt watching her go from that sweetness to . . ."

He searched his brain for words, but how did one convey that sort of horror? ". . . madness. There's no other word for it."

"But surely an innocent child can't take on her mother's madness."

"I didn't think so, either," he answered. "But then I did some reading on the subject, and I found out that children often do inherit insanity from their parents."

"Not Bunny, not such a beautiful little girl."

He gazed into Isabel's face and found sympathy, understanding. "I felt the same way. I'd look into her eyes, so like my own. And I swore she was whole, healthy."

"As well she is."

Waitangi Nights

"But a tiny doubt always niggled at the back of my mind," he went on. "Was I blinded by my love for her? Were the signs present, but I refused to see them?"

"So you watched her constantly."

"Yes," he answered, the word escaping his chest like the much welcomed confession it was.

"And you roamed the halls at night."

"Louisa didn't sleep when the madness was on her. She didn't eat, couldn't sit still in a chair for more than a minute at a time." He took a deep, shuddering breath. "I thought at least if Bunny could sleep, the demons would leave her alone. Naive, I know. But it was all I had."

"Oh, my poor . . ."

Richard gazed at her. She'd stopped herself, but she'd called him hers. He needed her strength tonight, and right now he needed most to tell her the entire story. "One night, in my wandering, I heard Bunny singing," he said. "A perfectly normal little girl's voice, that time."

"Oh, Richard."

"There wasn't anyone else in the room—only Bunny, sitting in her bed, singing to herself. At first I thought little of it, just a child's game. But then, it happened again, a few months later."

Isabel squeezed his hand. "And you heard the other voice? That thing we saw tonight?"

"I ran to Bunny's room as quickly as I could, but there still wasn't anyone else there, despite the other voice," he answered. "The window was shut tight. No one could have left without my seeing them."

"So you assumed Bunny had made the other sounds as well."

"What else was I to think?" he demanded. "Louisa could make the most ungodly noises in her frenzy."

"I'm so sorry."

"Then Bunny began to tell me stories—or what I assumed were stories—about a *turehu* who visited her room. They terrified me. Louisa's demons always came from Maori mythology, after all. *Taniwha, wairua, ngerengere*, quaint, harmless delusions at first. Later they became vicious tormentors. They tore at her."

"I see."

And she did . . . Richard knew that. She saw, and she understood. A magnificent woman like Isabel Gannon would. Strong, beautiful, compassionate, she looked up into his face, slipping her arms around his neck and pulling herself against his chest to comfort him.

He clutched her to him, selfish as it was. Just for a moment, he'd allow himself to lean on her strength, to bask in her compassion. "That part's over now," he sighed. "My daughter's sane."

"But, Richard," she said, looking with wide eyes into his face, "what was that thing?"

"I don't know."

"It just disappeared. As though it had never existed at all."

"I'd never have believed if I hadn't seen it with my own eyes."

"And it seemed so evil," she said.

"Whatever it was I'll find it and destroy it. I'll keep Bunny safe. I can do that now." He took a breath. "Now that I know she isn't mad."

"Yes."

The sound of a throat clearing came from the doorway. Richard pulled out of Isabel's embrace and turned toward the voice. Sammy stood on the threshold. "The men are ready," he said. "And there's something else."

Before Richard had a chance to respond, another man entered the room. Short and squat but powerfully built, the man carried an air of authority, not in the least created the impressive tattooing on his face.

"Henga," Isabel whispered.

"You know this man?"

"He's the local magician," she said. "He dropped by to see Samuel one evening. We didn't think it important enough to tell you."

Waitangi Nights

"Well, it wasn't," Richard replied. "And it isn't now."

"You should listen to him," Sammy said.

"Very well, I'll listen, and then I'll do what I planned to do. Find that thing and kill it."

"I told him that," Sammy said. "He says Anui won't let us find him."

Bloody ignorant oaf. "Then you can tell the man we're not looking for Anui. We're looking for a female."

"I did. Henga says that one was sent by Anui, the chief of the *turehus* here. The spirits of the place."

"Well, you can tell him I don't care who I have to fight. They'll not have my daughter."

Sammy repeated something in Maori, and Henga launched into a heated monologue. Sammy turned back to Richard finally. "Henga says Anui doesn't want a little girl."

"Then what in blazes has his *turehu* been doing in Bunny's bedroom?"

"He might keep her as *mokai*." Sammy struggled visibly for an English word. "A pet. But what he really wants is the *hine*, the woman. Miss Gannon."

Beside Richard, Isabel turned ashen, and she swayed, grasping his arm for support. "Me?"

"Yes, miss. That's what Henga says. *Turehus* take women, not children."

"Dear Lord," she whispered.

"He won't have you," Richard gritted. He raised a hand to her face and rubbed his thumb across her cheek. "I'll die first."

Isabel pulled a chair to the window and sat down. She propped her elbows on the sill and gazed outside. From here, her old sitting room on the second floor, she could watch for the returning men. But it had been hours since the searchers had left, and there'd been no word, just that light in the distance and the music, mocking them all.

Finally, the men came back, straggling up the gravel

walk from the direction of the glasshouse, torches and weapons in hand. Some carried rifles, others hoes and garden implements, still others took knives from the kitchen.

Samuel appeared on horseback after them, slowly approaching the house. He stopped his mount, dropped to the ground, and gave the reins to one of the others, who then led the animal in the direction of the stable. Samuel crossed the terrace and entered the house. The rest of the men headed off toward their quarters, but still Richard didn't appear.

What if he refused to come back without finding the *turehu*? What if he insisted on continuing the search on his own? He'd do that, the stubborn man. He'd run himself into the ground for the sake of his daughter and for Isabel's sake, and she'd adore him for it, love-besotted fool that she was.

She couldn't hide from the truth any longer. She loved Richard Julian, no matter how hard she had fought her feelings. She wanted to be with him every minute. She warmed herself in his smile and craved his touch in her most secret places. What she'd do with all these hungers, she hadn't the faintest idea. She'd have to protect herself from them somehow.

Richard occupied a different station in life than she did. Perhaps he harbored some affection for her, but he couldn't love her as she did him. And despite all the best intentions in the world, he couldn't bring her anything but heartbreak.

He came into view finally, on his black stallion. In suspenders and shirtsleeves, he looked like any ordinary man, much like her father at the end of a long day of exploration, in fact, tired and hungry and discouraged.

Samuel reappeared on the terrace and walked to Richard's stallion, taking the reins. Richard swung his leg up and over the horse's neck and then dropped to the ground. He put his hand on Samuel's shoulder in a ges-

Waitangi Nights

ture of gratitude and said something Isabel couldn't make out. Samuel nodded and headed with the horse toward the stable. Richard watched him go for a moment. Then he turned and went into the house.

Isabel rose and walked away from the window. She went toward the boudoir door and then stopped. In the middle of the room, she stood, frozen. She ought to rush downstairs, meet Richard in the parlor where he had left her. But she didn't really want Samuel to find them together when he came back from putting the stallion away. She didn't want the staff's eyes on them if she took it into her head to rub Richard's shoulders as she had done for her father.

Nonsense. Cursed, stupid nonsense. She couldn't touch Richard without giving in to urges that she didn't dare express. So she wouldn't touch him. She'd go downstairs, after all, no matter whether they were seen. She only wanted to find out about the search, and as such, she had nothing to be ashamed of.

Too late. His step sounded on the staircase and then continued down the corridor, passing by the room where she stood and then proceeding to his own suite. His door opened and closed, and all was silent.

Isabel walked to the sitting room door and opened it. She glanced down the hallway to Richard's bedroom. She should just slip out quietly, go to her cottage, and get some sleep. In the morning she could find out how the search had gone. By the light of day she could face him, not tonight.

She took a few paces in the direction of the stairs and had to stop. She wouldn't leave him alone, it was foolishness to pretend she would. She turned, walked to his door, and put her ear against the wood. Silence. She pushed, and it swung open silently. She stepped inside and found herself in his sitting room.

Richard stood at the entrance to his bedroom, his hand stilled in the act of removing his collar. He hesitated for a moment and then finished the task, dropping the stiff neckwear onto the top of a rolltop desk at his elbow. "You waited up for me," he said.

Isabel nodded.

"Thank you." He unfastened his sleeve buttons, removed and dropped them next to the collar. Then he rubbed his hands over his face.

"Did you find her?" Isabel asked.

"No."

"Where can she have gone?"

"I don't know," he answered, shrugging out of his suspenders and leaving them to hang from the waist band of his trousers. "We followed that light. It was like following a rainbow. No matter how close we seemed to get, it still remained at a distance."

"Anui is not letting you find him."

"I don't like to give credence to anything Henga said, but yes, Anui kept us at bay most effectively." He pulled his shirttails out of his pants and proceeded to unbutton his shirt.

Isabel stood and regarded him, fascinated. She'd seen the male form nearly naked in the past, but she'd never actually watched a man undress. Even her father hadn't removed his shirt in her presence. And none of the men in their company, white or native, had ever tempted her in the least.

But this man, the man she loved, filled the room with his presence, his scent, his beauty. And she wanted to see what he looked like under the trappings of civilization. Would he have hair on his chest? Would his skin be smooth over those powerful muscles? Would it be warm to the touch? What would that part of him look like?

He started to take off his shirt, revealing curling dark hairs where Isabel had imagined them. But he stopped, apparently thinking better of showing himself to her, and pulled the muslin back over his shoulders. He walked to an arm chair and sank into it. "You shouldn't have stayed up," he said. "It's late."

Waitangi Nights

"I didn't mind."

He gestured toward a straight-backed chair on the opposite side of a small table from where he sat. "Then sit down. You must be tired."

Isabel joined him, taking a seat and folding her hands in her lap. So close to him, the temptation to touch his shoulder, his chest, his face grew almost unbearable. But there was still so much she wanted to learn.

"Tell me the rest," she said quietly, "about Bunny's mother."

"Louisa . . ." He pressed the heels of his hands to his eyes and sighed. "Louisa was the daughter of an innkeeper in Paihia, a white man. Her mother was Maori."

"That's where Bunny gets her complexion."

"Yes." He lowered his hands and looked at her. "I thought I was in love—I even asked Louisa to marry me."

Isabel sat silently, waiting for him to go on.

"My father flew into a rage, as I had expected," he continued. "What I hadn't expected was for him to threaten to disown me, cut me off without a penny."

"And so you . . ."

"And so I moved Louisa into the house and lived in sin with her," he said.

"Didn't your father disown you then?"

"Oddly enough not." He paused. "Maybe he didn't relish the idea of tossing us out on our ears publicly. Maybe he preferred to keep us with him and make us rue the day we were born."

"Could he do that?" Isabel asked.

"Oh, yes. And he did." More silence. "He began a campaign of verbal abuse—insults, criticisms, slights. The men in my family are rather good with words, as you may have noticed."

Indeed she had.

"I had grown up with him, so I was used to the venom of his tongue," he continued. "But Louisa . . ."

He clenched his jaw and stared into the darkness.

Alice Gaines

"Louisa was oversensitive," he said after a moment. "She was vulnerable. The rough customers who came into her father's tavern took advantage of her. I thought I could rescue her."

He rested against the back of the chair and stared some more, this time at the ceiling. "Instead I destroyed her."

"No." Isabel reached across the table and rested her hand on his arm. "How could you have?"

"I got her with child." He turned to Isabel, gazing into her eyes. "I swore then we would be married, and to hell with what my father said. But she . . . she changed."

"How?"

"She pulled away from me," he said. "She'd always had a vivid imagination. She entertained me with stories from her mother's folklore."

"What you told me about tonight."

"Yes," he answered. "After Louisa conceived Bunny, all the fantasy became real for her. Perhaps because of the changes in her body. Perhaps because of my father's ever-increasing insults. Perhaps because of my complete inability to understand, to reach out to her."

He put his own hand over Isabel's and stroked her fingers. "She retreated from reality further and further. By the time Bunny came, she'd gone quite mad."

"I'm so sorry," Isabel said.

"The pretty stories she'd told herself before had grown dark and cruel. And they held her in their grip. She mumbled, cried, screeched. But her laughter was the worst—frenzied, insane."

Isabel squeezed his fingers and waited for the rest, knowing from the expression on his face that the tale wouldn't be pretty.

"Mrs. Willis was the one who heard Louisa's final screams," he said. "From one of the upstairs suites, muffled by distance and by doors, three of them. She'd locked the sitting room door, the bedroom door, and finally the bathroom door. Then she'd slashed her wrists with a kitchen knife."

"Oh, dear heaven."

"By the time Mrs. Willis found me and I kicked in all the bloody doors, it was too late. She was gone." He took a deep, shuddering breath. "I had every lock removed from the inside of the house that very afternoon. My father didn't argue, he was afraid of me most likely. I think I'd gone a bit mad myself."

"And Bunny?"

"Bunny was just a tiny baby," he answered. "She doesn't remember any of it, thank God."

"Thank God," Isabel repeated. "But what you've been through, Richard, what you've had to face all on your own."

"No more than I deserved. I used Louisa to satisfy my lust, to irritate my father."

"That isn't so."

"I have to take responsibility for my actions, Isabel." He lifted her hand from his arm and set it on the table. "And now I have to take responsibility for dragging you into this."

"It isn't your fault."

He looked at her, a deep sadness filling his eyes. "I've put you in danger."

If only she could tell him that it didn't matter. If only she could tell him she loved him, that she'd brave any danger to be with him. If only she had the courage.

"If I can't find that *turehu* and her master and destroy them both, you'll have to leave here," he went on.

"Surely that won't be necessary," she protested. "Perhaps I can help you."

"No," he said, and the word had a frightful weight to it. "I can't have you hurt. I can't live through that again."

She stared at him, at the rigid outline of his jaw. She couldn't let him send her away when he and Bunny needed her, and yet she hadn't the backbone to tell him how much they had come to mean to her. She hadn't the words. Most important, she had no right to insist on staying if he truly wanted her gone.

After a moment he sighed. "I'll see you're cared for somehow," he said, "but I won't be part of another woman's ruin."

Chapter Fifteen

Isabel sat at a wrought iron table in the garden of Willowbrook Manor, sipping tea out of a delicate china cup and enjoying the play of a warm breeze over her skin. This was her fourth trip now. Each grew just a little bit longer and more familiar, as she'd grown closer to Olivia and Hugh.

"I'm so glad you could come for luncheon today," Olivia Farnsworth said. "All our visits have been taken up with my new glasshouse. I wanted us to be friends."

"Thank you. I'd like that, too."

In truth, Isabel needed a friend. She'd had to make so many decisions in the last few days since they'd found the *turehu* in Bunny's room. She'd finally faced the fact that she loved Richard Julian, and now she had to face the fact that he wanted her gone, if not from his life, at least from his house.

Every night that he set out in search of that light and came home having found nothing, his desperation grew. And he reminded her over and over that she'd have to leave for her own protection. Worse, he grew further and further away from her, emotionally distant and cold. She saw him every night at dinner, and she missed him.

He watched her sometimes, though. Every so often she'd turn and surprise him in the act of scrutinizing her, the old, hungry look in his eyes. He'd cover it quickly by looking away, but some spark must still burn there, just as it did in her own heart. On several occasions she'd had to keep herself from reaching out to touch him.

". . . business in town," Olivia said.

Isabel snapped back to the present. "I beg your pardon."

Olivia smiled at her. "You've been woolgathering."

"I'm sorry."

"Think nothing of it." Olivia reached over and patted Isabel's hand. "My mind often wanders on afternoons like this. The garden is so lovely."

"You were saying."

"Edward and Hugh are on a business errand in town, something about Hugh's school. But they'll be back soon. Hugh would never forgive me if I let you go without seeing him."

Hugh was Isabel's real reason for this visit. She didn't need to know much about men to know that Hugh loved her and planned to ask her to marry him. And he was the most logical solution to her problem. She had a way to leave Harrowgate with her dignity intact.

"I suppose I want the entire world to be as happy as I am," Olivia continued. She smoothed an errant strand of blond hair back from her face, tucking it into the knot at the nape of her neck. "I've just discovered that I'm going to have a baby."

"Olivia," Isabel exclaimed. "How absolutely wonderful."

"I feel a bit foolish talking about it as though I were a young bride." Olivia blushed and smiled shyly. "I'm

Waitangi Nights

rather old to be having my first child."

"Oh, but you'll be fine. The baby will be fine. Everything will be fine."

Olivia laughed. "I'm not sure about Edward. He's being quite silly about it, fretting and fussing over me."

"He'll be fine. He only worries because he loves you."

"As I love him." Olivia turned to Isabel, her eyes alight with joy. "If anyone had told me two years ago when I was still living with my parents, an abandoned old maid—"

"You couldn't have been," Isabel protested. "Not you."

"If anyone had told me that today I would have a husband, my own home, a baby on the way . . ." Olivia's voice trailed off, and her eyes misted over. "Well, it's more than one person deserves."

Was that true? Was that all too much for one woman to hope for? Would she always have to settle for the best she could do and never have the love she really craved?

"And so," Olivia continued. "I'm on a crusade to make sure that everyone around me finds as much happiness as I've been given. You, my dear, are my next project."

"I?"

"Hugh's given me permission to discuss his intentions with you. 'Softening you up' he calls it."

Isabel looked down into her lap. "That sounds like him."

"He blunders about sometimes, but he's a good man, Isabel."

"I know he is."

"You and he have been keeping company for weeks now. Hasn't he declared himself to you?"

Bless him, he'd tried, several times. But she'd found a way to fend off the words on each occasion. If he'd come right out and asked her to marry him, she'd have had to tell him something. But if she postponed the inevitable for a while, maybe she could find a little passion for him in her heart. Then she'd be able to give him the answer he wanted, the answer she would have to give him or end up an "abandoned old maid" herself.

"I think the world of Hugh," she said.

"But he's not any woman's dream man. I know," Olivia said. "I had my doubts about marrying Edward. He's almost old enough to be my father. Now I thank the Creator that I took the chance."

"I'll think about what you're saying, Olivia."

"Hugh's a decent, loving man. He wants to share his life with you, his dreams. He'll make you happy if you give him a chance."

"I'll think about it."

"Hello," a voice called from behind them.

Olivia turned to glance down the gravel walk, and she smiled. "Hugh, you're back finally."

"I say, look who's here," he declared, quickly covering the distance to the table. "My two favorite ladies."

Olivia turned her face up, and he planted a kiss on her forehead. "You missed luncheon," she said.

"Had something in town."

"You almost missed Isabel, too," Olivia chided.

"Now, that I would never have forgiven myself for," he said. He walked around the table and took Isabel's hand. "My dearest Bella."

Olivia averted her eyes but smiled nevertheless. "We've been discussing you in your absence, Hugh."

"Do tell." Hugh dropped Isabel's hand, stuck his finger under his collar, and yanked at the stiff material. Isabel recognized the gesture now—she'd seen it every time he got nervous about something. He knew very well what the discussion had been about. No doubt he planned to continue it as soon as they were alone.

Olivia yawned elaborately. "I'm dreadfully tired all of a sudden," she said.

"Probably your delicate . . ." Hugh began and then shut his mouth abruptly.

"It's all right, dear," Olivia told him. "Isabel knows."

"Then you pop on into the house," Hugh ordered.

Waitangi Nights

"Edward's waiting to make sure the little mother has her nap."

Olivia rose from her chair. "A nap sounds wonderful." She gazed down at Isabel. "You'll consider that little matter we discussed?"

"I will," Isabel answered.

Hugh cleared his throat and shifted his weight from one foot to the other. "Can I help you indoors, Livvie?"

Olivia patted his arm. "Good gracious, I can still walk. You stay out here and keep Isabel company."

"Right you are," he declared.

Olivia walked briskly up the pathway. Hugh followed her with his eyes for a moment. Then he pulled her chair close to Isabel's and sat down. "Bit of good news about the baby, eh?" he said.

"Wonderful."

"Livvie looks fabulous, don't you think? Ever since she got . . . that is, since she's been . . . blast it, you know what I mean."

"She's glowing," Isabel said.

"You should see Edward." Hugh grinned at her. "Normally such a stout fellow. He's gone clean out of his head. Can't decide whether to dance with joy or worry himself to death."

He took her hand in both of his and studied her fingers for a minute. "Not that I don't understand exactly how he feels," he said softly. "The woman he loves carrying his child, maybe a son to carry on his name. I hope to find myself in that position soon."

"Hugh—"

"Livvie's told you my feelings, hasn't she?"

"Yes."

"I've started to tell you myself, dozens of times. Somehow I just never get to the meat of it."

Isabel covered his hand with her own. "I've known."

He expelled a sharp breath. "I've never been any good with matters of the heart. On the cricket pitch I'm your man. But around women . . ."

Alice Gaines

"You're doing fine," Isabel said quietly.

He gazed into her eyes and smiled, showing the gap between his teeth. "I am?"

Isabel pushed a stray lock of straw-gold hair from his forehead. "Yes, you are."

"Well, yes, I say." He swallowed hard. "I want you to be my wife. I've never loved anyone the way I love you, Bella. Say you'll marry me."

Isabel hesitated, still looking into his dear face. She ought to accept, say yes now and get it over with. She was going to marry him eventually, so why not give him the words now?

"You have doubts," he said.

"Surely that's not so unusual," she answered.

"I've been thinking, Bella. If it's the physical side of marriage you're worried about . . . if you think that I expect you to be . . . that is, if you aren't quite as . . . oh, dash it all."

He shot out of his chair and began to pace up and down in front of the table. "We're neither of us children. I've had some experience in the boudoir, if you catch my meaning. And you, with your long expeditions surrounded by men . . ."

Isabel watched him in amazement. "You think that I've had knowledge of a man."

He stopped in his tracks and shoved his fists into his trousers pockets, pushing his jacket up and over his wrists to do so. "I don't think anything," he said. "Only if you've, well, enjoyed the pleasures of the flesh, I want you to know that I understand."

Understand? He understood a great deal better than she did. He didn't care if she was a virgin. She ought to be offended, highly offended. But, dear man that he was, he only meant well. He was offering his love to her unconditionally, without regard for convention. And how could she be angry with him for that?

"What's sauce for the goose and all that," he said. "I can't judge you for doing what I've done myself."

Waitangi Nights

She rose from her chair and approached him, resting a hand on his sleeve and looking up into his face. "You're a decent man, Hugh Bridgewater Upton. And I want you to know that when I marry you, you'll have my every thought, every bit of affection I have to offer."

He grasped her arms, none too gently, and pulled her closer. "Then you will?" he exclaimed. "Oh Bella, you will?"

"Yes."

He yanked her against his chest and pressed his closed lips to hers. Her first instinct was to pull away, but she didn't. She did clench her hands into fists and close her eyes. A tiny voice sounded in the back of her brain. *No. This isn't it.*

Bloody hell. Richard found it frustrating to have to sit through an entire dinner tied up in knots. Knots of jealousy whenever Upton looked at Isabel, which had been constantly. Knots of lust whenever he looked at her. And he hadn't been able to take his eyes off her all evening.

Thank God for clothing, at least. He would have been damned humiliated, too, if Isabel and Upton could see the condition of his body. For days now, he'd wanted Isabel Gannon more desperately than he'd ever desired a woman before. She'd sat close to him through every dinner, so close. Just an arm's length away. But he couldn't have her, and somehow he was going to have to make his body understand that fact. Isabel Gannon was not his.

He poured two brandies, turned, and looked across the parlor at Isabel and Upton where they shared a love seat. She and her stories would forever haunt the dining room of Harrowgate Manor, and Richard wanted it that way. So as soon after dessert as possible, he'd moved his two dinner companions to the parlor, where Upton's cheerful jabbering wouldn't taint his memories of his

Alice Gaines

petite nurseryman and the magic she could work on him.

"I've found just the spot for our school, Bella," Upton declared, gazing into her eyes. "The owner of the estate is itching to move on to Australia and will sell for half of what the place is worth."

"It sounds wonderful, Hugh," she answered softly. "I want you to tell me all about it. Later."

"We can set up in the main house at first," the man rambled on, squeezing her fingers between his own. "Later, when the student body has grown, we'll add a separate building for classrooms. The place already has a cricket pitch."

"Splendid," Richard muttered.

Isabel glared at him, warning him with her gaze. Oh, hell, what did she expect? Civility? He'd had to watch Upton devouring her with his eyes all through dinner—when the bastard wasn't outright looking down the front of her bodice.

She'd worn one of the dresses he, Richard, had paid for. The garnet-colored satin made her skin seem to glow. It also offered more than a hint of the swell of her breasts, so smooth and tempting. He'd taken one look at her and turned into a territorial male animal, with one half of him dying to take Upton apart, limb by limb, and the other half aching to rip that dress from her body and bury himself inside her.

And the hell of it was, he couldn't even turn away, gaze out the window, think about sheep ranching, count flowers on the wallpaper. She occupied every primitive place in him, demanding that he watch another man claim her, take her from his own preserve. Now he stood staring down at her, helpless in his own parlor.

Richard crossed the room and shoved one of the snifters under Upton's nose. Upton jumped, dropping Isabel's hand, and took the drink from Richard.

"Thanks so much, old chap," Upton gushed. "I say,

though, it really ought to be champagne."

"Do tell," Richard answered, using one of the fellow's favorite phrases. Upton had looked ready to bound out of his chair all evening. Clearly, the man had an announcement to make, most likely not something Richard wanted to hear.

Richard glanced down at Isabel and offered her the second drink. "Miss Gannon?"

"Thank you," she murmured, nearly in a whisper. She took the glass and settled it in her hands in her lap, toying with the stem.

She looked uncomfortable, guilty even. He'd seen her nervous before, on the first day she'd shown up at Harrowgate. But this was different. The way she stared down into her drink, fidgeting with it, as though she'd done something momentous but maybe not quite what she'd intended.

Her uncertainty tore at Richard, as did Upton's exuberance, both so obviously meant that Richard was about to lose her. He turned away and walked back to the occasional table that held the decanters. He picked up the brandy again and poured himself a drink.

Behind him, Upton cleared his throat. "I see no reason to keep the secret any longer, do you, Bella?"

Richard set the decanter back down very slowly and carefully. He closed his eyes and listened for her reply, listened for a denial, or perhaps an announcement that she'd agreed to join Upton's faculty when the school opened. A year from now, maybe five, maybe ten. Instead she mumbled something he couldn't make out.

"Right you are," Upton said. "Well, Julian, I'm afraid you've lost yourself a nurseryman. Miss Gannon's agreed to be my wife."

Richard's snifter came down on the tray. Hard. He couldn't tell how that had happened, but only that it had, firmly enough to snap the stem. He looked at his hand and found that his fingers were gripping the glass so tightly his knuckles stood out, white. He released it, and the bowl tipped drunkenly, spilling its contents. "Clumsy of me," he mumbled.

"Please do join us in a drink," Upton said. "We want you to share our happiness."

Did they, did they indeed? Did she? Was she happy? let her be happy. *Only get her out of my house, out of my sight, quickly.* He found another snifter and poured a second drink, putting more liquor into it this time. Then he turned and lifted his glass to them. "Mr. and Mrs. Hugh Upton," he toasted.

Upton hefted his own snifter and took a sip of brandy. Isabel did the same, pointedly avoiding Richard's gaze, glancing first into her glass and then to the far wall.

"Decent of you to take the news so well, Julian," Upton said. "It's hard to lose a valued member of one's staff, especially after having her for such a short time. How long did you say it's been, Bella?"

"A few months," she said quietly, now studying the arm of the love seat. "Since the end of January."

"The beginning, rather," Richard corrected. "The ninth."

She looked at him then, her eyes widening to an expression of surprise and something more. Something very much like a plea. But what the hell else could she want from him? He'd given her a job, given her a room in the house and then the blasted cottage. He'd let her get close to his daughter, to himself. And now she was leaving him. She'd have to take care of herself from here out.

"So, when's the happy day to be?" he asked Upton.

"As soon as the lady'll have me," Upton answered, all puppy-dog eagerness.

And why not? As soon as he married her, he could bed her. The damned fool probably didn't realize what he was getting. Oh, he'd know she was beautiful—he'd have to be blind not to see that. But he wouldn't know how she could melt against a man, lean into him and warm to his touch, until her breath came in little gasps

Waitangi Nights

and her skin flushed with readiness.

He had to get his thoughts under control. He was already hard for her. In another minute, he'd cross the room, lift her bodily from the love seat, and claim her in a kiss. He'd show Upton who she really wanted. He'd show her whose touch could take her to heaven and keep her there until she begged for release.

Upton put his glass on the table at his elbow. Then he reached his arms over his head and stretched elaborately. "I say, it's late," he said. "I think I should see my intended to her cottage."

She gripped her glass tightly, staring down at it where she held it in her lap. "That isn't necessary."

Upton took her snifter and set it next to his own. "You have a husband now, Bella." He laughed briefly. "A fiancé, I mean."

She fidgeted for a moment. "Really, Hugh . . ."

"A man takes care of his bride-to-be, doesn't he, Julian?"

"I wouldn't know," Richard answered. "I haven't had any experience in that area."

"Well, certainly he does." Upton rose and smiled down at Isabel as if he already owned her. She got up, too, and stood beside him. She glanced at Richard briefly and gave him a little smile and a nod. Then she turned back to her fiancé.

"Thanks for dinner and all, old chap," Upton said. "Needn't see us out. Bella can show me the way."

"Of course."

Richard watched them go, watched Upton put his hand at the small of her back. A protective gesture, a gesture of ownership, tender but possessive. Upton would make her a good husband. He'd share his name with her and his respectable reputation. He'd build her a decent home, nothing remarkable, just solidly middle-class. He'd give her children, little blond ones or maybe miniatures of their mother. Richard would encounter them in Paihia from time to time. Mr. and Mrs. Hugh

Alice Gaines

Upton, with another little one on the way. *Dammit all to hell*.

Richard turned and walked to the hearth. He set his drink on the mantlepiece and stared at his reflection in the glass chimney of an unlit decorative lamp. A haggard face looked back at him, the image distorted by the curves of the glass. Wild hair, even wilder eyes.

What else could he expect? The mere idea of her pregnant by another man was more than he could bear. How would he survive having to see her on the street, having to watch her grow radiant and heavy with another man's issue? How could he sleep at night knowing how those babies had come to be conceived in her belly? Imagining the details?

He rested his forearms on the mantle and put his face onto them. Think. He had to think of something safe, something that would get his mind off making frantic, passionate love to Isabel Gannon. Something had to drive the images from his brain, or he would surely go mad.

Closing his eyes only made the pictures more vivid. Isabel, standing in the lantern light on a warm evening, her lips parted, her breath coming in sweet, labored sighs. Isabel, slipping her fingers into his hair as a waltz played in the distance, enchanted music for their intimate dance. Isabel, rising up on her toes to offer her lips to him. All those things, and more that he could only dream of. And Upton would have them.

But the man was an oaf. He couldn't possibly know the subtleties of coaxing a woman to passion, not with the way he galumphed through things, with his "stout fellows" and "I says." Fine for a schoolmaster, fine for a batsman. But as a lover? The man would bumble his way through years before he developed the right touch. Before he got the sense of when a woman wanted slow loving and when she wanted to be taken—quick and hard. He'd learn at Isabel's expense. He'd experiment with her, damn him.

Waitangi Nights

For all Richard knew, he was doing it right now. He might be standing inside the nurseryman's cottage this very minute with his hand down the front of her dress, groping her roughly in his ignorance. She wouldn't protest, of course. She was too generous. No, she'd put up with his fumbling without complaint.

The fool probably didn't even know she was a virgin. He'd probably fallen for her pretended sophistication. He wouldn't think before he took her. He'd just barrel on through their first coupling, with no thought about handling her delicately. He'd hurt her.

Wedding night, hell. He might be hurting her right now. Men were supposed to wait until after the marriage vows, but they didn't always. Richard knew that well enough. Even the upstanding types like Upton couldn't always control themselves until everything was neat and legal. And that cottage would make the perfect setting for an illicit tryst, isolated as it was from the main house. Upton might be out there this exact moment, violating the woman Richard loved, taking her clumsily, hurting her. On Richard's own property.

"No," he roared. He lashed out with his arm, clearing the mantlepiece in one motion and sending everything flying—brandy snifter, lamp, anything else in his way. Something flew against the near wall and broke into bits. Something else fell to the hearth stones, also shattering. Violent sounds, satisfying sounds. But not enough.

He straightened and turned. No one would have Isabel Gannon on his property. No one. He'd go out to the cottage, and if he found Upton there, if the man had so much as touched her, Richard would murder him with his bare hands.

He found her, alone, sitting on the bench just outside her cottage. In the light of the waning moon, she looked unhurt, unruffled, serene. But as soon as she saw him, she jumped up, and her hand flew to the bodice of her

Alice Gaines

dress, what little there was of it. The action proclaimed her guilty of something, even though there was no sign of Upton about. Maybe the bastard was waiting for her inside.

"Where is he?" Richard demanded.

"Richard, what's wrong?" she answered. "You look—"

"Never mind what I look like. Where is he?"

"Who?"

Who, indeed? Curse Upton, and curse her, too. "Upton," he growled. "Who else?"

"He's gone home."

"Did he hurt you?"

She stared at him as though he'd lost his wits. And maybe he had. But the question was simple enough. Why in hell didn't she answer it? "Did he hurt you?" he repeated.

"No, of course he didn't. What on earth has gotten into you?"

"I need to know . . . dear God . . . if I'm ever to have any peace . . . I need to know."

She put her hand on his arm and stared up into his face, sincerely concerned, if the warmth in her eyes could be trusted. "Need to know what, Richard?"

"Has he been with you?" There, he'd asked. He shouldn't have, had no damned business asking. But he had asked, and now he'd have an answer.

Her brow furrowed as she studied him. "Yes, Hugh's been with me. You saw us together at dinner less than an hour ago."

"Dammit, woman. Don't act stupid," he said. "Has the man been with you?

"Been with me," she repeated, throwing her hands into the air. "How am I to understand that? Been with me."

"Has he lain with you? Known you, in the biblical sense. Plowed you, frigged you, swived you."

Her fingers flew to her mouth. "Dear God."

Waitangi Nights

"Answer me," he commanded.

"How can you ask such a thing?" She turned as if to go into the cottage.

But he caught her and pulled her up, almost off her feet, until she rested against his chest. "Answer me."

"No, he hasn't," she shouted into his face. "Not that it's any of your concern. But, no, he hasn't been with me."

"But he's kissed you," Richard said more quietly.

She twisted, trying to break free of him. "This is ridiculous."

"Tell me, Isabel."

She glared up at him, her expression a jumble of defiance, hopelessness, and misery. "I'm engaged to him."

"Then he has kissed you."

She slumped in his arms, falling against him. "Yes."

"Tonight? Just now?"

"Yes," she sighed, all the air going out of her at once. "Yes, yes, yes."

"I won't have it," he muttered. "Not on my property."

She tipped her head back and stared at him, tears shining at the corners of her eyes, barely caught in the moon's dying light. "You have no choice."

"Like hell I don't."

He kissed her then, fiercely, roughly. He captured her lips with his own, devouring her. And he pulled her hard against him, molding her body to his until he couldn't tell where he ended and she began.

She answered him. She moaned deep in her throat and opened her mouth under his. She dug her fingers into the fabric of his sleeves and rose on tiptoe, bringing herself to him. She straddled his leg and moved herself against him. Against his throbbing manhood, rubbing. Rubbing.

Fire and lightning she was. Molten heat and sweet agony. Passion enough to make him weak. Pleasure almost unbearable in its ecstasy. He clutched at her, grabbing, grasping, defenseless against his own need.

Alice Gaines

Cloth ripped. He heard it somewhere in the back of his brain. He'd torn something, torn her, torn something. He lifted his lips from hers and gaped down at her dress. He'd ripped it along the back somehow, and it hung off her shoulders, threatening to fall completely. Her breasts rose and fell erratically, now almost fully exposed to his view. Soft, round, alabaster in the moonlight. He gazed down at them, aching to release them from her corset and sample their weight in his palms. Needing to feel the nipples harden against his fingers.

Her hand stroked his face, her skin oddly cool against his own.

"Richard," she whispered in a voice grown low and dark with desire. "Richard, please."

"Oh God, Isabel," he answered.

She pressed her mouth to his, at first softly and then with more authority. She brought her tongue to his lips and teased them apart. He met her tongue with his own, darting, stroking. She fumbled with the buttons of his jacket for a moment and then pulled herself against his chest, never taking her lips away from his. Her soft breasts crushed against him, and she let out a whimper.

What a woman. Such response, such searing heat. He lowered his face to her neck and kissed her there, tasting her and nipping at her skin. She tilted her head, exposing the entire length of her throat, and he took it all, covering every inch with caresses from her earlobe to her shoulder.

He reached her bosom, perfumed like wild flowers and soft as powder. Gently, reverently he reached below her chemise and freed her breast. It was beautiful—round and firm, heavy and tempting. He circled the nipple with his tongue, and she gasped and shuddered against him. Finally, after an eternity of watching and waiting and wanting, he took the delicate bud into his mouth and sucked.

"Oh, dear heaven," she cried. "Oh, Richard, please."

He slipped the other breast from its linen prison and

Waitangi Nights

caressed it, too, tugging gently with his lips and tongue. She writhed against him, making animal sounds in her throat.

She was his now, and she'd deny him nothing. He could lower her to the ground, rip open any of her small clothes in his way, and plunder her. He could unbutton his trousers, take out his stiff, hot sex, and plunge it into her. Hard, if he wanted to. Over and over until he satisfied his lust. He could put his mark on her and ruin her for any other man.

But, no, he couldn't. Dammit all, he couldn't.

He rested his face in the crook of her neck and worked for breath. He couldn't ruin her—he loved her. Hurting her would kill him. She'd come to hate him if he took her. And then he'd hate himself, and he'd want to die. He would die, a little at a time, from the inside out.

"We have to stop," he muttered into her throat.

"Richard?" she cried.

One word, his name. But it held a world of uncertainty and need. And accusation. He'd made her want him, and now he was backing away. She'd despise him, she probably loathed him already for what he'd done to her. Well, let her loathe him. That would work out best for them both.

He straightened, put his hands on her shoulders, and pushed her away. The sight of her, standing there, trembling with unsatisfied passion, almost unmanned him. Her lips were soft and full from kissing, her eyes glazed over with desire. Her breasts stood high and full, the nipples erect and still moist from his kisses.

How he wanted her. What he wouldn't give to carry her into the cottage and lose himself in her. Still, he couldn't, not if he was to live with himself afterward.

"Go inside," he whispered, his voice coming out raw with emotion.

"But Richard," she said, reaching out to him, promising him heaven, if only for one night.

Alice Gaines

A merciful God would spare him, release him from these blasted scruples. Where had they come from, anyway? He didn't used to think beyond pleasing a woman, making sure that she enjoyed herself as much as he did. What had changed?

He had. She had changed him, with her openness, her talent for giving of herself. Even now she stood before him, offering her innocence, no matter the cost to her. Well, he wouldn't let her make the sacrifice. He loved her, and he wouldn't hurt her.

"Go inside," he repeated, the order gritting out from between his clenched teeth this time. "Now."

"I don't want to," she answered.

He shoved her away from him, walked to the cottage door, and yanked it open. "Do it!"

She pulled her chemise up and over her nakedness, lifted her chin, and walked by him, pulling the door closed behind her. He turned and frustrated, he slammed his fist into the old wooden planks.

Chapter Sixteen

The kitten tumbled in Isabel's lap, rolling over and pulling the ball of yarn against his belly, clawing at it with his back paws. His bright little eyes flashed furiously as he demolished his prey. Mighty predator, innocent babe—he was completely oblivious to the turmoil of the woman who held him.

Isabel clutched her wrapper tightly around her throat. A full quarter hour had passed since she had taken off her ruined gown and buried what remained of it in a drawer of the old dresser. Then she'd slipped out of her corset, untying the laces with shaking fingers, and put on as many clothes as she could without getting perfectly silly about covering herself. Now here she sat, in her rocker in front of the fire clad in drawers, chemise, nightgown, cap, and the most virginal wrapper she owned, its collar so high that her chin brushed lace whenever she turned her head.

And still she trembled. Still she craved Richard's touch. Still her heart leapt at every sound, as though he

Alice Gaines

might yet come through the door and take her back into his arms.

"Oh, Tigre," she sighed, "what am I to do?"

The yarn slipped from her lap, and Tigre bounded to the floor after it. It took some doing, of course, for such a tiny animal to make such a huge jump. And Tigre executed it with his usual enthusiasm, overbalancing and almost landing on his head. Isabel would normally have laughed, but not tonight. Tonight nothing could distract her from her thoughts of Richard and how deeply she had fallen under his spell.

She loved him. She'd known for days that she loved him, but she'd believed she could rein in her feelings, control her behavior. What a fool. She couldn't stay with him and not give in to him, even beg him to take her if he wouldn't do it willingly. She wanted him too much.

Was it natural to crave a man that badly? To turn to custard inside at his touch? To go all breathless and limp with his kisses? To throb in that secret place between her legs, when he hadn't even touched her there?

Natural or not, she did all those things, and the wickedness of it all was that she wanted more. She had promised herself to Hugh Upton, but she couldn't imagine living the rest of her life without having Richard Julian. Being with him, as he had put it, the way a woman should only be with her husband, making love with him.

Love—she always came back to that word. Could it be so wrong to give herself to him if she loved him? Hugh didn't think so. He'd told her straight out that he didn't expect her to have saved her virginity for him. Of course, he hadn't meant for her to lie with another man now, after they'd become engaged. He'd meant that he'd forgive her for her past, if she had one.

But would it make that much difference, really? Whether she had lost her innocence last year in the Amazon or tomorrow night in New Zealand. The effect

Waitangi Nights

would be the same—a tarnished bride. Hugh expected no more than that, a woman who had known another man but who nevertheless came to him, and his bed, freely. A woman with some knowledge of love who could devote herself completely to him.

And she would. As soon as she left Harrowgate Manor as Mrs. Hugh Upton, she'd forget about Richard. She'd dedicate herself to Hugh and his school—their school—and perhaps someday their children. She'd make him a good wife, the best wife in the world. If only she could have Richard for one night first, so that she could know true carnal pleasure, love's deepest intimacies. Did she dare?

She rose, walked to the hearth, and picked up the poker. A few prods at the fire, and a log split in two, cracking into flame and heat. She set the poker back and watched the log burn. She would shatter like that, shatter and burn, if she could have a night of passion with Richard. She might never put the pieces of herself back together again, at least not in quite the same order. But the flames of her love might forge her into something stronger than she was now. If she already understood passion when she married Hugh—if she knew what was meant to happen between men and women—perhaps she could bring a greater joy to her marriage bed than she could now. Perhaps she could teach her husband to be her lover.

It was worth a try. What choice did she have, anyway? If she stayed one more day with Richard, if she found herself alone in the moonlight with him one more time, she would make him make love to her. He'd resisted so far, but even an unschooled virgin could tell he wanted her. She only needed to figure a way to bring him to her, here in the cottage, where they would be alone.

Something tugged at the skirt of her wrapper. Isabel glanced down to find Tigre, lying on his back, all four paws tangled in her hem. She bent and picked him up, gently pulling his claws out of the cotton as she straightened. She held him for a moment and scratched behind his ear.

"How shall I trap him, little one?" she asked her pet. "How shall I draw him into my lair?"

Tigre squirmed, twisted onto his back, and batted at her fingers with needle-sharp claws.

"I see," Isabel whispered. "I prick him somehow, make him angry, and then sit back and let his temper bring him to me."

She scratched Tigre's tummy, and he purred, all the while doing battle with her fingers.

"Defiance, that's it," she said. She chuckled for a moment. "I won't show up for dinner. That will make him furious. Then I'll wait here for my punishment. Yes, that will work."

Pain shot through her thumb, tiny but burning. She looked down at the kitten. "You've bitten me, you little scamp," she declared, tapping his nose with her fingertip. "If I didn't love you so much, I'd throw you right out on your ear."

He squiggled again, still purring. Isabel pressed against the almost invisible puncture in her thumb, and a bright red drop of blood appeared against her skin.

"Are you sure you're quite well, miss?"

Isabel leaned her shoulder against the inside of the cottage door and curled her fingers around the edge. She rested her head on the old wooden boards and applied just enough force to block her lady's maid's well-meaning and very determined attempts to enter from the outside. For her plan to work, she had to remain on this side of the door, and Clarice on that.

"It's only a headache," she called through the door. "I'll be fine in the morning."

"Still, I don't think I should leave you alone," Clarice insisted, her fingers curling around the edge of the wooden plank and almost touching Isabel's.

Waitangi Nights

"I'm not a child," Isabel said. "I'll see you in the morning, Clarice."

"But," the words came softly, "what will I tell the master?"

"Tell him whatever you want. Tell him I have a headache."

"He'll worry about you," Clarice said.

"Don't tell him anything, then," Isabel said. "I don't owe him an explanation. Just tell him I'm not coming to dinner."

Silence greeted that declaration, as well it ought. Clarice knew exactly how the master would react to any sign of defiance from his nurseryman. His temper was what Isabel was relying on, so why not make the message unmistakable?

"In fact, you can inform Mr. Julian that I'll dine with him when it suits me, and tonight it doesn't suit me."

More silence. "Are you sure you want me to tell him that?"

"That and more," Isabel replied. "You can add that I'm tired of being ordered about. I work hard every day on his orchids, and I don't care to perform at his table every night as well."

"Oh, miss, you really do have a headache."

"Just tell him what I said."

Clarice would never repeat any of that, of course. But, as forthright as she was, she wouldn't be able to look Richard in the eye, and she'd mumble some excuse or other. Her behavior would give her—and Isabel—away.

Clarice's fingers disappeared from the edge of the door, and a deep sigh sounded on the other side. "I'll come back in the morning, miss. I hope you'll be feeling better then."

"Thank you, Clarice. I'm sure I will."

Isabel closed the door, turned, and leaned against it. She took a breath and scanned the room, the scene of her soon-to-be loss of innocence. She hoped. Everything was neat and clean, of course, from the cheerful

Alice Gaines

gingham curtains at the windows to the firewood stacked with precision by the hearth. She'd set the table as best she could, but the slightly frayed linens and mismatched china only made the room homey. Not at all the setting for an illicit affair.

She glanced over at the chest of drawers. On top sat a bottle of whiskey and a pair of crystal tumblers that she had "borrowed" from the manor house. She hadn't taken a decanter, of course, and the master would have to have his whiskey poured straight out of the bottle. Again, not very elegant, but the best she could do.

Tigre sprang out from under the bed, batting his ball of yarn in front of him. Oh dear, what did one do with one's cat during a seduction? Would it be proper to put the little fellow out of his own home for the duration? What if he set up a howl to get back in?

He rolled onto his back on the braided rug, now wrestling with the yarn, his eyes aglitter with kittenish mischief. She'd better put him out. She certainly didn't want him watching her do . . . that. And knowing Tigre, he'd be likely to pounce at the worst possible moment.

She crossed the room and bent to scoop him up but was interrupted by a hiss of steam from the fire. The *mole* had boiled over again. Isabel flew to the hearth, grabbed the cloth and long wooden spoon from the mantle, and used the spoon to swing the pot out toward her. With the cloth in hand, she lifted the lid and took a sniff. Nothing smelled burned, thank heaven. She stirred the *mole* for a moment, replaced the top, and pushed the pot back to one side of the fire where it would stay warm without scorching.

She stood and looked down at herself, and her heart sank. What on earth did she think she was doing? Even she knew that for a tryst, a woman dressed in frilly things, bordered with lace and revealing in the front. But all she owned were practical, unattractive clothes. With nothing better to wear, she had stripped naked and then put on a cotton nightgown and wrapper. In a

Waitangi Nights

desperate attempt at a seductive appearance, she'd buttoned and unbuttoned the wrapper half a dozen times, but it looked silly both ways.

"Silly," she muttered. "This whole situation is silly, Tigre. The room looks silly. I look silly."

Tigre ignored her and continued to play with his yarn.

"I haven't the faintest idea how to seduce a man. Why should I try?" She set the spoon and cloth back on the mantle and began to unbutton her wrapper in earnest, crossing to the dresser as she did. "I won't, then. With any luck I can get dressed and up to the house before Richard even realizes I'm late."

The cottage door flew open, slamming against the wall. Isabel jumped and turned toward the sound. Richard stood on the threshold, and as the door bounced back, he caught it in his fist. "What in hell do you think you're doing, woman?" he bellowed.

Tigre arched his back and spat. Then he charged toward the door, ducked around Richard's feet, and dashed outside.

"Dammit, I thought we had this settled," Richard roared. He towered in the doorway, his face a perfect mask of rage, nostrils flaring, fire burning in his eyes.

Isabel raised her hand to her throat but stood her ground. Silly or not, she was stuck with her original plan—seduction, tonight—and she'd have to do her best. If only her heart would stop jumping around in her chest, "Won't you come in?" she asked as calmly as she could.

"Come in?" he repeated.

She straightened her shoulders and walked to him, taking his free hand in both of hers. "Come in, sit down, join me for supper."

He glanced around him as though seeing everything for the first time, rather like someone who'd found himself in an utterly foreign place. He looked at her finally, his gaze fixing at the bodice of her nightgown. "Bloody

Alice Gaines

hell, what's the meaning of this?"

"I made our dinner."

"You what?" he demanded.

"Don't you think you'd better come inside?" She tugged at his hand until he released the door and took a few steps into the room. He stopped, his chest still rising and falling with rage, no doubt, and from an excursion down the path at that near-run he broke into whenever he got angry.

Isabel dropped his hand and went behind him to shut the door. She took a steadying breath and turned to look back at Richard.

Somewhat calmer now, he stood in the middle of the room, studying everything—the fireplace and the pot that hung over the embers, the table with its two settings and crude candle holders. After a moment his gaze settled on the bottle of whiskey.

"Would you like a drink?" she offered, glad for something to make conversation about. "I don't have a decanter I'm afraid, but I suppose the bottle will do. There isn't any soda, either."

He turned his head and stared at her then, still not quite comprehending what had happened to him, if she could read the bewilderment in his eyes correctly. "I don't take soda," he said after a moment.

"No, of course you don't," she answered. She walked to the chest of drawers and opened the whiskey. "I knew you didn't. I suppose I just forgot."

He watched her, his gaze following her every movement. She poured some liquor into a glass, and saints be praised, her hands didn't shake, at least not much. "You've poured me so many glasses of sherry, and this is the first time I've served you," she rambled on, making herself sound thoroughly ridiculous. "You've even cooked for me. So, I thought I'd return the favor."

She walked to him and handed him the whiskey. He took it and stared down at her. A tiny smile curled his lips. "You cooked for me?"

Waitangi Nights

She smiled back, and pounding of her heart skipped one of its beats. "I've made a *mole*, a simple sauce from Mexico. Peasant food, but I thought you'd like it."

"Isabel . . ."

The word, her name, held a hesitancy, an uncertainty that she couldn't, wouldn't hear. She walked to the fireplace, picked up the cloth and spoon, and opened the pot. "I had quite a time finding chile powder, I'll tell you," she said in another attempt at talk. "The grocer in Paihia had an old jar that was covered with dust. I'll be amazed if it tastes like anything at all."

"Isabel," he repeated. "I can't stay here."

But you can't leave. And yet he would. She'd made herself laughable, and now he would leave. "I don't know what I'm thinking," she babbled on. "This isn't one of Mrs. Willis meals. I've nearly burned it twice. It's been so long since I cooked over a fire. And it has chocolate in it. Can you imagine? A proper gentleman would never eat a chicken stew with chocolate in it."

Behind her, he walked to the table. His glass settled audibly onto the cloth. "Do you know what you've done?" he said softly. "Do you know what will happen if I stay here?"

So, that was it. He wasn't rejecting her after all. He was only trying to act nobly, to preserve her virtue. She put the lid back on the pot and looked at her hands. "I think I know."

"I'm only human. I can't resist you forever."

She carefully set the spoon and cloth back on the mantlepiece. "I don't want you to resist me."

"But I really can't stay," he said. "I have to continue the search."

"Not tonight." She took a deep breath. Now. She had to find the courage. Now. "Spend one night with me, Richard. Just one."

"Dammit, woman," he said. But his voice didn't have any anger in it, only resignation. She turned and found the man she loved—tall and beautiful and hers for one night. "Please," she said.

He stood, looking at her for what seemed like an eternity. "Do you want me, Isabel?" he asked finally.

Not trusting her voice, she nodded.

"Then heaven help us both, for you shall have me."

He opened his arms wide, and she ran to him. She slid her own arms around his waist and tipped her face up to his. He closed his eyes, long lashes brushing his cheeks. Then he bent and took her mouth.

Heaven. The man and his kisses were pure heaven. His lips moved over hers, urgent and gentle at the same time. She pulled herself against him and answered with her own lips. She could have him now, every inch of him if she wanted. And she wanted, how she wanted.

She opened her mouth under his, releasing a rush of breath against his skin. He groaned and slipped his tongue between her lips, searching, probing, sending a current of heat through her blood. He lifted her against the hard length of him, and she floated in his embrace, lost in his scent, his heat.

He tore his lips from hers and lowered them to her neck, nipping at her skin. All the while his fingers played in her hair, and hairpins dropped to the floor behind her. "Sweet Jesus," he murmured against her throat. "I've wanted you for so long."

She stroked his face, his hair, and buried her nose in his curls. "Richard."

"I've burned for you," he muttered. "Until I thought I'd die."

"Take me then."

He slipped the wrapper over her shoulders and let it drop. Next he started in on the buttons of her nightgown, fumbling with them for several seconds. "Get this off before I have to rip it from you," he growled. "I can't wait another minute to touch you. I've waited too long already."

She obeyed, her own fingers suddenly clumsy. He

Waitangi Nights

watched her undo each button, a ravenous gleam in his eyes, his hot breath grazing her cheek. After she had the gown unfastened, she lifted it over her head. Finally, she dropped it and stood before him, naked.

He took a sharp breath and stepped back, his eyes growing wide. "Isabel," he whispered.

She tried to stand perfectly still, really she did. But with the cool air washing over her skin and with him staring like that, she couldn't help but tremble. She'd give anything to make him happy with her. Anything. But she wasn't tall and elegant, never would be. She was only Isabel Gannon, who loved him and wanted to show him her love.

She tolerated the silence for as along as she could. When she couldn't stand it a moment longer, she lifted her chin and looked into his face. "Do I please you?"

"Woman . . ." He swallowed hard. "You humble me."

She released a breath slowly. "You find me beautiful?"

"Beyond description."

"Touch me."

He reached out, slowly, gingerly, as though she might vanish if he moved too quickly. He stroked her shoulder with the tips of his fingers and then trailed them down her arm to her bosom. When he touched that sensitive flesh, she shuddered.

"Are you cold?" he asked softly.

"No."

He slipped his fingers under her breast and lifted it, cupping it with his palm. "So lovely."

He ran thumb over the peak, and a little cry escaped her throat. The nipple stiffened until it stood erect, rosy and puckered.

"Do . . . what you did," she murmured. "Last night."

"You liked that?"

"Oh, yes," she sighed.

He took her back in his arms and then bent and put his mouth to her breast, sucking on the tip and stroking it with his tongue. A shock ran through her, from where his lips caressed her, to the base of her spine, down all the way to her toes. Her knees buckled, and she clutched at his shoulders. Hot moisture gathered where her thighs met, a sweet rush of sensation. Tonight he would teach her about the throbbing there. He'd teach her how to soar, make her a complete woman.

He caressed the other nipple, now making soft noises in the back of his throat. He reached behind her and cupped her buttocks, kneading them rhythmically. He bent farther, and his hands slid to her thighs. From behind, his fingers slipped between her legs, so close to the need. But not close enough. She twisted, stretching for his touch, not even knowing what she sought.

He straightened, took her face between his hands, and gazed into her eyes. "You've burned, just as I have. I've dreamed of making love to you, but even in dreams I couldn't hope you would flame so brightly."

Words. Here she stood, naked and trembling. Wanting him with every inch of her flesh, and he was talking. She slipped her arms around his neck, rose up on her toes, and pressed her lips to his. They opened for her instantly, and she tasted him with her tongue. She pulled herself against him and felt his hardness against her hip—thick and long. She rubbed against it, and he let out a low growl. He grabbed her buttocks again, roughly this time, and pressed his maleness into her.

"God, woman," he gritted. "Another moment of this and I'll have to throw you over the bed and take you like a beast."

"I want you to."

"No, you don't," he answered. He released her and took her chin between his thumb and forefinger. "You want gentleness, and I'm going to give it to you, even if I die in the process."

But she didn't want gentleness. She wanted him. She slipped his coat over his shoulders and let it drop. His waistcoat went next. Finally, she pushed aside his sus-

Waitangi Nights

penders and unbuttoned his shirt, pressing her nose into the hairs on his chest, breathing in his scent. "Take me now," she sighed. "I'm ready."

He laughed, deep in his chest, a rumbling, happy sound. "Yes, I think you are."

He took her by the hand and led her to the bed. Once there, he laid her on the counterpane and kissed her gently. "Towels?" he asked.

She shook her head, trying to make sense of his question.

"I need something for the bed," he said. "A towel perhaps."

She pointed toward the chest of drawers.

He smiled. "Of course."

He walked across the room, his easy strides emphasizing the length of his legs, his broad shoulders rippling under his shirt. Isabel watched him and marvelled at herself and her soon-to-be paramour. She'd been naked many times before, often to bathe in a jungle stream, but she'd never exposed herself to the intent gaze of a lover.

She'd imagined herself with a man before, too, but she'd never dreamed she'd have Richard Julian. She'd heard stories from the native women of South America about the pleasures of the marriage bed, but she'd never guessed a touch could set her pulse to racing and light a wildfire in her heart.

Now she would learn, and from a man so tall, strong, and magnificent, she could hardly bear to look at him. But neither would she look away. Tonight was all she would have of him, and she wouldn't waste a minute.

He rummaged about in the dresser until he found a towel. Then he closed the drawer and turned to her. His gaze travelled from the top of her head to the bottom of her feet, and he smiled again. The expression was wicked and wild, but it was also warm and tender—a contradiction, just like the rest of him.

Alice Gaines

He walked to the bed and sat down on the edge. "Lift your hips," he said quietly.

Isabel obeyed, and he slid the towel underneath her.

"Good God, you're beautiful," he murmured. "Far more than I deserve."

He stroked her cheek softly, lazily, then her throat and her shoulder. His fingers moved over her breast, teasing the peak, descended to her ribs, and slid slowly over her belly. The fire kindled in her core again, the heat moving from her very center to the juncture of her legs. The aching, the moisture, the hunger for his touch. She arched into it, a purely instinctual motion, seeking the pressure of his caress against that hidden spot.

He knew somehow, because he slipped his hand between her legs and touched her. Jolts of pleasure shot through her, burning arrows of delight radiating outward. She fell helpless under the assault, her hips moving of their own accord.

"That's it, isn't it, sweet?" he whispered.

"Oh, Richard," she gasped. "Oh, dear heaven."

"You're so hot here. So wet. So beautiful."

He rubbed her, each stroke taking her higher, closer to some carnal reality, and she reached for it, pressing her body against his touch. His hand moved, sliding a finger into her—another sensation to steal her breath, her sanity. He probed gently and then more firmly. Suddenly, pain mingled with pleasure as she stretched, as something inside her threatened to tear. She opened her eyes.

"It will only hurt for a moment," he said. "I have to do this if we're to make love. And I have to have you."

She bit her lip and stared at him.

"Do you understand?" he asked.

She nodded, and he began again. His thumb teased her to breathless excitement, while his finger still pressed against the obstruction inside her. She closed her eyes and concentrated on the pleasure. This was joy not to be denied, ecstasy beyond belief, and if it came

Waitangi Nights

with some pain, that would soon pass. She let her body dictate its own rhythms, rising in concert with his touch. One more sharp jab, one more stroke on the throbbing seat of her pleasure, one more movement up to meet him, and the barrier broke, his finger entering her fully.

"That's it, my sweet, that's over," he whispered. "Now the satisfaction."

He stroked her again, firmly and in a maddening rhythm. She closed her eyes and sank into the mattress, dissolving into a helpless creature as he moved her closer, closer. Breath didn't matter now, nakedness didn't matter, nothing mattered but his touch. Something deep and primitive inside her coiled—delicious tension, irresistible, overpowering. She stiffened, tightened from the inside out as it claimed her. Blazing light played at the corners of her eyelids as she shuddered and finally exploded, letting loose a lusty cry.

Then came sweetness, soft and drowsy, as something at her core continued to spasm around his finger. She sighed, smiled, and sighed again. "Oh, Richard."

"Yes, my lovely nymph. How you respond. You make me feel like the most gifted lover on earth."

"You are the most gifted lover on earth." She lifted a heavy arm and stroked her own throat, feeling the skin as though she'd never touched it before. But then she hadn't, not really. Until a few moments ago, she hadn't known her own body, hadn't realized what it was capable of.

"And now," she murmured. "There's more."

"Much more," he answered. His weight lifted from the bed, and his footfalls crossed the room. She opened her eyes in time to see him remove another towel from the dresser and take it to the sink. He moistened the cloth, came back to the bed, and sat on the edge. He parted her legs and gently cleaned her where he had stroked and then probed and then driven her to madness. The towel came away spotted here and there with her blood. "I knew you were a virgin, you know. You never fooled me with all your claims of worldly experience."

"I never lied to you."

He dropped the towel to the floor. "No. You didn't."

She stretched and turned onto her side. "You now," she said. "I want to see you naked."

He slipped out of his shoes and socks. Then he pulled out of his shirt and tossed it aside, baring his chest completely. He rose, and the bulge in his trousers stood out against the fabric. She watched it as he undid the buttons. He slipped the pants low on his hips, exposing a few more inches of skin.

"You don't wear underclothes," she breathed.

He smiled, a purely wicked grin. "What else would you expect from a heathen like me?"

Her throat suddenly went dry. "You mean . . . those times when you held me against you . . . there was nothing between us except your trousers?"

"And your many layers of skirts," he answered. "Do you disapprove?"

"No," she answered immediately. And she meant it. The thought of his hardness pressing right against the fabric of his pants gave her a restless feeling in her belly, a surge of desire. She licked her lips. "You're not undressed yet."

He laughed. "Brazen little thing, aren't you?"

"I'm no delicate creature; I told you that from the first."

"We'll see about that." Still grinning, he pushed his trousers the rest of the way down and kicked out of them. Finally, he stood naked for her inspection. And what a glorious sight he made—broad shouldered and finely muscled, his hair haloing his face and setting off the glow of his eyes. And there, at the base of his torso, stood his manhood, proud and erect, compelling and, yes, beautiful. But perfectly huge. How on earth would she take him all?

Waitangi Nights

"Not feeling quite so brazen now, are you?"

"You're . . . well . . . impressive," she mumbled. "Yes, all in all, very impressive, Mr. Julian."

"Then it's time I impressed you thoroughly, Miss Gannon." He sat beside her on the bed, took her hand in his, and raised her palm to his lips. "I won't hurt you."

"I know you won't."

He bent and kissed her, softly. But she'd graduated from gentle, maidenly kisses, and she greeted his mouth with parted, hungry lips. He lowered himself onto her, his skin against hers everywhere, his heat enveloping her. She'd never touched anyone like this— with all of her. She slid her arms around his neck and pulled him down to her, revelling in the way her nipples grazed his chest, buried in the soft, curling hairs there.

He moved against her, his hardness insistent against her hip. He let loose a muffled groan and moved again. "Ah, God. I'm sorry, I can't wait."

"Now, Richard."

He shifted, moving his body lower on hers. His lips captured hers in a savage kiss, and he plundered her mouth with his tongue. No more careful wooing—this was an animal move, full of hunger and ferocity. She gave to him—her breath, her heart. She ran her hands over his back and to his buttocks and stroked him. He moved again. This time the tip of his manhood pressed against her own budding desire, and she cried out her pleasure.

Over and over he brought himself to her, moving his hips slowly. Delirious with bliss, she wrapped her legs around him and answered with her own motions. The pressure built again, threatening to erupt, as he urged her on.

One more tiny shift brought him to the entrance of her womanly core. He pushed, and the tip of him entered her. Her body had to stretch to accept him, but there was no pain. Only a fullness and joy to have him inside her. She moved up to bring him deeper, but he took a sharp inward breath and held back. He trembled in her arms, all of him leashed strength and desperate need. "Damn, but you're tight."

"Give me all of you, Richard," she whispered. "I'm ready."

"Tight," he gritted. "So tight. I'll spend before you're done."

"Now, Richard, please."

On her command he surged forward, filling her completely, shouting out in triumph. He drove deep within her, again and again, his breath coming in rhythm with his thrusts. She abandoned herself to the feelings, to the sensation of knowing him totally, the rising passion, the fire in her own belly. She rocked with him, uttering little cries into his ear, an alien language of love and carnal pleasure. The galaxy of sensation grew white hot around her.

Richard stiffened in her arms, and her body responded. The spasms started deep inside her again, grasping at him where they were joined. She shook and clutched his shoulders, gasping for breath. He roared into her hair, thrust deeply one more time, and finally collapsed onto her.

"Isabel," he whimpered. "Oh, Isabel."

Chapter Seventeen

Richard opened his eyes to find the ceiling of the nurseryman's cottage above him, firelight flickering off the heavy beams. He'd dozed off in Isabel's bed. And why the devil not? Lovemaking like he'd just had could knock the sense out of anyone.

He stretched and took a deep breath, hard work for a fellow whose limbs had turned to lead. No, not lead. Pudding, rather. Something soft and unresisting. Honey-warm, pliant, and satisfied. Good God, he was turning into a bloody poet.

He turned onto his side and propped himself up on his elbow. Isabel stood at the hearth, facing away from him and stirring something in a pot that hung over the fire. She'd put her nightgown back on, a demure thing that buttoned up to her chin. But backlit by the fire, the cotton showed off her every curve in silhouette. What a sight—just revealing enough to set fire to the imagination.

She picked up a plate from the mantle and ladled

something from the pot into it. A pungent aroma greeted Richard as she did, setting his mouth to watering. She set that dish back above the hearth and filled a second one. Finally, she turned, a plate in each hand, and took a step toward the table.

He sat up in bed and smiled at her. She stopped dead in her tracks and just gazed at him out of her big, dark eyes. Standing there, a tiny figure with hair trailing down her back and bare toes peeking out from under the hem of her pristine white gown, she had a sort of vulnerability to her, as though she wanted to please but wasn't sure how. She just stood there and stared at him.

"Our dinner, I presume," he said softly.

"Yes."

"It smells delicious."

That got a smile out of her finally. She finished her journey to the table and set the plates down. Now that the food was closer, he could get a better sense of its aroma. Unusual definitely, and tempting, rather like the woman who served it, who just now seemed an enigmatic combination of schoolgirl, pixie, and seductress—most certainly a seductress.

He climbed out of bed and found his trousers where they lay in a heap on the floor. He stepped into them and buttoned them up but didn't bother to pull up the suspenders or put on his shirt. With the room cozy and warm, the dinner aromatic, and the company so inviting, why bother to get dressed?

Isabel pulled out a chair and sat down. She very primly set her napkin in her lap and then filled two water glasses from a pitcher. Richard sauntered over and took his own seat, staring at her in the light of the fire the entire time, feasting on her with his eyes.

She smiled again, very sweetly, picked up a bread basket, and passed it to him. "I bought the rolls in town," she said. "I didn't dare ask Mrs. Willis to bake me some."

He leaned his elbows on the table and gazed at her

some more. "This won't do," he said after a moment.

She peered into the basket and then back at him, uncertainty returning to her eyes. "They won't be as good as you're used to, but they were baked today. The man assured me."

"The rolls are fine," he answered quietly. "What won't do is the distance between us."

"Distance?" She set down the rolls and looked back at him, questioning. "We're just across the table from each other."

"Much too far away."

A gleam of mischief entered her ebony eyes at that. "It's a very little table."

"Pick up your plate and bring it over here," he ordered.

She did as she was told, the feet of her chair scraping against the floorboards as she rose. She approached him slowly and put her dish right next to his own. "Is this close enough?"

"Almost," he answered. He pulled her into his lap. "Ah, now that's close enough."

She laughed. "Richard, this is silly. I can't eat my dinner sitting like this."

"Why the devil not?"

"Because . . ." She bit her lip and looked around her. ". . . because I don't have any silverware."

"Then I'll feed you."

She laughed again, more loudly this time. But she ran her arms around his neck, too, and she squirmed in his lap. A delightful sensation. If she did much more of that, neither of them would get any dinner.

Reaching both arms around her, he picked up his knife and fork. He sliced off a piece of chicken, swirled it in its sauce, and brought it to her mouth. She held her hand underneath to catch drips, and her fingers brushed his. Finally, smiling, she opened her lips and took the food from the fork.

"Good?" he asked.

"Passable," she answered. "But I wanted to serve you."

He set the silver back onto the plate. "Fine. Serve me."

She twisted in his lap, creating more friction between their bodies, and his sex reacted, stiffening in his trousers.

She turned back to him, a piece of chicken between her fingers, the sauce dripping along the side of her thumb. He took her hand in his and brought it to his mouth, licking the red-brown gravy from her skin.

She giggled and squirmed again. "That tickles."

"Does it, now?"

"Yes."

He tipped his head up and took the morsel of chicken between his teeth, nipping her fingertips in the process. She pulled them back and scowled at him.

He chewed slowly, savoring the variety of tastes and textures. Spice, almost fiery enough to burn his tongue, and smooth darkness. "This has chocolate in it?" he asked. "It isn't sweet."

"Chocolate isn't sweet without sugar," she answered. "It only makes the sauce rich."

"Huh," he grunted. "We'll see about that."

He reached around her and dipped his index finger into the bowl, bringing it away with the tip coated in sauce. He lifted it to her lips and gave them a generous coating of the brown liquid. Finally, he raised his mouth to hers and tasted her. "Mmmm," he murmured. "Tastes sweet to me."

"Let me see," she said. She dipped her own finger into the sauce and coated his lips with it. Then she bent and kissed him.

Her lips moved over his gently, coaxing them apart and sampling them. Her breath grew hot against his skin, and she moved her bottom against him. After a moment, she raised her head and looked down at him, her eyes feverish and heavy lidded. "You're right," she whispered. "Definitely sweet."

"Listen woman," he said. "We can't do this again. Not yet."

"Why on earth not?"

"You only lost your virginity a few moments ago. You'll still be sore."

She lowered her lips to his jaw and laid a trail of kisses to his ear. "I don't feel sore," she murmured. "I feel . . . oh, Richard . . . I feel so naughty."

He laughed and pulled her firmly against him, moving his hips under her, feeling his manhood harden further.

"I want you," she crooned. "I don't care how long it's been. I want you to make love to me again."

Oh hell, why not? Maybe he could be gentler with her this time, maybe he could make the pleasure last for both of them. "Let me make you ready."

"Please."

He bunched up her nightgown and slipped his fingers under the hem. He stroked her slowly, past her knee, over the soft skin of her thigh. She sighed and parted her legs for him. He touched her sex, opened the petals of her beautiful flower, and rubbed the hard little nub between them.

"Oh, yes," she whispered. She moved against his hand, instantly growing hot and moistening his fingers. Miraculous creature.

He lifted her into his arms and rose, heading for the bed. He set her down gently and watched while she slipped her gown over her head. His own fingers fumbled with the buttons of his trousers as he hastily stripped for her. Finally, they were both naked, gazing at each other.

"Now I want to make you ready," she said.

"You already have, madam, as is easy to see."

She stared at his sex where it stood proudly erect, waiting to enter her welcoming softness. "I want to touch you," she whispered. "I want to feel you."

"Then you shall."

Alice Gaines

He lay down beside her, flat on his back, open to her exploration. He didn't have to wait for it. She immediately reached over and circled his hardness with delicate fingers. She caressed him slowly, firmly—now over the tip, now along the length of the shaft. Over and over, until his hips answered, rising to her touch. Until he had to work for breath, had to grit his teeth for control. Until he went nearly mad with hunger. Enough.

He slipped his hands around her waist, lifting her. She rose and straddled him, somehow reading his intention and not hesitating in the least. She curled her fingers around his member again and brought him to her. He lowered her slowly, and she took the tip of him inside her.

She gasped and tilted her head back, closing her eyes. "Yes," she moaned. "Yes, Richard, yes."

He gazed in wonder at her beauty, revealed by the flickering of the hearth fire. He studied the length of her throat and the sable hair cascading around her shoulders. Her breasts, high and firm, and the curve of her hips. Her belly and the curls that covered her sex. He looked at where they joined, his hardness entering her body, and he almost came apart right then.

He bit his lip, hard, and lowered her a bit more. Her hips moved gently, and she brought herself down to him, taking all of him inside her. Then she rocked, forward and back, squeezing the length of him.

He couldn't last—she gripped him too tightly, too deliciously, like a moist fist or a heated kiss. If he didn't get himself under control, he was going to spend, and soon. So he held himself perfectly still. He pressed his thumb against her womanhood, where her every move would bring her against it. She cried out and moved harder, shuddering each time he touched her.

A strangled cry erupted from her throat, and she tensed all around him. The spasms came, her sweet release. He gave in to his own lust, thrusting into her, letting the fire loose in his loins, shouting out his love

Waitangi Nights

into the night. He erupted inside her and then rested back against the mattress, pulling her down onto his chest.

She settled nicely there, snaking her arms around his waist and nestling her head into his chest. Her breath came in short, happy gasps for a moment and then eased into a softer rhythm. His heart nearly burst—with love and possession and shame.

Damn him for a selfish sinner, he hadn't meant to seduce her, hadn't meant to take her innocence. He'd fought his feelings for so long, at first denying the need and then trying to hold it inside. In the end, he'd had no choice—he'd had to have her.

Worst of all, he'd put her in danger. Whatever it was out there that wanted Bunny wanted Isabel even more. He should have let her go. But he couldn't, and now she was his. He couldn't, wouldn't live without her. If he could manage it, he'd never let her out of his sight for the rest of their lives.

He squeezed her more tightly in his arms. Shame solved nothing. Somehow he'd protect her. He would, he'd simply have to. If he kept her with him every minute, nothing could get to her.

He sighed and held her close to his chest as the rhythm of her heart returned to normal, beating next to his own, where it belonged.

Isabel awoke in the morning to Richard's arm flung across her body, his head burrowed into her shoulder, his hair hanging over his face. She brushed it back and curled a lock around her finger. There was nothing supernatural about the color, after all, only red highlights in a warm brown. But when she lifted it to a shaft of sunlight that was pouring in from the window, it performed its magic, turning into gold and flame all at once. She sighed, dropped the lock of hair, and cradled Richard in her arms.

He stirred in his sleep, mumbling something and clutching her tightly. It was a possessive gesture, and she revelled in it. She'd only have him for a few moments more. He'd awake and go back to the manor house, and she'd remain behind, making plans to marry Hugh and leave Harrowgate.

He nipped her shoulder, a playful little bite.

"Ow," she cried. "What do you think you're doing?"

"What do you think you're doing, woman," he growled, "pulling my hair like that?"

"I had to wake you up so you'd release me from your grip."

He raised his head and looked into her face, his blue eyes twinkling in the sunlight. "You want to be released?"

She studied him, his devilish smile and the dimple in his cheek, and his beauty stole her senses. So she shook her head, dumbly answering his question. No, she didn't want to be released.

"Still, one of us will have to get up," he said. "The fire's out, and I'm ravenous."

"You're always ravenous," she said, "in one way or another."

He grinned. "Yes, I suppose I am. And I further suppose I'd better earn my keep by getting some heat in here."

She shrugged, feigning indifference when in fact she ached to keep him right where he was. The sooner they got up and dressed, the sooner she'd have to tell him good-bye.

He slid out from under the covers, naked as the day he was born and handsomer than any human had a right to be. "Damn, it's cold," he cursed as soon as his feet hit the floor. He hopped about for a moment.

She couldn't help herself—she giggled, pulling the covers up under her chin and keeping warm herself. He found his trousers and pulled them on, buttoning them quickly and leaving the suspenders to dangle from the sides. Then he picked up his shirt and shrugged into it. He walked to the hearth, scooped up some kindling,

Waitangi Nights

and laid a fire. A live ember caught instantly, making a warm blaze to which he added more wood. "There, your ladyship. You can get your delicate toes out of bed now."

She threw back the covers and rose. Despite the renewed fire, the air still held a chill, and she shivered. Richard stared at her, his eyes wide with something like reverence. "Isabel," he whispered, "I don't think I'll ever get used to the sight of you."

She bent and searched the floor for her nightgown. She had to cover herself immediately so that he would stop looking at her. If he continued to gaze at her with that longing in his eyes, she'd never be able to let him leave. And she had to let him go, she had to.

She found the gown and lifted it over her head. With fingers clumsy from the cold, she buttoned the bodice as quickly as she could. Avoiding Richard's gaze, she glanced around for her wrapper. "I'll make us a pot of tea," she said.

"Never mind that," he answered. "Mrs. Willis will have an enormous breakfast waiting at the house. If she's forgiven our not appearing for dinner last night, of course."

She picked up her wrapper and slid her arms into it, still not daring to glance at Richard. "You go on up. I'll make myself something here."

"Don't be absurd."

"I have a great deal to do today."

"It can wait."

"No, it can't," she answered quietly. "I want to finish the repotting soon so that all will be in order for my replacement."

Silence greeted that—cold, stony silence. "What?" he said after a long moment.

She looked at him then and found pain mixed with disbelief in his eyes. "What replacement?" he demanded. "What in blazes are you talking about?"

"Hugh and I will be married soon," she answered

evenly. "You'll need a new nurseryman."

"No, I won't. You're not going anywhere."

"We both have obligations, Richard. Nothing's changed."

He ran his fingers through his hair, making it wild in his distraction. "How can you say that?"

"Very simply," she answered. "Nothing's changed."

"Well, I'll be damned." He stood and gaped at her, all shining beauty and little boy disappointment. "I've had no experience at all with virgins, I'll admit. But I thought that giving a man your innocence meant something."

"It does," she said. It did—it meant the world and more. Moisture welled up behind her eyes, and she fought it back. If she admitted to him just how much their loving meant to her, the tears would spill out, and she'd be lost.

"And still you'd leave me?" he demanded. "After everything we shared last night?"

"That was last night."

"Bloody hell." He pounded his fist against the mantlepiece. The blow didn't make much sound, flesh against stone, but it must have hurt like the devil. "And today?"

"Today you're the master of Harrowgate Manor," she managed to choke out. "And I'm engaged to Hugh Upton."

He ran his hand over his face, over his eyes and his mouth, and he began to tremble. Dear heaven, she couldn't stand to see him hurt. "You must understand. You have to protect yourself and your daughter. If that spirit is after me, my very presence endangers Bunny."

"But how can I protect you if you're not here?" he demanded. "I got you into this, after all."

"Most likely I'll be safe if I only leave Harrowgate. I can hardly picture a Maori devil haunting a little house in Paihia. In any case, protecting me will be Hugh's concern."

Waitangi Nights

"I won't be able to watch over you. I won't have any right. For the love of God Isabel, I won't even know if you're safe."

She threw her arms into the air. "But you told me I'd have to leave. Over and over. You told me."

"That was before last night."

Last night, last night, last night. What had she done? She thought she'd had everything planned, but once again Richard Julian defied understanding.

He crossed his arms over his chest. "You can't marry Upton in any case. You're not a virgin anymore."

"He doesn't expect a virgin," she answered. "He told me so."

"Jolly good for him," Richard snapped. "But I'll wager he doesn't expect a pregnant bride."

She covered her mouth with her fingers. "Pregnant," she gasped.

"You could be."

Of course, she could. Why on earth hadn't she thought of that? Richard's child, growing inside her. Dear heaven, if only that were true.

"You'd never be able to explain the timing to him," Richard went on. "Unless he beds you in the next week or so." His eyes grew wide. "Will he? Is that how you've planned it, going from me straight to him?"

"No! I haven't planned anything, I swear it," she exclaimed. "I just wanted you so much. So much I couldn't think."

"Well, now you have me. I won't hear any more talk about Hugh Upton."

"What am I to do? I can't stay here as your kept woman."

"You can stay here as my wife."

She reeled at the word. Wife? He wanted her to be his wife? "You're offering me marriage?"

He walked toward her, stopping only a foot away, towering over her. "I'm not offering it. I'm demanding it."

"But that's impossible."

He took her chin in his hand and pulled her face up to his, rivetting her with the fire of his gaze. "Why?"

"It isn't done."

"Bloody nonsense."

"The staff will never accept me," she said.

"They work for me, not the other way around."

What a fool she'd been, in more ways than one. She should have known he'd do this—propose marriage to her. As much as he liked to present himself as a rake, he was a decent man at heart. Now that he'd taken her virginity, he'd do the honorable thing, even if he didn't want to. But she couldn't let him marry her out of a sense of duty. She'd rather die.

He sighed. "I know I'm no great prize, despite my money. I've a foul mouth and a worse temper."

"Oh, no," she cried. "You're wonderful."

"And I have a daughter. Perhaps you don't relish sharing your husband with another woman's child."

"I adore Bunny," she answered. "I'd love for the three of us to live together as a family."

"Then I don't understand."

How could she explain, when she didn't understand herself? She wanted him so badly she could hardly breathe at times, and she loved him with a ferocity that shook her to her core. But how could she marry him, knowing that she'd trapped him into it?

"You're mine now, Isabel," he said softly, reaching out and stroking her cheek. "I can't lose you. Forgive my weakness, and stay with me."

"I would," she whispered. "I want to, only—"

"Only what?"

"You don't love me."

"Don't be silly. I've loved you since the moment I laid eyes on you."

Her breath caught. "You have?" she managed to whisper. "You love me?"

"Of course." He ran his thumb over her lower lip, and

Waitangi Nights

it began to tremble. "Haven't I told you?"

Her eyes misted over, blurring his image. She bit her lip and shook her head.

"What an ass I am, expecting you to read my mind," he went on. "I love you woman, and I think after some time you might even come to love me."

Laughter choked its way from her chest through a throat grown tight with tears. "Come to love you, you bloody great fool?"

He laughed, too, a hearty sound. "Such language."

"Come to love you?" She pounded his chest with her fist. "I've made myself sick with loving you."

"And so you became engaged to another man."

"I had to. I had to find some way to leave you because you didn't want me."

"What a pair you and I make—two pig-headed idiots." He glanced at the bed and grinned. "Damned lucky our bodies overruled our pride."

Warmth rose over her cheeks, and she smiled back.

"You'll marry me, then?" he asked.

"Try to stop me."

He straightened and opened his arms wide. She walked into his embrace and laid her head against his shoulder. His warmth, his scent enveloped her, and she burrowed her nose into his chest, listening to his heart beat. Her love, her life.

Her husband-to-be. Oh dear heaven, now she had two of them.

Chapter Eighteen

So, now he had a daughter and a fiancée to protect and damned little idea how to go about it. Richard opened the drawer of his desk and found the satin box he'd placed there, not so long ago, really, but so much had happened since. He'd discovered that Bunny wouldn't join her mother in madness but that another threat existed. One he'd been unable to conquer so far. He'd made some very brave noises to Isabel this morning—he'd always been good at making noises—but this time he'd bloody well have to follow through. He had to protect his daughter and his wife.

Dear God, his wife. He'd almost lost her, through her pride and his own. But he'd keep her with him now, and he'd ask for help from the devil himself if he had to. Pride be damned.

"Richard?" a voice said from the threshold.

"Ah, Sammy. Come in and sit down. I need your advice."

Sammy crossed the length of the study and took a

Waitangi Nights

seat on the other side of the desk. "Whatever you want."

Richard took a breath. "What do you know of this fellow Henga?"

Sammy thought for a moment. "He says he knows the spirits. Ngapuhis respect him."

"Do you think he can help us find that light and whatever's in it?"

Sammy shrugged. "Worth a try. Nothing else has worked."

That was certainly true. Night after night they'd gone searching, following the light and never getting any closer to it. It eluded them, coming first from this direction and then from that, never far away, but always unreachable.

"Ask him to come and talk to me, would you?" Richard said.

"Yes." Sammy rose from his chair.

"In a moment," Richard added. "I need your help with something else."

Sammy sat back down.

"Miss Gannon will be moving into my rooms."

Sammy's eyebrow went up. "Richard."

"We're going to be married."

Sammy reached across the desk and clapped Richard on the shoulder. "Great news, man. But then, I knew all along."

"Am I that transparent?"

"You always had an eye for each other," Sammy said, smiling rather more smugly than he ought. "Then, last night neither of you appeared for dinner. And you didn't sleep in your bed."

"I suppose the whole staff noticed."

Sammy didn't answer but just kept grinning. Richard groaned. Sammy patted him on the shoulder again. "Don't worry, man. We all understand."

"Even Mrs. Willis?"

"Ah now, she may be a bit hard."

"I want them to get along. Mrs. Willis has been so

275

Alice Gaines

good to me over the years." Richard sighed. "I don't know what I would have done if she hadn't looked after Bunny these last few days."

"She's glad to do it. She loves the two of you."

"I want her to love Miss Gannon . . . Isabel, too," Richard said. "See what you can do to urge Mrs. Willis to accept my wife, will you?"

"I knew it," Sammy crowed. "I knew that woman would be good for you."

"What in blazes are you talking about?"

"You're doing less shouting, more reaching to others for help. She'll make you into a new man."

"She may as well," Richard grumbled. "There was precious little to recommend the old one."

Sammy laughed outright at that.

"Now then, go find that Henga and tell him I want to see him."

Sammy's brow raised again.

"Oh very well," Richard said. "Ask him very respectfully if he would pay me a visit."

"That I'll do." Sammy rose, chuckling, crossed the room, and stepped into the hall.

Less shouting and more reaching, indeed. Perhaps Sammy was right. He was in no position to turn down help at this point. He had to solve the riddle of the *turehu* and make his family safe. And heaven help him, right this minute he had to devise a way to convince Isabel that she had to share his rooms, even before they married, and to stay, safely, with the household staff while he went off to do battle with Anui.

He removed the satin box from the drawer, opened it and removed the *tiki*. After setting the box aside, he studied the greenstone. Maybe the thing was a good luck charm. Maybe it could help Isabel to see sense.

He closed his hand around the carving, just as he heard her approaching. He recognized her step now, that quick, light tread. Sure enough, she appeared at the doorway. She stepped inside and smiled at him.

Waitangi Nights

His heart nearly burst with love and pride. How on earth had he ever earned this woman's love? Her trust? That serenity he'd noticed at the first, that inner confidence, somehow she'd bestowed them on him. She'd granted him the serenity of knowing he was loved, and she'd given him the confidence that whatever obstacles lay ahead, whatever dragons he had to kill, he could best them. With her love and faith and strength he could do anything. What had he ever done to deserve her?

"What are you thinking?" she asked quietly.

"I'm thinking that you're the most beautiful woman on the face of the earth."

She laughed. "We'd best have you some spectacles made, then."

"Come here."

She did as she was told, for once, approaching the desk, her gaze never leaving his face, as though she couldn't get enough of the sight of him.

"Now, turn around and close your eyes," he ordered.

She did that, too, miracle of miracles. He rose and walked to her, stretching the delicate chain with its pendant out between his hands as he did. Once beside her, he hesitated only briefly to enjoy the scent of her hair and then slipped the necklace around her throat and fastened the clasp.

Her eyes still closed, she searched her chest until she found the jade charm and studied it with her fingertips. "The *tiki*," she exclaimed.

"No reason for you not to have it now," he answered.

She opened her eyes and turned to face him. "Oh, Richard, I love it. I've loved it, and you, since the night you gave it to me."

He slipped his finger under her chin and tipped her face up to his. "And you trust me? Completely?"

"Of course."

"Then do something for me. Move into the house, into my rooms."

"Richard—" she started to say. But he put his thumb over her lips, stilling her.

"I'm not doing this to control you, or even to satisfy my lust." She blushed very prettily at that. "Although I do plan to satisfy my lust whenever you'll allow me," he said. "It's for your safety."

"But what will the others think?"

"That's truly unimportant, my love. All that matters is that I don't lose you. I don't think I'd endure it."

"Oh, Richard."

He pulled her into his arms, stroking her back and holding her as close to him as physically possible. "Please, Isabel. Just do it. Stay with me. Let me protect you."

"I say," came a voice from the doorway. A man's voice. "What's this? What in hell is this?"

Hugh. Isabel pulled herself out of Richard's embrace and looked toward the threshold. Hugh stood there, his eyes wide, his face rapidly reddening.

"What's going on here?" Hugh demanded. His gaze travelled from Richard to her, accusation clear in his eyes. "Bella?"

"How did you get in here, Upton?" Richard asked.

"Your man let me in. Seems a decent chap," Hugh answered his voice rising. "Probably didn't realize you were . . . were . . . what were you doing?"

"We . . ." Isabel began. But she didn't finish. That sentence didn't have any decent end.

She'd have liked to slip between the floorboards. Hugh was such a dear, and now he had to learn that the woman he'd loved and trusted had betrayed him with another man. She'd have done anything to spare him the pain of that discovery, but he'd found out about her infidelity in the most humiliating, crushing manner imaginable. If only she could wish the last few minutes away. But she couldn't, and the clock continued ticking the seconds out, sounding very loud in the stillness of the room.

Waitangi Nights

Hugh's gaze wandered from Isabel back to Richard, the fierce glint in his eyes growing even keener. "Damn it, man, you had your arms around my fiancée," Hugh thundered. "I think you owe me an explanation."

"Try to understand, Hugh," Isabel begged. "Try to forgive us."

"Forgive what?" Hugh demanded. "Is there more here than I've already seen?"

Richard ran his fingers into his hair. "There's a great deal more," he answered. "We're in love with each other."

"Love," Hugh repeated, his face twisting with the word. "Love, Bella?"

She crossed her arms over her chest and hugged herself tightly. "I'm so sorry, Hugh," she whispered. "I never meant—"

"I don't blame you, my darling," Hugh said. "You wouldn't be untrue." He stared into her eyes, tearing her heart to pieces. "You couldn't, not you."

"Don't say that, please."

"This bounder, on the other hand," Hugh continued, gesturing toward Richard with an angry sweep of his arm. "This fine fellow is notorious all over North and South Islands."

Richard straightened and glared at Hugh. "I know you're upset, Upton, but take care what you say," he warned.

"Livvie's tried to put a good face on your past behavior, Julian, decent soul that she is, but I can always spot your sort."

"And what sort is that?" Richard replied quietly, all too quietly.

"The sort who treat women like playthings," Hugh declared. "Is that how you get these little cousins of yours? By toying with other men's fiancées?"

"Really, Hugh," Isabel gasped.

"Everyone knows the child is his daughter. By a woman he didn't have the decency to marry." Hugh turned on Richard. "Is that what you have planned for Bella? Genteel prostitution?"

"You have every right to be angry," Richard said evenly. "So I'm going to forget your last few remarks."

"Damned sporting of you," Hugh snarled. "I ought to take you out right now and pound your face to a pulp."

Richard's hand curled into a fist by his side. "One more insult and I'll give you the pleasure of trying."

"Stop it," Isabel ordered. "Both of you."

Hugh turned to her, pain and disappointment clear in his eyes. "How could you do this?" he asked. "After all the plans we made."

"You made the plans, Hugh. I only agreed to them."

He stiffened, reeling backward as though he'd been hit with a physical blow. "Why?" he said. "If you didn't believe in me, Bella, didn't want to share my dreams, why did you agree?"

"To make you happy," she answered. Oh God, that sounded terrible. But it was true. Everything she'd done, had promised, had been what she'd thought she ought to do, to promise. And now Hugh would pay for her dishonesty. "I'm sorry. I'm so sorry."

"Has Julian had his way with you?" he said.

"Bloody hell," Richard muttered.

"Has he?" Hugh repeated.

Isabel couldn't answer, so she just looked at Hugh, at his warm brown eyes, once so full of trust and hope, now full of anger and disappointment. She looked at him, and words wouldn't come.

"I see," he said from between clenched teeth. "Damn, I see."

"It isn't her fault," Richard said.

"I know that perfectly well," Hugh replied, glaring at Richard. "This is all your responsibility, and you'll do the honorable thing by her, or I'll throttle you."

"Of course, I will," Richard replied. "We'll be married as soon as possible."

Hugh turned back to her. "Is this what you want,

Waitangi Nights

Bella? Do you want to marry him?"

She straightened and looked Hugh in the eye. "Yes," she answered. "I love him."

"All right," Hugh gritted, setting his jaw. "But don't expect him to look pretty for the wedding. I'm going to push his nose into his face. Right now."

"Don't be an ass," Richard answered.

Hugh lifted his fists and assumed a boxer's pose. "Come on, Julian, act like a man. Or is seducing women your only understanding of manhood?"

Fury flashed in Richard's eyes briefly. Then they narrowed into an glare. "I don't want to hurt you," he answered, his voice as cold as ice. "You being the aggrieved party and all."

"Don't worry about that," Hugh snapped. "I can thrash you in here or out of doors if you prefer. Which'll it be?"

"Don't, Hugh," Isabel begged. "That won't prove anything."

"Come on," Hugh urged. "Which?"

Richard shrugged out of his jacket and tossed it onto the desk. "Outdoors, I think."

"Richard, no," she cried. "Both of you, don't. Please."

Just then a piercing shriek rang out. A woman's voice. After only an instant, it sounded again. "God help us."

Clarice. Dear heaven, it was Clarice. In the kitchen, if Isabel could make out the direction correctly.

Richard flew from the room. Isabel followed him, Hugh hot on her heels, down the hallway and into the kitchen. When she got there, the reason for the shouts became abundantly clear. Mrs. Willis lay in a heap, unconscious, beside the main work table. Clarice hovered over her, and Richard knelt beside her, pulling her to a sitting position. Her eyes fluttered open but didn't focus.

Richard shook her gently. "What's happened, Mrs. Willis?"

She rested a hand on his shoulder. "I don't know, sir. One moment the little miss and I . . ."

"Bunny," he said quietly, but there was no mistaking the panic in his voice. "Where's Bunny?"

Mrs. Willis glanced around the room, her eyes still glazed over. "She's here. Isn't she?"

"No," Richard said. "Dammit, she's not here."

"But where could she be?" Mrs. Willis asked. "She knows she's not to leave me even for an instant."

"Oh, Lord," Clarice cried, clutching her fist to her breast. "God help us."

Isabel spotted the thing first. No one else seemed to notice it. A pile of feathers, splotched with blood, sat on the table. "Richard, look," she said, pointing.

He rose and looked where she indicated, and his face registered revulsion. "Dear God," he said. "It's a *tui*, and its heart has been punctured."

"What in blazes is going on here?" Hugh whispered by Isabel's side.

She ought to tell him, ought to explain. But in truth she'd slipped out of the scene, as though she were standing off to one side, observing but not able to participate. The music, that was it, the flutes. Couldn't the rest of them hear?

She looked around her. Everything seemed unreal, as though seen through water. Every detail shone clearly, more clearly in fact than possible in everyday existence. Magnified by something.

It was light. The light was in the room, along with the flutes. Why couldn't the others see, hear?

Richard swam in it, only a few steps away but unreachable. He ran his fingers through his hair, casting about him in desperation, as though Bunny were only hiding in a corner of the room. But Bunny wasn't here, Isabel knew that.

"See here, man," Hugh said, "I don't know what's happened, but if your little girl has run off somewhere, we'd best organize a search party."

Waitangi Nights

"She hasn't run off, Upton," Richard shouted. "She's been taken."

Hugh's eyes widened. "How do you know that?"

"Bloody hell, don't you think I'd know? Something's been after her. Something horrible. It has her, and I don't know what it'll do to her."

"I say, then," Hugh said. "All the more reason to move quickly."

Richard looked at Hugh, as though seeing him for the first time. He seemed to regain his senses. "You're right. I'll round up my staff. You see what help you can get in town."

"Right you are." Hugh hurried from the room. He must have hurried, but to Isabel his motions appeared more like a slow dance than the pace of a man on an urgent mission.

Whatever had happened to her, whatever the light had done to her senses, she had to get to Richard and comfort him. She managed to get her feet to move finally and walked toward him, finally reaching up to place her palm between his shoulder blades. "We'll find her."

He turned and looked down at her, pure panic in his eyes. "We have to. Oh God, we have to."

Clarice helped a very shaky Mrs. Willis to her feet. "Don't you worry, sir," Mrs. Willis said. "We'll find whoever took her, and then they'll have me to answer to."

Samuel appeared in the doorway. Henga stood right behind him. "Richard, what's happened?" Samuel asked.

"Bunny's gone, and we found this," Richard answered, gesturing toward the dead *tui*. "Does Henga know anything about it?"

Samuel said a few words to Henga in Maori, and the man entered the room. He looked around carefully, as though the corners of his eyes might catch something the others had missed. After a few steps, he stopped and turned his head, now this way, now that. Then he

Alice Gaines

looked Isabel full in the face.

Dear heaven, he saw the light. He heard the music. None of the others sensed them, but Henga did. A dreaded recognition passed between them. They both knew who the chief *turehu*, Anui, wanted. Anui wanted her.

After a moment, he approached the work table and glanced down at the *tui*. He lifted it, and its head hung limply on its chest, brushing the area splotched with blood. Richard had been right, it appeared. The bird's heart had been punctured.

Henga grunted and dropped the bird back to the work surface. "Anui," he said.

"Damn," Richard growled.

Henga spoke to Samuel for a moment, and Samuel turned to Richard. "He says Anui took the little miss and left this in exchange."

"He did, did he?" Mrs. Willis said, her eyes narrowing. "You get that Anui, sir, and bring him back to me. I'll show him the sharp edge of my cleaver, that I will."

"Ask Henga if he'll help us," Richard said. "We have to find Bunny. We have to save my little girl."

Samuel spoke to Henga again, and Henga nodded in agreement.

"Good then, gather the men and meet me outside," Richard ordered. "Hurry!"

Samuel guided Henga from the room, and Richard turned to Isabel. "I want you to stay with the others, preferably two or three at all times. Don't set foot outside the house."

"But you don't understand," she answered. He didn't. He wouldn't be able to find Anui, because Anui didn't want him. Anui wanted her. Only she could follow the light, follow the music of the flutes. Only she could find Bunny.

"I mean it, Isabel." Richard took her head between his palms and pulled her face up to his, none too gently. He glared into her eyes. "If I'm to concentrate on the

Waitangi Nights

search, I need to know you're safe. Now, stay here."

"But—"

"For once, do as I say," he ordered. "Promise me."

She didn't answer. He didn't see the light and wouldn't understand.

It was evening before Isabel was able to escape the others and their inquisitive looks. All day she'd been keenly aware that every eye was on her. From the minute Richard had ordered her to stay inside, Mrs. Willis had watched her with a combination of curiosity and hostility on her face. Clarice, on the other hand, seemed more protective, as though her constant hovering could keep Isabel safe. No matter. She'd remained wrapped in her cocoon of light, knowing that one way or another, she'd find an opportunity to get away from them.

The opportunity had come when Clarice stepped out to bring in some washing. Mrs. Willis was so busy preparing dinner for all the people from town who were helping with the search, she'd forgotten she was to stand guard over the upstart Miss Gannon. When she'd disappeared into the larder for several minutes, Isabel had simply put down the vegetables she was paring and slipped out of the kitchen. She'd made good her escape, walking over the grounds until she was well out of sight of the house.

Now she stood, her shawl wrapped around her, under a clump of red pines, and waited for the last rays of sun to give way to darkness. In that darkness she could best find the direction of the light, and night's silence would reveal the source of the music. She'd have Bunny back before dawn.

The sound of flutes came to her. Softly at first. Odd how the music had seemed eerie when she first heard it. The tone was lovely, actually, haunting. Not exactly like a European flute, more like something produced out of bamboo, with breathy, complex overtones.

Darkness overcame the sunlight slowly, stretching

out shadows across the meadow before her, until the trees in the distance grew indistinct in their detail. The light glowed from behind them, and a mist appeared, whispering through the trees and creeping over the meadow toward her.

She smiled. The mist had come to guide her. The others could search all they wanted. They'd never find that mist. It had come for her and her alone. She headed toward it, first at a brisk walk and then at a run.

Chapter Nineteen

The canoe made its way over the bay with no help from its human occupants. Richard sat in silence between Henga in front of him and Sammy behind. Whatever magic guided their little boat, it had better take them to Anui. The *turehu* chief had somehow gotten Isabel, too, and Richard couldn't possibly survive losing both of them.

What had possessed her to set off on her own? She knew Anui wanted her even more than he wanted Bunny, and yet, she'd slipped away some time before dark. If they hadn't found her shawl in the meadow, they wouldn't even have known what direction she'd gone in.

That had been over an hour ago, and now, here he sat in a canoe that propelled itself somehow, prepared to carry out a rescue that might have been orchestrated by a lunatic, and under the complete command of a shaman he had only met a few days before. He had no choice in the matter, no blasted choice at all.

Alice Gaines

Waves lapped against the side of the canoe, setting up a gentle rhythm to underscore the music of the flutes. The unearthly sound grew stronger as they got farther and farther out onto the bay, leaving behind Paihia and any semblance of the ordinary world. The canoe answered with its own song, vibrating out of the very wood it was fashioned from. The magic was impossible and yet undeniable. It was Richard's only hope that he'd find his daughter and the woman he loved.

He glanced over his shoulder toward Sammy. "How does Henga do this?" he whispered.

"Not Henga," Sammy answered. "The wood is *tipua*, enchanted. From a log that used to float the rivers, singing to anyone who could listen. Henga captured the log and made it into this canoe."

"I didn't think you believed any of the folklore," Richard said.

"I didn't."

Richard turned and studied Henga's back. The man hadn't moved since they'd left the shoreline of the bay.

Richard hated having to depend on all the hocus-pocus. Singing logs. Canoes that didn't need to be paddled. Witch doctors who spoke no more than two words an hour. It all went against everything he knew about reality. But good, old-fashioned beating the bushes with dozens of men had gotten him nothing, and he had no choice but to follow Henga's instructions to the letter.

The canoe approached a small island, little more than a hill sticking up out of the water, indistinguishable from the dozens of other tiny islands that dotted the bay. The canoe emitted a high-pitched note that sounded for all the world like a greeting. The island answered with a fanfare of flutes. Richard could have sworn just a moment ago that the music had been coming from another direction. Then the top of the hill began to glow, giving off the light that Richard had seen from Bunny's window the night they'd first seen the *tur-*

Waitangi Nights

ehu. The light he and his men had followed nearly every night since then.

"Look at that," Sammy whispered from behind Richard. "*Tipua* brought us where good sense couldn't."

Indeed, it had. As much as Richard would have denied it only days before, some enchantment was at work here. Was it completely and utterly evil? And if so, had it already destroyed the two people he loved most in the world? No, it couldn't have. He wouldn't allow himself to think in those directions. Henga had said that Anui wanted Bunny as a pet. She'd be here, and he'd get her away.

But what did Anui want of Isabel? Henga hadn't volunteered that little bit of information. If he wanted from her what mortal men wanted from women, who knew what the foul creature might have done to her?

That didn't matter. If she were alive, nothing else mattered. Richard would take her home and care for her. He'd make her well. He'd been precious little use to anyone in his life, but he'd heal Isabel. He'd erase any memories she had of horror and replace them with new, joyous ones. So help him, he would.

The canoe circled around the island, revealing a tiny beach. Another canoe rested on the sand, also oarless, like the one they rode in. Was this how Bunny and Isabel had arrived, guided as they had been, by *tipua*?

The canoe beached itself and fell oddly silent, as though it hadn't been singing in the first place. Richard jumped out, landing in a foot of bay water. Sammy and Henga did the same. Henga grabbed the prow of the canoe and pulled it farther onto the beach, anchoring it there. After all, it was their only way back to the rational world.

Henga retrieved his greenstone warclub from the canoe and padded silently up the beach. Richard reached inside and grabbed the two bags he'd prepared according to Henga's instructions. One held a tub of red ochre and the other cooked food, *kumara*, a dozen or so of the fleshy tubers. Preposterous weapons, but absolutely essential, if Henga was to be believed. Mrs. Willis hadn't seemed to suffer the same skepticism that Richard had. She hadn't even remarked on having to cook for a rescue but had gone about the preparation as though it was the last meal she'd ever make.

Henga crouched where he was and motioned for Sammy and Richard to join him. Richard squatted in front of him and watched as the man reached into one of the sacks and pulled out the ochre. With one hand he tipped Richard's head roughly up toward the light. The other he smeared into the ochre, coating his fingers with the stuff.

He turned Richard's head one way and painted circles over his forehead, cheek, and chin. Then he tilted Richard's face the other way and repeated the process. Finally, he scrutinized his work and grunted in what sounded like approval. He released Richard and turned to Sammy, who had dropped to his own knees in front of the magician.

Richard rose, stretching his legs, and surveyed what he could see of the island. The hill rose steeply in front of him but should be possible to scale. He could barely make out a palisade of sapling trunks at the top. It was Anui's pa, or fortification, with his own daughter and his fiancée held prisoner.

He glanced over toward the beach. Henga had finished adorning Sammy's face, who for the first time resembled a fearsome Maori warrior. He was grateful that underneath the paint was his childhood friend, a trusted ally who had seen him through adventure and tragedy. He'd never needed Sammy's help more than he did right now.

Henga smeared his own chest with the ochre and put it back into its sack, lifted the other bag, and handed it to Sammy. Without a word, he turned and headed up the hill, signalling them to follow.

The footing was loose, making their ascent a scram-

Waitangi Nights

ble. But an occasional skitter of a falling pebble didn't cause the music to diminish as it would if someone or something were listening for the approach of three ochre-painted men. In fact, the closer they got to the summit, the louder the flutes became, and singing could clearly be made out, the same unholy, disembodied song that Richard had heard coming from Bunny's bedroom. How on earth could he have ever thought that his precious daughter had made those sounds?

At the top of the hill, the climb eased, and the *pa* came more clearly into view. It appeared clumsily constructed, saplings tied together loosely with vines. Anui must have felt confident that none would dare attempt an assault on his stronghold, for the fortification wouldn't hold out against any type of war party. More likely, Anui depended on magic of the sort that had allowed him to send the search parties off in all the wrong directions.

Behind the last clump of sheltering shrubs, Henga crouched again, and Richard and Sammy joined him. The man whispered in Maori for a moment. Richard turned to Sammy for the translation.

"He says Anui will be feasting."

"I hope Henga didn't bring us here just to deliver the meal."

"*Turehus* don't eat cooked food," Sammy replied. "Henga says that dead *tui* Anui left in the kitchen would have been his meal."

Dear God, and this vile creature had his daughter? "So, what are the *kumara* for?"

Sammy repeated the question to Henga, who answered briefly in Maori. "He says the spirits are afraid of two things, cooked food and the red-ochre. He plans to send the *turehus* into confusion by tossing the *kumara* into the compound. Then we can follow inside."

"Does he know if Isabel and Bunny are safe?"

Sammy spoke to Henga briefly, who replied in even fewer words. "He says he doesn't know everything."

Alice Gaines

Hell. Bloody hell.

Henga said a few more sentences, performing a pantomime as he did, aping the motions of dipping his fingers into something and then smearing his hands over his face.

"He says that when we find Bunny and Miss Gannon, you're to do as he did to us," Sammy volunteered. "Put as much red ochre as you can on them. It will protect them."

"All right. Tell him I'm ready."

Sammy repeated that in Maori, and Henga nodded to Richard. Crouching low, he covered the distance between the shrubs and the compound, finally hunching down just outside the palisade, at what appeared to be a door. Richard picked up the sack holding the ochre and joined him. Sammy made up the rear with the food. On a hand signal from Henga, Sammy reached into the sack, removed a tuber, and tossed it over the top of the palisade. That finally got the attention of the beings inside, and the music and laughter stopped abruptly, only to be replaced by shrieks equally as inhuman as the singing had been.

Henga slid his arm along a sapling, apparently searching for the door's closure, as Sammy tossed a few more *kumara*. Richard clutched the bag with the ochre to him and waited for a signal, for Henga to get the door open, for some sound that would tell him his loved ones were inside the compound and still alive. Anything.

Sammy continued to throw cooked food into the enclosure, and the din inside swelled. Henga continued to battle with the vines and saplings that formed a gateway. The single obstacle keeping them outside. How long would the presence of the *kumara* hold the creatures at bay? Would they overcome their initial shock and regroup? Might they be murdering Bunny and Isabel right now? Damn it, if Henga didn't get that door open in another minute, Richard would tear it open with his bare hands.

Waitangi Nights

Finally, Henga managed to flip up some unseen fastening on the inside and pull open the door. Richard crashed past him into the *pa* and searched it frantically for Isabel and Bunny. All he saw were hideous creatures, just like the one he'd surprised in the nursery that night. Dozens of them, some male and some female. All had garish red hair, skin the color of moonlight, and no light of humanity in their colorless eyes. They cowered, huddled together in groups, trying to crawl under each other as he turned his painted red face toward them.

"Richard," came a faint cry from behind him. Isabel, oh God, Isabel.

He turned and found her, sitting in a corner with her back propped against the palisade. Bunny was in her lap. He flew to her and dropped to his knees, fumbling with the sack. Finally, he got the pot of ochre out and shoved it into her hands.

"Put as much of this on you as you can," he ordered. He dipped his own fingers into the stuff and then painted Bunny's face with it.

"Thank heaven you've come," she answered, clutching Bunny to her and looking around frantically. "I knew you would. I knew you would."

He stopped his work on Bunny and ran his hand over Isabel's face. "Here, my love, like this."

She came around finally, as she dug her hands into the pot and began to apply the ochre to her own face, leaving Richard free to finish with Bunny.

"Samuel," Isabel cried.

Richard glanced over his shoulder. Sammy and Henga had entered the compound, and Henga now stood brandishing his warclub and sticking his tongue out in the traditional warrior's expression. He chanted something guttural and nearly as frightening as the sounds of the spirits around him. The beings still held themselves away in a trembling, moaning knot, but who knew how long that would last?

"We have to get out of here quickly," Richard said. "Can you walk?"

Isabel nodded.

"Up with you, then." He rose, pulling her to her feet, and took Bunny from her. Isabel wobbled and steadied herself against him. Richard finally looked at his daughter, really looked at her. She hadn't stirred or made a sound since he'd found her. She appeared to be asleep. What had they done to her?

The moaning behind him stilled, leaving a silence that was louder than the earlier commotion. He turned, holding tightly to his daughter. The *turehus* parted, slinking back against the palisade. A lone figure emerged at their center.

Anui. The thing had to be the leader. He had the same appearance, the same unnaturally pale skin and eyes, the same flame of hair. But he didn't shrink from the humans and their weapons. Instead, he walked, very cautiously in Richard's direction. One slow step at a time.

Henga jumped in his path, raised his warclub, and issued a series of deep shouts that might have been a predator's bark. That stopped Anui, as his eyes widened, and he bared his teeth and growled.

"Get out," Sammy shouted. "Now, Richard."

Clutching Bunny in one arm and Isabel's hand in the other, Richard made for the gate. They reached it and left the *pa*, Sammy and Henga hot on their heels. Sammy stopped just for a moment and laid the rest of the *kumara* across the threshold, blocking the *turehus'* exit. The four of them scrambled down the hillside, Richard carrying Bunny.

They found the canoe at the beach. It was humming again in an agitated rhythm, as though resonating with the discord still audible from above. Richard climbed in and sat on the bottom this time, cradling Bunny in his lap. Isabel joined him quickly, and he slipped an arm around her. He had his family back now, and he'd

Waitangi Nights

hold them as close to him as humanly possible.

Sammy and Henga pushed the canoe off the sand and jumped inside. Henga uttered a brief chant, singing softly to the canoe, and it headed out over the bay.

Isabel began to tremble, shivering. Richard stroked her roughly. She felt so cold, even through the cotton of her dress.

"Bunny hasn't moved once since I found her," she said between chattering teeth. "She's breathing, and her heart's beating, but she hasn't moved."

"Hush, my darling. We'll get her back home to her own little bed."

"You don't understand, Richard. Anui can charm his victim. I'd never have left without you except that I was under his spell. You must know that." She looked up at him, begging with her eyes. "I'd never have left you."

He pulled her head down onto his shoulder. "I know."

"They tried . . ." she began in a tiny voice, muttering into his neck.

"What did they try, my love?"

She shivered again, a tremor running along the length of her body. "They tried to make me eat . . . oh dear God. They tried to make me eat the raw flesh of a bird. I watched them kill the poor creature. They speared it with their long fingernails. Horrible."

"That's all over now. You're safe."

"I resisted." She pulled away and looked up at him. "No matter how deep the trance Anui had me under, I wouldn't do that."

"Hush."

"But Richard, what if they succeeded with Bunny?"

Richard gazed down at his daughter. She looked normal enough, as though just sleeping. But why wouldn't she wake up?

Isabel pulled the nursery door closed behind her, tugged her shawl tightly around her shoulders, and headed toward the kitchen. The longest, hottest bath of her life had failed to warm her through, but maybe a cup of tea could fix that. And she'd bring one back to Richard. He wouldn't leave Bunny's side until she came around.

Along the corridor she went, and down the back stairs. All the nights she'd walked these hallways before Richard had had her cottage fixed. They all seemed so long ago. Dinners with him and laughter, delightfully indecent jesting that she'd known she should object to but somehow never found the desire to stop.

The laughter was gone now, replaced by the haunted look she'd seen in his eyes when she'd first caught him prowling the house. Without even knowing what she'd been about, she'd banished the darkness from his eyes. But it had returned now, with a vengeance. If Bunny didn't recover she'd never rid him of the sorrow again, and she did want her devilish lover back. She needed him as much as he needed her.

She found herself at the kitchen door, not even aware of having reached it. A light came from inside, just the normal, human variety. But in the middle of the night, who would be awake?

Isabel looked inside and found Mrs. Willis. Of course. No one else would venture into the kitchen without Mrs. Willis's permission. She turned as Isabel entered, and studied her, her expression unreadable. "Can I do something for you, miss?"

"I thought I'd make a pot of tea."

"I'll do it," Mrs. Willis answered. "You're to be the lady of the house, I hear. I'll be working for you."

"Quite."

"Before you are, then, while we're still both employees, I'll speak my mind," Mrs. Willis answered. "If that's all right with you."

"Certainly." Isabel crossed her hands in front of her skirts and waited.

Mrs. Willis indicated a chair by the work table. "Please, sit down."

Waitangi Nights

Isabel walked to it and sat. Mrs. Willis pulled up another chair and joined her, finally resting her arms on the table top.

"I've been horrid to you, and I'm very sorry for that," she said after a moment.

Isabel's mouth dropped open. "No, you haven't."

"That's very kind of you. But I have. I hope you'll accept my apology and an explanation."

Isabel sat, speechless. With all the possibilities she'd entertained—silence, dismissal, disapproval—she'd never expected an apology.

"I just couldn't stand to see Mr. Richard hurt again," Mrs. Willis continued. "The other one—"

"Louisa?"

"Rest her soul," Mrs. Willis answered. "I know I shouldn't speak ill of the dead, but that woman and her madness near to tore Mr. Richard apart. The elder Mr. Julian only made matters worse. He seemed to enjoy her falling apart, as though it was some sort of judgment against his son." She snorted softly. "He was big on judgments, that one."

"Richard's told me very little about his father," Isabel said.

"I wouldn't have stayed in that man's household at all," Mrs. Willis went on, "if it hadn't been for Mr. Richard when he was a child. I can always get a good position, you know. A competent cook is hard to find."

"We're very lucky to have you," Isabel answered.

Mrs. Willis huffed. "I hope you won't take to flattering me," she said. "I can't abide flattery."

"No, ma'am," Isabel said.

The cook's features softened. "If only you'd seen the master when he was a lad. Such a scamp, into everything. But you couldn't stay angry with him, not after he looked at you out of those blue eyes. How they sparkled."

"They still do."

Mrs. Willis cleared her throat. "I was all he had when

297

was little, the poor mite. His father badgered him mercilessly, and his mother did nothing to stop it. Then Sammy came, and at least he had a friend."

"Samuel?" Isabel asked.

"Mr. Richard found him someplace, by the side of the road, he said. Sammy seemed to have no one, so we kept him."

"That's why Samuel and Richard are so close," Isabel said. "They spent their childhoods together."

"Sammy worshiped Mr. Richard. Followed him everywhere. Got him out of more than one scrape, I can tell you. They grew up to be two of the finest men you'd ever hope to see."

"You should have seen them fighting Anui," Isabel said. "Along with Henga. The three of them were so brave."

"You were very brave to go after the little miss."

"To the contrary," Isabel said. "That was very foolhardy of me, but I didn't seem to have much control over my actions."

"But you found her and kept her safe."

"Did I?" Isabel sighed. "I wonder."

Mrs. Willis paused, and her chin began to tremble. "Do you think she'll recover?"

Isabel reached over and squeezed Mrs. Willis' hand. "Of course, she will. She must."

"She's such a tiny thing, and Mr. Richard loves her so." Mrs. Willis studied their intertwined hands in silence for a moment. "If she doesn't come back to us, it'll kill him."

"Then we'll just have to make sure she does come back."

Mrs. Willis looked into Isabel's face. "You're good for him, miss. I should have seen that from the first. You truly love him."

"He's easy to love."

"He needs taking care of, too," Mrs. Willis said. "All men do."

"We can do that together."

"That we can." Mrs. Willis dropped Isabel's hand and swiped at her eyes. "The thing's still out there, isn't it?"

"Yes. I can hear it yet, very faintly. Can you?"

Mrs. Willis cocked her head. "With me it's more a knowing than a hearing."

Isabel rose, pulling her shawl around her and walked to the window. The glow still hovered near the horizon, no brighter or dimmer than the first time she'd seen it. Anui was out there, and he'd send his mist for her again, or perhaps he'd come in person. She shuddered. "I should leave here," she said softly. "It's me he wants. That's what Henga said."

"No," Mrs. Willis protested instantly. She joined Isabel, sliding an arm around her waist. "We couldn't protect you if you did that."

"But I might be able to draw Anui away."

"Now, don't go talking that way, miss. When he comes, we'll be ready for him. You have family now."

Isabel turned and gazed into Mrs. Willis' face. "Thank you."

"Besides," Mrs. Willis said, "the filthy beast hasn't felt the edge of my cleaver yet."

Isabel rapped softly and then nudged the nursery door open. Richard sat on the edge of the bed, as if he hadn't moved so much as a finger the entire time she'd been in the kitchen. She set the tray on Bunny's dresser, poured a cup of tea, and took it to him. "Drink this," she ordered.

He took the cup from her and just stared into it. "Nothing," he said. "She doesn't answer to her name. I even pinched her, and she didn't jump."

Isabel looked at Bunny where she lay, absolutely still, as though death had already claimed her. The bed had always seemed so small before, but now Bunny appeared lost in it. And the lambs on the headboard mocked the poor humans about them with painted-on innocence. What if nothing ever changed? Would those lambs stand perpetual guard over a child hovering somewhere between life and not-life?

Enough of such thoughts. They wouldn't help Bunny *or* Richard. "What did the doctor say?" she asked.

"He said he didn't know what was wrong." Richard closed his eyes. "Oh God, Isabel, she's so cold."

Isabel shuddered in spite of all her good intentions. She knew that cold, still felt it in her bones. She didn't remember much of her hours in the *turehus'* compound. She had fleeting images, and none of them were pleasant. How much had Bunny seen?

"Did you tell the doctor what happened to her?" she said.

Richard opened his eyes again and shook his head. "He already knew she'd been abducted. Upton had half of Paihia out looking for her. A decent fellow. You'd have married him if I hadn't stolen your innocence."

She put her hand on his shoulder. "And I'd have been miserable spending the rest of my life without you."

"And what are you now?" he asked, his voice barely audible.

"What I am is worried about Bunny." She took a breath. "So, the doctor isn't to know about Anui?"

"I hardly know how to explain Anui to a Christian man of science. Henga will do the witch doctoring. He's rather good at it."

Isabel sat on the bed beside him. "And what does Henga think?"

"Henga thinks Anui's bewitched her. He said some incantation or other, but it didn't work. He thinks it'll come down to a confrontation, and we'll have to kill the monster to save Bunny."

"Then that's what we'll do."

Chapter Twenty

Isabel stood at the nursery window, watching the light and listening to the distant sound of flutes, flutes that also played inside her own skull. Tonight. Anui would come tonight.

She turned and gazed at Richard where he sat on the edge of Bunny's bed. Three days had passed, and he'd only left his daughter's side long enough to care for the most basic needs. He hadn't washed and hadn't eaten. He'd slept for only a few moments at a time. He'd grown haggard and unkempt, three days worth of beard giving the contours of his face a ragged look. Most likely, he'd cried more than a few tears when no one else was around to see them.

Her Richard. Her dear, dear Richard. Whatever was to happen, he wouldn't have to wait long now.

She walked to him and put her arms around his shoulders, pulling his face against her breast and stroking his hair. "It's time, my darling," she whispered.

He pulled back and looked up at her. "Anui?"

Alice Gaines

She didn't answer but merely nodded.

He ran his fingers through his hair. "No. Hell and damnation, no."

"Richard, we've discussed this."

"I don't like the plan," he said. "It puts you in too much danger."

"There's no other way. Anui is going to come for me. We have to be prepared."

He stared down at Bunny, and his jaw clenched. "I can't lose both of you," he whispered. "I can't."

A soft rapping came at the door. Clarice stood on the threshold, her brown eyes wide. "Samuel says that Henga fellow wants you, sir. And Miss Gannon."

Richard didn't move for a moment, he hardly seemed to breathe. Finally, he bent over slowly and pressed a kiss to Bunny's forehead. Then he straightened and cleared his throat. "Tell Sammy we're on our way."

"Yes, sir." Clarice didn't leave but stood in the doorway, her eyes downcast. "Mr. Richard?"

He rose from the bed. "Yes, Clarice."

"I'm frightened, sir."

"Run and get Ned, then," he said softly. "We can wait with Bunny until you get back."

Clarice curtsied, and then left. Isabel turned to Richard and walked into his arms.

The pleasure of his embrace still astounded her. The joy of being held, the warmth, the pure privilege of having his love—it all amazed her. It felt as though she'd found one last, unopened Christmas present, only to discover it paled all the others in its beauty and worth. Every time Richard held her, she found something else to cherish about the man, something to hold next to her heart. Whatever waited for her outside tonight, she'd have that. No matter what her fate, she could confront it, knowing that in this lifetime she'd been well and truly loved.

She tipped her face up to his, to study it one last time. She found her brave and beautiful pirate gazing back

Waitangi Nights

at her, with his dazzling blue eyes and impossible hair. The last several days had frayed him a bit around the edges, but he was still the most beautiful man in the world. And he loved her.

He bent and brushed his lips over hers. He let the kiss linger, as though it had to hold an eternity of loving in it. Isabel leaned into him, revelling in all his textures, giving every ounce of herself to him. Pledging him her life.

Someone cleared his throat, and Richard looked up. Isabel held her arms around his waist, though, and rested her head against his chest. Clarice and Ned stood on the threshold, back so quickly. Too quickly.

"Very well," Richard said, the sound of his voice rumbling through him and into her. "We've discussed the preparations. You know what you're to do."

"Yes, sir," Ned answered.

"We'll be going, then," Richard said.

Richard studied Isabel's back, the absolute straightness of her spine, and his heart nearly burst with pride. The tiny woman who'd stood up to him on her very first day under his roof had more courage in her than any three men could muster among them. She'd trembled more than once since she'd taken up her stance between two of the topiary figures. She'd claim it was from cold, no doubt, but he'd felt her heart fluttering moments before in the nursery. Standing there, unprotected by any magic whatsoever, inviting Anui to come for her terrified her, as well it should.

Crouching behind a hedge, his own face smeared with ocher and armed with a razor sharp kitchen knife, Richard shared her terror. He could only trust that Sammy and Henga could spring with him to her defense from their own hiding places. That the three of them—and his love—could defeat the *turehu* chief and end the horror.

A figure approached from the house, headed straight

toward his hiding place. What in hell? Skirts.

Mrs. Willis crept right up behind him. "Any sight of that creature?" she whispered.

"Get back inside, Mrs. Willis," he ordered.

"With all due respect, sir, no."

"I need you to care for Bunny."

"Clarice and Ned are with her. They've painted her and themselves with the red stuff, and the windows and doors are secured with cooked *kumara*. They don't need me."

"Mrs. Willis," he said.

"That vile thing knocked me cold and took the little miss. He'll feel the edge of this," she said, brandishing her favorite cleaver.

Richard had never won an argument with this woman, and her face was covered with ochre. Perhaps she could help. "Very well, but you must follow my instructions."

"Yes, sir."

It started then, at that exact moment. The music, the flutes, and a tiny whimper, too, from Isabel.

Richard parted the leaves of the hedge just enough to see a mist creeping through the distant trees and heading in Isabel's direction. It held the light in it, shining and evil. Long, cold fingers of it snaked their way over the grounds, across the lawns, approaching her. She swayed briefly, leaning toward the fog. Richard tensed. If she became entranced and ran into it, as she'd done before, he'd have to run and catch her. Her only hope lay in staying here, where Anui could be trapped and destroyed.

On and on it came, and Isabel stood her ground. More music and singing and laughter. A male voice this time, inhumanly low and grating, as though produced by some hellish instrument. Isabel clutched herself and trembled, but still she held firm, waiting, waiting.

The mist enveloped her. Why hadn't they thought of that? Why had they assumed the beast would show

Waitangi Nights

himself clearly? She cried out, a strangled plea for help.

"Now," Richard shouted, rising and vaulting over the hedge. "Now."

He covered the short distance to where she had stood and charged into the fog. He barely made out two forms, struggling. Straight ahead of him. No, left. No, right. Damn. "Isabel," he shouted.

"Richard," she said, her voice weak but still there.

He headed toward the blessed sound. If the monster wanted Isabel, it would have to kill him first. A shape loomed ahead, shimmering in the fog. He lunged for it, and his hand made contact with something cold. Something like ice. His fingers froze, the thing was that cold.

"Richard," Isabel called again, off to the left this time.

"I have her, man." A very human voice. Sammy. "She's safe."

The thing in Richard's hand twisted. The cold crept up his arm, stealing all his strength. He couldn't hold it much longer, but he couldn't let it go. He pulled the thing to him, squinting through the fog, through the light. It took form finally, revealing itself to him. Hell stared him right back in the face.

It was Anui, of course. His skin glowed with the light around him, and his eyes shone with an evil both demented and cold. He opened his mouth in a parody of a smile, baring his teeth. The music came out of it and then laughter and then singing, even though his lips never moved. More music followed, haunting, slipping into his brain.

Richard's fingers grew weak, and the knife slipped from his hand. Anui's smile grew broader, and Richard's grip on his icy flesh loosened. He had to hold on or the monster would have Isabel.

He lifted his arm and grabbed Anui with both hands, hanging on despite the freezing cold. He shook his head, clearing it. "Here," he shouted. "I have him. Here."

Something blurred past him and crashed into the

skull of his enemy. The music changed to shrieks, as Anui writhed. Another blow whizzed past Richard and into the monster's head. And another and another. The very mists around him keened and wailed, piercing his ears and reverberating around his head.

Anui slipped from his hands, and he covered his ears, trying to shut out the pain of those shrieks. Still the blows came, and still he heard them, even through the other noises.

One last blow, and the fog dissolved. Slowly, at first, allowing Richard to make out more shapes around him. Then faster, it sparkled and crumbled and fell apart. No more than three feet in front of him Henga stood over a lifeless form. He held his warclub high above him and gave out one of his barking chants. The thing at his feet—what was left of Anui—didn't move or make a sound.

Richard glanced over at where he had last heard Isabel's voice and found her, leaning weakly against Sammy. When their gazes met, she straightened and walked unsteadily toward him. He met her halfway and pulled her into his arms where she melted against him.

"It's gone," she whispered against his chest.

Richard stood, holding the woman he loved, and listened to the night. No more flutes, only natural, earthly sounds, a bird in the distance, a gentle wind in the trees. The glowing mists had disappeared, too, leaving nothing more than starlight.

"Yes, it's gone," he murmured. The words felt so good.

Sammy walked to Richard's side and clapped him on the shoulder. "Some work, man."

"The monster's dead, isn't he?"

Sammy nodded. "Henga will deal with what's left."

"What will he do?"

"Best not to ask."

Right. He didn't need to know the details, and Isabel certainly wouldn't want to hear them. Henga knew

Waitangi Nights

what he was about. Anui wouldn't bother Richard's family, or anyone else's, ever again.

Just as Richard allowed his shoulders to relax, shouts came from the house. "Mr. Richard. Hurry, sir, please."

What now? Richard relinquished a shaken, unsteady Isabel to Sammy and turned toward the house. Clarice leaned out of an upstairs window, shouting, "Oh please, do hurry!"

Richard took off at a run. Bunny, it had to be Bunny. What could have happened to her now?

He was over the lawns, onto the terrace and across it in three strides. He charged to the door, threw it open, and ran inside. From the entryway he could make out the sounds from upstairs. Screams. His daughter was screaming.

He took the steps two at a time, his heart pounding. His mind raced back to that sunny afternoon, when Mrs. Willis had called him. He hadn't heard Louisa's screams then, and he'd been too late. By the name of everything holy, tonight he couldn't be late. He had to get to his little girl in time.

At the nursery doorway he hesitated for no more than a second. Clarice and Ned hovered over Bunny, Ned sitting on the bed and holding her. She flailed about, thrashing and uttering her screams, as though something was tearing into her. He flew to her, pushed Ned aside, and held her himself. She struggled against him. Against him. Against the father who loved her more than life but had never revealed himself to her.

"What happened?" he demanded.

"I don't know, sir," Clarice answered. "One moment she was lying there all silent-like, and then she started hollering and twisting. She nearly flew off the bed."

"Oh, God," he murmured into her hair. "Hush, precious. I'm here now. Hush."

Still she fought him, her tiny fists pummeling his chest and shoulders. Was it the madness, after all? Now that he'd battled the *turehu* and won, would he lose her, anyway? Would he always fight for the ones he loved, only to fail? "No," he cried. "Bunny, you have to come back to me. I love you. I need you."

A weight joined him on the bed, and a hand touched his shoulder. Isabel. He turned toward her, still holding Bunny, still trying to quiet her. "I'm going to lose her," he whispered. "All the battles have come to nothing."

"Oh, my dearest," she answered.

Tears burned in his eyes. The rest of them would see, but he didn't give a damn. He was losing his little girl, and nothing else mattered. Her screams tore through his heart. Her every blow against him might have come from Henga's warclub. How could she fight him like this? Why wouldn't she come back to him?

"Richard, listen to me," Isabel said softly. "There's one thing you haven't tried."

"What?" he demanded. "Anything. Anything."

"Tell her you're her father. If she can't come back for her cousin, maybe she can for her father."

"God, yes. How bloody stupid of me." He pressed his lips to Bunny's ear. "Listen, precious, it's papa. I'm not your cousin Richard. I'm your father. I should have told you sooner, but I loved you too much to see you hurt."

Nothing changed, she still twisted and cried out. He clutched her harder. "I'm your papa, and Isabel will be your mama. We'll go riding together. We'll have so much fun, you'll see. Only you have to come back to us. You have to come back to the parents who love you."

She went absolutely still, hanging limp in his arms. She wasn't dead, he could still feel her breath against his shoulder. He gently put her back in bed and stared down at her. She was still his Bunny, his little girl. Her long, black eyelashes still fanned over her glowing skin. Her tiny mouth still promised giggles and childish kisses. Her beauty still stopped his heart. And yet, he'd lost her.

He took a shuddering breath and reached out to smooth a strand of hair from her cheek. Her eyes

Waitangi Nights

opened. Dear God, they opened, so clear and blue, so like his own. She looked at him for a moment and then smiled. "Papa?"

He scooped her up again, cradling her in one arm while slipping his other around Isabel, and he gave in to the tears.

Epilogue

The garden at Harrowgate Manor made a perfect setting for an intimate wedding. The enormous reception following, which seemed to include most of the population of Northern New Zealand, Maori and *pakeha* alike, filled most of the rooms on the first floor. Dozens of people lined the refreshment tables around the dining room, and more swirled over the parlor's makeshift dance floor to the tempo of a lilting waltz. When the European part of the program concluded, Henga, their honored guest, would lead his clan in traditional Maori chants and dances.

She stood to one side of the room and marvelled at it all. She'd have to accustom herself to being wealthy, it seemed. With Richard's family safe, he'd proceed with his plans to form a sheep ranching cooperative, and Isabel would have to serve as his hostess and confidante, when she wasn't busy with the orchids.

She was certainly playing the part of mistress of Harrowgate Manor today. She'd forgiven herself one little

Waitangi Nights

deception and worn a snowy white dress of Madame Arlee's creation, this time designed to her own very explicit directions. She carried a bouquet of white *cattleyas* that Clarice had fashioned from the flowers available in the glasshouse.

Her glasshouse. She ran her finger over the velvet of one blossom to the sparkling yellow in its throat. Her orchids. Her home. Her husband. Her daughter. When she'd climbed out of bed this morning, she'd still been Arthur Gannon's spinster daughter. Now she was Richard Julian's wife and Miss Beatrice Julian's mother. Would miracles never cease?

"There you are, Bella."

She turned to find Hugh approaching, his long strides covering the polished floor. He reached her and handed her a glass cup full of punch. "Thought you might need a spot of something wet."

"Thank you."

"Thirsty affairs, weddings." He reached to his collar and tugged on it with his forefinger. "You're standing up well, though. I must say, you look positively radiant."

She couldn't stifle a smile, a grin so wide, in fact, that she must look perfectly ridiculous. So she took a long drink of punch to hide it and then discovered that she'd drained the glass. She had been thirsty.

"You're happy, aren't you, Bella?" Hugh asked quietly, taking the empty glass from her hand.

"Deliriously."

"Good, then." He turned to gaze across the room and squared his shoulders. "I'm still glad I gave Julian a sound thrashing, though. He deserved it for taking you away from me."

Isabel snuck a peek at Hugh from the corner of her eye and smiled again. No doubt it would prove useless to point out that Hugh's own lip still showed evidence of swelling and a cut at the corner where Richard's fist had connected with it. The whole incident had seemed dreadfully violent at the time. But now that both of them were recovered—if a bit battered—their brawl could be forgotten. It was no more than a bit of family history. And the fight had allowed the two of them to vent their anger and become neighbors, if not actual friends.

"I say," Hugh remarked. "Do you suppose I might kiss the bride?"

"Of course." Isabel rested her palm on his arm and tipped her face up to his.

He bent and planted the most pristine of kisses on her cheek. Then he straightened and cleared his throat. "Damn, but Julian's a lucky chap."

"Kissing my wife, Upton?" Richard sidled up behind Isabel and slipped his arm around her waist. "Do I have to trounce you again?"

" 'Tain't the way I remember it, old fellow," Hugh answered. "And your black eye says I'm right."

Isabel glanced up at her husband. "Black eye" was overstating the case a bit. But Richard did still sport a purplish bruise at the end of his cheekbone. That and his pirate smile contrasted with the starch of his collar and the impeccable cut of his tailcoat to produce the most delightful image of a rake, a tempting scoundrel. He was her very own for every day and every night the rest of her life.

Richard raised his fingers to the bruise and smiled. "Perhaps you're right, Upton. But your own face looks a bit the worse for wear."

"You gave me a deuced good fight," Hugh admitted, sticking his hand out toward Richard. "If you're as good a husband, I won't have to drub you again."

Richard took his hand and gave it a firm shake. "No need to worry on that score."

"Hello, there," came a musical female voice. Isabel glanced around Richard to find Olivia and Edward Farnsworth approaching. Olivia's lips were curled into a mischievous smile.

Waitangi Nights

"I think you need a word with your daughter, Richard," Edward Farnsworth said as he and his wife joined the little group. "She's telling anyone who'll listen that you're her father and you've just married her mother."

"Oh, dear heaven," Isabel exclaimed.

Olivia's brown eyes sparkled. "Those of us who know you understand, but there are a few others . . ."

Isabel looked up at her husband. "You'd best stop Bunny before everyone's heard her tale."

He snuggled Isabel against his hip. "I wouldn't dream of it," he replied. "She's a Julian, and she's expected to raise eyebrows. Besides, it's the truth."

"She's certainly the most beautiful flower girl I've ever seen," Olivia said. She placed her hand over her slightly rounded belly. "If I have a little girl I hope she's as pretty as Bunny."

"As lovely as her mother is, Livvie, she will be," Hugh said.

"Or perhaps you'll have a boy," Richard added. "He can marry our daughter, when we have one, or teach our son to climb trees. Join our families." He clapped Edward on the shoulder. "What do you say?"

"I'd say you're getting a bit ahead of yourself, don't you think?"

"Nonsense," Richard answered. "We'll have five or six children. Your boy can have his pick."

"Really, Richard," Isabel said. She smiled to herself. He'd been full of the most improbable promises ever since Bunny had recovered and they'd been sure that all the danger was over. Living to age ninety-six together, dozens of grandchildren, hundreds of nights of love as good or better than their first. And she believed every one of them. Every single one.

A most unusual couple passed by on the dance floor, both dark of skin, the man towering over his tiny partner.

"Well, I'll be damned," Richard declared. "My daughter and my valet dancing."

Alice Gaines

He was right. Bunny stood on Samuel's feet as he guided her in the waltz. She gazed up at him primly and properly, the very image of a lady.

Olivia laughed. "Aren't they darling together?"

"Just what do you think you're doing with my daughter, man?" Richard called. "Bring her over here."

Samuel stopped dancing and nodded toward Richard. The perfect gentleman, he turned to Bunny and bowed deeply. She curtsied and then took his hand. The two of them headed for her father, who had removed his arms from around Isabel and crossed them over his chest, feigning a scowl.

It didn't fool Bunny. She walked directly to her father and extended her arms. He scooped her up and planted her on his hip. "What's this?" he demanded. "Dancing with another man?"

"I couldn't find you, papa, and I so wanted to dance."

He raised an eyebrow. "And you encouraged this behavior, Samuel?"

Samuel put his hands behind his back and made his face into an impassive mask. "The little miss ordered me, sir."

"Rubbish," Richard said. He looked into Bunny's eyes and pretended at a frown. "Is he as good a dancer as I am?"

"Well," she answered, appearing to consider the question.

He buried his face in her hair and made growling noises into her ear. She squirmed in his arms and giggled. "No," she cried. "Oh, papa, no."

"That's better."

They laughed for a moment, all of them. Such a happy sound. "Well, well," Olivia said finally. "What a young lady you've become, Miss Bunny."

"I'm big enough to go to South America," Bunny answered. "Mama's going to show me the orchids where they really, really live."

Mama. The word still went straight through Isabel.

Waitangi Nights

The silly grin got the better of her after all, and she reached up to stroke her daughter's cheek. "Not for a few years yet, dear."

"But why? I'm old enough, even papa says so."

"Because we're all staying safely at home for a while, precious," Richard said. "We'll have more adventures later on."

"Of course," Isabel agreed. "We have all the time we want now."

Richard gazed at her, pure love and happiness in those remarkable eyes. He smiled, an expression for the first time free of any glimmer of pain or fear, an expression that was the greatest gift she could ever have wanted.

"All the time we want," he repeated softly. "All the time in the world."

Don't Miss These Haunting Love Stories By
SABINE KELLS

"A major new voice in the supernatural/fantasy romance sub-genre has arrived!"
—*Romantic Times*

Shadows On A Sunset Sea. The ghostly legends of Thornwick Castle can't be true. Tiernan O'Rourke lived nearly three hundred years earlier; he couldn't still walk the great halls, waiting for the return of the woman he lost. Carolyn wants to deny the irresistible spirit that calls to her from a wondrous realm of rapturous passion and unknown peril. But in the fading echoes of her ancestral Irish home, secrets of the past sweep Carolyn to a time she's never known—and into the arms of the lover who is her destiny.
_51984-4 $4.99 US/$5.99 CAN

A Deeper Hunger. A romance in the immortal tradition of *Interview With The Vampire*. For years, Cailie has been haunted by strange, recurring visions of fierce desire and an enigmatic lover who excites her like no other. Mysterious, romantic, and sophisticated, Tresand is the man of Cailie's dreams. Yet behind the stranger's cultured facade lurk dark secrets that threaten Cailie even as he seduces her very soul.
_3593-6 $4.50 US/$5.50 CAN

Dorchester Publishing Co., Inc.
65 Commerce Road
Stamford, CT 06902

Please add $1.75 for shipping and handling for the first book and $.50 for each book thereafter. NY, NYC, PA and CT residents, please add appropriate sales tax. No cash, stamps, or C.O.D.s. All orders shipped within 6 weeks via postal service book rate. Canadian orders require $2.00 extra postage and must be paid in U.S. dollars through a U.S. banking facility.

Name_____
Address_____
City _____ State_____ Zip_____
I have enclosed $_____in payment for the checked book(s).
Payment <u>must</u> accompany all orders.☐ Please send a free catalog.

Second Chance
Lori Handeland

Second Chance is a small Missouri town where the people believe that anyone who has done wrong deserves another shot. All the condemned man needs is someone to take responsibility for him. And that someone will never be Katherine Logan. With a bad marriage behind her, and the bank note on her horse ranch coming due, the young widow has neither the time nor the inclination to save a low-down bandit.

But the sight of the most wickedly tempting male ever to put his head through a noose changes her mind real quick. Although the townsfolk say Jake Banner will as soon shoot Katherine as change his outlaw ways, she won't listen. Deep within Jake's emerald eyes lie secrets that intrigue Katherine, daring her to give him a second chance at life—and herself a second chance at love.

_51966-6 $4.99 US/$5.99 CAN

Dorchester Publishing Co., Inc.
65 Commerce Road
Stamford, CT 06902

Please add $1.75 for shipping and handling for the first book and $.50 for each book thereafter. NY, NYC, PA and CT residents, please add appropriate sales tax. No cash, stamps, or C.O.D.s. All orders shipped within 6 weeks via postal service book rate. Canadian orders require $2.00 extra postage and must be paid in U.S. dollars through a U.S. banking facility.

Name_____
Address_____
City _____ State_____ Zip_____
I have enclosed $_____in payment for the checked book(s).
Payment <u>must</u> accompany all orders.☐ Please send a free catalog.

LORI HANDELAND
ROMANCES WHICH TRANSCEND HUMANITY!

Full Moon Dreams. Though born into the magic and mystery of the circus, Emmaline Monroe is not prepared for the frightening reality of a dark myth. Fellow performers have met suspicious deaths on nights when the moon shines full and bright, and Emma and the others have been warned to trust no one. But the lovely tiger trainer is finding her attraction to Johnny Bradfordini impossible to tame. Each time she looks into the handsome stranger's silvery-blue eyes, she feels pulled into an all-consuming passion—and an inexplicable danger.

Violent dreams and bizarre episodes on full-moon nights have left Johnny fearing his darker side. Yet Emma's sweet, soft kisses remind him of all that is good and worth fighting for. Is he endangering the life of the woman he loves by letting her get too close? Or will the fiery beauty save his soul with her eternal love?
_52110-5 $5.50 US/$6.50 CAN

D.J.'s Angel. D.J. Halloran doesn't believe in love. She's just seen too much heartache—in her work as a police officer and in her own life. She vowed a long time ago never to let anyone get close enough to hurt her, even if that someone is the very captivating, very handsome Chris McCall.

But D.J. also has an angel—a special guardian determined, at any cost, to teach D.J. the magic of love. Try as she might to resist Chris's many charms, D.J. knows she is in for an even tougher battle because of her heavenly companion's persistent faith in the power of love.
_52050-8 $5.99 US/$6.99 CAN

Dorchester Publishing Co., Inc.
65 Commerce Road
Stamford, CT 06902

Please add $1.75 for shipping and handling for the first book and $.50 for each book thereafter. NY, NYC, PA and CT residents, please add appropriate sales tax. No cash, stamps, or C.O.D.s. All orders shipped within 6 weeks via postal service book rate. Canadian orders require $2.00 extra postage and must be paid in U.S. dollars through a U.S. banking facility.

Name_____
Address_____
City _____ State_____Zip_____
I have enclosed $_____in payment for the checked book(s).
Payment <u>must</u> accompany all orders.☐ Please send a free catalog.

Spirit of the Mountain

FELA DAWSON SCOTT

Bestselling Author Of *Black Wolf*

She has befriended the cougar, tamed the wild wolf, and survived alone in the wilds of the Great Smoky Mountains, until finding true peace living as one with the Cherokee people. She is also the loveliest woman Nathan Walker has ever laid eyes on, and as far as the handsome trapper is concerned, the wilderness is no place for her. Determined to lead the orphaned beauty back to civilization and a heritage she has never known, he vows to be prepared for whatever dangers cross their path. But what he doesn't count on is his growing passion for the remarkable woman they call Spirit of the Mountain.

_3817-X $4.99 US/$5.99 CAN

Dorchester Publishing Co., Inc.
65 Commerce Road
Stamford, CT 06902

Please add $1.75 for shipping and handling for the first book and $.50 for each book thereafter. NY, NYC, PA and CT residents, please add appropriate sales tax. No cash, stamps, or C.O.D.s. All orders shipped within 6 weeks via postal service book rate. Canadian orders require $2.00 extra postage and must be paid in U.S. dollars through a U.S. banking facility.

Name_____
Address_____
City _____ State_____Zip_____
I have enclosed $_____in payment for the checked book(s).
Payment <u>must</u> accompany all orders.☐ Please send a free catalog.

ATTENTION PREFERRED CUSTOMERS!

SPECIAL TOLL-FREE NUMBER
1-800-481-9191

Call Monday through Friday
**12 noon to 10 p.m.
Eastern Time**
*Get a free catalogue;
Order books using your Visa,
MasterCard, or Discover;
Join the book club!*

Leisure Books

Love Spell